THE
TAKEN
ONES

BOOKS BY RUHI CHOUDHARY

THE DETECTIVE MACKENZIE PRICE SERIES

Our Daughter's Bones

Their Frozen Graves

Little Boy Lost

THE
TAKEN
ONES

Ruhi
Choudhary

bookouture

Published by Bookouture in 2022

An imprint of Storyfire Ltd.
Carmelite House
50 Victoria Embankment
London EC4Y 0DZ

www.bookouture.com

ISBN: 978-1-80019-888-3
eBook ISBN: 978-1-80019-887-6

Previously published as *The Dying Game*.

To Sasha

PROLOGUE

The booming sound of a gunshot punched through the silence.

"Nick!" Mackenzie screeched, her voice cracking.

She shot through the winding woods. Her knee throbbed, hot and heavy. Her breath came in gasps. But the searing pain was drowned as adrenaline flooded her. Her legs leapt, taking long strides, like a predator chasing her prey. All she could think about was Nick.

The forest was thick and the path led downhill. The trees were tall and barren, black branches and trunks crisscrossing the darkening sky. The deeper she ran into it, the faster her heart raced, as if trying find a way out of her body and escape this horrid place.

"Nick!" Her voice was carried by the wind. But there was no response.

She stopped when she saw something on the ground. Blood.

Her legs trembled, following the trail. Then she saw it. Behind a tree lay a body, face down. His back was shredded by the gunshot. His jacket torn. Blood flowing out.

Mackenzie dropped to her knees; a sob caught in her throat.

"Please. No. Please." She prayed for the first time in her life.

She had to see. She had to turn his face. It was eerily quiet now—the wind had died down and the clouds had stopped swirling. It felt like a moment frozen in time. Then a hand came to her shoulder and Mackenzie's hand went to her gun.

ONE

By the time Detective Mackenzie Price's car rolled onto the street lined with semi-detached homes and apartment buildings, it was raining cats and dogs. She easily spotted the house. It was the one with the CSI van and squad cars in front of it. The red and blue lights refracted through the water droplets. Cops and technicians were gathered outside in raincoats, filtering in and out of the front door.

Mackenzie parked the car and climbed out. She ducked under the yellow crime-scene tape, already drenched in the rain.

"You'd think you just moved to town." Detective Nick Blackwood, her partner for nine years and closest friend, came to her side, holding an umbrella over them. "Not knowing to carry an umbrella at all times." He towered over an already tall Mackenzie, strapping, with a chiseled jaw, black eyes, and black hair that was gray around the temples.

She shivered. "This is *my* umbrella, Nick. You stole it."

"Oh." He frowned and shrugged.

"Who's our vic?"

Justin Armstrong, a junior detective with the unit, stood in the porch. He was big, with a bushy mustache that hid his upper lip and a perpetual look of paranoia on his face. He was known for his military-like demeanor and staunch discipline.

"Apparently her name is Mia Gallagher." Justin joined them, handing them the protective gear.

"Apparently?"

"You'll see. It's on the second floor."

Mackenzie braced herself and followed the directions. The loud pitter-patter of rain grew faint when she walked into the apartment, with Nick right behind her. The entire floor was crowded with uniform cops, barricading the unit away from prying neighbors who stood with their doors ajar, curious to see what the commotion was about.

The living room was filled with CSI. The first thing that hit her was the metallic smell of blood, stinging the inside of her nose.

She took in her surroundings.

The living room looked like a tornado had torn through it. The couch had shifted, center table toppled, the TV mounted on the wall drooped on one side, and the curtain was ripped off. A concrete pillar by the kitchen had bloodstains.

"What the hell happened here?" she murmured.

"A neighbor had just gotten home and saw the door was open. He peeked and called 911," Justin replied.

"Guess nosy neighbors aren't always a bad thing." Nick's eyes searched the space. "So, where is she?"

Becky Sullivan, the chief medical examiner, emerged from one of the rooms with a look of resignation. "There's no dead body. What am I even doing here?"

"Is this an abduction?" Mackenzie gestured at the dried blood on the pillar. "That's a lot of blood loss."

"Not enough to kill her. Enough to knock her out, perhaps," Becky replied.

"Did anyone hear anything? Looks like the attack was vicious," Nick said.

"The neighbor she shares a wall with is an eighty-year-old man who uses a hearing aid. Peterson talked to him, and he said he was lights out hours ago. And it's been storming." Officer Peterson was a uniform who had recently begun assisting on cases. Justin handed Nick a purse in an evidence bag. "This was recovered next to the front door."

Nick turned it over. "It still has her wallet and credit cards."

"And that's an expensive bag," Becky remarked. "It's Gucci."

Mackenzie mused. "It doesn't look like a robbery gone wrong. First thing they'd take is the purse."

"We also haven't been able to find her cell phone. And her car is in the parking lot."

Mackenzie exchanged a loaded look with Nick. "Maybe it was on her when she was taken. Assuming the blood belongs to Mia."

"The neighbor who called 911 rang Mia several times, but she hasn't picked up," Justin added.

Nick nodded. "Let's ping the carrier. And flag the phone in case it's switched on at any point."

Mackenzie walked around the apartment, careful not to disturb anything or get in the way of tech collecting evidence. This was somebody's home; there were plants by the windowsill that were probably watered every day and a book-case that was filled with stories. But everything was destroyed now and a bunch of strangers, including Mackenzie, had descended to dissect and inspect every inch of it with detachment.

She noticed a bloody handprint on the fireplace and directed the CSI to it.

There were no signs of forced entry. The front door was

screwed to the hinges with the lock intact, no signs of tampering. Mia's purse and car were here, but she wasn't.

Mackenzie spotted a framed picture of a young woman standing in front of the Eiffel Tower. The woman was strikingly attractive, tall and slender with blond hair being whipped by the wind. There was another picture of her sunning on a beach in Santorini. Her lips were full and wide. She had a long neck and a perfect string of teeth. Mackenzie wouldn't be surprised if she were a model or popular on social media. She had a way of posing for the camera, knowing what angles and dips of her body to flaunt.

Mackenzie imagined how the attack might have played out. Her surroundings vanished and shifted as the scenario she predicted took shape in her eyes.

Mia Gallagher returned home after a long day. She entered her apartment and just as she closed the door, someone grabbed her from behind and lifted her. He clapped her mouth with his hand. Her screams were muffled. Her long legs and toned arms flailed and thrashed. She bit him. He released her, and she began throwing things at him to get away. He chased her around the apartment. The rugs shifted. The lamp and the fruit bowl fell. The clock and the paintings moved. He caught her and slammed her head against the pillar. She started fading, blackness dotting her vision. She stumbled away, leaving her bloody handprint on the fireplace. But this time she couldn't get away.

Mackenzie's vision faded, and she turned to Nick, who was discussing getting the surveillance footage with the super. "How did the perp get inside?" she asked.

"What?" Nick frowned, letting Justin take over with the super.

"There is no sign of forced entry. Unless he had a key, which probably means it's someone Mia knows."

Nick rubbed his chin. "There is a balcony."

He led her to the door at the end of the narrow hallway next to the kitchen. The balcony was small, with one chair, which was toppled from the storm. The lashing rain blurred the view of the woods that the balcony overlooked.

"The door was unlocked when we got here." Nick raised his voice over the booming thunder.

Mackenzie stayed inside, inwardly wincing at the rain spraying on her boots. She checked the flimsy door that hung loosely from the hinges. There was a dent in it. "Someone broke through this."

Nick inspected it and gave it a shake. "It's easy to break this down, I suppose. It's the second floor. They probably just climbed up the pipe."

"Can we get someone to lift any prints here?" Mackenzie gestured at the door when she noticed a faint outline on the floor, catching light from the thunder. "We got a footprint here!"

Nick knelt next to it. "It's a partial."

"Looks like a man's."

"We should check her car. See if it has a GPS system that can tell us where she's been lately," Nick said.

"Good idea. I also want uniform to talk to all the neighbors to check if someone was visiting frequently or hovering."

On her way out, Mackenzie glanced at the smeared blood on the wall and tried to settle the whirring in her gut.

TWO

OCTOBER 11

It had been forty-eight hours since Mia Gallagher was brutally snatched from her apartment. And there was no trace of her. The weather in Lakemore had dried up after ferocious rainfalls, but the mornings had been cold and unforgiving. By the time Mackenzie barged into the office, the skin on her cheeks was cracking.

"Are the posters up?" she asked.

Nick and Justin were standing around her desk, engaged in a serious conversation.

"Yes, ma'am." Justin tipped his head. "This morning we got a team putting them on all bus stops and train stations."

"Just talked to the guys at Olympia and Riverview. They've got the case on their docket," Nick added, pouring himself coffee. "Want some?"

She rolled her eyes. "No thanks."

Mackenzie resisted anything that felt too good. She was Mad Mack—always in control. She prided herself in not having any vices, unlike most of her colleagues. Mad Mack wasn't addicted to caffeine or alcohol or pills. She didn't wear her emotions on her sleeve for the world to see. Over the years, she had crafted layers of apathy to hide herself from the world.

She rubbed her forehead. "Justin, can you check with Clint if we have her phone records yet? The court order was served yesterday."

Justin nodded and left the room.

"Rough night?" Nick ventured a guess, wheeling closer to her desk.

"It always is when a woman goes missing. Especially when she's a young and attractive one." She sighed, looking at Mia's picture clipped to the bulletin board on her desk. Her silky golden hair fell in curls around a brightly smiling face. It made her heart twist, thinking about where she could be right now.

"I got the video from the restaurant Mia went to the night she disappeared." Nick set his coffee on her desk and opened his laptop.

"Who did she meet with again?"

"Another model. Peterson talked to her, and she said that Mia was acting normally and didn't mention anything suspicious. But she said they weren't too close."

Mackenzie leaned over and watched the video of the dimly lit restaurant. She immediately spotted Mia, sitting at the bar with another girl equally as glamorous. While they chatted and ate freely, Mackenzie was more focused on the other patrons.

"What are the chances that someone followed her from the restaurant?" Nick picked up his mug and pressed it against his head.

"You're the unofficial profiler in this unit. You tell me."

He cracked his neck. "She was snatched in an almost crude manner. Her place was in a mess. There was a struggle involved, but the CSI has not been able to pick up any useful prints or DNA..."

"Which suggests the perp cleaned up the place."

"But not entirely. They could have staged it to look like

there was no abduction. Wiped the blood and bolted the door shut. We wouldn't have assumed she was abducted so easily then." He paused when a man appeared in the video to talk to Mia and her friend, but Mackenzie's shoulders sagged when she realized he was just a server.

"Maybe they were in a rush," she continued.

"Or we could be looking at someone new to this."

Two hours elapsed on the tape. Mia and her friend were leaving the restaurant. No one approached them. No one followed them. No one even watched with interest.

Mackenzie sat back on her chair, deflated. "That was a dead end. Did you get in touch with her family?"

"They live in Kansas. She grew up in a big family but wasn't close to anyone. Her parents are dead. A cousin mentioned how she was always different and wanted the big city life."

"So no roots."

"No roots."

Mackenzie's mouth flattened. Neither had she—for a very long time. Her parents had died a long time ago, as had her grandmother. She didn't have any siblings. Her parents' lies and deceit ensured that she didn't really grow up around any extended family. She had always felt unmoored, sometimes even inconsequential. Like she was a blip on this planet.

Her computer chimed with a notification. "Justin just forwarded us Mia's cell phone records."

For the next hour, they picked apart Mia's life. Mackenzie always found this uncomfortable. The necessary invasion of privacy. But as she became more and more absorbed in Mia's life through her pictures, videos, and messages, her confusion grew.

"She doesn't have a boyfriend or a girlfriend," Mackenzie noted aloud. "She isn't even on any dating apps."

"Maybe she just wanted to be single." Nick shrugged.

"Could be..." she trailed off, going through the hundreds of pictures Mia took of herself. "But for someone who is so out there, it's a bit strange. There's no one who particularly features in her pictures either. No regular contact with family either."

"There is one person she talks to a lot." He pointed at a number on the screen. "This shows up a lot. There are messages making plans to meet many times. Nothing romantic about the exchange from what I can tell."

Mackenzie skimmed through the content of the messages. "His name is Wren."

"If he's on social media, she should have added him." He whistled. "There you go. Wren Murray. I'll get his address from the DMV."

Mackenzie nodded absentmindedly, staring at a text sent by Wren to Mia that had caught her attention.

I'm sorry, Mia. I didn't mean to offend you. Please meet me again. I just really think you need to get yourself out of this situation.

THREE

On the radio, the spokesperson for the Lakemore PD read a statement asking the public for help to locate Mia Gallagher.

"If anyone has any information regarding the whereabouts of Mia Gallagher, please call 555—"

Nick changed the channel to some mundane football commentary. Mackenzie didn't complain, preferring the white noise over the constant reminder of what they were dealing with.

"She didn't even visit her family for Christmas," Mackenzie remarked, still scrolling through Mia's pictures on social media. "She was somewhere in Africa. Did we get her bank statements yet?"

"No, but we'll have them within forty-eight hours. Based on statements from her friends, she just had random gigs. How did she afford all those luxury bags and trips to Europe?"

She frowned. "She hasn't even tagged anyone in the photos of the trip. It looks like it's solo travel. It's kind of sad..."

"What is?" He looked at her.

"She smiles a lot but appears to lead a very lonely life," she replied. Even Mia's text messages revealed mostly impersonal conversations. Her life was all glitter and grandeur but empty.

It was something Mackenzie identified with. On the surface, she had everything. She was on her way to become a decorated detective in her small town. It was a job she loved. She was young and attractive, living in a nice house. But that was where it ended.

She came across a picture of Mia with a raggedy-looking doll. According to the caption, it was the only thing she had preserved from her childhood. It reminded Mackenzie of a doll she'd had when she was a little girl. She had called it Patch. It was a rag doll that had been squashed under the tire of her bike and the wheel of an ice-cream truck. One of its eyes was missing. Its clothes were torn. And half of it was stained from the many things Mackenzie had accidentally spilled on it. After years of being distorted and sullied, Patch finally gave up one day.

"Do you want me to fix it, Mackenzie?" Melody, her mother, asked her softly, stroking her hair.

"Can you? It's beyond repair, I think." She sobbed. She was eleven. Too old to love a rag doll to bits and pieces. But when her nights were spent listening to her drunken father beat her mother, she was willing to cling to whatever shred of innocence she had left.

"Nothing is beyond repair, sweetie." Melody dabbed her tears, wincing when her hand grazed a fresh bruise on her cheek. She took Patch from Mackenzie. "No matter how much something is broken, you can always fix it. You just have to look hard enough for that one rip and seal it. The rest will begin to fall into place then."

It took her all night. The next day, Patch looked as good as it did before. And there was hope in Melody's eyes.

The car went over another pothole, but the memory burned behind Mackenzie's eyes. She hadn't thought much of what

Melody had said. But now she did. Maybe her mother was onto something. Maybe Mackenzie could get better, if she found that one rip. Maybe she would plug that hole in her life and stop feeling empty.

Nick pounded his fist into a shabby-looking door in an apartment building with paint peeling off the concrete walls. The door swung open revealing a short man with stringy brown hair touching his eyebrows and a portly frame, wearing bedraggled clothes.

"Yeah?" He rubbed his eyes like he had just awoken from a nap.

Mackenzie flashed her credentials. "Mr. Murray? Can we talk?"

Wren's forehead crumpled, but he let them in. Mackenzie quickly scoped the apartment. It was a studio with a small kitchen, a couch and a bed in the corner. A chunky brown dog panted and drooled, hopped off the couch and began sniffing around their feet. She stiffened, knowing dogs smelled fear.

"How can I help you?" Wren asked. "Don't worry, he's harmless."

"You know Mia Gallagher?" Nick asked.

"Yes..."

"She's been abducted."

Wren blinked like there was dirt in his eyes. "What?"

"Haven't you been watching the news?" Mackenzie raised an eyebrow. "She's been everywhere."

He shivered and crossed his arms. "No. I just got back from Wichita last night, that's why I was sleeping in."

Mackenzie picked up on his drawl. "You knew her from back home?"

"Yeah, yeah. We lost touch but reconnected when I moved to Washington. She got out of that life back in Kansas only to live in another small town. Except nobody back home knew, of course."

"What do you mean?"

"You've seen that life she showed online. Everyone thought she was living some glamorous life out of her suitcase." He took out a joint. "May I?"

"Sure. Did she tell you how she was able to afford her travels and luxury items?"

He shrugged. "She was evasive about it. I figured it was either some boyfriend or... sex work. Don't want to jump to any conclusions, but what else could it be, right? Do you have any idea who did this?"

"We're hoping you could help us." Nick eyed him. "Do you know anyone who could have wanted to hurt her? Was she seeing anyone?"

"No." He looked appalled. "She was easy-going. An introvert. I didn't really know her other model friends, but she never mentioned any problems..."

"Then why did you send her this text?" Mackenzie read aloud the message. "What situation were you recommending she get out of?"

"It was around a month ago." His voice had an edge. His dog must have sensed his distress and barked at Mackenzie, making her jump. "Sit down, Rocky. Sorry about that. Where was I? Yeah, we met for coffee, and she looked like she had been crying. She said something about how she was sick of being forced into things but didn't have a choice. When I pressed for more, she said it was some stupid audition," he recounted, the corners of his eyes collecting tears. "I don't know, now... now I just keep thinking about every interaction. She was my oldest friend. We met when we were seven years old, and she stole my juice box." He looked away, sniffling and turned back to her with a puffed chest. "She has to be alive, right? Why would anyone do this?"

Mackenzie's neck felt like a block of concrete had settled on her shoulders. "We'll find her."

"Please do." He ran an impatient hand through his messy hair. "I can't believe this. If there's anything I can do to help..."

After getting his contact information and asking more routine questions, Mackenzie and Nick were on their way back to the car, the sound of their steps bouncing on the staircase.

"Being forced into things..." Mackenzie repeated Wren's words, baffled. "She hadn't signed with an agency, had she?"

"No. She was freelance. But I'll ask Jenna to focus on Mia's gigs from around a month ago." He was already on his phone. Nick's face was grave. "If she was being forced into something, it's a good bet that her disappearance could be related to that."

"Could it be drugs?" Mackenzie suggested. "It's common for models to use. But we didn't find anything in her apartment."

Mackenzie's stomach dipped, thinking about what possible thing was Mia entangled in. And where she was at this very moment.

FOUR

Later in the evening, Mackenzie unholstered her Glock, faced the paper target squarely and pushed her feet shoulder-wide apart. She extended her arms and pointed the gun ahead, lining up the sights. Bracing herself, she pulled the trigger.

Pop!

Pop!

Pop!

She didn't stop shooting the 0.45 and absorbed the recoil every time a bullet barreled out and struck the target. Shell casings popped out and scattered on the floor. The muffled sound reverberated throughout.

The shooting range in Lakemore was in a remote location at the end of a narrow drive surrounded by sparse woods and abandoned construction sites. She was alone at the range—it being ten in the evening. The office was locked, and she had been instructed to lock the gate on her way out.

Pop!

Pop!

Pop!

Adrenaline flowed in her like rocket fuel. It was the rush of holding a weapon that could take a life instantly by putting the slightest pressure on a tiny little part. She had been visiting the range frequently in the last few months. She gravitated to this place whenever she needed to think without any distractions.

And now all she could think about was Mia.

Instead of reloading the magazine, Mackenzie removed her earplugs and safety glasses and got ready to pack up.

She took a quick detour to the restroom and splashed cold water on her face, analyzing her reflection. Blazing red hair tied in a tight ponytail, symmetrical face with a long nose and thin lips, big brown eyes and high cheekbones. The hardness she had spent her life faking was now a permanent fixture on her face.

Unlike Mia who had softness and cheer and sunshine dripping from her face. Did someone take advantage of that vulnerability? Did she trust the wrong person, or did she inadvertently catch the attention of someone evil?

Uniform was still in the process of canvasing the crime scene and reaching out to all of Mia's contacts. No one claimed to know anything. Yet.

Mackenzie left the building and walked toward her car, eager to get her hands on Mia's financial records. The answer to how she was affording a luxurious lifestyle had to be hidden in those statements. Maybe they could point to whatever she was drawn into doing.

Lakemore was going through an unusual hot spurt for a rainy and gloomy Washington town. It was the brink of fall, but the air was balmy and saturated with moisture. The scent of cedar lingered in the hot air. Mackenzie's feet sank into the patches of peat. The silver moonlight threaded through the wispy clouds, making shadows appear and disappear on the ground.

Suddenly, she came to a halt.

After nine years of being a detective, Mackenzie's senses

were finely tuned. She spun around, her hand hovering over her Glock, quickly assessing her surroundings.

It was dead silent except for the occasional rustling of the leaves. The building was empty. The lot was behind a concrete barrier with a razor wire strung atop. Beyond it were the woods, but they weren't thick. Not nearly as dizzying as the woods in Lakemore could be.

Mackenzie was standing in open space with her car a few feet away from her. But there was uneasiness in the pit of her stomach like she was being watched. She looked around, trying to catch anything out of the ordinary.

But it seemed that she was alone in the dark in the middle of nowhere.

Her phone rang, the sharp sound puncturing the tense silence.

"Detective Price," she answered without looking.

"Mack? I'm sending you an address. Get there." It was Sergeant Jeff Sully, who headed the Detectives Unit—a team in Investigations Division at the Lakemore PD. "Looks like we found Mia Gallagher."

"On my way." She sprinted to her car, forgetting all about the feeling of having eyes on her.

Mackenzie drove through the narrow roads of Lakemore surrounded by dense foliage and tall trees, making it seem like she was in a tunnel. Lakes were sprinkled all over the town, but at this time of night they looked like pools of ink, so deep and dark that even the moonlight couldn't touch them.

Lakemore was known for three things: rain, crime, and football. The small town loitered and dwindled, impoverished and boring. Some viewed it as a breeding ground for crime and laziness. The poster child for inertia. The kind of town you escape for a brighter future. But Mackenzie had grown to love it. It had character; it had heart.

A row of drab and similar-looking houses across a vast lake surrounded by a knot of trees was a common sight in Lakemore. It was the juxtaposition found almost everywhere in this town. A scenic place with lakes and woods that harbored darkness and secrets. A little town tucked next to Olympia, often overlooked and overshadowed but with a fighting spirit and bursting talent.

For almost fifty years, Lakemore had gained prestige in the state for high-school football. The Lakemore Sharks were the sparkling crown of a failing town. It was Lakemore's one claim to fame. Its one badge of honor. The reason why Friday nights at bars were packed. The foundation upon which a community had built itself for the last five decades.

Mackenzie parked the car in front of a half-constructed building illuminated by balloon lights. A group of workers in hard hats and orange jackets stood around a work zone, scowling at the police that had infiltrated their space and disrupted the night construction.

"Did Sully tell you anything else?" Nick joined her with a coffee in his hands.

"Nope."

They had reached the landing when Officer Peterson approached them. His young face was pale. "T-there's something you should see."

Mackenzie made a face and followed Peterson toward a half-assembled elevator. There were a few uniform cops surrounding it; all looked like they'd seen a ghost.

"The construction guys reported the elevator was jammed. When they tried fixing the problem, this is what they found." Peterson gulped and slowly raised his head.

Mackenzie followed his gaze. Ice crawled up her spine.

Nick swore under his breath.

The doors were forced open. A hand—half bone and half

red flesh—dangled at the top, peeking out from above the elevator. From the shape and size and the green color on the three nails that were still intact, the hand belonged to a woman.

"Someone shoved her down the elevator shaft," Mackenzie whispered.

FIVE

OCTOBER 12

"So, you're a detective," the blond man sitting across from Mackenzie chirped. "How many serial killers do you know?"

Mackenzie's cheeks strained as she tried not to let her polite smile fall. "One too many."

He waggled his eyebrows in excitement. When the waiter arrived with the food, she got some respite as they busied themselves.

Mackenzie was seated by the window in a restaurant filled with the drone of cutlery clanking and people murmuring. It was one of the few restaurants in Lakemore that was appropriate for a candlelight dinner. Shadows of the patrons danced on the walls. A harp's gentle notes reverberated throughout. She kept checking her phone sneakily for any updates.

"I can bench-press around two hundred pounds. What about you?" His eyes sparkled, trailing over Mackenzie's arms. "You look like you work out."

Mackenzie stifled a groan by gulping down some wine.

"Last year, all I ate was chicken," he went on. "Added some hot sauce and just baked in the oven. Though the jury is still out on spot reduction, it's the best diet for washboard abs." He patted his abdomen. "I guess you'll see later." He winked at her. She almost choked on her quinoa. "Are you okay, Mackenzie?"

"Yeah." She coughed and drank more wine. "I'm fine."

"You know our jobs are kind of similar." He puffed his chest. "You catching killers and me developing code to detect bank fraud. We're both putting bad guys away."

Mackenzie wanted the earth to split and for him to fall right through it. She blinked, wondering if Becky had pranked her by setting her up with him. Was he a paid actor?

"Tell me more about your job," she said, knowing he'd talk about himself for ten minutes and she could use that time to think about Mia Gallagher.

The body they had recovered from the elevator shaft was beyond recognition. But the clothes matched Mia's description. The CSI had spent the entire night gathering tissue and bone fragments in the shaft. Mia's phone had been switched off, with the last known location being her house. Her car GPS had shown that she had returned from the restaurant in Tacoma that Mackenzie and Nick had seen her at on tape, reaching home around eight in the evening. The 911 call was made at ten.

She looked at her phone. Becky was conducting the autopsy on the mangled remains right now, and she was desperate for news.

"Mackenzie?" Chad asked. "Am I boring you?"

"No," she said truthfully. He was pissing her off.

The last few days she had felt like a fish out of water. It had been a few months since her divorce, and she was ready to dip her toes into the dating pool. She hadn't realized how much her ex-husband, Sterling Brooks, had worked hard to bring her out of her shell.

Chad sighed and put down his cutlery. "You know, I think we're both attracted to each other. I'm not sure if we're... intellectually the same." He made a pretentious face. "I'm all brain and data analysis and you're all punching and kicking people. But I think we can have a good time tonight. For a few hours. If you're willing?"

"Huh?"

Chad gave her a dazzling smile and held her hands. "Come on."

She stared at him, wondering how much long-term damage smashing a plate in his face would do. Her phone rang. Relief burst inside her. She snatched her hands out of his clammy ones and answered abruptly.

"Is someone dead?"

"Yeah…" Nick said slowly. "That woman in the elevator. Most likely Mia. Remember? Peterson threw up."

"Oh, do I have to be there now?"

"What?"

She continued the façade, watching the hope in Chad's face fade away. "Okay then. I will be there."

"You're acting weird. Meet me at the morgue. Becky's done with the post." Nick sounded bored and hung up.

Mackenzie couldn't hide the delirious enthusiasm clouding her face. "Sorry, Chad. A woman got mulched in an elevator shaft. I have to go."

He winced. "That's gross."

"Yeah, I have to punch and kick the truth out of suspects." She didn't bother hiding the bite in her tone.

Chad fumbled for words while Mackenzie threw a hundred-dollar bill on the table and made a beeline for the exit, never having been so grateful for a postmortem in her life.

The morgue was inside a concrete building in Olympia, which was around a thirty-minute ride from Lakemore. The newly renovated building shone brightly against the velvety black sky, sheltering the horrors and macabre expected from a place surrounded by thick trees and impenetrable darkness.

Mackenzie climbed out of the car and almost tripped over her dress. It was long, reaching her ankles in the back. It seemed appropriate considering the fancy restaurant she had gone to. Now, as she took the stairs to the dingy basement, she felt ridiculous wearing pink.

A cool current of air brushed her bare arms, sprouting goosebumps on her pale skin. She shivered and noticed Nick sitting on a steel bench against the yellow-tiled wall.

"Hey," she said, reaching him.

He was absorbed on his phone and muttered a "hey", briefly glancing at her. Then he did a double take. "What the hell are you wearing?"

She frowned. "A dress."

He raised his eyebrows, scanning her from head to toe. "I didn't know you owned a dress."

"I have many dresses."

"How many?" he challenged with a knowing smile.

Mackenzie had bought the dress last week. She huffed, dodging the question, and headed toward the examination room. "Did we get anything from the surveillance in Mia's apartment building?"

Nick walked behind her, amused at her struggling to walk fast in heels. "We can see Mia entering the building at fifteen past eight in the evening and never leaving. Some residents came in after that. All have been questioned and accounted for. But looks like whoever took her, snuck up to her balcony... So, why are you dressed up?"

"I had a date," she mumbled, embarrassed.

"A date?!" He stopped in front of the examination room.

She glared at him. "Why can't I have a date?"

"You can." He looked like he was trying to hold his laughter. "You just look very angry for someone who had a date."

The door opened, and Becky popped her head out. "Thought I heard you two bickering outside. Oh, sorry, Mack. I forgot you had your big date tonight." She let them inside and went to the sanitization station to collect gloves and skullcaps.

The examination room was bright and roomy. There were four downdraft postmortem tables situated in the center, pull-through fridges on the back wall, and a wall-mounted dissection bench running along the right side. Two doors were situated on the other end, leading to the utility room and transit area for staff.

"Did everyone know about this date but me?" Nick asked.

"I was the one who set her up. Chad's a family friend."

"*Chad?*" Nick laughed. "You set her up with a guy called *Chad.*"

Becky jutted out her hip, placing her hand on it. "Yes, Nick. What's wrong with Chad?"

Mackenzie focused on putting on the skullcap and trying to hide her flaming cheeks.

"For starters, she's thirty-three years old, not twenty-one."

"*She* is standing right here." Mackenzie growled. "No more comments on my date with Chad. There won't be a second one anyway."

Becky raised her hands in surrender and gestured them to follow her. "That is Mia Gallagher."

Mackenzie regarded the bones lying on one of the tables under the forensic light with a forced detachment. In some ways, it was easier this way, to visualize a victim without skin that once tanned under the sun, hair that someone must have run their fingers through lovingly, and eyes that watered and sparkled. The bones felt less human to Mackenzie, reminded her that, underneath, everyone could be stripped down to something so rudimentary and clinical. But the closer she got, she saw that even bones looked distinctive. There were little cuts, dents, and angles—evidence of a life lived.

"Angela Weiss was kind enough to send over her interns to clean the bones for me and help with the post," Becky said. "As you know, I prefer to have more flesh and tissues on my bodies, but this one was so messed up that it was better to scrape it all off."

She referred to the leading forensic anthropologist of Washington State, who consulted on high-profile cases for the Lakemore PD.

"Was she alive when she was thrown down the shaft?" Mackenzie asked.

"Nope. She was already dead, based on the hemorrhaging tissue," Becky confirmed.

"It looks like she was dumped in from the machine room up top," Nick said. "Justin said the lock was jimmied. It's a construction site, so no security or surveillance."

Becky did some calculations in her head. "That would be concurrent with the hairline impact fissures on the lateral epicondyle, the bones outside the elbow joint, which are consistent with falls. I estimate she fell at least fifty feet, which brings us to that height."

"How do you know she's Mia Gallagher?"

"We couldn't do a dental since all her teeth were knocked out postmortem in the shaft and her DNA is not in the system, but fragments of her clothing match exactly what Mia was seen wearing in that footage." She pointed at the bagged clothes behind her, ready to be dispatched to the crime lab.

Mackenzie shuddered at the little pieces of bones arranged in the correct order. "That's a lot of damage."

"Comminuted fractures in upper and lower extremities and sheering of the spinous processes—the little extensions found along the vertebrae—are all postmortem. She also suffered from burst fractures in her lower back and bilateral compression fractures in the ribs that aren't remodeled."

"So they happened recently?" Nick sighed.

"Right before death. Ante-mortem. She was beaten up. But not too badly."

"She probably got into it with her attacker." Mackenzie's mind reeled. "Think she scratched them?"

Becky smiled. "She definitely did. There's DNA under her fingernails. I'm checking the state and federal databases for a match."

Mackenzie hoped there would be a hit and they could wrap up this case. "Any signs of sexual assault?"

"It's hard to say," Becky pressed her lips in a thin line, "because of all the postmortem damage, but I found no evidence of it. She was tied up, based on the ligature fractures around her wrists."

"I'm guessing you're still running the tox screen?"

She nodded. "If she was drugged, we'll know."

"And the cause of death?" Nick prodded.

"Manual strangulation is a reasonable conclusion." Becky looked uncomfortable. "The hyoid bone is fractured and compressed, but it's tricky to distinguish between postmortem and ante-mortem damage. Her hyoid bone was found lodged in a hook that connected the cable to the elevator."

"Jesus," Nick muttered. "What about time of death?"

"She's still in rigor mortis, putting the time of death at least around twenty-four hours ago."

"The construction crew hadn't worked on the site for almost a week. Yesterday was their first day back," Nick added.

Mackenzie stifled the discomfort brewing in her gut. An attractive model who always had it together was stashed down an elevator and broken into chunks. Nothing in her text messages or call logs indicated that she had a boyfriend. None of her co-workers or friends said there was anyone who could have wanted to hurt her. Mia's behavior in the days leading up to her disappearance was described as normal.

"What are you thinking?" Nick read Mackenzie's absorbed face.

Mackenzie stared at Mia's skull and her empty eye sockets, almost seeing the eyes there. "I'm scared this is the work of a serial killer."

"Why?" He crossed his arms. "We only have one body. Nothing ritualistic about the killing apparently."

"I know. But I'm thinking if this was personal then there should have been *some* evidence of something out of the ordinary in her life. But there's not a shred of anything odd."

Nick considered this but wasn't convinced. "I think it's too early to assume anything."

"One more thing." Becky picked up a bone and pointed at two tiny stained holes. "These are puncture wounds. Based on their diameter and the distance between them, I say it's from a stun gun or a Taser."

"It was probably used to subdue her after she fought that hard." Nick connected the dots. "She was probably thrown into the trunk of a car he had parked behind the building and driven to where he held her."

"I'll ask CSI if they found any Taser confetti in or around the site of abduction," Mackenzie said, referring to the colored tags that were dispensed whenever a Taser was fired. Each tag was marked with an ID, allowing the police to track the owner of the weapon. "If we can get the AFID serial number, we can trace it to the buyer. Provided it was a taser gun."

Mia Gallagher had fought back. In her final moments, she'd left them the best evidence an investigator could hope for. This could have been a slam-dunk if they found a DNA match. But then why didn't Mackenzie feel even a shimmer of hope? Her nerves fluttered at the sight of Mia's bones, an instinct developed and honed over years whispering that there was something more to this.

SIX

OCTOBER 13

Mackenzie fiddled with her cuffs. They were ironed, but she saw one crease and diligently tried to smoothen it. Her boots weren't scuffed, the black sheen as shiny as ever. Her neck sat stiff on her shoulders.

"Why don't you try to relax?" Valerie Cohen suggested in a sweet tone that had undergone years of vocal training to sound perfect on camera. "Remember, just look at me."

Mackenzie noted how relaxed and poised Valerie was. Her legs were casually crossed; she sat back, her neck swiveling with grace and ease. It was the fluidity that Mackenzie lacked and envied. How Valerie blended into the world, unlike her, who constantly felt like a skeptical spectator.

They were seated in the conference room at the Lakemore PD station. A few months ago, Valerie and her crew had arrived intending to make a documentary about female detectives in Washington. Lakemore, wanting to participate to rehabilitate its image following the negative publicity it received from the backlash of a big case, suggested Mackenzie's name. To Mackenzie's agony, she couldn't refuse her superiors or ignore Nick's incessant teasing. Fortunately, the documentary crew had been good at staying out of the way and didn't seem to be in a rush. She was able to squeeze in short interviews over the summer, often when she was taking a lunch break or waiting for reports or leads to turn up, or during those two rare weeks when she was working on a cold case and there was no urgent crisis in Lakemore.

Mackenzie was far from the "cool" and "charming" cop Valerie had envisaged. Instead, she was guarded, stoic, and sometimes brutally honest. She rarely opened up to people she knew, so having a stranger ask personal questions about what shaped her and motivated her had been beyond agonizing for both of them.

The documentary had been completed, but Valerie was back to reshoot some scenes they realized during final edits could have come out better. Which was a polite way of saying that Mackenzie needed to appear less wooden.

"Let's roll the camera," Valerie said to the camera guy. "So, Detective Price, how long have you been with the Lakemore PD?"

"Nine years now."

"And before that you were in New York?"

"That's right."

"What a strange move, from New York to Lakemore. As a police officer, what's the difference between a big city and a small town like this?"

Mackenzie's eyes found Nick standing by the door, behind the camera, watching with a grin, and stifled a groan. "New York registered over three hundred murders in the year 2015 alone, and that's *just* homicide. We don't see those numbers here. Every murder and abduction ends up getting coverage and attention and becomes the talk of the town. We face more pressure and scrutiny in some ways."

"Do you find law enforcement to still be a man's game?" Valerie asked. "Do you feel you have to go an extra mile to exhibit your toughness so that people take you more seriously?"

Mackenzie paused, feeling her ears burn from the giant, imposing black camera pointing at her and recording every twitch of her face. "Fortunately, or unfortunately, no one's ever accused me of being soft or sweet, so I don't have to consciously do anything."

Valerie let out a forced chuckle, which confused Mackenzie since she wasn't joking. She gestured to the cameraman to stop recording and leaned forward. "I know you're nervous, Detective Price, but can you elaborate on your answers more? Don't keep them too short or to the point. You know, loosen up a bit."

A bark of laughter came from the door. Nick and Troy Clayton, another detective in Mackenzie's unit, reined in their mirth.

"You clearly don't know her. At all," Troy quipped.

"I'm just not someone with a lot of words, Ms. Cohen. More of an action woman."

Valerie's eyes widened and she clapped her hands. "What an excellent idea! We should follow you on the field! That's exactly what we were missing in the edits."

"I didn't mean—"

"Of course, we would stay out of the way!" she went on.

"I don't think—"

"This will give our viewers some really edgy footage." She turned to the cameraman to discuss details, forgetting Mackenzie, sitting there with her mouth open.

Mackenzie shot up from the chair and marched toward Sully's office with purpose.

"I would *pay* to watch you get interviewed again." Nick was at her heels.

"I didn't sign up for this." Mackenzie gritted her teeth. "I hate talking about myself. Why didn't they ask for you? All those lights and cameras and attention are right up your alley."

Nick was the only son of Senator Alan Blackwood and had descended from a long line of senators and governors and other highly ranking public servants—a tradition he broke when he declared his intentions to forever stay away from politics. But, of course, the documentary was about female detectives—which was just Mackenzie's luck.

She knocked on the door and entered without waiting for a response.

Mackenzie and Nick both froze.

Sully's office was small, with a map of Washington State on the right wall and a whiteboard on the left. A window behind his wooden desk looked over the parking lot. The small space was usually filled with boxes and whatever random hobby the quirky sergeant had selected to obsess over this week everything from model-building to origami. But now not only was the office the most organized and empty they'd ever seen it, but Sully sat at his desk, his gray hair dyed jet black.

"S-Sully?" Mackenzie found her voice eventually. "A word?"

Sully was engrossed in trimming his mustache. "Make it quick. I'm up next with Cohen," he informed them, looking very pleased. "Pam's been telling all her friends at the club that I'm going to be in a documentary. I have to look good. My wife can't lose face after all the bragging she did."

"Valerie suggested she go with us on field," Mackenzie said sharply. "Clearly she's way over her head. Can you put a stop to this?"

Sully didn't flinch. "No can do. Captain Murphy's orders. She can do whatever she wants as long it doesn't interfere with an active investigation."

"Really?" Nick raised an eyebrow. "I didn't realize the brass were giving her such a long leash."

The scissors made a sharp snipping sound. "We need some

good publicity, Nick. Especially the mayor after everything that has transpired this past year."

"How will we accommodate her if she is to stay away from active investigations?" Mackenzie asked.

"Just take her on patrol. Bust a few dealings. That will be enough. She'll be out of your hair in no time."

"But we don't go on patrol."

Sully set down his scissors and sighed. "Mack, be a team player."

"I *am* a team player."

"Yeah, right." Sully snorted and exchanged a look of disbelief with Nick.

She pinched the bridge of her nose, feeling irritation nip at her skin.

"What do we have on Mia Gallagher?" Sully asked, standing up and changing his tie to a blue one.

Mackenzie's chest caved. "The DNA under her nails isn't on any database."

"And the CSI found no confetti in her apartment from a Taser," Nick added. "But we're sure that her apartment was the site of abduction. Maybe a stun gun was used to subdue her."

Sully sighed, picking up a pair of shoes to buff them. "Keep me informed."

Mackenzie returned to her desk and pinned Mia's picture on the board. Dissecting and picking apart others was easier. It was when she turned her skills to herself that she feared the pieces she was made of.

"We just got her finances." Nick wheeled into her cubicle, giving her a file.

"Great. This might explain things." She took it from him and began skimming.

Mia had been a country girl who had left her small town in Kansas to chase big dreams in LA. But when constant rejection crushed those dreams, she found herself in another small town.

Except this life came with little luxuries. Somehow Mia had found a way to thrive, well above her means.

She was immersed in her task, tracking down how Mia had managed to afford the trips and pretty things, when her phone rang. "Detective Price."

"Ma'am, it's Peterson." A gravelly voice filtered through the phone. "We need you and Detective Blackwood at 2401 Maple Street."

"Okay, what is it?" she asked, detecting a note of indecision in his tone.

"Looks like a suicide... But we have reason to believe it's related to Mia Gallagher's murder."

SEVEN

"So what was Chad like?" Nick asked stopping at a red light.

She rolled her eyes. "Why are you so curious?"

"I just don't know anyone who ever went on a date with a *Chad*."

"You really hate that name." She chuckled. "He was a jerk. Self-obsessed. Superior. But that's not what bothered me the *most*."

"Then what did?"

The engine roared to life again.

Mackenzie fiddled with the watch on her wrist, given to her by her uncle. "This is embarrassing. But he propositioned me." She felt the pink bursting on her cheeks.

Nick was baffled. "Why is that a bad thing? Wait. Did he force himself...?"

"No!" She dropped her head back. "It was nothing like that. He *asked* me. So I know it wasn't creepy, but I was still offended, which is strange. Nothing wrong in an adult man asking an adult woman if she's interested in spending the night with him. Am I a prude? Do I have a stick up my ass?"

"You don't have a stick up your ass..." He shrugged casually.

"I mean, not a *big* stick. I wouldn't even call it a stick. A twig. You have a twig up your ass."

Mackenzie glared at him, the corners of her lips threatening to break into a grin. "A *twig*?"

He blew out a breath. "You know what I mean. If he was being a dick to you and then propositioned you, then it is offensive. It means he thinks he can treat you like shit and you'd still want him. Sounds like the guy is just dumb as rocks."

"This conversation has been mortifying." She zipped up her leather jacket like it was her shield.

"Are you really ready to date?" Nick asked softly.

Mackenzie felt the air in the car shift. Nick had been her best friend since she stepped foot in Lakemore and mistook him for a mugger and hit him with a pipe, only to find out the next day that he was her partner. He knew everything about her, including her past. Which was why Nick understood how it was a big deal for her to even entertain the possibility of companionship after Sterling had shattered her trust by cheating on her. Just like so many others in her life, her ex-husband had joined the list of people who had betrayed her. For Mackenzie, who hid from the world behind her tough and reserved façade because she bruised too easily, dating was a huge step.

A step that left her stomach feeling hollow.

"Baby steps," she chanted aloud. "Baby steps."

Nick nodded. "Yeah. Just don't date another guy called *Chad*."

"What other names should I avoid?"

"Channing. Zeke. Trey. Chaz."

"Chaz is a name?" She smirked.

"Hoo, boy. Oh yeah." He groaned, turning into Maple Street. "Did Peterson give any other information?"

"No. And from what we know, nobody Mia knew lives on Maple Street."

The street was lined with cardboard-cut-out houses. They all looked the same, box-shaped with a shingle roof, front yards with clothing lines and overflowing garbage bins in the front. Stray cats sashayed around like it was their territory.

But the dirt-ridden street had speckles of beauty. Orange gilded leaves floated down after being plucked off trees. Mackenzie looked up at autumn kindling the tops of trees, the colors of scarlet and gold bursting across the canopy. It was her favorite season.

When they climbed out of the car, the chilly air kissed her skin. Slight winter blusters. It was a dry morning. No hint of moisture in the air and no wisp of cloud in the sky.

The house had been secured with a crime-scene tape. A squad car and a morgue van were on standby. They ducked under the tape and were joined by Peterson on the front porch.

"Glenn Solomon," Peterson said. "The guy he owed money to came to collect and found him hanging instead."

As soon as Mackenzie entered the house, she saw a hefty man dangling from a ceiling fan. A stool was toppled over, not too far from his feet. He was dressed in gray sweatpants and red T-shirt that rode up revealing his hairy torso, bulging out. His eyes were closed; his neck limped over to one side.

Some uniform cops on the side were interviewing a jittery man wearing a fedora.

"The door was open?" Nick asked.

Peterson nodded at the man in the fedora. "He broke it down."

"How do we know it's a suicide?" Mackenzie asked, her eyes scanning the room for any signs of struggle. But the space was undisturbed and filled with minimal, second-hand furniture—plastic chairs, a coffee table with a broken leg—and there was a humming sound that came from the refrigerator.

"He left a note." Peterson handed her a piece of paper inside an evidence bag.

The handwriting was messy and hurried. Some of the ink was smudged like tracing a tear rolling down the paper.

> I killed her. Mia Gallagher. I swear I didn't want to. But I had no choice. It was either her or me. But I can't live with myself anymore. I'm sorry. I'm so, so sorry.

EIGHT

OCTOBER 14

The morning in Lakemore was wet and shiny. Mackenzie's feet rang against the glistening concrete as she ran, causing jets of water to fan out. The sky was thick and gray, hanging low. It had rained the entire night. The little Washington town was left drenched like a towel, dripping and heavy. The earthy perfume slithered up Mackenzie's nose.

It had all almost come crumbling down over a year ago when Mackenzie had solved a case. Lakemore had changed. The past year it was left licking its wounds and reflecting upon its shameful past and tepid future.

Mackenzie came to a halt, her breath coming hard and squeezing her lungs. She took off her earphones, soaking in the silence of the early morning. The vast lake had waters so still that it looked like a painting. She recalled going for an impromptu swim in one of the lakes as a child. She saw a faint image of herself, zipping past her so fast, disturbing the air around her. Just as quickly, the little Mackenzie disappeared.

It was a simpler time, when Mackenzie wasn't aware of how the world worked. It was a simpler time, when the little and big blows of life hadn't hardened her.

"Sometimes I want to chase the wind," Melody had muttered aloud one time.

"What do you mean?" a ten-year-old Mackenzie had asked.

Melody looked out the window as wind whipped through the trees. "I want to run like I used to when I was kid."

"Why don't you? No one is watching."

Melody had sighed, wistfully. But her voice had an edge of scorn. "It's not about that, Mackenzie. Innocence once lost is almost impossible to recapture. Always keep some of it bottled away if you can. Because one day the reality of this world will tire you."

Melody had gone back to scrubbing the dishes clean and Mackenzie went back to reading her copy of The Hardy Boys.

Now Mackenzie stood by the lake, and after all these years she understood her mother's words. The desire to break free made her heart boil. She wanted to do something out of character, something crazy but not irresponsible. Anything to make her feel *something*. She could swim in the lake for a bit. But her feet were heavy like iron, rooted deep into the ground, like it was a part of the earth. They just wouldn't move.

Stupid, stupid idea.

She shook her head and bit her tongue. Steeling her spine and schooling her face, she crept back behind her reliable armor.

She sprinted past a poster that caught her eye.

Football coaching was starting again. Lakemore Sharks were on track to reclaim the Olympic Championship—a local football tournament.

It gave her hope.

Mackenzie tapped her fingers on her desk and glared at Glenn Solomon's suicide note.

But I had no choice. It was either her or me.

A junior detective with their division, Jenna, strolled in wearing her standard knee-high boots. "I heard back on the handwriting analysis." She placed an elbow on Nick's cubicle wall and only addressed him, giving Mackenzie a cold shoulder.

Nick closed a file and rubbed his eyes. "And?"

"It's authentic." She handed him a file, while Mackenzie peeked over his shoulder. "The connecting strokes to letters, slant and even him going off baseline alignment. We matched it to some documents we found at his place."

"Becky will be performing a post tonight, but based on her initial assessment, it looks like suicide," Mackenzie said, pulling out pictures of the body. "No visible injuries. He wasn't beaten up."

Nick scratched his ear. "Did you do a background check?"

Jenna shrugged. "He has no priors, no record. He has an accounting degree from the University of Michigan but has done mostly freelance work or odd jobs for twenty years."

That caught Mackenzie's attention. Glenn Solomon had a respectable education from a good university. Remembering the house and the second-hand furniture, she wasn't surprised that he didn't hold a steady job. "Has he ever been married?"

"Divorced around twenty years ago." Jenna kept her eyes on Nick, pointedly ignoring Mackenzie. "No kids. It was around then that he was fired from his last stable job at a small steel manufacturer company, Acorn Metals."

Nick turned to Mackenzie with a grave look on his face. "Maybe he went down a spiral after losing the job and wife."

"What was his link with Mia? And why was he talking like that in his suicide note?"

Jenna cleared her throat to get their attention again. "We found some pills in his bathroom. The bottles had an expired label on them so we're running them down right now."

"If he'd been misusing drugs, then there might be no logic to any of this." Nick rolled his eyes. "Thanks, Jenna. Let us know when you find out more."

"Will do." She turned on her heel and barreled out of the office with stiff shoulders.

Mackenzie watched her leave. They had never gotten along, for no reason at all as far as she could fathom. "What's her deal today? Did I do something?"

Nick snorted and picked up his coffee. "Nah. She's just taking it hard that the documentary chose to focus on you."

"What?"

"She's also a female detective in our division. She's feeling overlooked."

"Oh, she can gladly take all the spotlight." Mackenzie shuddered, remembering that they had to take Valerie Cohen on a drive-along in a few hours. It made her nerves scratchy to think how she was going to be more accessible to the public. Pushing it away, she focused back on the case. "We should pull Glenn's finances."

"You think Mia was a murder for hire?"

"He was struggling for money. He had taken loans from people. Maybe someone who wanted Mia dead found the perfect person to do the job." She pointed at the suicide letter in the evidence bag. "It would explain what he meant by he didn't have a choice. As in he was desperately in need of money, but then felt guilty after the fact."

Nick nodded. "Yeah, okay. I'll get those. Who do you think would want Mia dead? Wren Murray didn't think anyone had a problem with her."

Mackenzie was at a loss. She picked up Mia's picture, trying to deconstruct the staged photo of a pretty girl lounging on the beach with a seemingly perfect life. "Jealousy? What if someone in her life was jealous of her?"

"We still don't know how exactly she was able to afford all

this," Nick mulled. "She was making significant cash deposits every month that didn't come from her salary."

"Who was paying her in cash?"

"Detective Price!" Lieutenant Atlee Rivera emerged from Sully's office. The strapping woman with olive skin and long dark hair had joined the Lakemore PD merely few months ago and had already made a mark. "Can I see you for a moment?"

Mackenzie exchanged a nervous glance with Nick. Why was only she called? It had to be something to do with the documentary. Pulling back her shoulders, she went into Sully's office. There was a blank canvas on a wooden table easel with a tray of acrylic paints and brushes. "Painting?"

Sully adjusted his belt buckle over his drum of a belly. "I want to give something to Pam for our thirtieth wedding anniversary."

"Usually, people stick with just jewelry." Mackenzie took a seat next to Rivera, who put her spectacles on and opened a file.

"Wanted to add a personal touch."

"How did your reshoot go?" Rivera asked in a clipped tone, absorbed by the file she was reading.

"Fine. I don't want to think too much about it. But why am I here?"

Rivera's watchful gaze drifted to Mackenzie. "Just a quick question. Did you know Detective Austin Kennedy has been looking into his fiancée's disappearance?"

She took a small intake of breath. The new detective had joined the force with the intent to hunt down his fiancée, who was last seen in Lakemore over a year ago. "Yes. He told me about it. I helped him this summer, but nothing came of it," Mackenzie replied. It was the truth. She had helped her colleague while he frantically pored through records and statements. But his fiancée, Sophie, had disappeared like footprints washing away on the shore. "Is anything wrong?"

"No." Sully frowned. "We just didn't know about this. He

sent an informal request to Riverview PD, which got flagged, as I never approved it."

"Oh, okay." She played with her fingers. "Um, anything else?"

"No." He was evasive. "You've stopped looking into it, right?"

"Yeah. There was nothing there. At least not in our jurisdiction."

"Okay." Rivera looked satisfied. "Detective Kennedy has breached protocol a few times and has tried to hide this from us. He has promised to stop looking, and we have decided not to reprimand him, because we... sympathize with his situation. Provided that there is nothing under the table moving forward." She pinned Mackenzie with a hard glare.

The lieutenant was a stickler for protocol. She brought in the necessary discipline that the department needed. A chain weaved through the town, connecting everyone and everything. When prosperity and doom were pooled together, it was only natural for seeds of corruption to grow. Heavy silence pressed in the room. Mackenzie felt the air become sharp with tension.

"Okay then," Sully forced a smile, dismissing Mackenzie. "Good luck with your ride-along today. Glad this chapter is closed."

She stood up slowly and left the office. On her way back, she spotted Austin sitting at his desk, talking on the phone. His blond curls had grown longer and wilder, almost covering his entire forehead. His pale skin had thinned over his strong bones. His blue eyes collided with Mackenzie's. He gave her a courteous nod.

Mackenzie stifled an uneasy feeling. Austin had seemingly agreed to stop looking for Sophie. But hope was stronger than love—harder to kill and nearly impossible to resurrect.

NINE

To Mackenzie's annoyance, her car was covered in soaked leaves. They stuck to the windshield, leaving water rings. The silver-black sheen was sprayed with stains like ink splats. She didn't dare to look at the tires. She knew what she'd find—wet mud mulched in between the ridges.

Today, the rain came in bursts. Thunder grumbled, shaking the ground, beckoning another splash.

"We're going to have to postpone our ride-along to tomorrow." Valerie opened an umbrella with bright pink polka dots. She looked up at the darkening sky with a scowl. "We won't get good shots with this weather."

Mackenzie's chest fell in relief. "Perfect. See you tomorrow." She opened the door to Valerie's car, ushering her away.

Valerie chuckled at Mackenzie's blatant attempt to get rid of her. "See you, Detective Price."

Mackenzie pulled up the hood of her jacket as the car pulled out of the parking lot.

Nick came out of the building, wearing his coat. "You not going?"

"Nope." She beamed at him. "I can actually spend my time doing something productive. You got anything?"

"I was going to speak with Glenn's therapist." He walked over to his car with Mackenzie following him.

"He had a therapist?"

"Jenna found a diary in his room. Every Tuesday evening, he had an appointment. I thought this doc could tell us about those pills and Glenn's state of mind."

"I'll come with."

On their drive, Mackenzie studied Mia Gallagher's case file. It was a bad habit, always triggering her motion sickness. She could already feel vomit bubbling in the back of her throat. Seeing her go green, Nick popped open the glovebox with his free hand and threw Gravol on her lap with a silent disapproval. She swallowed the large pill dry and went back to reading, unable to sit idle while riding.

Mia had been abducted from her home after she returned late at night. Her mangled body was discovered on the other side of town in the elevator shaft of a construction site. Glenn lived around halfway in between.

"I can hear you thinking," Nick commented.

"I'm wondering how they could be connected." Mackenzie did a quick check on her phone. "Not on any social media platform from what I see."

Nick's thick eyebrows dipped. "Maybe there is a connection between them, but we haven't found it yet. Though, to be honest, I don't see them crossing paths. I also didn't find Glenn's number on Mia's phone."

It wasn't a surprise. Mia was the poster child for the new era in social media. She looked flawless, planning every angle of her face and twist of her lips for the camera. She ate at trendy restaurants outside Lakemore and conversed in the new-age lingo.

Then there was Glenn, whose life was a question mark. Mackenzie looked at an old picture of him taken twenty years ago—the last time he had a steady job. He looked well groomed, clean and had that spark of confidence. A man who had it together. A jarring contrast to the unkempt man hanging from a ceiling fan, bordering on depravity.

"She was abducted," Mackenzie wondered aloud. "So he must have wanted something from her. Statistically speaking, it was sexual. Too bad we can't confirm that. But Glenn has never been a person of interest in any investigation. He's not in the system. Things that are typical for someone who hurts random women."

"That's a more likely profile of a serial killer. You think Mia could be his first victim?" Nick asked.

"Maybe. But how many potential serial killers have you heard of who committed suicide out of guilt after their first kill?"

There was a reception desk underneath a bright white light at the end of the narrow hallway. It reminded Mackenzie of that tunnel many people who've had near-death experience report about. They walked down the claustrophobic path, reaching the end—bright and airy. The reception desk was white and glass with the name of the practice in block letters on the wall behind. It almost pained Mackenzie's eyes how white everything was—from the white roses in white vases to white plastic chairs. Like abundant positivity was being shoved down her throat.

The wiry man behind the desk typed deftly on his computer. "Do you have an appointment?"

Mackenzie showed her badge. "We're here to talk to Dr. Adeline Kane."

The man didn't show any reaction, like he was used to the police barging in and interrupting the schedule. "You can go in now. She just finished with a patient."

Mackenzie and Nick were directed to one of the rooms, with Dr. Kane's name written on it.

Nick whistled at the robot cleaner mopping the floor in a corner. "This place sure looks fancy. Didn't expect anything like this in Lakemore."

"The rent is dirt cheap here compared to Olympia. How the hell did he afford therapy at this expensive place?" Mackenzie took in the inspirational quotes framed on walls about changing and healing. She didn't realize when her feet stopped moving. "Do you think they do anything?" she whispered.

"Words?"

Mackenzie pressed her eyes close. Her stomach sagged and fold onto itself. A white-hot sensation pulsed through her, her mind briefly catapulting to another time in her life when she felt something. But her stupor crackled when the door opened and a tall, dark woman with sharp-edged features came out.

"Dr. Kane." Nick stepped forward and did the introductions. "We have a few questions for you."

"Of course."

"We believe Glenn Solomon was one of your patients."

Dr. Kane's face twitched. "I'm sorry, but what is this about?"

Nick dropped his voice. "He committed suicide."

Her shoulders fell. She blew out a staggering breath. "*Really?* Oh, dear God." She rubbed her forehead and began pacing back and forth.

"We have a few questions for you," Nick said.

"Yes, yes." She crossed her arms and chewed her lower lip until it looked shredded. "I saw him once a week."

"How did he afford therapy? We looked into his finances, and he wasn't doing well."

Dr. Kane hesitated. "Well, Glenn and I went to university together. Our majors were different, but we lived in a coed dorm. We reconnected after his divorce. I felt bad for him, so I offered him free services."

Mackenzie raised an eyebrow. "That's kind of you."

"I pull in an easy six figure a year. It really isn't a big deal to listen to an old friend one hour a week without charging a fee."

"We are looking into his suicide," Mackenzie continued. "We have reason to believe that he was involved in a serious crime. Did he mention anything to you?"

"Well, I don't want to break confidentiality..."

"Since Mr. Solomon was never an official patient, I'm guessing he never signed a confidentiality agreement?" Mackenzie said.

"Look, doc." Nick put her at ease—his general role in their dynamic. Where Mackenzie pinned them with a hard look, using her tall height and sharp eyes to instill nervousness to get people to talk, Nick used his crooked smile and charm to lure information out. It had been the perfect balance for the last nine years. "I get you want to be respectful of your late friend, but you can help clear his name. Someone is dead, and Glenn looks like he was involved. We just need to get this case off our docket."

Dr. Kane nodded. "I wasn't aware of Glenn dabbling in anything illegal. There were a couple of times he tried convincing me to prescribe him Vicodin, but I refused."

Mackenzie thought about the pills found in his bathroom. "To your knowledge, did he acquire pills from any other source?"

"No. Around a few months ago, he stopped asking. I presumed he gave up..." She blinked rapidly. "How did he kill himself?"

"He hanged himself," Nick said. "You didn't think he was suicidal?"

"*Never*." She glared at them horrified and indignant. "Not once did I suspect he had those tendencies. If I did, I would have done something about it. He was depressed, but that doesn't necessarily imply suicidal tendencies."

"He had been divorced for many years. Was he seeing anyone lately? A close friend, perhaps?"

She shook her head. "I encouraged him several times, but he was a loner. He just gave up all those years ago. It doesn't seem like a big deal, considering the awful things people go through, but I see it a lot. Some people just don't know how to stand up again."

"Did he ever mention anyone by the name Mia Gallagher?" Mackenzie inquired.

"Not at all. Who is she?"

"In your professional opinion, do you think Glenn had violent tendencies?"

Dr. Kane's eyes enlarged. "*No*. Glenn was harmless. What do you think he did? What's going on?"

Mackenzie scribbled notes in her diary. They weren't at liberty to reveal anything to someone who wasn't his next of kin. But Glenn Solomon had no next of kin. Neither did Mia Gallagher. One was a loner with his life in shambles and the other shared too much of hers.

"In his sessions with you, did he say anything out of the ordinary in the last few weeks or months?" Nick pressed.

"*No*." She insisted. "The strangest thing he did was cancel his appointment with me last week. He just told me he wasn't feeling well. He was a bit abrupt. I didn't think much of it. I thought I'd ask him about it the next time I see him..." her voice trailed off. Her alert eyes suddenly turned haunted. "I'll never see him again. I failed him."

Nick took out his card. "If you remember anything about him later, get in touch."

Dr. Kane took the card with trembling fingers and swallowed hard. She pocketed it in her coat and checked her watch. The blank face dissolved into a welcoming smile when she peeked over them to address a patient in the waiting area at the end of the hallway. "I'm ready for you!"

They turned to leave after finishing their inquiry, but Mackenzie's mind still reeled.

"She looked positively shocked that he killed himself," Nick muttered, taking out his lighter and flicking it open and close. "But some professionals get it wrong. He must have been good at hiding it."

Mackenzie pressed the button to the elevator. "He was depressed for years. Why *now*?"

"He said it was either him or Mia. Sounds like he was delusional."

They entered the elevator and the doors closed. The shaft moved with a creaking sound. Idly, Mackenzie looked up, wondering how Mia's body would have been moved and crushed. "Yeah, but Dr. Kane would have had *some* inkling. She has been practicing for years. How good could he be at hiding it?"

Nick's hand playing with the lighter paused. "He was on those pills and didn't tell her, so he wasn't completely honest with her. Maybe his issues were worse than he let on and he had some psychotic episode during which he killed Mia?"

"But why her? Where did he hold her hostage? What did he want from her during that time?"

Nick didn't answer when the elevator doors opened. His phone pinged. He checked it and exhaled. "There you go. PCR confirmed that the DNA under Mia's fingernails is a perfect match for Glenn Solomon."

It was the most damning forensic evidence that sealed the

deal. Glenn had not only confessed it in his suicide note that he murdered Mia, but there was also irrefutable physical evidence. But still Mackenzie couldn't shed a strange feeling swirling in her gut. Like a false note in a song. Like that intangible shift in the air when someone has been in a room. It blared loudly like a siren.

Something was amiss.

TEN

Night was drawing in. The station was slowly emptying, but the lights in the Lakemore PD remained on. Being surrounded by trees and a poorly lit parking lot, the building looked like a lantern. The shadows surrounding it deepened. The darkness lingered among the trees, like it was stuck there.

Mackenzie pressed her hand against the window and felt coolness seeping into her skin. It was a chilly night. She was left alone in the office. All her co-workers had families to go home to. Nick lived alone, but he had dinner plans with his daughter, Luna. Mackenzie had nobody waiting for her at home. In the beginning, it had upset her. It left her chest prickly and full. But now she finally saw the silver lining. She was free. She didn't answer to anyone. She only had to think of herself.

Then why wasn't she happy?

Shaking her head, she returned to her desk and opened an email containing the video attachment from the restaurant Mia had frequented the night she was snatched from her home. The case was essentially closed.

But Mackenzie *knew* something was wrong. It was an itch that wouldn't go away no matter how much she scratched.

Glenn Solomon had no history of mental disorders. Could he really be this good at hiding it? Would he be good at fooling people if he was completely delusional? But then why would he confess to killing Mia? A depressed man surviving on the fringes of life used a stun gun on a woman to abduct her and then kill her two days later. It was too abrupt for her to digest.

What irked her was *why*. Why would Glenn go to such extreme lengths because of Mia?

By the time Mackenzie reached home, she was bone-tired. She moved sloppily, her legs woolly and head foggy. She didn't even remember crawling into bed. But before she knew it, she was fast asleep.

A few hours later, the sound of wind slamming against the windowpane almost stirred her awake. She found herself stuck in that little space between sleep and awareness. Her room was swathed in darkness. The only shimmer of light came from the fluttering curtains, throwing shadows on the wall.

It was then she heard a sound.

Someone breathing.

She felt it on her arm.

Hot breath brushed against the hair on her skin.

Heart thumping uninhibited in her chest, she turned over. It was only for a second. But she saw her. Mia. She was sitting on the bed next to her and watching her with a blank face but yearning eyes. But her image was already fading. When Mackenzie blinked, she was gone. It was like trying to catch a reflection in a pond. Before a coherent thought could form in her head, sleep was dragging her back under. But a familiar voice weaved its way through to her. It was her mother.

You'll figure it out, Mackenzie.

ELEVEN

OCTOBER 15

Sully twirled his mustache and assessed everyone in the room crabbily. "Everyone's had their coffee?"

A stream of grunts echoed in the conference room. It was the weekly meeting of the sergeant addressing the Investigations Division. Mackenzie stood at the back of the room with Nick, so that he had the closest access to the espresso machine. Justin stood alert, while Jenna, Ned, Troy and Finn, the other detectives, were seated around the table. Austin leaned against the desk, repeatedly checking his phone. Mackenzie wondered if it were some official case or if he was discreetly looking into Sophie.

"Justin, I want you splitting your time with Ned on the Sidorov case. Seems like it's linked to some drug operation so Special Investigations is in on it too. Our budget for it just blew up." Sully read out from the file like he hated his life. But Mackenzie knew better. Despite Sully's grumpy attitude and preference for random hobbies, he was dedicated and never cut corners. In a town like Lakemore where, over the years, she had realized how many people in power were corrupt and negligent,

Sully was a hidden gem. "Finn and Troy, we need to add one more case on your docket."

"Did Chad message you?" Nick whispered while Sully gave the others their orders.

Mackenzie stifled a laugh. "I had totally forgotten about his existence. But I have another date tonight."

He frowned. "That explains it."

"Explains what?"

"Why you cleaned all our desks last night." The corner of his mouth tugged in a smile, as he teased her over her habit.

He was right that Mackenzie had taken out her cleaning supplies and decided to disinfect all surfaces in the office the night before. It wasn't anxiousness about the date, but her mind was preoccupied with Mia and Glenn.

"What's his name?" Nick asked, sipping his coffee at leisure, his eyes not leaving Sully.

"John. That mature enough for you?"

"Meh."

"What's wrong with *John*?"

"It's too common." He shrugged.

She scoffed. "Okay, *Nick.*"

"Mack and Nick!" Sully said, drawing their attention. "We're closing the Mia Gallagher homicide? Looks like we got enough for the DA."

"We need one more day to confirm something," Mackenzie said, feeling Nick's surprise gaze on her.

Sully sighed. "Confirm what? The guy confessed in a suicide note and his DNA was under her fingernails."

"The motive is still—"

"He was deranged. Didn't he have drugs on him?"

"Amphetamines," Jenna pitched in eagerly. "They were illegally obtained and can cause psychosis."

"There you go!" Sully said.

Mackenzie hissed through her teeth. She had no logic to back up her argument.

"Just a formality. Want to make sure the story holds," Nick said with an easy smile like it wasn't a big deal. Then he pressed Mackenzie with a frown and whispered, "What's that about?"

"Later."

"Wrap it up fast. Austin, where are you on the disappearance of Veronica Fang?" Sully asked.

"It's been forty-eight hours. MUPU has posters out and patrol units have been notified. Media will broadcast information tonight." Austin drummed his long fingers on the table, referring to the Washington State Patrol Missing and Unidentified Persons Unit.

"Veronica Fang?" Mackenzie piped up. She had seen the name on the bulletin yesterday but didn't think much of it.

Sully's mouth flattened. He knew how her brain worked. "A thirty-eight-year-old Asian-origin with black hair. Has nothing in common with Mia."

It was a long shot. Mackenzie was grasping at straws, trying to find anything tangible to explain the queasy feeling gnawing at her.

Once they were dismissed, she waited around to catch a moment with Austin.

"Austin?" She walked alongside him.

He didn't look up, reading a file intently. "How can I help you, Mackenzie?"

She saw the crime-scene pictures he was looking at. It was of a pavement next to a tire. Chalk marked the asphalt circling around what looked like clots of black deposits. "What's that?"

"Abduction site of Veronica Fang." He brooded. "She was taken from a parking lot with no surveillance late at night."

"And that black thing?"

"It's silver according to the crime lab."

"Silver?"

He shrugged and closed the file. "What's up?"

She released a breath and lowered her voice. "I just wanted to check if you were okay. I'm assuming Sully and Rivera spoke with you about... your investigation."

Austin had come to Lakemore to look for his missing fiancé, and Mackenzie had helped him all summer only to meet one dead end after another.

His jaw tightened. "Yes, yes, they did. It's nice of them to let this one slide."

"Are you going to stop looking?"

Pain flashed across Austin's face. The corners of his eyes crinkled. His nostrils flickered. Like he was on the verge of tears. "I have to. I have to... move on, I suppose."

She patted him on the arm and turned around when he said, "Thanks. For helping me out."

"Don't worry about it." She couldn't bear to look at him again.

Living without knowing and forever wondering was a fate she didn't wish upon anyone.

TWELVE

The car jolted up a rutted and muddy track, bouncing over potholes and making growling sounds of protest. Valerie yelped in the back seat, her head smacking against the roof of the car.

"Sorry," Nick mumbled, turning sharply around a bend into a narrow street.

The border Lakemore shared with Riverview was the roughest and most dangerous neighborhood. Crime spilled from Riverview—a town too rotten and far gone to rebuild. It was what Lakemore could have been if it weren't for football. Sometimes that was all it took. One hobby to grow into a passion, and eventually to the most important thing: a source of income.

The farmlands were left far behind. They were at an abandoned chemical plant with tattered, graffitied walls, cracked windows covered in rusted bars and unhinged doors. The ground was littered with scurrying cats, plastic bags and rotting food. The dumpsters lined up on the street hadn't been emptied in days.

Mackenzie saw raccoons feasting on them. "It can't get worse than this."

Nick parked in an alleyway behind a dumpster, concealing

the SUV. They had a view of the adjacent street even though a broken wall separated them. "A lot of deals happen here. We just have to wait."

"Isn't it dangerous?" Valerie asked in a shrill voice. "Don't you need more backup?"

"It's going to be low-key. Dealers don't move big shipments during the day. You'll get enough juice for your video." Nick gave a Cheshire cat smile through the rear-view mirror at the rolling camera held by a silent crew member.

Mackenzie stifled a yawn and began reading Mia's autopsy reports for the hundredth time, hoping to find some detail she had missed. She couldn't ignore what Wren Murray had said. Was it what he thought, that Mia was struggling just because of a bad audition? Or was she being forced into something? Could it be related to her death?

"Might as well make use of this time and get some extra information on the two of you." Valerie perked up from behind. "So how long have you been together for?"

Mackenzie and Nick slowly looked each other—partly baffled but mostly alarmed. At the same time, they broke into hysterical laughter.

"Did I say something funny?" Valerie asked, confused.

Mackenzie couldn't rein it in. She clutched her stomach, chuckling, while Nick's grating laugh echoed in the car. "We're not... we're not together."

"I see."

Nick wiped a tear from his eye. "Jesus. The last time I had to clarify this was when Luna asked me three years ago."

"Luna?" Valerie asked.

"My daughter."

"Oh, I didn't know you were married."

"I'm not. Never was."

"Interesting."

Mackenzie noted the slight tilt in Valerie's tone. She eyed

her from the side mirror to find her tucking her hair strand behind her ear and glancing at Nick with blatant curiosity. She rolled her eyes and went back to reading through Mia's text messages, hoping to discover *anything*.

"Mack, what is it?" Nick asked quietly, while Valerie was instructing her cameraman on something. "Why are you so hell-bent on this?"

"It bothers me."

"What?"

"That I don't know everything. Where did he keep her? Why did he take her? How was she making all that money? Doesn't it bother you?" She searched his eyes.

Nick stared at her for a few seconds and then sighed. "All right. You continue looking into Mia. I'll go through Glenn's movements and cross off the places he went to. Maybe we'll find where he held her. I'll delay the report to the DA."

A small smile broke on her face. "Thanks."

"Don't thank me. You're right. It's better to be safe than sorry."

Mackenzie turned back to the file while Valerie engaged Nick in mindless chatter.

"There we go. Some kids over there," Nick said after a few minutes. "Last time I was in a patrol like this was before I made detective."

Everyone in the car became eerily quiet. The group of teenagers looked no older than sophomores in college. Dressed in hoodies, they stood around, exchanging wads of cash.

"Will you turn on the siren?" Valerie asked.

"They'll just run. Easier if we approach them," Nick said.

"I'll go," Mackenzie decided. "The car's a bit overcrowded anyway."

"But—"

"You need to stay here. Don't want to leave them unsupervised in case something goes down. They're basically kids."

Mackenzie was out the door, ignoring Nick's protests. It was a hot afternoon. The sun was blazing, sending waves of heat dancing on her skin. She adjusted her leather jacket, striding toward the teens, wearing her fierce expression.

They spotted her and one of them whistled.

"Does the carpet match the drapes?" he cackled.

Mackenzie glared at the three boys. She was taller than them with a strong build. Up close, she realized two out of the three boys looked barely sixteen. They flinched at her sharp gaze. She didn't have a soft face. It was hardened after she had to grow up too fast and the lies she carried further steeled her. The third one who had mocked her wasn't deterred. He leered at her openly. She casually flicked the hem of her jacket aside, revealing her gun tucked in the holster. "What's going on over here?"

The two young boys stepped back and looked at each other, while the third one piped up.

"Just hangin' out. That illegal now?"

"No. But that is." She looked pointedly at the plastic bag with white crystals poking out of his pocket. "Meth?"

The boy cursed under his breath.

Mackenzie turned to the two boys—their breathing quickened, sweat beading on their foreheads. "How old are you?"

"Fifteen."

"Fourteen."

"Christ. Okay." She wagged her finger at them. "Consider this your first and last warning. If I catch you two ever again, I will throw you in prison personally. Go to school, keep your heads down, and do not get involved with scum like him. It's not worth it. Am I clear?"

"Yes." They nodded, swallowing hard.

"Run along then."

They hurried away like little kids who were out on their first adventure turned dangerous.

"Little shits like you lure them in young now."

"Not my problem they come looking," he bragged.

Mackenzie turned him around and took out her handcuffs; she'd had enough of him. But as she did, he jammed his elbow into her stomach.

"Ah!" Her body bowed, her entire breath leaving her lungs in a single shot.

The boy stumbled away and picked up pace, running away from her. His outline blurred and rippled under the sunlight. Anger and adrenaline surged through her, and she chased after him. She was a runner—the fastest one in her class in the academy. Her long legs carried her closer, until she reached him and wrapped her arms around his torso. She picked him up and threw him behind her, falling back in the process. The back of her head slammed into concrete. She was dizzy for a few seconds, the blue sky above flickering like glitches in a video. He moaned in pain behind her. Getting to her feet, she quickly inspected him and noted that it didn't look like he had broken anything. By the time she pulled his wrists behind his back, Nick caught up with them.

"Mack! Are you okay?" he asked.

"Yeah..."

"Do you need a doctor?"

"No. I'll be fine." She shoved the boy into Nick. "Let's take him to the station to get processed."

Behind Nick, an excited Valerie and her cameraman had recorded the entire thing. The plastic bag had dropped on the ground next to the boy's feet; its contents spilled next to his shoes.

His shoes.

Mackenzie couldn't stop staring at them, feeling a realization lingering right at the corner of her mind. She tuned out the conversation around her. The voices sucked away into a vacuum, until all she heard was the movement of air.

THIRTEEN

Mackenzie picked at her food and looked up at John sitting across from her. The date had dragged. Her mind had been stuck on the case, but she didn't want to cancel last minute. Her head had throbbed after the arrest, and she had popped an over-the-counter painkiller. Heat swam behind her eyes. She blinked and guzzled water.

"Are you feeling well?" John asked, fixing his glasses. "You've been flushed all night."

"Yes, sorry." She shook her head. "I hit my head at work today so I'm a bit out of it."

"You should get that checked out."

She gave him a teasing smile. "You're a doctor, right? You can give me a free check-up."

John pressed his lips in a thin line. "I'm a schoolteacher."

Mackenzie's smile fell. She bit her tongue. She really hadn't been paying attention. "I'm so sorry."

He shrugged and went back to his food.

Mackenzie wanted to cower in the awkward silence. He hadn't been inappropriate like her previous date, but he was immeasurably dull. Or perhaps she hadn't given him a chance.

How could she when her mind kept wandering back to Mia and Glenn?

"So what do you teach?" she asked.

"Chemistry."

"Ah." She struggled to make conversation. "We deal with a lot of forensic chemistry in our field."

"Oh, really!" He wiped his mouth with the napkin, his dull face lighting up. "I'm always trying to get kids interested in chemistry. Maybe this fact will. Clearly none of my experiments work."

"Kids are a tough audience," she said wistfully. It was the reason why her ex-husband had cheated on her—kids. He wanted them and she didn't. And that was how he'd punished her for lacking a parental instinct, even though he had called it dealing with the pain. "What kind of experiments do you do for them?"

"The general. The Mentos trick, dry ice, litmus tests, and all that."

"Oh litmus tests. The ones that change color," she remembered, having gathered a lot of knowledge over the years. Then she paused. A thought came to her. "Does silver change color?"

"Silver?"

"Yes, I mean, any interesting reactions from it?"

He beamed, eager to share the knowledge. "Silver chloride or nitrate crystals change color in the sun. They break down into silver, which is black or gray. It's called a photolysis reaction."

Mackenzie's brain jumped into overdrive. Austin said there were traces of silver in the parking lot where Veronica was abducted. It wasn't found in Mia's apartment—but silver chloride was. She had absorbed every detail from crime scene, including the details of the partial footprint discovered.

It gave no information about the shoe size and was too faint to match anything belonging to Glenn. But there were deposits in it—dark-brown gravelly loam soil, typical of Washington State, and some white crystals, almost powder-like—silver chloride. Mackenzie had no idea what any of it meant. It wasn't specific enough to narrow it down to any place Glenn could have frequented. What did it mean that it had been found at both Veronica and Mia's abduction sites?

"If there is no sunlight then it won't decompose to silver?" she asked.

"No. The reaction needs UV light."

"That's why it didn't convert to silver inside Mia's apartment," she muttered to herself.

He leaned forward. "Excuse me?"

"I have to leave," she said abruptly.

Her hand almost shook with a sense of urgency. Her nerves twisted and knotted under her skin. If there was a slightest chance that what she feared was true, then there was no time to waste.

"What?" John asked with his mouth full.

"I'm so sorry, but you can tell your students that you just helped solve a case." She gave him a swift kiss on the cheek and left bills on the table. "The least I can do for abandoning you. Thank you."

Mackenzie parked haphazardly at the station. A fork of lightning released angry rain. When she opened the door, a strong wind whipped it back shut. She pushed her weight into it, wrestling against the droplets blown in her direction. Somehow, she managed to open an umbrella and finally climbed out of the car. It was so loud—the popping of water on concrete and splashes from water spraying as cars zipped past close by. Another gust of wind, and the umbrella distorted and broke.

"Damn it." Quickly, she rushed inside and headed to the second floor with water dripping from her dress. But all she could think about was checking and comparing the CSI reports. No way sleep would come to her when her brain was buzzing.

The wet dress clung to her skin. Goosebumps rose on her arms from the air conditioning.

"Mackenzie?" Austin looked up from his desk when Mackenzie tottered in.

She had been hoping nobody would be in. "What are you still doing here?"

He shrugged at the paperwork in front of him. "It's getting bad out there, isn't it?"

A loud bang of thunder punctuated the brief silence. "Yeah, probably best not to drive until it gets better."

She logged in to the server and accessed the CSI reports on Mia's apartment. Flipping through the images, the one she was after popped up. There was a partial print in a kitchen corner, tucked safely away from any window.

Mackenzie scrolled through the report. Mass spectrometry results from the crime lab showed that loam was present at the largest quantity—matching the soil in the vicinity. There were significant amounts of Douglas fir seedlings as well, presumably from the woods around the apartment. But an unusual finding was highlighted: trace amounts of silver chloride. Despite the low quantity, the detection was within acceptable confidence intervals. Mackenzie even checked the chromatograms, seeing neat, albeit small peaks.

"Austin? Can I ask you a favor?"

"Yeah," he called from his desk on the other side.

"Those results you were looking at today. The silver powder found in the parking lot where Veronica Fang went missing. I think we should compare our reports."

After a bated breath, Austin walked around to her desk carrying the file. "Why?"

"We found traces of silver chloride in Mia Gallagher's

apartment." She nibbled on her thumb. "Which decomposes to silver in the sun."

The dots connected in Austin's head and his lips parted. "Same trace elements found at two abduction sites. But silver chloride is used for a lot of things. From photography to as an antiseptic."

"I guess. But how many people would have silver chloride under their shoes?"

"We also found confetti under her car."

She sat up straight. "Confetti?"

"Yeah. Like from a Taser." He showed her a picture of the hot pink marked confetti on the ground.

"Mia was stunned or tasered. We didn't find any confetti though..."

Confusion marred his face. "But I thought you caught your guy. Well, he had killed himself."

"He did. And this is one hell of a coincidence."

If Glenn Solomon didn't hurt Mia, then why did he lie in his suicide note? And who abducted Veronica?

FOURTEEN
OCTOBER 16

Veronica Fang had disappeared over seventy-two hours ago from the very spot where Mackenzie stood. The crime scene unit had finished sweeping the area, removing the markers and the yellow tape. Now this lot stood empty with just one car other than hers.

It was still early in the morning. Clouds stacked on top of each other in the sky. Blue-gray shafts of light leaked through, casting soft but dull hues around. The parking lot was behind a dingy bar with barbed fence. Dense woods crowded either side of the concrete clearing. The only way out was a dirt road that merged with one of the main streets zigzagging through downtown Lakemore.

It was eerily quiet. No singing birds or whistling winds. It was like the thick trees had absorbed all sound. They stood tall around her, close together. They weren't lush woods but prickly, the kind that wouldn't swallow but cut and slash when walking through.

Mackenzie pulled up a picture of Veronica on her phone. She had straight dark hair and small eyes. Her face was angular and sharp. She wasn't smiling. Unlike Mia who looked like she should be sunning by the French Riviera, Veronica had an air of efficiency around her. She looked like she belonged in a boardroom.

The door to the back of the bar swung open, and a lanky man came out carrying a crate.

"Can I ask you a few questions?" Mackenzie flashed him her badge.

The man sighed and put the box on the ground. He was heavy and tired, with yellow fingers. "I already told the cops I saw nothing. I don't know what happened to Ronnie."

"Ronnie? You were familiar with her?"

"Yeah, she used to visit twice a week. Liked to sit in a corner booth and work."

"Why here?"

"Her friend is a waitress, so she gets free drinks." He shrugged like it was no big deal. "I think they live together."

"Can you give me her contact information?"

Mackenzie made a note of the details.

"Can I get back to work?"

She glanced at his yellow fingernails. His stale, smoky breath had been overbearing enough. "You must take smoke breaks back here. You never saw anything? Anyone paying special attention to her or followed her out?"

He frowned. "Not that night."

"So some other night."

"Last week I was out here taking a drag, and she was walking back to her car," he recalled. "There was another car slowly crawling up the dirt road toward the lot. A little too slow. But then I noticed she'd dropped her scarf by the back door, so I picked it up and went up to her. That's when the car suddenly started going back. I thought they probably lost their way."

Mackenzie dismissed him, tapping her pen to the page, her mind stretching in all directions. Had someone lost their way, or had they been following Veronica and backtracked when they realized there was a witness? To take Veronica from a parking lot that wasn't monitored, they must have scoped the area. They must have known about her movements.

But who carried around taser guns? There had been some planning go into it. It sank onto Mackenzie's chest like a heavy rock how two women were tasered and snatched. It was brutal and cold. At the same time, methodical and efficient, but vicious too. It was a dangerous combination—someone calculative who had control over his or her darkest desires.

Rivera's office was what Mackenzie aspired to have if she were to get a promotion and have her own space. The only decorative item was a bamboo palm slate by the window and a row of framed awards she had received over the span of her career. There was nothing unnecessary or sentimental. The lieutenant even took off her wedding ring on duty, leaving a faint groove around her ring finger, the only evidence of the steely woman having a heart.

Her chair squeaked when she sat on it, peering over her glasses as she read the report. Mackenzie paced the office, her pulse jumping. Nick stood behind a chair, and Austin was seated, his long legs spread lazily.

"Why do you think the cases are linked again?" Rivera demanded.

"Mia Gallagher was tasered, according to Becky," Mackenzie explained, drawing her attention to the close-up of Mia's pelvis. "The barbs penetrated the bone. And the silver chloride, presumably from shoe deposits."

Nick leaned on his elbows, resting them atop a chair. "We found no confetti in her apartment."

Rivera raised a cynical brow. "No confetti? A single cartridge discharges like thirty of those. They're tiny but color-ful, easy to spot. Maybe they used a stun gun?"

"That's what we assumed at first, until I realized what these are in the crime-scene pictures." Mackenzie showed a picture of the protective cover. "These shoot out of Tasers along with the confetti. There are two, but we only found one. It was under the couch, so we didn't catch it before."

Rivera's sharp eyes drilled into the picture. "And Veronica?"

"She went missing in a parking lot," Austin said. "There were a lot of cars moving around. There was also a storm later that night."

"You think most of the confetti got blown away or got stuck underneath tires?"

He nodded. "We found a few in a puddle under the car and were able to extract the AFID number from them."

"We should immediately trace the cartridge it came from," Mackenzie said, unable to conceal her eagerness. "The killer was careless with the second abduction. Veronica might still be alive—"

"No."

"Huh?"

Rivera's voice punctured Mackenzie's train of thoughts and actions. "I don't think this is enough to suggest that these cases are related." Her finger tapped the two files. "Especially when we have Glenn Solomon's confession *and* DNA under Mia's fingernails."

Mackenzie's forehead wrinkled. "Lieutenant, what are the chances that two young women were tasered and abducted within a week by different people? Lakemore is a small town. And Glenn had amphetamines, which could account for delusions. He could have been experiencing some kind of delusions for all we know."

"I understand, but that DNA evidence is damning and far more concrete than this Taser and silver chloride link."

Mackenzie looked at Nick, whose mouth was flat. He agreed with Rivera. Helplessness clawed at her. "Glenn could have been an accomplice to the crime. That's how his DNA ended up on Mia. And that's why he felt guilty, for the role he played in Mia's death."

Rivera's mouth pinched in consideration. She eyed Austin, but Mackenzie detected a hint of scrutiny. "What do you think, Detective Kennedy?"

"I have to agree with Detective Price. I'm still new to Lakemore, but in the last few months I've realized this town isn't big enough for this to be a coincidence."

"But these two women are so different," Rivera said skeptically. "They have nothing in common. Ethnicity, age, physical description, education. On what basis is he targeting them? And you found no confetti in Mia's apartment?"

"No, ma'am," Nick said. "Once Mia was subdued the killer had time on his hands to clean up the confetti. But the parking lot was a public area. They couldn't stick around to get rid of evidence and risk being seen."

"Detective Kennedy, have you interviewed Veronica's friends and family?"

"I talked with her family over the phone," he informed. "They live in China and haven't seen her in over two years, since she last visited them. I was going to talk to her roommate today."

"Detectives Price and Blackwood will do it. Give them everything you have gathered so far."

"What? Why?" His tone was almost accusatory.

There was a pregnant pause in which the atmosphere in the room tightened. Mackenzie felt Nick's puzzled eyes on her, but she couldn't look away from Rivera and Austin.

"Finn is injured. He broke his leg, and Troy needs a partner. His caseload is heavy. I want you working with him," Rivera replied calmly.

"I'm ready to work with Troy, but this is my case. I can multitask."

She didn't waver. "I know you can. But if the cases are linked, which I will concede is possible, then it's better for Mack and Nick to absorb this one, since Mia Gallagher was the first victim."

Mackenzie could tell that Austin was attempting to poke holes in her logic, even though it was sound. Yet even she could sense the distance and wariness with which Rivera regarded Austin. It was something Mackenzie had experienced herself briefly last year when she had disobeyed orders and almost blundered a case. Rivera didn't like mistakes. It took her time to trust again.

Austin gave her a curt nod.

"Dismissed." Rivera sighed.

As the three of them poured out of the office, Mackenzie could feel the tension radiating from Austin's rigid shoulders. He barreled past them to his desk, avoiding their eyes.

"What the hell was that about?" Nick whispered. "Austin can just work this case with us. She didn't have to freeze him out."

"I know. But I think she wants him away from it."

"But why?"

"She doesn't trust him. I'll tell you later."

Austin returned with a file. "Here's everything. It's also up on the server; I'm sure you'll have access to it now."

"Thanks." Nick took it from him. "I'm guessing Veronica's family has no idea what happened?"

"None at all. They weren't very close. She's unmarried, single, and lived with a roommate over at Burrows Avenue. I didn't get a chance to run a background check on Veronica yet."

"I don't think her name came up when we looked into Mia," Mackenzie rehashed her memory. "Rivera is right. They're too different-looking. Either our killer is targeting women with no discernible pattern, or they have some connection."

"I was wondering how the killer cleaned up the confetti at

your victim's apartment," Austin said. "Did Mia have a vacuum cleaner? Did you check it?"

She paused. "We didn't. I think she had one. I remember seeing it in the kitchen."

"That's how I'd do it."

"Good point." Mackenzie made a note of it. "I'll ask the team to sift through that."

"What did Veronica do for a living?" Nick asked, flipping the pages.

"She was a personal assistant to a wealthy businessman." Austin looked at the file. "I forgot his name. Oh, there it is. Baron Wildman."

"Shit." Nick hissed through his teeth.

"What?" Mackenzie asked. "You know him?"

"Sort of. He owns the Wildman Group. It's a huge conglomerate. They're expanding in Washington now that a lot of competition has been squeezed out since Perez Industries went under."

The last time Mackenzie had dealt with powerful people, the entire fate of the town had changed. "Great. We're going to need to talk to him too."

FIFTEEN

Mackenzie looked at the pictures of Mia's body brutally forced down the elevator shaft. As the elevator had moved up and down, the body had pressed and broken against the walls. It didn't even look like a body anymore, but a distorted puppet.

It was one of the worst she had seen in her career. She still felt that relief that at least Mia was already dead before being thrown in.

"Why do some people find violence attractive?" She voiced the question that she had once been asked.

"We evolved from predators." Nick scowled at the parking meter and sieved through the coins in his pockets. "Some instincts are just wired in us, I suppose."

"But finding it *attractive*? That's different from occasionally wanting to beat someone up."

He glared at her like she had grown two heads. "What is up with you?"

"I'm contemplative."

"You're never contemplative verbally."

"I'm trying to grow as an individual."

"By asking weird questions?"

"How is that weird? I'm trying to understand human psychology."

"But you don't believe in psychology," he reminded her flatly. "You think it's mumbo-jumbo for people who like to overthink."

Mackenzie looked around, hoping nobody had heard that. But the parking garage was empty. "Okay, don't repeat that in front of anyone else. Ever. But maybe I'm wrong. Maybe I need to be more open-minded."

Nick shoved his hands in his coat and stared at her with furrowed brows and narrowed eyes. "I think you have a concussion from that fall. You should see a doctor."

"Shut up." She marched toward the staircase.

Burrows Avenue was a street consisting of townhouses and apartment buildings occupied by the youth who worked in Olympia or Tacoma but chose to live in Lakemore for the cheap rent. It faced one of the lakes and had a row of benches with trees lined on either side forming a canopy. Mackenzie glanced around, wondering if she should consider moving here. The townhouses seemed far more practical than the big house she resided in.

She took a whiff of the crisp October evening. The setting brilliant orb over the horizon slowly peeled the light off from the mackerel sky, making the stain of darkness grow larger. The ground underneath Mackenzie's feet was covered in leaves: fireside reds and browns.

A little boy ran past her, trying to catch a football. A girl tackled him to the ground, and they wrestled, giggling. Their parents watched from one of the benches. Simple and peaceful moments like these were why she worked hard. She watched that family just be around each other, not talking but sharing smiles and looks of concerns; a deep bond tethering them to each other. But Mackenzie was far removed from them. She felt like an outsider looking in.

"That's the apartment building," Nick pointed out.

"How do you know the Wildmans?" Mackenzie asked. "I didn't want to ask in front of Austin."

He looked uncomfortable. "My father knows them. I saw them around a lot growing up, but not in recent years."

"Anything I should know before we meet them tomorrow?"

"They'll probably just be cagey and not without a lawyer." He shrugged. "Typical rich-people stuff."

They reached the apartment and knocked on the door. A woman with tawdry clothes and ropey hair hanging limply around her face opened it. "Yes?"

"We're from Lakemore PD. This is where Veronica Fang lives?" Nick asked.

Her eyes grew wide, and she swung the door open, thrusting her eager palm into theirs. "Yes, yes. I'm Casey. Did you find her?"

"Not yet. Can we ask you a few questions?"

Casey let them inside. Mackenzie made a quick inspection of the space; there was nothing to write home about. A kitchenette, living room with a laundry pile sitting on an armchair, and a little balcony from where the cool breeze floated in. There were a few pictures hanging by the television of Casey and Veronica at bars and on hikes.

"You were the one who reported her missing?" Mackenzie asked.

"Yes." Casey nodded, rushing to close the balcony door. "I had left before she did that night. I had a date. When I got home, I assumed that she was already asleep in her bed. The next day when I went to work, I saw her car was still there and the door was open." Her forehead crumpled. "I rang her a bunch of times and then I realized her phone was under the car. I immediately contacted the police."

"Did you recognize either of these people?" Mack showed her pictures of Mia Gallagher and Glenn Solomon.

Casey took her time staring at them and shook her head. "I'm sorry; I don't. Who are they?"

Mackenzie was disappointed. "We are just exploring some avenues."

"Do you think she's alive?" Her pleading eyes flitted between them. Her breath was slightly stale and her eyelids puffy. "I don't know what to think."

"We can't say anything definitively yet," Nick replied. "Have you noticed anyone following her? Anyone strange lurking around?"

Casey's lower lip jutted out as she shook her head helplessly. "Sorry, I haven't noticed anything."

"How was her behavior in the last few days? Any changes?"

"Well, yes." She scratched her head, exhausted. "She wasn't happy at work. Didn't think she was getting paid enough. But I figured that's normal. I feel the same way. Who doesn't?"

"Was she considering switching jobs?"

"I don't think so. She said she had something in the works. Whatever the hell that means."

"Was there anyone she had gotten particularly close to lately?" Mackenzie asked.

Casey's eyes rolled back, trying to remember. "No... honestly, she's always so busy."

"You don't think there's anyone who wanted to hurt her, perhaps?" Mackenzie was grasping at straws. The last thing she wanted was this to be a random event, everything picture perfect and someone randomly deciding to pluck a young woman out of that picture.

Casey chewed her lip. "Well, there was something."

Mackenzie's spine snapped straight in attention. "What is it?"

"She said something about someone harassing her at work. She didn't say a name, or if she did, she mentioned it in passing and I can't remember. But she had complained a few times about it. It was around a month ago, I think."

"Was she scared of him?" Nick pressed. "Did she give you any more details?"

"She was more annoyed and nervous. But her work troubles took over lately. I can't remember anything else." Her face morphed into desperation. "I'm so sorry! Please find her. I can't sleep thinking what might be happening to her right now. She's my best friend. We've been living together for years."

The thought of whatever was happening with Veronica made Mackenzie's stomach churn too. Like a sore patch of skin she couldn't bear to touch, she was determined to keep those thoughts at bay.

After exchanging more information, they were back on the way to the car. The temperature had nosedived in the last twenty minutes and Mackenzie shoved her freezing fingers inside her pockets.

"I was really hoping she'd recognize Mia or Glenn," Nick said, taking out his cigarette case and running his hands over it. "Whoever was harassing Veronica might be a promising lead though."

Before Mackenzie replied, her phone rang. Looking at the screen, she said, "It's Justin. I asked him to run a background check on Veronica." She put him on speakerphone. "Did you find anything?"

"Veronica has no priors or even a parking ticket to her name," Justin's deep voice replied. "But she had filed a restraining order two weeks ago."

Mackenzie's head snapped to look at Nick, who stopped playing with the case. "Against whom?"

"Someone by the name Bobby Wildman."

Nick pinched the bridge of his nose. "That's Baron Wildman's younger brother."

SIXTEEN

OCTOBER 17

Mackenzie's head was pounding. She'd slept through her alarm and missed the time to go for her morning run. As a result, her muscles ached in rebellion, demanding to exert and burn. Instead, she was plopped at her desk, sedentary, and trying to absorb whatever she could find about the Wildmans.

But her brain didn't seem to want to hold on to the information. She growled and closed her laptop, pulled out a disinfectant wipe and cleaned the inside of her drawers. The smell of the cleaning solution wafted up to her nose as the wipe collected more and more dirt. The tension gripping her uncoiled and she breathed easily.

"Look, Mack! You're a GIF," Troy quipped at her side. They shared a cubicle wall.

She looked at his mop of carrot-like hair and dimpled cheeks. "What?"

He showed her his monitor with a mischievous glint in his eyes. "I asked Valerie for the footage of you doing that German suplex on the dealer."

To her mortification, Mackenzie watched a clip of her

throwing an adult man on his back over her head. "What is that?"

"A GIF. I made it."

"What's a GIF?"

He shot her an indignant look. "Dear God, woman. Do you live under a rock?"

"I don't like it." She turned away. "I'm finally done shooting for that documentary. It's a closed chapter. I don't need… GIFs."

Troy chuckled. "You don't. But we definitely do. Especially this one."

Mackenzie bit her tongue, knowing Troy irked her just to get a reaction.

She was checking her emails from the crime lab when a shadow loomed behind her. Turning around, she jolted.

It was Captain Murphy—a tall and large man with loose skin, a sneer, and lazy and offensive habits. Mackenzie always tried to stay out of his radar, fearing she'd snap at him. Murphy was an inert component in investigations. A vestigial organ at the Lakemore PD, solely there due to his friendship with the mayor. The only cases he inserted himself in were the ones involving big names.

"Where is Nick?" he demanded.

"He's dropping off his kid. Her mom had to go to work early."

He made a face, like speaking with Mackenzie was an undesirable option. "You traced the weapon from those AFIDs found at the crime scene?"

She quickly hid her surprise that Murphy remembered case details. "The number wasn't too clear since they were sitting in a puddle for hours, but the crime lab just cleaned some up." She gestured at the email. "A team was dispatched to the other victim's house, and they found some AFID tags in the vacuum cleaner garbage. Justin is tracking down the user."

"Huh? Another victim?" Murphy scowled.

It struck Mackenzie that he had only bothered himself with Veronica's case due to her association with the Wildmans.

"What else you got?"

She held his sour gaze unflinchingly. "Veronica had filed a restraining order against Bobby Wildman. We'll talk to him today."

He pretended to think, tracing his lip with his finger. "Hmm. Keep him happy, all right?"

There it was. The reason he had sought her out. She set her jaw hard. It peeved her to no end how brazenly Murphy demanded unethical behavior.

"We'll treat him fairly." She chose her words carefully.

He sighed impatiently. "The last thing we need is the Wildman Group as our enemy. We have a bad rep anyway."

"Ironically, that was because the department favored powerful people. You sure you want us to continue that trend?" she asked reminding him of an old case.

Murphy's face turned red. The sound of Troy typing came to a grinding halt. Movements around them froze. Mackenzie felt eyes on them. She knew she had messed up, but that voice was too faint. "I don't need you telling me how to run my department, young lady."

"And I don't need you telling me how to solve my case." She held her ground, despite her anger rising like a tide. "I have a solid success rate, Captain. I know how to handle them."

Mackenzie wasn't stupid. She knew she had to deal with the Wildmans with tact. If she went in guns blazing and hurling accusations, then they'd lawyer up as Nick had warned. And rich people could afford good lawyers. It would essentially stonewall the investigation.

Murphy grumbled under his breath, his eyes twitching as he glanced around, before he stormed back to his office. Mackenzie's cheeks heated and heart thumped. She had never been this confrontational with a superior before.

"You got some balls, Mad Mack." Troy whistled.

"I've decided to be more honest with people around me and stop keeping things to myself," she said, still breathless from the episode. "Which reminds me. Please get a haircut."

Justin hastened into the office. "Ma'am." He tipped his head.

"Don't call me ma'am, Justin," she singsonged, like she had for the last few years.

"Clint and I traced the cartridges that were fired at the scene of Veronica and Mia's abduction sites." He referred to their IT guy.

Mackenzie's back snapped straight. "You got a name?"

His frown was deep, his eyebrows dipping low into his eyes. "Wren Murray."

"That's Mia Gallagher's friend."

Mackenzie recalled Murray's pain and confusion over Mia's disappearance. Was that all an act?

SEVENTEEN

The water came up in huge arcs on either side of the car, almost soaking a pedestrian.

"Sorry," Nick grumbled, waving a hand. "Damn this weather."

He slowed down, and the car merely trudged along the shoreline overlooking the sea. Mackenzie didn't join in Nick complaining about the weather. She pressed her nose against the window, gazing at the vast sea and water falling into it causing little dents and ripples. White-capped waves crashed into the rocks and the tiny sliver of beach below. It was damp and windy. The sounds *shush, shush, shush* echoing. Visceral and feral.

"Maybe I should live close to the sea," she said. "It will be hell of a commute, but I think I'll like it here." She could picture herself taking walks along the path, basking in solitude.

"You're thinking of moving?"

"The house is too big. Not to mention, I almost died there." She opened the visor and examined her reflection.

Nick's grip on the wheel tightened. "Yeah. You know you

can talk about it once in a while. I know you spent a few hours with some therapist which was mandatory but—"

"It's fine." She shrugged. When he raised his eyebrows, she insisted, "Really. I know these days it's all about verbalizing your feelings, but not everyone needs that. I certainly don't. I resolve things better inside my head."

She wasn't lying. She just didn't bother to mention the fact that she had no feelings that needed verbalizing. There was nothing but a void inside her. Earlier in the year, she was almost killed in her own home by someone she'd trusted. An enemy she didn't know she had, but who had festered and grown and lurked too close to her, exacting a decades-old revenge plot.

"You're lucky," Nick replied.

She ran her finger over her father's watch on her wrist. "My mother taught me well."

"Why don't you talk to someone?" Mackenzie had begged. "A friend?"

Melody wiped her tears and forced a smile. "Not everything needs to be shared, Mackenzie."

"But maybe it will make you feel better. Maybe you'll feel lighter."

She clasped Mackenzie's chin, meeting her pleading eyes with her hardened gaze. "Sometimes sharing increases the burden, sweetheart. Not everything has to be said. Some emotions should be kept private. There's dignity in that."

Mackenzie looked outside the window again, catching her reflection. Instead, she saw Melody. It was very brief. Only a moment. She told herself it meant nothing. After all, she looked exactly like her. Same eyes, same bone structure, same lips, and same blackened heart.

"There it is." Nick killed the engine in front of a shack that sold equipment for beach activities. "Wren Murray. He has known Mia since they were kids, he said. What could be his motive?" he mused. "She rejected him?"

"But why would he take Veronica?"

What was the connection between Mia and Veronica? It was the million-dollar question.

They huddled under an umbrella and walked into the shack. It was dingy, with sunhats, beach bags, and sandals stacked in one corner. Surfboards and leashes hung on one of the walls. Another corner had swimwear and beach towels.

Wren Murray sat behind the table, playing on his phone. When he saw them, he stood up. "Detectives! Did you find anything?"

"Not beach season," Mackenzie said, ignoring any pleasantries. "Why are you here?"

Wren licked his lips.

Nick made a show of scoping the place, his tall and muscular build meant to intimidate.

"There has been a development in the case," Mackenzie tested Wren's reaction. He looked eager. "We found confetti in Mia's apartment from a Taser. The AFID tags traced it to you."

His eyes darted between them. "What?"

"Your Taser was also fired at another site of abduction."

"Am I in trouble?"

"Definitely," Nick said. "We have grounds to arrest you."

"*Shit!*" Wren stood up from his chair abruptly, toppling it. He ran his hands through his sandy blond hair, his chest falling in waves. "I swear I didn't hurt Mia, or anyone!"

"Your Taser, Wren. How do you explain that?"

He was torn. "I... I can, actually."

Mackenzie waited.

Wren almost recoiled being cornered by the two of them, his eyebrows kissing his hairline. "I had a break-in."

"That's convenient," Mackenzie retorted.

"Please. I bought some guns, Tasers, and other stuff, and then sold them at a higher price. But about two weeks ago, someone stole a whole bunch of my stash." He shook his head.

"Shit. Shit. Shit. I didn't know this would happen. What are the chances?"

"Yeah, what are the chances?"

"Look, I know it's wrong, but I don't have a steady job. This shack sells stuff only for a few months. I need the money. I can't go back to my hick town."

"And why should we believe you? Your story is convenient," Mackenzie said.

He took off his chain, which had a key for a padlock. He unlocked a cupboard behind him and displayed the contents. Weapons from handguns, pistols, Tasers, stun guns and even packets of weed. "I sell to some regulars, but two weeks ago, I showed up and the lock was broken. Half of the stuff inside was missing."

"Did you go to the police?" Nick asked.

His face was red.

"Ah. Confessing to illegal sales of firearms." Mackenzie took out the handcuffs.

"It's better than going to jail for *abducting* someone!" he cried, not resisting when she turned him around. "You have to believe me. I had *nothing* to do with that! I don't know what happens to these guns after I sell them. Once they're on the streets, they can go anywhere."

"Provide us a list of all your regulars and maybe we can put in a good word for you with the DA," Nick said.

Wren nodded, desperately. "Yes, yes. I'll do anything. But I didn't hurt Mia! I have no reason to."

Mackenzie nudged him forward, escorting him out to the car. "Did you like her, Wren? Did you want her, but she didn't want you back?"

He scowled. "No! I didn't see her that way." Then he paused and glared at them, his eyes shining with tears. "Think about it. I know how Tasers work. After all, I've sold a lot of them. I know they release confetti that is difficult to clean up. If

I had to abduct someone, why would I use a Taser that leaves evidence?"

Mackenzie pushed him inside the car, closing the door. "He's got a point," she said to Nick, who already had an unlit cigarette between his lips. "He could have used a stun gun. They don't have confetti."

Nick regarded Wren's face; it looked even smaller and more desperate. Like a child who had tried something dangerous but wanted to rectify his mistake immediately. "He confessed to his side gig easily. Offered it to us on a platter. His record is also clean."

"But what are the odds that Mia was taken by someone who used her friend's Taser on her? Do you think it's a coincidence?"

Nick spoke around the cigarette. "Not at all. I think Mia was being watched before she was taken."

"They must have known about Wren. She met with him often."

"And they found out about Wren's side hustle. Realized a Taser is a good way to subdue a target before taking it but didn't know it would leave trackable confetti behind."

"We might be dealing with a novice criminal," Mackenzie suggested.

Nick's lips turned into a shrewd smile. "Let's hope that's true. Because it means they're going to slip up at some point."

EIGHTEEN

Being wealthy wasn't like being in a bubble. It was like being on an island. A bubble could be easily popped, but an island was remote and hard to access. The outside world was visible from inside a bubble, but being on an island created so much distance that the entire concept of the real world could become hypothetical and abstract.

As Mackenzie watched the champagne fountain in front of her, waves of conflicting emotions hit her. It was unnecessary, gaudy, and downright absurd. But at the same time, she wanted to be around it and keep looking at it.

"What event is this?" she hissed at Nick, who was unaffected by the crowd in designer clothes, the foie gras and beluga caviar being carried around, and the string quartet playing music.

There was a marquee in the massive backyard of Baron Wildman's mansion. There was polite laughter, constrained movements, and side-eyes. All the guests followed the code of conduct: being contained and civil. All emotions diluted in the name of propriety.

Mackenzie blinked, the image of Mia's body still fresh in

her mind, a stark contrast from the perfection around her that was so distant from violence.

"Probably some merger." Nick shrugged, stuffing his mouth with cupcake. "Might as well."

But Mackenzie wasn't hungry.

A tall man with gray sideburns and deep lines in his large forehead approached them wearing a solemn expression.

"From Lakemore PD?" he asked.

They had called ahead. "Yeah, I'm Detective Price. This is my partner, Detective Blackwood."

"Dominic Childs," he said. "I'm Baron Wildman's personal lawyer. Let's talk inside."

Mackenzie exchanged a guarded look with Nick. Before she had even set eyes on Veronica's employer, he sent his lawyer, his first line of defense.

They left the marquee as the wind started picking up. Her hair flung around her, slipping out of the hair tie. They climbed up a rolling green hill to the Victorian mansion sitting atop it with the view of snow-tipped mountains behind. A strong gust almost caught Mackenzie; she looked over her shoulder down below to the flaps of the marquee thrashing in the wind. Thunder clapped. The first rain drizzled upon them just as Dominic ushered them inside.

"It wasn't supposed to rain today. According to the weather report," Dominic muttered, taking them through a long hallway with arched ceiling and past the staff dressed in whites and blacks. "Not that it helps much in Washington. It's always raining."

There were oil paintings on one side of the wall of stiff men with a hook of a nose from the early seventeen hundreds. It was always just the men. The history of wives, daughters, and sisters clearly too irrelevant to be preserved.

"All that wealth and ivy league education doesn't always

equal progress, does it?" Mackenzie whispered in Nick's ear, disapproval leaching her tone.

Dominic stopped short in front of a double door with gold pulls shaped like lion's heads. There were torches on either side of the entrance with flames flickering from a draft that made a soft, keening sound among the stones. He opened the door to reveal a library. The bookcases were built into the curved wall running from floor to ceiling. There was a fireplace and four leather armchairs in front of it, the French windows overlooking the party wrapping up in the backyard. It was all brown and woodsy, with the smell of dust and whiskey in the air.

A man stood, his thick finger trailed the spines of books that hadn't been removed for a long time. Mackenzie recognized him from her quick internet research. It was the same tall, bald man with a stubble and strong jaw. His body was lean and eyes black but shining. He moved toward them with the grace of a predator.

"Nick, it's been a while," he remarked in his slightly British accent, and Mackenzie remembered from her research that Baron had spent a decade in a boarding school in England before moving back to the United States.

"Baron." Nick shook his hand.

"I saw your father the other day. You know how fond I am of him. I would love to contribute to his campaign, but we bat for different parties." He chuckled as he sat on one of the chairs. "Please sit down."

Mackenzie took a seat gingerly, feeling out of place. "We are here about Veronica Fang. Your personal assistant."

It was the first time Baron acknowledged her existence. He almost blinked, like he was surprised she talked. He took his time, pulling out a cigar and lighting it. Taking a few puffs, he sat back. "She has been out of reach for the last four days almost. Haven't heard from her at all. That's what we told the police when they called two days ago. Did you find anything?"

"She was abducted," Nick said.

Baron glanced at Dominic next to him. "I see."

"When was the last time you saw her?" Mackenzie asked.

"Four days ago."

"And did anything strange happen?"

Dominic cleared his throat, his Adam's apple bobbing as he spoke. "My client has no knowledge of anything that could help you. His personal assistant seemed a bit distracted the last few days, but that was about it."

"Do you know why?"

Before Baron could answer, Dominic spoke up. "My client kept things strictly professional with her. He has no knowledge that could you help your investigation."

"Is it seriously going to be like this, Baron?" Nick sighed. "We're just here to talk."

Baron crossed his legs. "Sorry, Nick. You know how these things go."

Mackenzie turned to Dominic. "When was the last time *you* saw her?"

"*Me?*" he gasped.

"Well, you're his personal lawyer and she was the personal assistant. I'm sure you've worked together."

"Of course." He plucked at his collar like it was strangling him. "I saw her around the same time as Baron did, I suppose. To be honest, Veronica was never the type to draw attention to herself. Most of the time, I barely noticed her in the room."

"She was good at her job," Baron declared. "Efficient and discreet. Even though the last few days her productivity had decreased, I have no complaints. She was the best assistant I've had."

"Her roommate stated that she was unhappy with the pay she was getting."

"Who isn't?" Dominic rolled his eyes and poured a glass of

whiskey with shaking hands. "I tell Baron all the time he should pay me double for everything I do for him."

Baron snorted. "I bring in ten million to his firm every fiscal year and he still complains. Lawyers!"

Dominic's laughter was forced; his body angled away from Mackenzie and Nick, almost in a cowering position. She wondered why a lawyer would be nervous talking to the police.

"Do you have any leads?" Baron asked in his rich, deep baritone. He had a commanding voice and an astonishing amount of confidence.

Nick clicked his tongue. "She filed a restraining order against Bobby a couple of weeks ago."

Baron let out a deep sigh and looked at the flames of the fire, dancing like little men and women. "Dominic. Please find Bobby and bring him in." His voice was tight.

Dominic staggered out of the room, almost bumping into a table.

"Bobby still giving you trouble, Baron?" Nick asked.

"Blood is thicker than water, Nick." He sucked on the cigar, tendrils of smoke escaping from his nostrils. "But there are moments I wish we could choose our family." He turned his scorching gaze to Mackenzie. "Do you have anyone you're responsible for, Detective Price?"

The question gutted her. She spoke in a measured tone to not betray the emptiness in her life. "No."

"You're lucky."

The doors opened again. On the heels of Dominic was a rugged man, a younger reflection of Baron, but with greasy, long, disheveled hair. His shirt was tucked out of his pants and his tie askew. A naughty grin on his face blared loudly how he was up to no good.

A woman also came in, dressed in a tight blue dress that looked difficult to breathe in. Her arms and legs were pencil-thin, but her breasts were inflated and sitting high. She was as tall as Mackenzie, and from the way she walked comfortably in stilettos, Mackenzie predicted she had been a model. Her features had been attractive at one point, but Botox had stretched her skin a tad too tight.

"I'm Linda Wildman, Baron's wife." She flaunted her perfect veneers. "Nice to see you, Nick."

"Ah, you too." Nick gave her a quick kiss on the cheek. "This is my partner, Detective Mackenzie Price."

"Is that Nick Blackwood?" the man snickered. "The last time I saw you, you tried dunking me into the pool at that White House luncheon."

Nick gave him a reluctant hug. "Well, you did key my father's car, Bobby. You deserved it."

Bobby threw his head back and laughed. When Nick made the introductions, his depraved gaze slid over Mackenzie. "I've always had a thing for redheads..."

"Bobby!" Baron gritted his teeth.

Linda rolled her eyes and mouthed, "Locker-room talk."

But Bobby shrugged unaffected. "My brother's a bore. I'm the fun one."

"And the useless one," Baron muttered under his breath.

Bobby's lips curled in a sneer. His eyes were glazed. Mackenzie caught a whiff of bourbon in his breath. "What is this about? I was busy. Do you know what it's like to have a hundred grand between your legs?" When Mackenzie's eyes bugged out her sockets, he winked. "I meant the Ducati Desmosedici. It's a motorcycle. Linda gifted it to me."

"Wisely spending the money *I* earn," Baron groaned, not sparing his wife a glance.

While they bickered, Mackenzie's attention was focused on Dominic. He was standing now almost obediently, peering out into the mist pressing up against the window. It made the room smaller and claustrophobic. But his silence appeared tumultuous. He kept swallowing and the corners of his mouth kept twitching.

"Veronica Fang is missing," Nick said.

"That's terrible!" Linda gasped. "I had a bad feeling when we couldn't reach her. It's very unlike her."

"Oh." Bobby wrinkled his nose. "Poor girl. What does this have to do with me?"

"She filed a restraining order against you, Bobby, and her roommate said she was upset that she was being harassed at work." Mackenzie spoke slowly like he was a child. "She rejected your advances and now she's missing."

"Please! I'm a flirt." He uncorked a bottle of wine lying around and sipped directly from it. "A lot of women have filed restraining orders against me. I like playing with them! Too bad some women don't have a sense of humor. Do you think Baron's forty-year-old assistant is so special that I'd hurt her? I have Victoria's Secret models on my speed dial. When you're rich enough, you can have anyone."

Mackenzie almost flinched at his words. She had seen blood, corpses, rotting flesh and charred bones. But there was something so much fouler about men like Bobby. The arrogance to belittle and insult, to slowly destroy a person without having to resort to violence. It was fiendishly clever but downright despicable.

"I suppose it's easier to buy consent than to gain it. The latter requires good character and intelligence," she bit out.

"You wound me, Detective Price," Bobby mocked, but his eyes spelled bitterness.

"Now, now," Linda tried pacifying them as the air cinched with tension. She was all about smiling and being polite—the perfect trophy wife. "You have to excuse Bobby, Detective Price. He has a crude manner of speaking, but he means well."

"Where were you on the evening of October thirteen?" she asked.

"Probably buying someone's consent. I'll give you the number of the agency. You can confirm."

"We most definitely will."

Nick showed them Mia's picture. "Do any of you recognize her? Her name is Mia Gallagher."

Baron barely took a peek before shaking his head.

"I think I would have remembered that one," Bobby smirked.

Linda squinted at the picture. "She's very pretty, isn't she? I don't remember her."

Dominic took a moment longer than the others. "I don't think so. Sorry."

"What about him?" They showed them Glenn Solomon.

When they all denied knowing him as well, Mackenzie's spirits shrank. Mia and Veronica seemingly never crossed paths. Were these abductions random? She hoped not. A pattern was easier to handle. But someone deranged snatching women on a whim was a greater challenge.

Mackenzie and Nick took their leave. Walking out of the library, she looked behind at their little unit. Baron was captivated by the fire, while Bobby and Linda were engaged in an animated conversation. The three of them untouched by the woman they saw almost every day for years suddenly gone missing. Except for Dominic. He dabbed his sweaty forehead with a handkerchief.

"He knows something," she whispered in Nick's ear.

"But will he talk? A lawyer on the payroll of a wealthy man."

"How the hell are we going to break through to them?"

NINETEEN

OCTOBER 18

"Lakemore PD is asking for the public's assistance to help them track thirty-nine-year-old Veronica Fang, who went missing from the parking lot behind The Lake Tavern," Debbie Arnold, the most salacious and watched reporter in Lakemore, said to the camera. *"The details of the investigation are being kept private at the moment, but the police have reason to believe that Fang might still be alive."*

Sully turned off the wall-mounted television in the office. "The last thing we need is to listen to that voice." Mackenzie's head jerked up to find Sully's sullen face eyeing everyone in the office, forcing them into action. His fat fists were at his sides, squeezing tension balls, while he breathed like a bull. "Mack! Nick! I need an update. Now." He stormed back into his office.

"What's wrong with him?" Mackenzie asked Nick.

"I'd say he hasn't found a new hobby."

Walking inside his office, she realized Nick's guess was correct. There was no hint of activity for the sergeant to help him focus on work. Without his amusements, he was too tethered to this job, being grazed by the responsibility it entailed.

Sully fell onto his chair. "What do you have?"

"Wren Murray has been charged with multiple accounts of illegal sales of firearms," Mackenzie informed him. "But he is more than willing to cooperate, so the DA has decided that if his cooperation leads to any significant arrest, he will seek only two years of prison time, followed by two years of parole."

"He's smart," Sully pointed out. "Unlike those idiots who like throwing in guys for decades for selling weed to make an example instead of trying to catch the big fish. Well, what does Murray have to say?"

Nick unbuttoned his cufflinks, rolling up his sleeves. "He has provided a list of his regular customers. The cartridges that were used to tase Mia and Veronica were not in his possession and sold to different people. Justin is tracking them down as we speak."

"If those weapons are on the streets, then they might be gone forever," Sully said. "Most of the times, it's bouncers selling them behind clubs and they end up with gangs. Was there anything useful on Veronica's phone?"

"No." Mackenzie grimaced. "But we believe Dominic Childs is hiding something. The Wildmans denied knowing anything, but Childs was acting strange." She recalled the sweat beading on his forehead and the nervous twitch of his face. Classic telltale signs of someone feeling cornered. Coming from a lawyer it was more surprising. "If I can pull him into one of the interrogation rooms, I'm confident I'll get something out of him."

"You're going to need a lot more than Childs acting strange to haul him in for an interrogation." Sully guffawed at the ridiculous idea. "Baron sure as hell won't be happy. He relies on Childs too much."

The image of them in that wooden paneled library flashed in Mackenzie's head. They were an impenetrable unit, cohesive despite the tense undercurrents. Dominic knew Veronica;

something could have transpired between them. But Mia and Glenn's connection loomed like a shadow.

"Do we have anything on Glenn?" Sully asked. "Any connection with Mia or Veronica?"

"No." Nick shrugged. "We have alerted Riverview and Olympia. The sheriff's department is featuring Veronica's information on their website as well."

"Mia was killed in forty-eight hours," he glowered. "We're way past that deadline for Veronica."

Sully's words caused an unpleasant tide to rise inside Mackenzie. A uniform, informing them that someone had come to see them, interrupted them.

Mackenzie left Sully's office feeling indigestion in her chest. It was probably too late—and they weren't close to finding out who had taken her.

"Detectives!" It was Casey, Veronica's roommate, holding a tote bag and wearing a jumpsuit. Her grubby hair was twisted in a bun. "Did you find anything?"

"Not yet." Mackenzie swallowed down the lump in her throat. "We have patrols on the borders and all departments in surrounding towns are cooperating."

Casey nodded in jerks, gulping blocks of air incessantly, like she would tip over to hysteria anytime. "I remembered something."

"What?" Nick leaned closer.

"It might be n-nothing..." Her voice was hoarse. "But the Monday before she went missing, she came home late from work. I asked her if Baron had her running late errands again, but she said something weird. She said she took care of something and now has *insurance*."

"Insurance?" Nick repeated puzzled. "Did she elaborate?"

"She kind of said it in passing and I was busy in the kitchen, so I didn't exactly pay attention. Should I have? It must be something, right?" She was like a scared kitten; she had chewed her nails right off. "Oh God, why wasn't I listening to her?"

"I'll bring you some water." Nick shot Mackenzie an exasperated look behind Casey's back.

"You did well, Casey," she assured her. "If you remember anything more, come to us."

While Casey chugged down the water and calmed her erratic breathing, Mackenzie looked at Nick. Both were thinking the same thing. Bobby had been harassing Veronica—maybe it was *him* she had found insurance against.

Baron Wildman came from old money, but tragedy had struck him young. He was only sixteen years old when he lost both his parents and was left with a seven-year-old brother to look after. For someone who was handed everything on a silver platter, he still worked hard, taking his legacy very seriously. Glaringly different from his slimy younger brother whose legacy was making it to page six.

Mackenzie took in the multistory glass building with bridges extending up as far as the eyes could see. Plants and vines covered the walls. The roof had solar panels. Everything about the design of the building shouted eco-friendly. She even noticed the bamboo furniture and ergonomic keyboards. The people here were energetic, mostly young, but all determined. None of that usual trudging-along attitude that people of Lakemore oozed. She felt it in the air: ambition and greed.

Only big cities like Olympia had places like these. Lakemore was where back end operations were conducted. But towns like Lakemore were necessary. They fostered hunger. It was only after living in Lakemore where life and business was conducted at snail's pace that one valued what it meant to be in an environment that forced people to thrive, an ambience which nurtured growth.

When Nick's phone trilled with a notification indicating that the football game had started, Mackenzie was reminded that Lakemore wasn't all dull and mediocre.

"Who's playing?" she asked.

"Sharks versus Ravens."

"That's an easy win for us," Mackenzie said. "Uniform talked to Veronica's colleagues, right?"

He nodded. "Nobody knows anything."

Dominic approached them. All his jumpiness seemed to have evaporated from yesterday. "Detectives, how can I help you?"

"Do you work out of here, Mr. Childs?" Mackenzie smiled.

"No, but since the police were questioning Veronica's colleagues, we deemed it fit that there be an in-house attorney present," he replied smoothly. "You'd called ahead?"

"Yes, we wanted to figure out Veronica's movements at work the week she was abducted," Nick said. "Her roommate believes there was an incident."

He looked bemused. "Is that so? Did anyone say anything?"

"No. But maybe nobody else was involved," Mackenzie said. "Veronica had worked late into the night."

"There are security cameras in the building. Not everywhere. But the elevators and some sensitive areas..."

"If we can check those out that will be helpful."

"Sure. Follow me."

Mackenzie was surprised. She whispered to Nick, "He's cooperative."

"Or he had time to prepare. Pretty generous of him to just show us security tapes."

They were taken inside a dark room with monitors lined in rows. The glow from the screens infused the air with a bluish tinge. Tired men with bloated bellies sat in front of them, watching mindlessly and munching on takeout food. They straightened, seeing Mackenzie and Nick.

Dominic instructed one of them to pull up tapes from the day Veronica went missing.

"Well, you can just sit here and watch them. I'll be in my office," Dominic announced cheerfully and exited.

"Damn lawyers," Nick muttered, shrugging off his jacket. The room was almost blisteringly hot with the many machines running. "Dumping hours of tape on us to watch in a hot room that smells like old Chinese food. Clever move."

They sat in front of monitors that played events from that day. Two minutes in and Mackenzie knew how mind-numbing this was going to be. They had spotted Veronica and followed her around the building as she went to different desks, washrooms, conference rooms, and sometimes even out of the office. The resolution was better than most security cameras, but still it was hard to make out her expressions. Was she stressed? Was she fearful?

"My brain is melting," Mackenzie groaned.

"Looks like a regular Monday. Okay. Now it's after five," Nick narrated. "The building is emptying, but she is at her desk."

Mackenzie watched the numbers of the timestamp roll forward, hurling Veronica closer to a bleak future. Soon, Veronica put on her coat and went to the elevator. She hadn't carried her bag. The security camera on the elevator didn't show the floors, only a view of those riding. She got off and disappeared off camera.

"Where did she go?" Mack asked, her eyes searching the other monitors showing the footage from other cameras for that time.

"Christ, there are so many. Not the first floor."

"Oh, she's back in the elevator." Five minutes later, she was riding it again and then exited. "She got off on the floor where her office is."

Veronica went back to her desk and grabbed her purse.

Nick jutted out his lower lip. "Maybe she was leaving, but then remembered she had forgotten her purse or something."

This time, Veronica went back to the elevator and thirty seconds later was seen getting off in the lobby. She walked out the door and didn't return.

"Well, that was a waste," Nick snapped, irritated. "She went straight to the Tavern after this. Not enough time to account for a detour elsewhere."

"Which floor did she get off on the first time around?" Mackenzie murmured, lost in thought.

"What?"

"If she realized she had forgotten her purse, she would have stayed in the elevator and then gone back up again. But she went out for *five* minutes."

"To use the bathroom perhaps?"

Mackenzie turned to one of the security guys, discreetly watching the game on his phone. "Excuse me. Are all elevator exits covered by the cameras?"

He stifled a yawn. "Only some floors."

"Where did she go for five minutes?" Mackenzie said to herself.

"Let's check every camera facing the elevator," Nick suggested.

Together they spent the next few minutes playing and replaying the timestamp of Veronica exiting the elevator. If only the elevator camera showed the floors. A dull ache began to form under Mackenzie's eyes but she persisted. It was imperative to account for every movement. But Veronica wasn't seen getting off on any elevator. "It must be the floors that aren't monitored."

Nick clicked a pen. "We can eliminate the floors where she didn't show up."

"And we know it took her twenty seconds to reach the floor she was heading to," she said an idea taking shape in her head.

"That eliminates some floors too. We'll have to get in one and time ourselves."

Leaving the room choked with rancid smell and sweat, Mackenzie breathed deeply in relief. Her lungs worked better outside where the air was cool and crisp.

"No way I'm leaving here without finding anything useful."

"Dominic sure as hell is discouraging us without being uncooperative," Nick glowered.

"And he's hiding something."

They got inside an elevator and instructed everyone to empty it. She noticed Dominic watching them through the glass doors of an office.

"Veronica was on the fourteenth floor." Mackenzie punched the number. "And then it took twenty seconds for the elevator to reach her floor, not accounting for how long it takes for the doors to open and close. Up or down, we'll have to check both."

"Think it's related to Bobby?"

"He was the one harassing her. It's no joke to file a restraining order."

"You followed Murphy's advice of being nice to the Wildmans." Sarcasm dripped from his teasing tone.

She frowned. "I couldn't help it. Besides it's a good thing. I'm the bad cop. You're the good cop. It just makes you look nicer."

After minutes of going up and down, they narrowed it down to two floors.

"It's either the eighth floor or the twentieth," Nick said. "But the eighth floor is covered by the cams."

"So it must be the twentieth."

They rode the elevator back up. The twentieth floor housed three amenities: a meditation room, gym, and an indoor swimming pool.

Nick whistled at the facilities, where a few employees exercised. "Guess if you're living at work, you might as well have a swimming pool, right?"

"What the hell was Veronica doing on this floor?" Mackenzie inspected her surroundings. It was then she noticed the locker room. "I think I know."

There was a small locker room with separate sections for men and women, their names written on top of the lockers. Mackenzie walked past the names arranged in alphabetical order, until she reached Veronica Fang's. Just another steel box surrounded by a gazillion others. She could have left something here and come to collect it. Or she could have put something inside it.

Mackenzie pulled at it, but inevitably it was locked. "We need permission to break it open."

"I'll ask Dominic."

Mackenzie didn't have to wait too long before Dominic barged inside the locker room with beads of sweat under his hairline. "Detective Blackwood told me you want to access her locker?"

"Yeah, we just want to check if anything's in it."

His lips remained parted, his eyes like a deer in headlights. He struggled, scrambling for an excuse not to comply with the request. When he couldn't, he called for a receptionist and asked for the universal key to unlock the locker. He kept rubbing his lips and darting back and forth.

"You feeling all right, Mr. Childs?" Mackenzie asked in a harsh voice.

He almost looked dazed. "Y-yes. Of course."

When the receptionist arrived with the key, Nick unlocked the locker door; it opened with a creak. There were many things inside it, from a towel to a water bottle and some mild painkillers. But Mackenzie saw it instantly. It sat in the middle of the dark space, daunting and ominous.

A gleaming metal box.

When she took it out, she knew she was holding something important. It hid a secret.

Nick and Dominic closed in, wanting to peer at its contents. But Mackenzie gestured Dominic to move away.

Holding her breath, she flipped open the lid. There was a black diary inside it and a stack of pictures.

"What the hell." Nick grimaced at the pictures, as he flicked through them. "Mr. Childs, looks like your services will be required soon by your client."

Mackenzie's scalp cooled, but her ears burned. They were nude pictures taken from different angles of two people engaged in passionate lovemaking. One of them was Baron Wildman. The other was Mia Gallagher.

TWENTY

"Mia Gallagher and Baron Wildman?" Lieutenant Rivera repeated for the millionth time.

Sully chewed off the end of a granola bar, almost gagging.

"You okay, Sully?" Nick clapped his back.

The sergeant was seated inside the conference room with his carton of granola bars while Mackenzie, Nick, and Rivera stood around them. "Yeah. Pam has asked me to lose weight."

The compromising pictures of Mia and Baron were laid out on the table. They were almost lewd, not even erotic. When Mackenzie realized that pictures of gruesome dead bodies made her less uncomfortable, she questioned where her life was headed.

"Baron lied to us." Nick's voice brought her back.

Rivera recoiled at the pictures. "Make sure only the people you trust have access to this information."

Sully seemed to be the only one unaffected by their vulgarity. "If this leaks, it will be a media circus. And a huge divorce settlement for Linda Wildman."

"I care more about Veronica," Mackenzie said in a hard voice.

"We finally have a link between the two victims. Your hunch and reasoning was right, Detective Price." There was praise in Rivera's eyes. "But the reason I'm asking you to be careful is precisely for Veronica's sake. If the media gets wind of it, you can say goodbye to the attention Veronica's disappearance is getting right now. Rich people cheating is a story that tends to sell more, especially in a town with high crime rates where a woman missing doesn't quite strike a nerve with a desensitized population."

"And it will piss off the Wildmans," Sully said with his mouth full. "They're right in the middle of this. You'll need their cooperation moving forward."

Mackenzie had always been a direct person—sometimes even too direct. Even though part of being a detective entailed playing suspects and people of interest, it was the part she hated the most. As someone who had kept dark secrets all her life, she preferred honesty at work.

Nick shot her a pressing look, and she obliged. "Fine. I'll tone down my..."

"Mad Mack-ness," Sully finished.

She huffed. "Coming back to the point, it explains why Dominic had been so nervous. He clearly didn't want us opening that locker."

"Personal lawyers know more than spouses when it comes to these people," Nick said. "He must have known and was freaking out when we showed up."

Right on cue, Dominic and Baron appeared on the landing of the floor. Baron was stone-faced, regarding everyone around with him a stiff brow, like it was a huge inconvenience for him to be here. He kept checking his Rolex while Dominic was waved over to the conference room.

"Lieutenant Rivera?" Dominic shook her hand. "Captain Murphy said you'd be conducting this interview?"

She stifled her surprise. "There must be a miscommunication. Detective Price and Blackwood will talk with you. But I'm involved in the case, not to worry."

After more pleasantries and small talk, during which Baron remained glued to his phone, Sully and Rivera left the room.

"My client has taken time out of his very busy schedule to be here." Dominic pulled back a chair, jumping straight into a protective role. "I hope his cooperation is taken into consideration."

"Well, I'm not surprised he was able to find the time since his mistress was murdered," Mackenzie said, sitting down.

Baron's eyes snapped to hers and then to Nick. "Is this how it's going to be, Nick?"

Nick kept his neutral mask. "We're going to keep this professional, Mr. Wildman."

Baron's eye twitched. His long fingers drummed the table in contemplation. He gave a curt nod to Dominic, giving him the green light to continue.

"My client has no knowledge of what happened to Mia Gallagher and Veronica Fang."

"You lied that you didn't know who Mia was," Nick said.

"My wife was sitting there." He set his mouth in a grim line. "I'm not going to own up to an affair in front of her."

"Now we can have an honest conversation," Nick said.

"Veronica had these pictures in her possession." Mackenzie turned some of the pictures over, making Dominic and Baron look away. "She told her roommate that she had insurance against Bobby."

"What is that supposed to mean?" Dominic asked.

"It's pretty clear to me." She shrugged, pinning Baron with a hard look. "Bobby was harassing her. You wouldn't do anything about it. So she decided to blackmail you to do something about it."

"She had filed a restraining order against Bobby Wildman,"

Dominic argued. "She had already taken whatever measures she could, and he stayed away."

"We all know that a restraining order can't control your brother," Nick said. "And Veronica wasn't happy with her salary. Sounds like a way to kill two birds with one stone."

"I had no idea that Veronica was planning this blackmail," Baron insisted. "She never spoke with me about it."

"What about Mia Gallagher?" Mackenzie asked.

"What about her?" He shrugged, completely detached from the woman he had been intimate with, like she was a mere stranger.

"You have motive to hurt both women, Mr. Wildman. Did the affair with Mia turn sour?"

He barked a laugh. "There were no feelings involved! I paid her. In cash obviously."

That explained how Mia funded her lifestyle. "She told her friend that she was upset being *forced* into things. What was she talking about?"

"I don't know."

"Did she want more? More money or maybe she caught feelings for you? Were you tired of paying her because you got bored?" Mackenzie asked.

He rolled his eyes. "I used to like that she didn't demand things. I didn't realize she'd become a problem after she died."

Dominic clicked open his briefcase and pulled out a piece of paper. "This is Baron's itinerary going back two weeks that we are providing you out of goodwill."

"I highly doubt that Mr. Wildman would directly get his hands dirty," Nick scoffed. "We're not that naïve."

"We'll need to look at your financials," Mackenzie warned. "We can go get a warrant, but your cooperation now would be very much appreciated."

Dominic didn't need to check with Baron. Suddenly, the air hardened, and a wall erupted between them. "Baron Wildman is a prominent industrialist on the west coast, not your average Joe. You want his bank statements? You get a court order. We're done here."

Dominic and Baron left the conference room, without giving Mackenzie and Nick a chance to stop them. She watched their taut backs covered by tailored Italian suits. It didn't just stand for wealth; it was a symbol of how untouchable they were.

"Childs is smart," Nick said. "He knows we don't have enough for a judge to sign off on that court order. We need more than circumstantial evidence."

"Think you can ring your dad and ask for a favor?" she teased lightly.

"I'd rather swallow my own tongue."

"There is another person who had motive to hurt Mia," Mackenzie said.

Nick nodded, always in sync like a well-oiled machine. "Linda Wildman. It's possible she found out. But why would she take Veronica?"

"Why would even Baron abduct them instead of just having them killed? Mia was killed after forty-eight hours. And Veronica..." She couldn't keep the dread out of her voice.

"Maybe he wanted to reason with Mia first? No." Nick ran a hand through his hair. "He would have just talked to her, not tasered her and snatched her. She knew him."

She regarded Nick's tired eyes, the slight droop in his shoulders and messy hair. "You should head home. It's been a long day."

"Yeah." He pressed the heels of his hands into his eyes. "I'm going to hit the sack. Haven't gotten much sleep lately." He dragged his feet out from under the table and swung his jacket over his shoulder. "See you tomorrow."

"See you." Mackenzie lingered. She read over forensic reports and background checks and witness statements for Mia and Veronica—anything and everything she could get her hands on.

When her eyes began closing of their own accord and none of the words on the screen made sense to her, she decided to head home.

As soon as she reached the lobby, a tall, young man with chestnut hair falling over his forehead hurried over to her, looking frantic.

"Please! Can you help me?" he beseeched.

Mackenzie stepped back out of reflex. It took her a moment to adjust; her spent brain cells slowly began firing again. "I'm sorry?"

"Are you the detective that cop said he's getting for me?" he asked with wild and teary eyes. "My wife. She didn't come home. I *know* something went wrong."

"I'll take it from here, Mack." Austin's voice came from behind her, shooting her an apologetic look before turning to the man. "Mr. DeRossi? Let's go upstairs. I'll take your statement."

Hysterical words streamed out of his mouth as he walked past Mackenzie, leaving her to wonder if another woman had perhaps gone missing in Lakemore.

TWENTY-ONE

Entering her home, Mackenzie froze like she always did now. This time, a thought came to her. Until now, she'd had three *homes*, and each had seen death, including this one. The memory of what transpired in this house a few months ago was still fresh in her mind. The sound of the gunshots ringing. The weight of a lifeless body falling on top of her. It left her cold.

She went about the night robotically. She had gotten beyond tears and night terrors. Now she was numb, inert. Sleep had fled her. As she cleaned her already clean house, she wondered if she should seriously consider moving.

But it felt like giving up.

Twenty-one years ago, she left her first home after finding her father dead on the kitchen floor. A few years after that, her grandmother had died and took away her second home. And now it was this house and the violence it had seen so recently. It almost felt like she was always fleeing her rotten luck. And it would follow her to whichever house she moved to next.

It wasn't her job that had exposed her to the darkness of the world. It was when her mother had asked her to bury her father in the woods—and she had obliged. Something had changed inside her then, irrevocably.

Crime was a mystifying and bottomless abyss. It was easy to lose oneself in it. And Mackenzie lived and breathed that abyss. All of the team did. Except the rest of them had meaningful relationships that kept them bound to normalcy and sanity. She'd had it too when she was married. But now she was unchained. She was free but also dangerous.

"Do you feel like doing bad things too, Mom? Like Dad does?" Mackenzie had asked one stormy night.

"I have, Mackenzie. Unfortunately, I have." A fat tear had rolled down Melody's bruised cheek.

Mackenzie snapped out of her daze. It was one in the morning, but she played music and wore an apron. She set the oven to preheat and decided to bake a vanilla cake. A few minutes later, she became busy in her task and all her problems had fallen away.

The music suddenly stopped when her phone rang.

She wiped her hands and answered. "Justin, I didn't know you were on night shift today."

Justin spoke in a grave tone. The news cut sharply through the peaceful bubble she had built for the night.

"We just found Veronica Fang's body at Red Pond, ma'am."

TWENTY-TWO

Mackenzie focused on the rumble of the car underneath her. The road ahead unfurled like a dark gray ribbon. An icy storm had ushered in out of nowhere and was mounting. The hail was brutal, like the entire town was being peppered by gunfire. It slammed onto her car with such force that she was afraid it would crush it.

It did nothing to placate the doom she felt that Veronica had been discovered at a factory site miles away from where she was abducted.

Fifteen minutes later, Mackenzie saw the shadowy outline of a large structure against the velvety black sky. A swarm of cars and vans with lights stood in a cluster. She parked her car haphazardly and climbed out to the assaulting hail. A cop ran up to her with an umbrella and escorted her to the forensic tent behind the crime-scene tape. Another tent had been set up where uniform stood. Beads of ice were tangled in her red hair, running down her skin and leaving shivers in their wake.

A tall and bony man with clumps of white hair—Anthony, from the crime lab—instructed technicians. "Ah, Mack." He scowled, looking above. "You better hope this tent holds up against the hail. Fortunately, the winds are still mild."

As if on cue, a gust billowed the flaps of the tent and some officers rushed, helping to contain the crime scene.

"Where is she?" Mackenzie asked, taking the protective gear from him.

The tent mostly had makeshift tables and evidence boxes set up. Anthony hitched a thumb over his shoulder. "It's really been a pain in the ass to collect evidence in this weather. Becky has told us not to move her yet. She's over there."

Beyond the tent, there was a small pond bordered by cattails and bulrush. A shelter was held up above the pond to prevent the hail, but some of it blew in from time to time as the wind changed directions. A group was huddled around a body, while others collected samples from the water and soil and took photographs. Justin was also there, staying out of the way of the technicians but diligently noting all the protocol was being followed.

Mackenzie finally saw her.

Veronica lay with cloudy eyes and open lips. The skin on half of her body had almost melted away. The rest of her was intact—the left side of her body marbling and showing mild bruising.

"How do we know it's Veronica?" Mackenzie asked Justin. "Half of her face has melted off."

"She's wearing the same clothes Veronica was reported to have been wearing when she went missing. And there's a kidney-shaped birthmark on the bottom of her left foot, which is a match."

"Where's Nick?" Mackenzie looked around.

"He didn't answer his phone."

"He was beat the last time I saw him." She checked her watch. It was two in the morning.

"Who found her?"

"A maintenance worker." Justin pointed at a man, shaking under a blanket, in the other tent.

"At this hour?"

He huffed in disapproval. "He was dumping toxic waste into the pond when he saw her half submerged. He spooked and called 911."

"That's why her body is half dissolved," Becky piped up from next to the body. "This pond is full of sulfuric acid and other chemicals. Instead of treating their chemical waste, the factory has been dumping them in the Red Pond and one of the lakes."

"We'll inform the EPA first thing in the morning," Justin assured her.

"Good. Good. Becky, can you tell me anything?" Mackenzie asked.

"I have to open her up. With the body like this, I can't say anything."

Mackenzie rubbed her forehead with her fingertips. The sound of hail blasting increased, a keening wind almost toppled the shelter over.

"I want to move her *now!*" Becky shouted over the raging sound, struggling to keep her eyes open against the wind.

"We have to check in the pond," Mackenzie looked at the pondweeds and tape grass peeking out of the dark waters. "We can't go in if it has acid."

"The CSI will use nets to fish out any evidence," Justin said.

"Did you talk to the maintenance worker? Did he see anything else? Someone drive by?"

He shook his head. "No, ma'am. He said he dumps the waste alternate nights around this time."

"And he didn't see her two days ago?"

"No, he sounded very adamant."

Mackenzie looked over at the body again, which was now being lifted. There was a bit of a slope going into the pond where she was positioned. It appeared as though the body was intended to roll down into the pond but had got caught by the grass and ended up only half submerged.

"It's night-time. He could have missed it with all the weeds around it." She was unconvinced.

Justin pointed at a spot on the bank. "That is where he stood emptying the contents of the bins. He empties three, which usually takes him at least twenty minutes."

Mackenzie stood at the spot. It was in direct view of the body. If the worker had indeed been standing here for twenty minutes last time too, he should have seen her.

"Well, at least this tells us when the body was dumped," Mackenzie said. "Sometime within the last forty-eight hours. Where the hell was she for four days before that?"

Meet Lakemore's Mad Mack.

Mackenzie stared at her picture in the newspaper. She had crossed her arms and was smiling at the camera. A strand of red hair had strayed to the front of her face, flailing freely in the wind. She looked like an easy-going, cheerful, young woman, happy to be featured in the news. Completely opposite to how she'd felt. No one could guess how she'd glared at the makeup man, scaring him away, how the photographer had had to take at least a dozen shots begging her to smile, and how her cheeks had hurt, and she'd wanted to kill someone.

"The article has gotten a lot of hits," Troy reminded her, sucking on a lollipop. "Look at all the retweets. It's in the thousands!"

Mackenzie jerked at that and peered at his screen. "Oh God. It's just a silly article. Who cares what happens in Lakemore?"

Troy grinned. "Smart of the documentary guys to put out a few articles to generate publicity. Care to share the fame?"

Nick walked into the office, pressing the hot cup of coffee against his forehead. "Damn it. Sorry, Mack. I was out like a light and only saw the messages this morning." He shrugged off his coat. "When is Becky doing the post?"

"Right now." Mackenzie closed the newspaper with a wince. "She'll be ready for us this evening. And the tox screen for Mia came back earlier this morning. There were high amounts of chloroform in her system."

"Used on her while she was held captive, I bet. Any leads on Veronica?"

"Jenna is over at the factory collecting statements from workers if they've seen anyone scope the area or any security footage."

"We got the crime-scene photos." Nick opened them on his phone. "It's strange."

Mackenzie straightened her shoulders. "What do you mean?"

The Lakemore PD didn't have an in-house profiler; their budget simply didn't allow one. But Nick had been shrewd throughout his career. Capturing one of the most notorious child killers in the state of Washington on his first case had given him not only a distinguished reputation, but had also honed his skills of profiling. Mackenzie watched him carefully simmer in his own thoughts.

"They took Mia and Veronica at places with no witnesses or surveillance. They knew that Mia lived alone. They knew Veronica had a roommate, so she was taken from that dingy parking lot. They were both tasered from a weapon purchased from the streets, nearly impossible to track. They're planners, but then..." he frowned. "They dump their bodies in places where they could be found. They're almost careless about it."

"Maybe they *want* us to find the bodies? It's all a twisted game."

"They aren't staged. There's no ritual. These body dumps are not so public as to make a statement. It's almost like..."

"Like what?"

He blinked. "Never mind. We should talk to Linda Wildman today. I went over Veronica's phone records again but found nothing there."

"Maybe she'll slip something that can help us get a warrant against her husband's finances." Mackenzie could only hope.

"Or maybe she's the one we're after."

Light shimmered in the crystals of the Swarovski chandelier hanging above, casting slices of bright light across the walls covered in portraits and abstract paintings. Staff members moved around Mackenzie and Nick, dressed in uniform, wearing no decipherable expressions. The spacious living room was one of the many living rooms with more modern and sleek furniture and white walls as opposed to the plush rugs, wooden panels, and velvet sofas with gold trims of the library. The room opened to a mini garden with a giant tree at the end surrounded by bushes of brightly colored flowers.

Linda Wildman was there in a hat, watching the gardener snip out the weeds. They stepped out into the garden, Mackenzie's feet sinking into the thick, evenly cut grass. The weather had cleared suddenly; all the monotony and wildness from yesterday had given way to clear, bright skies.

"Mrs. Wildman?" Nick asked.

Linda turned around. "Oh! Nick!" She pulled him into air kisses and shook Mackenzie's hand eagerly. "Detective Price. I'm sorry I didn't recognize you the last time we met. But I read that article. Mad Mack, is it?"

She tried not to cringe. "It's just a silly nickname."

"Oh, please. I think it's fantastic." She beamed. "How can I help you? Are you here to see Baron? I'm afraid he flew to DC for the day."

"We're actually here to talk to you," Mackenzie said.

"Me?" She pressed a hand to her chest, her threaded

eyebrows raising over her Botox-filled forehead, like she wasn't used to people talking to her about serious things. "About what?"

"It's a delicate matter." Nick dropped his voice.

Linda moved away from the gardener under the shade of the tree. "Let's just talk here. It's way too hot today anyway. We keep having strange weather, don't we?"

The tree was tall and decades old, almost dwarfing the height of the house. Mackenzie glided her palm over the thick trunk. Above her, the branches extended in perfect symmetry. The branches and leaves formed a perfect triangle, the sides traveling up in slight arches and ending in a point.

"I have never seen such a symmetrical tree before," Mackenzie said in awe. "Must be a chore to keep it like this."

"We don't touch it. It's Baron's instructions. He and Bobby used to climb this tree when they were just boys. He loves it. Not because of nostalgia but because it represents perfection to him," Linda said with a strained smile. "Baron likes everything to be perfect." She fidgeted, grazing her thick hair.

Linda had toned arms and legs and a flat stomach. She was at least a decade younger than Baron—in her forties. But she made every effort to look even younger. It wasn't only her thick lips, shiny hair extensions, and face filled with Botox. But her posture was upright, her body language carefully crafted to be poised and feminine, her clothes always fashionable and expression welcoming and optimistic. Not a flicker of annoyance that she was having a bad day. Not a moment of her body slumping due to exhaustion. It was unnatural.

"Veronica Fang was found dead," Nick said slowly.

Her eyes widened. "Oh, dear God. That's horrible. Who did this?"

"We don't know yet. Did your husband ever talk about Veronica to you? Did you notice any tension between them?"

She laughed like the idea was ridiculous. "Baron and I don't talk, Nick. Well, except about the kids. And he's tense with *everyone*. I'm afraid, I don't know anything. Veronica was just one of the many staff members I'm surrounded by. She didn't work for me, so I don't think I even ever talked to her."

"Well, this is awkward..." Nick scratched his ear. "Veronica had intimate pictures of your husband... and Mia Gallagher."

Linda's face was straight.

"That woman we showed you a picture of who was murdered about a week ago," Nick elaborated.

"I see." She smiled tightly. "This is messy, isn't it?"

"Did you know about your husband's affair?" Mackenzie asked dubiously. When she'd found out her ex-husband had cheated on her, she'd gone into a state of shock followed by months spent in denial and trying to dissect what had happened before finding the strength to kick him out.

"It's Baron!" She waved a hand dismissively. "I'm not surprised. He's been unfaithful many times before. I don't keep track of his mistresses."

Mackenzie and Nick were stumped, staring at Linda's polite smile, which finally wavered and looked slightly wan.

"I know what this looks like to you, Detective Price. But, Nick, you shouldn't be surprised. Our world is different. Or maybe you really have stayed away from it for too long. What can I say? He looks elsewhere sometimes, and so do I. As long as we put our kids first and don't make a public scene, it doesn't matter."

"You don't care that your husband was sleeping with Mia?" Mackenzie asked, disbelieving.

She shrugged apologetically.

"You and Baron must have signed a prenuptial agreement," Nick said. "There isn't any infidelity clause?"

"No. Plus, if *I* leave him, I get nothing. If he leaves me, I get half. So the best scenario is for us to stay together and sleep with whoever we want to." Linda checked her watch. "Oh, dear, I'm sorry, but the redecorators should be here any minute I'm preparing the guest cottage for my dear sister. Are we done here?"

"Yes," Mackenzie said. "For now."

Linda smiled like she was playing a hostess at a party. "Stupid me! I never offered you water!" She gestured to one of the staff members, who carried over a tray of glasses and bottles with crystal lids shaped like chess pieces. "The water is from a spring in Japan. Enjoy!" She sashayed away.

Mackenzie took a sip of the water, coolness spreading through her chest. "So, water in Japan tastes the same as water in Washington."

"Except this bottle is over $200." Nick rolled his eyes.

Mackenzie almost spat it out, her body erupting into coughs as Nick patted her back. "Anyway, if Linda doesn't care about the affair and there is no infidelity clause, then does Baron still have motive to want Mia and Veronica dead? Would he care that Veronica planned to blackmail him?"

"Not for Linda's sake, but I don't think Baron would want Veronica to take this to the media. It would be an embarrassment. Wait for me? I'll just quickly use the restroom."

Mackenzie touched the tree again. It was more impressive than the sprawling mansion, exuding power, strength and perseverance. The heat began beating down on her. She wandered back inside, trying to soak it all in and momentarily getting lost in a world that was starkly different from hers. She was looking at a portrait of Baron's grandfather in a hallway when a voice echoed.

"You know there are no portraits of women in this house." Linda's heels clicked on the marble floor. "Only men."

"I noticed."

"I would blame the men. But I was shocked to find out that some women participate in this. My mother-in-law, for example. She lectured me on how my role is to stand in the shadows like a good woman. Thank God that old crone is dead. It's sad when women do it. Hypocritical of them, isn't it?"

"What do you mean?"

"Some women look down upon other women who fight for more. But they forget that the reason they can vote, travel without a chaperon, have claims to inheritance, and can own properties, bank accounts and their own money is because there were women who fought for these things before them. Not smart to discourage that behavior when they're living comfortably *because* of it."

Mackenzie couldn't hide her surprise. It was like she was talking to a different person. In this empty hallway away from any prying eyes, Linda had dropped her mannerisms and was almost relatable, showing that there was a strong, intelligent woman underneath the one that cooed at luxury brands.

She chuckled. "I know what you're thinking, Detective Price. I'm not offended. It's too late for me. Now all I can do is make the best of the situation while I encourage my Bette to be different. That's why I was so impressed with you from what I read in the paper. We need real female role models, not those fake ones. Not models that preach body positivity on social media but still look like sticks. Women who know more than just walking down a runway or using some Photoshop app. I want my Bette to be the first woman to go up on these walls. It will be hard. Baron focuses on Junior too much, grooming him to take over someday."

Before Mackenzie replied, a woman in uniform appeared at the end of the hallway, letting Linda know that she was needed. The fragile moment in the hallway was over. Linda transformed into the dutiful trophy wife, wearing her mask and fussing after the woman, complaining about how she only wanted mahogany antique.

"Mack!" Nick found her, striding to her with purpose.

"Remember that little black diary we found in Veronica's belongings? Next to the pictures?"

"Yes. We flipped through it, but it was empty."

"It's not." Nick showed her his phone. "Jenna went through it again in detail and found this."

On a page, there was a number scribbled with black ink—easily over ten digits.

"What's this?"

"No idea."

TWENTY-FOUR

Mackenzie and Nick climbed down the stairs at the medical examiner's office in Olympia.

Nick flipped open his cigarette case and perched one between his lips. "Any luck with that number she wrote?"

Mackenzie looked at the page with the number and counted the digits. "Thirteen digits. Not a phone number. Actually, there are two numbers. First one has six digits and then seven. There's a hyphen between them. I have no idea what this means."

"A birthdate?"

"No."

"We'll let Clint have a crack at it."

They reached the basement, where the air was thinner and colder and where sounds echoed. It was the floor the government didn't find it in its budget to renovate, leaving it with lime-tiled floors and gray walls where shadows flickered and danced.

"You're late." Becky let them into her office.

"Sorry. Traffic was crazy. And we had to swing by the station to collect something." Nick spoke around his cigarette and took a seat, resting his ankle over his knee. "We don't have to see the body, do we?"

"It's your lucky day." Becky sighed. "Dissolving bodies—I don't get a lot of those."

"Do we have cause of death?" Mackenzie asked.

"That's an interesting one. It was an aneurysm."

"What?" Mackenzie's eyes narrowed.

Becky showed them marked pictures of the partial skull, which was undamaged by the acid. "Veronica had an undiagnosed aneurysm. Thanks to hemorrhagic staining, I found some wounds in the ectocranial surface. The weapon perforated the thinnest part of the calvarium, which is the squamous temporal bone."

Mackenzie tried to make sense of it. "So, you're saying someone hit her on the head, which caused her aneurysm to rupture, therefore killing her?"

"Exactly. But then she was stabbed in the chest. However, there was no blood in the thoracic activity and her heart was perforated. Which means that she was already dead when she was stabbed."

"Is it possible that perhaps during a struggle the killer hit her on the head but didn't realize she had died so he stabbed her?" Nick asked.

"A likely explanation. I highly doubt that blunt force trauma was enough to kill her without the aneurysm. In my opinion, it should have just knocked her out."

"And the time of death?" Mackenzie inquired.

"Forty-eight to seventy-two hours before she was found. And your next question will be any signs of sexual assault." She pressed her lips in a thin line. "I found no lacerations, bruises, or abrasions in the vaginal and anal area. In fact, she hasn't had penetrative sex in a while. The minor injuries that occur during sex to the posterior fourchette—the skin at the bottom of the vagina—and labia minora are missing. UV showed no semen or mucosal injury. Even generally the body doesn't present any signs consistent with sexual assault, or any kind of assault."

Mackenzie sat back thinking. "Was she drugged?"

"Probably," Becky said. "I'm running a tox screen as we speak and have sent her clothes and shoes to the crime lab."

"And no DNA under her fingernails this time?" Nick asked hopefully.

"Unfortunately, not."

Mia had scratched and clawed, but Veronica had not. Had she been caught unexpected and didn't have time to react?

"Looks like Glenn's mystery partner has gotten better at snatching people," Mackenzie said. "Both Mia and Veronica are related to the Wildmans. They have a connection. How the hell does Glenn come into the picture? He was an unemployed man, living on the fringes of society."

Nick's face was grave. "And what do they want with these women if they aren't killing them immediately and not assaulting them?"

Leaving Becky's office with more questions, Mackenzie's head began to pound. She sat in the car, rubbing her temples, trying to dull the pain.

"You okay?" Nick asked from the driver's seat.

"Yeah, it's probably just stress." She hid the fact that it was happening a lot lately. The random bursts of headaches and strange thoughts plaguing her. It was everything, from this case to her face being in Lakemore's newspapers and magazines.

Mackenzie's phone gave a sharp ping. She frowned at the name.

"Austin?" she answered uncertainly.

"Mack?" His voice had an urgent edge, almost breathless. Like he was walking in a hurry. "It's important."

For a fleeting moment, she thought it was about his missing

fiancée and that he had refused to follow orders and give up on looking for her. But then he said something that made Mackenzie's veins crackle with electricity.

"I was looking into a woman who never returned home to her husband. Stella DeRossi. Just found out where she was taken from. Guess what else I found there? Taser confetti, the AFID tags match Murray's stash."

"We're on our way to the station." She hung up.

"What happened?"

"Another woman was abducted," she whispered.

Nick white-knuckled the steering wheel. "Damn it."

TWENTY-FIVE

"Is it possible that Stella DeRossi's abduction has nothing to do with Veronica and Mia's homicides?" Sully pressed, leaning against his desk. His latest hobby was discarded on the side. The sergeant was preparing to leave early tonight, but that plan was cancelled when Mackenzie, Nick, and Austin barged into his office, bearing bad news.

"The Taser fired came from a cartridge sold by Murray," Austin repeated. "In fact, the exact same Taser was used in the case of Veronica."

"How do we know that?"

"Some taser guns are equipped with two cartridges," Nick added. "Murray kept a detailed inventory of which cartridges were assigned to which Taser. We confirmed from the AFID serial numbers of the cartridge fired at Veronica and the one found where Stella was taken came from the same gun."

Sully twirled his mustache, staring at Stella's picture on his desk. "How is *she* related to Mia and Veronica?"

"We don't know yet," Mackenzie said. "Stella went to different schools. There are no mutual friends on social media. She worked as a pharmacist and had no connection to the Wildmans. We can't pinpoint how or where she would have crossed paths with the other victims. Uniform is talking to her co-workers and friends."

"The first two victims are related but the third one isn't. That doesn't make any sense!"

"Maybe she is. It took us a while to figure out the connection between Mia and Veronica. We will keep looking."

"Well, you don't have much time," Sully reminded sternly. "The first two victims were killed in a matter of days of being abducted after whatever the hell he wants from them. Did you get anything from Glenn Solomon?"

"There's nothing on his phone or email." Nick crossed his arms. "His neighbors said the only person who visited him was the man who had discovered his body. Jenna followed up on him, but he's just a local businessman with no connection to any of this and a solid alibi."

"If Glenn was working with someone, then why isn't there any evidence of it?" Sully asked.

There was no answer. Mackenzie felt inadequate—they all did.

"Patrol officers know about Stella?" Sully asked Austin.

"Yes, sir. The sheriff's office as well. Missing posters are up on all bus stops and bus stations. All exit points out of Lakemore are covered. Some sheriff deputies have volunteered to help with the on-foot search to comb through the woods where she went missing to see if there is any more evidence."

"All right. Well, Mackenzie and Nick, you're on this. Austin, I want you to stay with Troy. Hand over everything to them." He dismissed them.

Mackenzie didn't have time to feel bad for Austin nor to ponder over how Sully and Rivera were keeping him on a leash —or perhaps trying to keep them apart, knowing she had helped his mission.

"Stella's husband, Jonathan DeRossi, is an architect and has no idea who could have wanted to hurt her," Austin told Mackenzie and Nick outside. "He seems genuine. I didn't ask him about Veronica or Mia because I didn't know about the Taser back then. So do talk to him again."

Mackenzie added it to the list of things she had to do. "Okay, and where did she go missing?"

Austin showed them the crime-scene pictures. It was a wooded area with ground covered in moss and brown leaves. There was a thick log of wood lying with vines and creepers on it, along with bright pink confetti scattered over it. And a few drops of blood.

"Did you get a DNA confirmation from the blood?" Mackenzie asked.

"We will by tomorrow. But we found her earring under the leaves." Austin directed them to a close-up picture of a purple earring. "Which the husband confirmed she was wearing that day. And this place is close to her usual route from work to home."

"Her car?" Nick asked.

"She walked. The pharmacy was only fifteen minutes from their house. They only have one car and the husband works in Olympia so he's the one who uses it."

"Thanks, Austin," Mackenzie said.

He opened his mouth like he wanted to say something but settled on a small smile before leaving them.

"We don't have much time, Nick. She's been missing for twenty-four hours. And whoever this asshole is doesn't keep them alive for long."

Night had crept in, but neither of them left. Adrenaline was pushing hard inside Mackenzie, leaving her brain buzzing and her body shaking with untapped energy. She had decided not to sleep or go home until she made some progress, going over the crime-scene pictures and statements of Stella's friends and co-workers to see if anything was missed.

Stella's picture was pinned to her desk. She was a brunette, around forty years old but looked at least a decade younger. Stella and Jonathan had been married for over eight years, didn't have any children, but cared for a Golden Retriever they called Bean. Her parents lived on the east coast and were already on their way to Lakemore to help with the search.

Nick was in his cubicle behind her, poring over phone records, checking every text and call. His desk was littered with empty coffee cups to help him power through the night. Stella's phone had been missing and was last active around the area of her abduction. He had requested Clint to monitor it, to triangulate its new position if it were switched on.

"Anything?" Nick asked again.

"No," Mackenzie replied again.

"The body was dumped before the maintenance worker came around one thirty in the morning. Do you think that was a lucky shot?"

Mackenzie considered. "If they've been keeping an eye on their victims, then I reckon they must have done some research into where to dump the body without being seen."

Nick spun on his chair and logged in to the server again. "They must have moved the body at night to avoid eyes. The last worker's shift ends at ten in the evening."

"Okay, but the security cameras don't cover the pond." She wheeled closer to him, curious about where he was going with this.

"The factory is off Exit 98," he groaned. "Think Clint is working right now?"

"It's ten in the evening. He's definitely still in. Why?"

"I might have an idea."

Clint was the tallest member of the Lakemore PD with a giraffe-like neck that rose above his mountain of monitors in his office. He liked to work alone in the hum of running machines. When Mackenzie and Nick waltzed into his office, he didn't express surprise, but carried on tapping away on one of the keyboards.

"We need your help." Nick shoved his hands in his pockets.

"I still have to look at that number you gave me. Didn't match any database. I'll tell you that." His eyes didn't stray from the screen.

"It's not that. I want you to check some traffic cams for us around the factory off Exit 98."

Clint clicked his tongue and released a breath. "Guess I can use a break. Special Investigations has me working on that Simonds money-laundering case."

Mackenzie waited patiently while Clint pulled up the traffic cams in the area.

"We don't have a view of that exit." Clint sounded resigned.

Nick walked around his large desk and stood next to him, determined. "What's the best one you got?"

"This one on the freeway two exits after."

"Last shift ends at ten, so accounting for some buffer time... play the footage from ten-thirty to one last night," Nick instructed.

Mackenzie joined him in watching the grainy video of cars whirring past. "How will this help? We have no idea what car was used for the body drop. All tire marks were washed away by the rain."

Nick's hands twitched in his pockets. "I don't know exactly, but maybe—Wait! Slow that down!"

Clint did as told and played the video again.

"Look at the car speeding on an empty lane."

Mackenzie watched a car flying past others. The video quality was too grainy to confirm the license plate number.

"Clint, can you check if there was a speeding ticket given there around that time? I really hope one of our guys was eager to fill their quota and catch this one. It will be a pain in the ass to get the plate from this video."

"I'll just go to the traffic safety commission and download that data," Clint narrated.

Mackenzie nibbled on the pad of her thumb. She wouldn't have had any expectations if it weren't for Nick leaning in closely behind Clint.

"Officer Calloway issued a speeding ticket at ten past eleven four miles from Exit 98," Clint said.

"To whom?" Nick asked.

"Someone called Dominic Childs."

"Stella DeRossi has been missing for over twenty-four hours," Debbie Arnold announced with Stella's picture flashing next to hers. *"Our sources have confirmed that DeRossi's abduction is linked to the Mia Gallagher and Veronica Fang homicides. Do we have a serial killer on the loose in Lakemore?"* Her voice turned ominous. *"The Lakemore PD were tight-lipped when we reached out to them for a comment. But the residents of Lakemore, especially young, professional women, deserve to know if they are being targeted. Or do the police simply expect us to not ask questions because the public's new favorite Mad Mack is on the case?"*

Fury bubbled inside Mackenzie, and she closed the tab on her phone.

"Debbie gave you a shout-out?" Nick had heard as he walked around the car to join her. "You'll definitely be a household name now."

"Why would she throw my name around like that?"

"She's probably jealous about that article and now the documentary. Debbie loves attention."

They walked up the arching driveway to a house painted in

sky blue. Mackenzie dodged the water spraying from the sprinklers across the front yard. Dominic resided in Forrest Hill, an exclusive gated community in Lakemore, which housed retired football athletes, politicians, and businesspeople. A previous case had brought her here once and Lakemore was still healing from the consequences of that case.

When they rang the bell, Dominic opened the door, dressed in a suit and carrying his briefcase. For a fleeting second, panic rose in his eyes, his throat struggling to swallow. But he composed himself. "Detectives, I'm running late for a meeting." He pushed past them toward his Mercedes.

"Actually, you'll have to call an Uber." Mackenzie handed him a warrant with a smile. "The crime lab is towing your car to look for any evidence of Veronica Fang."

Dominic's nostrils flared. He read the warrant with gritted teeth. "You're wasting your time."

"You got a speeding ticket the night Veronica's body was dumped," Nick said, watching Dominic's face fall.

"That means nothing. I was speeding, so what?" he challenged. "I'll pay the fine."

"You were cruising at over 100 miles an hour on an empty lane where the maximum speed allowed was fifty-five. Your breathalyzer showed no alcohol in your system. Why were you in a hurry?" Mackenzie asked.

"I was going home! I had been working late."

"Your office is nowhere around that area. No reason for you to be on that highway."

"I was with a client," he asserted.

"Which one?" She took out her pocket diary ready to note down the details.

Dominic crumpled the warrant and shoved it into Nick's chest. "I don't have to talk to you." He stormed past them back into his house, just as a tow truck turned the corner to take his car to the crime lab in Olympia.

Mackenzie recalled Dominic's reactions since she'd met him. Unlike Baron, he was jumpy and nervous. She thought it was because he knew about Baron's relationship with a murder victim and fretted about how to protect his client. But now it looked like Dominic's involvement was deeper than she had imagined.

"He's not talking now, but he soon will once we find something in his car," Nick said. "Let's see if Stella's husband knows anything about her connection to Mia and Veronica."

Jonathan DeRossi's hands trembled as he carried two glasses of water from the kitchen to the living room. Mackenzie took the glass from him and went back to eyeballing the large wall above the fireplace, which had a collage of pictures. Stella and Jonathan getting married at city hall. Their reception at some barn, where guests sat on hay bales. Their holidays together in Paris, Las Vegas, and New York City. Their graduation ceremony. And there were more intimate pictures—Stella taking her morning coffee in her pajamas with her hair undone, Jonathan still sleeping in bed, Stella giving a bath to their dog, Jonathan lying on the grass getting his face licked by their Golden Retriever. It looked like they lived a happy life. Fragments of a young couple very much in love.

And suddenly that life had collapsed.

"My hand still searches for her in bed." Jonathan rubbed his tired eyes. "It's early in the morning when I'm somewhere between being asleep and awake. And when my hand finds nothing, I'm up feeling so heavy in my chest."

"I'm sorry, Mr. DeRossi," Nick said. "I understand you spoke with Detective Kennedy and stated you can't think of anyone who wanted to harm Stella?"

"I really can't. I have no idea. She got along with everyone. She was an easy-going and shy person."

"And she hadn't said or done anything out of the blue lately? Any money problems?"

"No. Stella got a huge inheritance from a grandparent when she was in college, so we never had to struggle, really. We were in fact looking forward to going up to Vancouver next weekend. We were going to get Bean neutered as well. Now Bean can't even stand to be in this horrid house." He looked around, wincing like he was in pain. "He was getting depressed, so I had to send him to my sister's for a while. We had all these plans and then she just..." He broke down.

"Did she know or speak about the Wildman Group?" Mackenzie asked. "Baron, Bobby, Linda. Or Dominic Childs. Any of these names ring a bell?"

"No. Should they?"

"It's just the first two victims had a connection to them."

Jonathan shot up from his seat, his hands fisting his hair. "Debbie was right?! Stella was taken by some serial killer? The first two women are dead! Does that mean that my wife is too?"

"We have no reason to believe that your wife isn't alive. But the cases do seem to be linked," Nick said.

"Why? Why her?" he beseeched. "There are hundreds of young women in town. Why my wife?"

It was a question that had plagued Mackenzie. This morning the DNA results came back on the blood found on the log at the abduction scene, confirming that it belonged to Stella.

Nick gave him his phone. "Do you recognize these two women and that man?"

Jonathan wiped the tears pooling in his eyes with his sleeve and took his time looking at the pictures of Mia, Veronica, and Glenn. "No. I saw them on the news and some missing posters before, but that's it."

"Mr. DeRossi," Mackenzie tried to soften her voice. She was always too cut-throat and direct in her approach. "Is there anyone else other than you that Stella was close to? A friend or a sibling? Maybe someone would know some—"

"Stella tells me *everything*," he glowered. "We don't have any secrets. And I told you, her nature is reserved. She doesn't have a lot of friends. She's never met or even heard of Mia Gallagher or Veronica Fang or that man."

Despite always suspecting the worst, Mackenzie found it hard to doubt Jonathan DeRossi. The house smelled stale; dishes were stacked in the kitchen sink with remains of food still welded to the rim of bowls. Dark circles ringed his eyes. He sat now, rocking back and forth with brimming anxiety. Mackenzie looked at Stella's picture again with Jonathan kissing his cheek, silently praying that she wouldn't have to be the bearer of bad news.

After questioning him some more, Mackenzie and Nick left the house.

"Damn, I feel like I can breathe better now." Nick opened an umbrella against the tapping rain. The weather was gray and uninviting, with a chilly wind blowing sodden leaves in their path. "Funny how the air changes when something bad happens."

Mackenzie nodded, feeling her breath tear in her chest. "There's something wrong about this, Nick."

He stopped. "What do you mean?"

"I don't know..." She couldn't explain it. "Mia's murdered. Her killer—or one of them—committed suicide. Veronica was killed. And now there's Stella with no connection to any of this."

Nick's phone rang. He handed the umbrella to Mackenzie and put the call on speaker. "You got anything from Dominic's car?"

Anthony gloated. "We got him. We can place him at the pond and Veronica inside his car."

TWENTY-SEVEN

Dominic Childs sat in the cold and clinical interrogation room. Mackenzie watched him through the mirror. He rubbed his hands and tapped his foot, buzzing and caged.

Nick leaned against a table, reading the reports Anthony had emailed one more time before they headed to question him.

Justin knocked on the door, peeking his head in. "Got a minute?"

Mackenzie gestured him to come inside.

"I couldn't find a connection between Glenn Solomon and Dominic Childs," Justin admitted reluctantly. The junior detective had high expectations of himself. "Solomon has received no significant payments in the last year, so he couldn't have been a murder for hire."

Then why would Glenn kill Mia? Was he a budding psychopath, whose conscience suddenly woke up, driving him to commit suicide?

"We'll have Childs's finances soon enough. Maybe that will shed a light," Mackenzie said, trying to stay upbeat. "Did you have any luck tracking the people Murray sold Tasers to?"

He nodded. "I've been working with Special Investigations. I can get you more information soon."

"Good. Stay on that." She turned to Nick. "Are you ready?"

Nick closed the file and fixed his tie. "Ready."

As they were exiting the room, Captain Murphy tottered in, without sparing them a look. Mackenzie and Nick froze, watching him take a seat without a word.

"What the hell is he doing here?" Nick murmured.

"Murphy giving a damn about a case. That's a new one."

They swung the door open. The temperature in the interrogation room had plummeted. Mackenzie set the camera on the tripod to record, while Nick read him his rights again since Dominic had been arrested and picked up by uniform. When he was done, there was a thin silence in the room. Mackenzie could feel the curious gaze of Murphy drilling into her back. For a moment, it felt like everything could fall apart. Like those agonizing seconds of watching a glass fall off a table before it smashes on the ground.

"We found evidence of Veronica in your car," Nick said.

"Veronica has been in my car a few times." Dominic shrugged, trying to look unconcerned, but it was forced.

"In the back seat?" Nick raised an eyebrow. "That's where we found her hair."

"Yes. She rode with me."

"There was also blood."

Dominic took a quivering breath. "I... One time she got a nosebleed. It must be from that." Despite being poor at veiling his fear, he was still a lawyer worth his dime if he had Baron as a client.

Mackenzie plastered her back to the chair and crossed her arms. "Are you ready to provide us with the information of the client you were meeting the night you were caught speeding?"

"I'll have to check my itinerary for that day," he replied evasively.

"Are you saying you weren't at or around Red Pond the night in question?"

His eyes registered fear. "Absolutely not."

"Are you sure?" Mackenzie bit back a sour smile.

"Yes."

She let it unleash on her face. They had him. She opened a file with chromatograms and a list of chemical structures with their scientific names. "Then how do you explain why your car tires have traces of water lettuce, tape grass, silt, and sulfuric acid among other things? Everything you find in the Red Pond."

A moment of panic. "I'm sure you'll find these things in other water bodies."

"Not sulfuric acid. You see, it doesn't evaporate easily."

Dominic scratched his temple. "Oh, that's from the battery. It got on the tire somehow. Is that it?"

"You're a good lawyer." Nick smirked. "Excuses are just sitting at the tip of your tongue, which is why we asked the crime lab to be more thorough."

Mackenzie relished Dominic's face darkening as she elaborated. "We found orthosilicic acid as well. Found commonly in water bodies."

"It could have gotten there from anywhere!"

"Except we identified diatoms that narrowed it down to a specific water body... the Red Pond." Mackenzie pointed him to another page. "Look at the chromatograms of samples obtained from your tire and from the Red Pond. It's a match. It's like finding a fingerprint—which reminds me... Nick?"

"We found a partial print on Veronica's clothing. Now that you're under arrest, you'll be processed and we will get your prints. We've got you cornered, Mr. Childs. Confess everything and tell us where Stella is."

Triumph flowed through Mackenzie, swelling inside her. She could feel Stella at the tip of her fingers. All she had to do was twist her hand and make a fist.

Then the unexpected happened.

Dominic began shedding tears. A flush spread up his neck and he hid his face in his hands, his shoulders raking with every sob. "I... I'm sorry. I swear I didn't want to. I *swear* to God I had no choice. It haunts me every single day what I had to do. I'm so sorry. I didn't have a choice."

The recollection of Glenn's memory came to her unbidden. *It was me or her. I didn't have a choice.*

She leaned forward. "Explain."

Dominic sniffled and withdrew a thick red envelope from his briefcase. "This was slipped under my house when I was alone. I didn't see who brought it."

Nick poured the contents of it. There was a single sheet of paper and surveillance pictures of young children—two girls.

"What choice did I have? Look at those pictures! They were followed at school, at their piano classes, their playdates... some were taken inside their bedrooms!"

Mackenzie picked up the paper and read the words printed on it.

Let's play a game. Kill Veronica Fang or I kill your daughters. If you choose the former, come to the Lakemore Gardens by the carousel at 4 p.m. tomorrow for further instructions. If you do not come or you tell the police or anyone, I know who to kill instead. The choice is yours.

TWENTY-EIGHT

"Why don't you run away, Mom?" Mackenzie had asked, both of them slumped against the foot of the bed. Outside, the storm had worn itself out. It was eerily quiet, the air too still.

"I told you, Mackenzie." Melody sighed, forlorn. "Sometimes choice is nothing but a hollow word."

Mackenzie's temples throbbed. Taken aback by the sudden onslaught of the pounding in her head, she drank some water.

"Someone blackmailed you to murder Veronica," Nick said softly.

Dominic nodded. "I couldn't believe what I was holding in my hands. I thought of going to the police. I thought maybe they weren't serious; just someone I pissed off at court. But those surveillance pictures terrified me. I... My girls were being followed! He has been in their bedroom!"

There were three pictures of the two girls sleeping. They were barely ten years old, tucked in and dreaming away while someone had stood next to their beds and taken photographs of them.

"You could have..." Mackenzie struggled to find her voice. "You should have still gone to the police."

"I couldn't risk it! These are my *children*." He implored to Nick, "You have a kid, don't you? What would you have done if you were in my place?"

Nick didn't answer. He didn't need to. Mackenzie knew that he'd do anything to protect Luna and deal with the consequences later.

"Do you suspect anyone? Have you noticed anyone around your kids?" Mackenzie asked.

Dominic kept shaking his head. "Not someone who would do something like *this*. Trust me, I've spent hours thinking about it, but I didn't see this coming."

"Did you meet them at the park?"

"No. I was sitting at a bench there by the carousel as instructed. It was very crowded. I didn't even realize when there was another envelope left on the bench next to me. It said to find Veronica under the old bridge in woods by Crescent Lake. I got there..." He wilted as he recalled the horrid details. "I waited until it was dark to get there. I found her half-unconscious and bound. Nobody was around... and I... I was so close to taking her to the hospital and calling the police. For God's sake, I *knew* the woman. But my girls. This person abducted and hurt Veronica. What was to stop them from harming my girls? I had a brought a knife. But I just bashed a rock against her head. I thought there'd be less blood that way. She went still, but then I got scared that maybe she was still alive, so I stabbed her. I had brought tarp. I wrapped her up in that and drove to that factory."

"Why that factory?" Nick asked.

"I knew about their illegal practices. One of my colleagues handles their account. They let it slip one night. I figured her body would dissolve but..." he trailed off, weary.

"You were careless."

"I just wanted to get out of there. Drive back home to my

girls and hold them and forget about what I did. But I... Dear God. I'm sorry. I didn't have a choice. Not really."

Mackenzie tuned out his earnest attempts to convince them how sorry he was. He was a mess. All that guilt had built up inside him and poured out in that interrogation room. She was still reeling from his revelation, unable to offer him any comfort. She left that to Nick. He was better at dealing with people anyway. Her head was ready to burst.

She stumbled out of the room, shouldered past the officers and stepped outside the building. In the cold air, she breathed better. She didn't know what had set her off. If anything, Dominic's confession had confirmed the niggling feeling of this case being more warped than it seemed.

The residue of that letter clung to her skin. The twistedness and brutality of it. Someone had abducted Mia and then threatened Glenn into murdering her. They'd snatched Veronica and then blackmailed Dominic into killing her. Now they had Stella.

This was a game. But whose turn was it this time?

TWENTY-NINE

Mackenzie poured a glass of water and pushed it toward Nick.

"Feeling better?" Nick asked.

She shrugged. "I don't know, I just keep getting random headaches."

"You should get it checked." He swallowed half of the water in large gulps. "You hit your head when you took down that dealer."

Her brain had floated loosely in her head. But she dismissed it. "It's probably just stress."

After putting Dominic in the holding cell, they'd realized that Captain Murphy had already left. They'd drove to Mackenzie's house where they now sat in the kitchen, still stunned.

"What do you think the DA will charge him with?" Mackenzie asked.

"He'll still be charged with first-degree. Though he shouldn't." His expression turned fierce. "He was being a good father."

"By murdering an innocent woman?"

"By making sure that no harm comes to his children. The day he became a parent, it was his responsibility to put them over anybody else."

She trailed her finger along the rim of the glass, pondering. "Did he do the right thing?"

"Doing something bad to protect your loved ones doesn't make you a bad person." His eyes held hers.

Mackenzie reined in her racing heart. She felt so exposed, so naked. That grisly horror of standing unprepared on stage in front of thousands. Nick was the only other person in the world who knew what she had done as a child. How she had helped her mother bury a body to protect her. How the remnants of that night had defined her for so long that she didn't know what she was without it.

She began cleaning the counter. "I suppose the jury would be sympathetic."

"Maybe. Now we know why they were held captive before they were killed. It was to account for the time to deliver the notes and to move the body."

"We didn't find any letter like that at Glenn's, did we?"

"No, I don't think so." Nick ran a hand through his hair. "He probably destroyed it. I'll ask Jenna to check more carefully now that we know what we're looking for."

"Why these players?" Mackenzie set the washcloth over her shoulder and turned to face him, crossing her arms.

"What do you mean?"

"What connects all of them? Mia, Veronica, and Dominic are related to Baron's company and his affair, but where do Glenn and Stella fit in? And on what basis were some selected to be murder victims and others their killers?"

Nick took a staggering breath. "And how many more will be forced to play the game?"

The game. It had to be someone clever and perceptive to force people to be part of this chain.

It was almost midnight, but neither of them was sleeping tonight. Not after the knowledge seeping in that someone out there was going to get blackmailed to murder Stella—if they hadn't already. By some silent understanding, both continued working at Mackenzie's kitchen counter. She had a study that Sterling used to use, but she wanted to convert it to a gym. Might as well.

"I'll send the CSI first thing in the morning to check the bridge where Veronica was found by Dominic." Nick muttered more to himself, "Ever feel there aren't enough hours in the day?"

"Every single day." Mackenzie sighed, realizing there wasn't much she was going to get from Stella's phone records. Just like Jonathan had said, her life had been uneventful, only to be cruelly interrupted.

She decided to switch strategy. What if another victim could lead them to Stella? After all, Veronica knew Mia—or at least *of* her.

Mackenzie pulled up the number written in the diary. She typed the number on Google and came up short.

"Come on," she groaned in desperation, drumming her fingers and staring at the number. What could it be? Not a bank account. Not a credit card. She'd confirmed all that. Plus the two numbers were separated by a hyphen. A password?

Maybe it wasn't a hyphen…

Mackenzie's heart sped up when an idea trickled into her mind. She wrote the numbers out separately and saw it clearly now. One quick check confirmed it.

"Nick! I think I know what this number is."

He stopped what he was doing. "What?"

"These are coordinates. It's not a hyphen. It's a negative sign. The first number is north latitude and the second is a west longitude."

"Where is it for?"

She showed him her phone. "Lost Woods Motel."
Nick was already on his feet. "Let's go. No time to waste."

THIRTY

It was a muggy night. When Mackenzie stepped out of the car, she felt the stickiness going down her lungs.

The Lost Woods Motel was aptly named, situated off a highway, being swallowed by surrounding dark woods. Creepers and ivy crawled up the walls. The sign of Lost Woods atop a pole flickered like a dying bulb. It looked more like an old three-story house with no decks or railings running around it. A macabre motel hidden from sight.

"Looks like a place where people come to get murdered." Nick stifled a yawn, trudging up the path lined with sticky soil bent on drawing their steps in.

Inside, there was a reception on the left behind a window with mailboxes across from it and a broad staircase was situated in the middle. Mackenzie knocked at the reception desk to wake up the slumbering man. It reminded her of a ticket counter at a train station.

His beady eyes with sagging cheeks glanced between them. "How many hours?"

"Sorry?" Mackenzie asked.

He opened the register, looking impatient. "How many hours do you want the room for? Two? Three?"

Mackenzie frowned and looked at Nick, whose face had turned red. It struck her then.

"Oh. *No*. We're from the Lakemore PD."

He shifted uncomfortably. "What do you want?"

Nick showed him the picture of Mia. "Recognize her?"

He evaded the question. "Nothing illegal is going on in my motel. Everything happens between consenting adults."

"That's not what we asked."

"Mia Gallagher. She's a regular. Though I haven't seen her in a while. She has a room reserved just for her. Nobody else uses it."

Mackenzie and Nick exchanged a glance. Veronica had obtained pictures of Mia and Baron. Perhaps they were taken in the motel room.

After managing to convince the man to allow them to see the room, they headed up to the room, walking past doors from behind which came noises of squeaking bedsprings and muffled groans. Mackenzie was suddenly acutely aware of Nick's shoulder brushing against her. She wanted to dissolve in a puddle.

"Maybe we'll find *Chad* in one of these rooms," he smirked.

"Oh my God. Shut up."

He looked pleased with himself.

They reached the brown, rusty door with the number 309 engraved on the white plate. Mackenzie used the spare key the man had given her to unlock the door. Pushing into the pitch darkness, her hand fumbled to switch on the light.

It was a usual room with a bed, a mini chandelier, a dresser, and a little sitting area. Nicer than what was expected at a motel, but the man had mentioned it was the most expensive room. It was clear, though, that it hadn't been cleaned in a while. Mackenzie ran her finger along the coffee table, collecting dust.

Nick took in the room. "This is where Mia and Baron used to meet? I guess Veronica found out and planted a camera."

Mackenzie threw open the cupboards. "Maybe there's something more here."

Together they searched the room, turning over the mattress and sifting through the chest of drawers. There was just some lingerie, a bag of toiletries, and condoms. Nothing out of the ordinary given the circumstances.

"Mack. Come here," Nick said, crouched on the floor facing the bottom drawer of the dresser. He revealed a black safety box inside a cupboard, the ones usually hotels were equipped with. "It's locked."

Mackenzie found a fire iron against the window and instructed Nick to move. She bashed it into the box repeatedly, denting the top, until the lock broke.

"We'll probably have to pay for that."

Nick dug through the box and pulled out two things: a film roll and a curated list of names with dates. "What is this now?"

Mackenzie took the film roll from him and looked at it against the bright light in the bathroom. She could barely make out any detail, but she didn't need to. From the outlines, it was clear that they were more intimate pictures. Presumably of Mia and Baron.

Disappointment flooded her. She had been hoping for new information. Anything that could lead them to Stella or move forward this tangled web of a case. But then she noticed something.

Her pulse galloped again. "Nick, I don't think they're all of Baron." The frame of the men was inconsistent: some stocky, others wiry, some towering and others short. When Nick didn't answer, she went back to the room to find him sitting on the bed, looking at the list of names like it was a puzzle. "What is it?"

He looked up. "I recognize some of these names. They're all influential businessmen and industrialists. Some of them have donated to my father's campaigns in the past."

Suddenly the film in Mackenzie's palm was too heavy and cutting, stinging her palm. Their eyes drilled into the roll. They knew that what she held was damning and bigger than the both of them. An icy tumble of panic unfurled inside her. They had opened the Pandora's box.

THIRTY-ONE

OCTOBER 21

Mackenzie had woken up with the sun. She turned on the blender in the kitchen, its grating sound scratching the air. She had just returned from her morning run. Sweat was cooling her scalp, and she was still catching her breath when her phone rang.

"You're not an early bird," she answered, turning off the blender and pouring the juice into a glass.

"I didn't sleep much," Nick replied. "I heard back from Anthony. There was nothing on the motel key. I sent the envelope and notes to him to swipe for any prints other than Dominic's."

"I don't think our guy is going to be dumb enough to leave prints on a piece of paper he's handing out like that." She took a few gulps, hoping that lethargy would leave her. "He has created this *network*. Cast a net to trap so many people without having to kill anyone himself."

"Everyone makes mistakes. We just need to find it." Nick sighed. "I'd called because Jenna got back to me. She found remnants of a red envelope covered in soot in a trash can at

Glenn Solomon's house. An exact match to what Dominic showed us."

"So Glenn tried to get rid of it."

"Yeah, the rest we couldn't salvage."

"We should run down the names we found at the motel. And get those negatives developed." Mackenzie recalled how silent the drive had been to the Lakemore PD when they went to put what they'd found in the evidence locker.

"I'm already on it. When will you be here?"

"Less than an hour." She hung up and clutched the phone to her chest.

A box was perched on the coffee table, filled with some of Sterling's things she had found around the house and gotten from the storage space. She crept closer, her breath hitching at her wedding picture on top.

Mackenzie wondered when it would stop, or if it ever would. She didn't love him anymore. But there was always this mild discomfort that flared inside her chest.

She checked the clock, her dread mounting as the hand went round and round.

And then the doorbell rang.

Without thinking, she swiped off her wedding picture and put it away in a drawer. Taking a moment to wear her mask of being aloof, she opened the door to find her ex-husband. He looked handsome as ever—tall and muscular with black hair growing into curls and frosty blue eyes, a stark contrast against his dark skin.

"Mack." Sterling smiled like they were old friends.

"Hello." She was taken aback when he gave her a quick hug.

He walked in and looked around the house. "Ah. You haven't changed it much."

"Haven't found the time." She leaned against a pillar, grinding her jaw. They were together again in the house they'd shared. His scent had already infused the air. The light had curved around him. "How have you been?"

"Good. Busy with work. You?" He removed his gloves.

"Same." They lingered awkwardly. "How's your new place?"

"It's great."

Are you seeing someone? The question burned the tip of her tongue. She didn't want to know. The petty side of her would throw a tantrum at how unfair it would be for him to find someone before her, when he was the one who had cheated. Not that she wanted to get back together with him.

"Well, this is the stuff." She handed him the box. "The last of it."

He swallowed hard. "Thanks. Hope it wasn't too much trouble."

"Not at all."

After a pause, he said, "I saw the trailer. You look great in it."

"The trailer?" Blood drained from her face. "What trailer?"

Sterling found her reaction amusing. He set the box down and showed her his phone. "It just dropped on YouTube a few hours ago."

Mackenzie watched in horror. Clips of her interviews with dramatic pauses and quick cuts of her walking down dodgy alleys, all against a background score that climbed to a crescendo. "Please make it stop."

Sterling chuckled and closed the tab. "I'm looking forward to watching it."

"That makes one of us."

"I'm surprised you agreed to it."

"Well, I didn't have a choice. Orders came from above. Publicity stunt to save our crippling image." She wanted to blend into her surroundings and never be seen again. She made a show of checking her watch. "Anyway, I have to head back to work. I'm sure you've seen the news."

"Third girl gone." He clicked his tongue. "I'm sure you'll find her alive."

His icy blue eyes pierced into her deep brown ones. He looked sincere—but that was Sterling, no matter what he felt inside, he always looked sincere. It had been a long and hard road to realize that she didn't really know the man she had spent six years with.

"Okay, then. I'll see you around. Thanks for this." He sauntered back to the door.

"Yeah. See you around." She shut the door and pressed her back against it, slinking down to the floor. He was the ADA and she was a detective. Their paths were bound to cross in the future.

The continuous trilling of the phones annoyed Mackenzie. "Peterson! Get more people on the phones!"

Peterson jerked up and hurried downstairs to gather more troops.

"You didn't run like a maniac this morning?" Nick muttered reading a file.

"I did. I just want more people doing their jobs and not make chitchat. A life is on the line, remember?" She glared at two officers who had been laughing and quickly went back to work.

The Lakemore PD had set up a hotline to get any tips regarding Stella DeRossi. Due to the urgency of the situation, they had also advertised a reward. Predictably, they were flooded with potential sightings and theories. Mackenzie knew from experience that most of them were hoaxes. But she had designated teams to check each tip.

"Looks like you watched the trailer," Nick commented.

"Please don't," she said in a hard voice.

"It's all about marketing yourself, Mack. No matter what your job is," Troy pitched in. "Optics trump substance in today's world."

She gave him a caustic smile. "Don't you have a ten-year-old cold case to solve or are you going to let another decade go by without any justice done?"

Troy raised his hands in surrender and wheeled away from her. He shook his head at Nick, looking frightened. "Good luck, buddy."

Mackenzie bit her tongue and focused on filling out a report. The stress had formed a film over her insides, spreading through her like a virus. When Rivera waltzed in, she prepared herself to hear an earful. But the lieutenant's expression was solemn and reflecting.

"This was good work, you two." Rivera held up the list of names in the evidence bag.

"Mack cracked this one." Nick shoved his hands in his pockets.

"Nick caught Dominic," Mackenzie added.

"Yes, everyone knows you work well together, but that's not why I'm here." Rivera leaned an elbow on the cubicle wall and placed one hand on her waist. "There are some powerful people on this list."

"Yeah, we're running the names—"

"I got something for you."

"What?" Mackenzie asked.

"Every single name on this list has invested in the Wildman Group. Not a shareholder, I will add."

Nick's jaw tightened. "That can't be a coincidence."

"Certainly not." Rivera's tone was almost menacing. "It looks to me that Baron Wildman was using Mia Gallagher to sleep with rich men and taking their pictures so that he could blackmail them into investing into his business."

"Mia had mentioned to Wren that she was sick of being forced into things," Mackenzie recalled. "She could be referring to this. Maybe Baron was pushing her into sleeping with potential investors."

Jenna interrupted them, entering the office out of breath. "I think I have something. Stella DeRossi attended the University of Washington from 1997 to 2000. Bobby Wildman studied there too, from 1995 to 1999. They overlapped for two years."

It wasn't enough. It was a big university. The connection was flimsy at best. But Mackenzie couldn't keep hope at bay. It wound itself into her bones. "Looks like we need to talk to the Wildmans again."

THIRTY-TWO

It was before noon, but Bobby had a little party of his own going on in a corner of the mansion.

"Should have dunked him harder in that pool," Mackenzie said to Nick.

Baron descended from the grand staircase, dressed in a suit and checking his watch—always looking at the time and acting like it was a precious commodity that he was kind enough to give away. An old but sturdy woman followed him. She was Dominic's replacement now that he had legal troubles of his own.

"He wasted no time," Nick muttered.

"What can I do now, detectives?" Baron sighed, exasperated.

"We're sure you heard about Dominic..."

"I didn't know that Dominic had hurt Veronica. Their interactions had always been professional. I can't think of a reason he'd want her dead."

Mackenzie and Nick exchanged a glance. The fact that there was a blackmailing angle had been concealed.

"I can think of a reason you'd want her dead." Mackenzie raised an eyebrow.

Baron snorted. "Like I said before, Linda knows about my transgressions. Veronica's blackmail scheme wouldn't have worked."

"I think it could have. Veronica found your little stash of your very married investors sleeping with your mistress," Mackenzie continued, watching the blood drain from his face. "Now that is a serious crime."

Baron fumbled, loosening his tie. He looked at Bobby and barked. "Get out of here! Now!"

The women with Bobby made skittish sounds and ran into one of the side rooms. Bobby wasn't flustered by Baron berating him, clearly used to it. He swayed toward them with a flask in his hands; his shirt was untucked and tie undone. When he got closer, Mackenzie noticed white powder under his nose.

"Ah, my favorite detective in Lakemore." He grinned. "I looked you up on the internet. You're a bit of a local celebrity in your small town, aren't you? Sorry, but I only date models. If only you were a few sizes smaller—"

"Watch it, Bobby," Nick warned.

"What's that under your nose?" Mackenzie asked. "Do I need to take out my handcuffs?"

"As much as I would love for you to use them on me, it's just talcum powder." He cackled, but froze when Nick fisted his collar, pulling him up to his eye level.

"Apologize." His black eyes burned with anger.

"*I* apologize." Baron separated them. "My brother is brash. I'm sorry, Detective Price."

Bobby pouted, wandering away.

"Do you have any actual proof of blackmail other than the pictures you obtained?" the lawyer asked.

"No," Mackenzie replied.

"Well then, you have nothing," Baron gloated. "If my investors were sleeping with Mia, then it's not my business. They're all adults."

"Well, we did find a ledger with dates and the names of your investors in the motel," Nick said. "We discovered an interesting trend that every investor on that list invested a significant amount in your ventures within two months of that date."

"Based on the motel records, those dates correspond to when Mia spent the night with them," Mackenzie added.

"Can you place my client at this motel?" the lawyer asked curtly.

"Not yet."

Baron rubbed his mouth, thinking. "I don't know what Mia was up to. Maybe she had taken it upon herself to do this."

"She told her friend that she was being forced," Nick added.

"This isn't our jurisdiction, but we've done our duty and informed the white-collar division at the FBI," Mackenzie said. "They will be getting in touch with you soon."

Baron jerked his chin at his lawyer, who immediately started making some phone calls. "Nick, I hope this isn't a personal agenda because I refused to donate to your father's campaign."

"You'll be surprised to learn that not everything is about politics."

"This doesn't look good for you, Mr. Wildman," Mackenzie said, raking her eyes all over his stoic face, looking for a crack. "Maybe you thought Mia and Veronica were loose ends in this giant operation that could bring down your entire empire."

"We're done here." The lawyer still had her phone pressed to her ear. She touched Baron on the arm and gestured him to leave.

Baron nodded. "I have no reason to kill anyone, detectives. I have enough money to silence anyone, and everyone has a price.

Please see yourselves out." He straightened his jacket and followed his lawyer.

"Ignore my brother." Bobby returned and poured himself another stiff drink. "He's been in a bad mood lately because of Cristane."

The name rang a bell in Mackenzie's head. She had seen it on the list. "Cristane?"

"Walter Cristane." He shrugged. "That timber guy."

"What about him?"

"Oh, you know, he's been riding Baron's ass these past few days." Bobby offered them drinks, but they refused. He wiped the powder under his nose and leaned against one of the high-backed chairs. "Came to blows two weeks ago. Cristane had too much to drink and almost gave Baron a black eye before I had to intervene."

One of the doors swung open, and a young woman wearing skimpy clothes emerged, giggling. "Bobby! We're waiting for you."

"Sorry, detectives. Duty calls."

"Not so fast," Mackenzie cautioned and showed him a picture of Stella. "Recognize her?"

He squinted with distaste. "A little too old for my taste."

"She's your age," Nick scowled. "Both of you overlapped at UW for two years."

"You know my type." He winked, hitching his thumb at the room filled with giggling girls.

"Enough, Mr. Wildman." Mackenzie raised her voice a notch, stepping toe to toe with him. Her tone was sharp, and her patience was running thin. "A woman is missing. I don't have time for your transparent attempts to gain attention because you are insecure in your brother's shadow. Next time I talk to you, I suggest you conduct yourself with some manners."

He flinched but his nostrils flared in indignation. "Do you know who you're talking to?"

"I know very well. So you can imagine how pissed off I must be." She had swallowed her anger before, but now she was like a boiling pot and the steam was dissipating out. "Once again, do you recognize Stella DeRossi?"

He made a show of finishing his drink at leisure. "Give me one good reason why I should cooperate after how you just talked to me."

"Give me one good reason why I shouldn't check how much *talcum powder* you have on you," she retorted.

Bobby ground his jaw. "I don't know her. I attended university with thousands of people, and I barely went to classes. I wouldn't recognize my own classmates! Now, if you don't mind." He gave them a lazy grin fraught with tension and sauntered away disappearing into a room; the sound of them tittering rang through the empty room where Mackenzie and Nick stood.

"Chad's a stand-up guy compared to this one." Nick tried to lighten the mood.

Mackenzie scoffed, the fire in her belly subsiding. Her eyes took in the extravagance of one of the living rooms. Above a large fireplace was a family picture. Baron sat on a chair with Linda flanking his left side. Bobby stood behind him. The children were at their father's feet. One of the blue bloods of Washington State, with Baron at the center, the leader, the one who held all the strings.

"Baron does make a point," Nick conceded. "It would have been easier for him to pay them off instead of arrange this killing network."

"Probably. But this is Baron's M.O. too," Mackenzie reminded him. "He blackmailed investors and now he could be blackmailing people into killing."

"We should talk to Cristane. That's another guy with a motive."

Mackenzie concurred. A deep frown marred her face. "I

can imagine a lot of these businessmen weren't happy about being forced to invest."

Nick paused, his hand running through his hair. "But where does Stella come into this?"

She loathed to say the words out loud. "I have no idea."

THIRTY-THREE

Walter Cristane was a temperamental man. The lumberjack-like man had grown up in Wyoming. Before he knew how to ride a bike, he knew how to wield an axe. He was rural and brash, unlike his peers in high society who often looked down upon him.

Mackenzie had scrolled through everything she could have dug up on him. He had had a few brushes with the law, mostly disorderly conduct, but nothing really stuck. He was known for losing his cool at parties. After finding success in Washington, he had brought over several of his old friends he had grown up with and given them lucrative positions in his empire.

Mackenzie came across a picture of Walter with his friends at a bar, drunk with sweaty skins, bald heads, and beer-stained clothes. Unruly and rebellious.

"Did you arrange a meeting with him?" Mackenzie asked Nick.

"His assistant told me to find him at some bar."

A group of children skittered past almost colliding into them. It wasn't too busy at the Lakemore Gardens, the brand-new development. It was not only Mayor Rathbone's dream project, but also his desperate attempt to garner votes for what was a very tumultuous term. Lakemore had weathered many storms in the last year alone. The mayor had been challenged every step of the way. Matters had finally begun to settle now, Mackenzie brooded, catching sight of a "missing" poster of Stella DeRossi stuck to a tree.

She should have known that the peace was only temporary, that eerie silence before a storm, that short sense of relief before everything came crumbling down. The little town was infected. No matter how many times she had weeded out criminals, new ones took their place.

She stared at Stella's picture. A happily married pharmacist who liked to walk her dog and dreamed of living at a beach. Was she even alive? How many more such women were to follow?

And why?

The carousel was moving with some children sitting on horses and unicorns. Their parents stood around, keeping watch and taking pictures. They didn't have long. A dark cloud was expanding in the sky above, casting a shadow on the park with new swing sets and hedge mazes.

"This was the bench Dominic was sitting on." Nick curled his hands around the back of the copper-colored bench dedicated to a deceased football player. "Uniform brought him here this morning."

Ahead of the chair was the carousel and behind were rows of trees masking a pavilion on the other side. A direct route from here to the pavilion was forbidden by the signs that were posted saying no one was allowed to walk through the trees.

"So they placed the envelope on the bench and then either disappeared into the crowd or headed back to the trees, not caring about the rules."

"I've asked parks and rec for assistance on the security

cameras that cover this area." Nick pointed at one. "Too bad Dominic didn't see anything."

"He was probably too spooked by the entire thing to be actually paying attention."

A scrawny young man with sparse hair, wearing a green shirt and khaki pants interrupted them. "Lakemore PD?" He fidgeted.

"Yes, we spoke on the phone. I'm Nick Blackwood and this is my partner, Mackenzie Price."

"H-hello. I'm Lance." He smiled feebly. "How c-can I help y-you?"

"Lance, we were wondering if we can check out the surveillance covering this area? We can get a court order, but we're running out of time and will appreciate you doing us a solid," Nick breezed.

"Is it about t-that w-woman?" he asked with puppy-dog eyes. "S-stella D-d-de-Rossi?"

"Yes. Will you help us?"

Lance smiled and gestured them to follow him. "We have a security room here on-site t-too."

"Didn't expect that from Lakemore," Nick scoffed.

"The mayor is very p-particular about increasing security."

Mackenzie walked behind them, envying how Nick easily put Lance at ease, chatting with him like they were old friends.

Lance led them into a small wooden shed with some monitors and a shelf of maps. He took one out and unrolled it on the table. "Only n-number 23 will c-cover it. What d-day are you looking at?"

Nick gave him the time and date as Lance set up the tape. Mackenzie watched the angle. The camera was on a tree, showing only a sliver of the bench, the rest being covered by the carousel. She picked at her cuticles, watching Dominic arrive and sit down. His eyes drifted around nervously as he fiddled with his cufflinks. He stood out in a suit at a park, presumably so anxious about the whole thing that he wore his go-to clothes.

It had been a crowded day, being the weekend. A chorus of children scampered around him, obstructing the view of him from time to time. Ten minutes later, an ice-cream truck pulled up in front of the camera.

"What is that?" Nick slammed his palm on the table.

"It c-comes every S-Saturday at the s-same time."

"Great. They planned this too," Mackenzie muttered and shook her head at Nick. "There was no way they were going to risk being seen after all the planning they did."

By the time the ice-cream truck moved out of position, it had been thirty minutes. Dominic had already left with his instructions. Nick cursed under his breath.

"Sorry we weren't of m-more help," Lance said meekly.

Nick clapped his back. "Not your fault a psychopath is on the loose."

The video kept playing, while Nick questioned Lance on anyone causing any trouble in the park, anyone suspicious lurking. Mackenzie noticed a highly concentrated beam of light reflecting on a shiny surface every few seconds. There was a huge slab of mirror lining the bottom of the carousel. She paused the video when the mirror wasn't glowing.

"Can we magnify this?" she asked Lance, who eagerly obeyed. The mirror reflected the empty bench where Dominic had been sitting. "And go back to when the ice-cream truck first showed up."

In the tiny mirror, they could see Dominic on the bench again before he left. He paid no attention to the ice-cream truck and kept looking at his watch and bobbing his knee, sweating bullets despite the pleasant weather.

But the truck caught the attention of all the kids and their parents. They swarmed toward it, a crowd descending on Dominic who was sitting close by. He got distracted. But

Mackenzie's eyes were stuck to the bench. And there was the drop. The red envelope.

"Freeze it here!" she ordered. "They just made the drop."

A fuzzy shape that looked like a hand had snaked out of the crowd behind the bench. Lance played the video at the slowest speed. But the figure the hand belonged to remained hidden in the throng of people.

"They probably moved away from the truck," Nick said. "Lance, what about the other cameras? Can they give us a view?"

As Lance played another set of tapes, Mackenzie's heart slowly sank into her chest. They were close to ending this. All they needed was one shot of the person who blackmailed Dominic.

"Look at that!" she said. The cameras showed the person with their arm over the back of the bench, dropping something while Dominic was distracted by the sudden onslaught of people around him. They emerged from the crowd, tall and broad.

He was wearing a ball cap and a hoodie and kept his chin down, his face was never visible. Dressed in blue jeans and boots, he turned into the woods behind where no one was allowed to go, only to disappear and not be picked up on any other surveillance.

Nick sighed. "At least we know we're looking for a man. Let's get this video to Clint. Maybe he can clean it up and get some detail we missed."

Mackenzie agreed, watching the repeated motion of the man disappearing out of frame. She knew he must have scoped the area.

THIRTY-FOUR

"What if Stella is already dead?" Mackenzie asked, her scalp prickling at the thought, before Nick started the car.

His hand paused at the ignition. "I doubt she's dead."

"Why?" Her fingers grazed her watch.

It was a habit she had developed in the past few months. The leathery, worn-out touch of it offered some comfort. This watch was all she had of a childhood she had forgotten over the years, the short period of her life when everything was how it always should have been before Melody's selfish and weak decisions ripped it apart. The memories of Robert, Mackenzie's legal father and the one who'd loved her, had withered over time. But one thing Mackenzie had realized was that feelings were never forgotten.

"Because he's blackmailing regular people to do the killing," Nick answered, the evening light falling on the sharp contours of his face. "They aren't experts at ditching bodies, which is why we have discovered them easily. Unless..."

"Stella's been buried or thrown into a water body," she finished his sentence.

He winced. "Shit. Well, no other woman is missing in Lakemore, right? I've been checking the bulletin every few hours."

"He does wait between victims. Doesn't hoard them together. But what if Stella was intended to be the last victim? What if his work ends there?"

"What is his work?" The engine came to life under them. "He isn't assaulting or torturing them. He isn't even killing them. It's not for fun." He hissed, "If we don't find a motive, we'll keep running in circles."

Mackenzie's mind reeled, a pressure building up in the center of her forehead. "Okay. Okay. It has to circle back to the Wildmans. It can't be a coincidence that two murder victims and one blackmail victim are connected to them."

"Stella's only connection is she attended university with Bobby. But I can believe that he didn't know her."

"Maybe we should try through Glenn..." she trailed off. "It's weird."

"What is?"

"Why did a well-educated man with a good career suddenly lose it over a divorce?" she wondered aloud. "I know that's what Dr. Kane said, but it doesn't feel like enough to me." She took out her phone, an idea taking shape in her head.

Look into Glenn Solomon's previous employment. Anything that can explain why he lost his way (other than his divorce).

Yes, ma'am.

Justin's reply was immediate, like he was waiting on his phone, hungry for orders. She knew he had taken it personally that he had been unable to track the taser guns in circulation so far. The young detective didn't rest until he had contributed. He worked like a machine.

"I've asked Justin to look into Glenn's background more."

"I heard talk that Justin is going to lead a case soon," Nick said.

"Oh yeah? About time. If we weren't short-staffed, he would have been promoted last year."

"They might pair him up with Austin. What do you think? You've gotten to know him very well." His voice was laced with restraint.

"Not really. I just know he's relentless in finding out what happened to his fiancée." Her eyebrows knitted. "But I guess he's dropping that now."

"Or he's just making false promises to keep his job."

Mackenzie looked out the window to the light draining away into dusk. They were driving under a canopy of trees; the barren branches braided above them, shutting out the dimming light. It was like they had entered the belly of a carcass. The leafless trees curved over the road like a ribcage.

For a moment, Mackenzie felt sick to her stomach. The darkness that had draped over them was crushing. There was no sight of any car or person. They were alone. It reminded her of the path she had set on. She was finally free from the chains of her past, finally free to move, but she didn't know where to go. Without her past, she was unmoored. She didn't have anything grounding her other than work. It was terrifying and almost brought tears to her eyes. She understood why Austin wouldn't want to let go. How an obsession didn't just end with answers but with meticulous rearranging of one's identity. Who was he if not a man determined to find his missing fiancée?

The bar in Olympia was lively and pumping. Beats of music reverberated, mingling with the sounds of laughter and glasses clinking. Mackenzie spotted Walter easily. The man towered over everyone around him.

Before Mackenzie and Nick could get closer, a man came to stand before them. He was tall and muscular, wearing a leather jacket and a sneer on his lined face. "Don't approach the boss," he said in a Texan accent.

Nick took out his badge.

The man's jaw ground.

Walter noticed them and shouted over, "It's all right, Romero!"

Romero flared his nostrils and jerked his head.

Mackenzie's shoulder brushed his, his pebble-like eyes glaring at her like *she* was the criminal. "Some bodyguard you got here, Mr. Cristane."

Walter's voice was low and guttural. "They're my boys. I trust them." He pointed at a table with similar brute-like men. They all looked like hooligans and not professionals.

"I wonder how many of them have a criminal record."

"All of them." He laughed. "Nothing wrong with that. They served time and now they're out and making an honest living by working for me." He sat on a high stool and slugged his beer. "Now, my assistant said you wanted to talk."

"We wanted to speak with you about Baron Wildman," Nick started, and Walter rolled his eyes.

"Oh, don't tell me he filed a police report because I roughed him up a bit? All those dollars and no testosterone."

His crew snickered in the back.

"It's not about that. Do you recognize this woman?" Nick showed him a picture of Mia.

Walter's face fell. He wiped the beer off his mouth with his sleeve. His posse noted the change and almost stood up, but he raised a hand. "What about her?"

"You didn't answer the question," Mackenzie said.

"It's no big deal. I slept with her." He shrugged, but his large shoulders were tense.

From the corner of her eye, Mackenzie spotted Romero circling them.

"Did you know that there are pictures of you with Mia?"

Nick asked. All the snickering and guffawing at the table collapsed into an awkward silence. "If you want, we can talk in private."

"No." Walter declared with an edge to his voice. "We are one. I'm not like those other prudes that just because I've made a buck means I'm above anyone. And, yes. I know. Baron used them to blackmail me."

"To invest in his business?"

"That's right. That energy company he set up."

"Why didn't you go to the police and file charges?"

He scoffed. "Can't afford my wife finding out!"

"Did he approach you to be an investor prior to black-mailing you?" Mackenzie asked.

"He did and I said no. I don't believe in the company. And I don't like putting my money into things I don't believe in. We live by a code where I come from."

"Do you know that Mia Gallagher was murdered?"

Walter stiffened. "I see. Terrible. She was a nice girl."

"And so was Veronica Fang. Baron's personal assistant who was threatening to expose him."

"What are you getting at?"

"I think it's fairly obvious," Nick said matter-of-factly. "You have motive to want those two women dead and they are."

Romero closed in on them, narrowing his eyes. But Walter gestured him to stay put.

"That's a serious accusation," he warned.

"I can imagine your wife finding out about this would be messy for you." Mackenzie tested the waters. "How much would she get in a divorce settlement if she can prove infidelity?"

He chuckled humorlessly. "I can guess that I'm not the only one Baron has blackmailed into getting money from to build his empire."

"You aren't. But you're the only one who has been incredibly pissed off according to various witnesses. Did you finally blow your lid?"

He stood up and slammed his beer bottle on the table, which rattled. His thin lips pressed in a line. "First it's Baron and now it's the Lakemore PD. This town really has a talent for getting on my nerves."

"We're just doing our jobs," Nick said. "If you have nothing to hide—"

"I have nothing to hide, but I do have a lot to lose," he gritted out, red creeping up his neck. "And so do you."

"What do you mean?" Mackenzie's voice was tight.

He pointed at the flat-screen TV playing the highlights from the game last week. Lakemore Sharks versus Titans. "Everyone knows how Lakemore works, detectives. It's no secret. The Lakemore PD is anti-business. You have a history of bringing down companies that almost destroy your little town. It's a blessing that some people are still willing to invest."

Her blood fizzed under her veins. "Are you threatening us, Mr. Cristane?"

"I'm stating facts. You lot really need to stop harassing businessmen." He scowled. "Next time you show up? At least have some proof. Romero!"

Romero, the loyal dog as Mackenzie had pegged him to be, stepped forward, shielding Walter and his posse. "Time to leave."

Mackenzie and Nick hovered, watching a visibly agitated Walter grumble to his friends and order another pitcher. Another table moaned in displeasure as the Lakemore Sharks had scored a touchdown. Their mouths hung open in shock. Their wide eyes were sparkling. Their entire bodies participating in the events that played on television. It was a peek at how Lakemore affected the world outside, how it mattered and was perceived. Mackenzie couldn't help but feel pride swell inside her.

A small town like Lakemore didn't have much in its arsenal; it hinged on raw talent and generosity of those who made it big. Which was why Walter's words had stirred a deeper fear inside Mackenzie. She had seen how Lakemore floundered when that support was ripped away. She didn't have the luxury to only worry about the crime she was supposed to solve. She had an entire town to think about.

"Fucking narcissist," Nick muttered as they left the bar. "He actually believes that we have some agenda against businessmen. Like we have nothing else to do with our time."

Before Mackenzie replied, she got a call from Justin. "That was fast."

"He must be really desperate for redemption."

They stopped by the car when Mackenzie answered and put the phone on speaker. "Did you find anything already?"

"Yes, ma'am." His gruff voice sounded relieved. "I looked into Glenn Solomon's last real employment over twenty years ago. He worked as the chief of accounting at a company called Acorn Metals, which was dissolved five years after he was let go."

"Okay..." Mackenzie absorbed his rapid stream of words.

"This company was a subsidiary of Crest Reliance Network."

Nick groaned and dropped his head low, pinching the bridge of his nose. "That belongs to the Wildman Group."

"Glenn Solomon was an employee of the Wildmans," Justin confirmed.

Another victim was added to the chain of connections to one of the most powerful families in Washington. Walter's veiled threats had more weight. The more they uncovered, the more they realized how entwined this case was with people who had the power to change the contours of Lakemore. Mackenzie took a shuddering breath and hung up.

THIRTY-FIVE
OCTOBER 22

"It's been four days since Stella DeRossi didn't return home to her husband," Debbie relayed to the camera. *"Her husband, Jonathan DeRossi, has offered a reward of twenty-five thousand dollars to anyone who has information that could lead to an arrest. This reward is double what the Lakemore PD has offered."*

The screen divided to show a clipping of the home video that Jonathan had recorded. His dark hair was uncombed and wild; his eyes were red and puffy. *"If anyone knows anything about my wife, Stella, then please, please, please come forward."* His dog, Bean, lay on the floor behind him. *"Stella is a wonderful person. She's shy, intelligent, and caring. I can't imagine anyone who'd want to hurt her. If you're watching, then please let my wife go. I can't even begin to explain how my life has come to a standstill since she was taken. It breaks my heart every day."*

Mackenzie's feet carried her to Hidden Lake to watch the sunrise. It was a long run from her place. It was in the woods of Hidden Lake where she had helped Melody bury a body.

Those woods were marked, forever haunted by the ghost of her past, forever echoing what she had agreed to do even if she was only twelve years old.

She panted and bent to breathe through the stitch on her side. The woods were across the lake; she stood on the other side. There was no wind. The water and the woods stood still, like a painting. The only sounds were the flapping wings of birds and the cry of a hawk. This is what Lakemore was at the core. Underneath the film of football, poverty, and crime, it was the place where regular people had dark secrets buried.

Mackenzie took a deep breath, the smell of pine needles and damp soil, along with something else. Something in the air that tempted people into doing horrible things.

She shivered and jogged back to her place, trying to shed away that fetid feeling that Hidden Lake always gave her.

When she reached her house, the sun finally rose over the horizon, spilling bright light everywhere. At her front porch, Austin was sitting, his blond hair fluttering in the wind.

"Austin?" she squeaked, aware that she was sweaty.

"Sorry, Mackenzie. But it was important."

"Come inside." She unlocked the door and let him in. It was seven in the morning. Did it have to do with his fiancée? Was he going down that path again? "What's up?"

"I'm sorry for showing up like this, but I think I found something that might help you."

"Oh. Of course." She went to the kitchen and ran some water to wash her flushed face.

"Some uniform had talked to Stella's co-workers at the pharmacy, and they'd said that she was acting normally in the days leading up to her disappearance," he recounted while she dabbed her face dry. "But one of her co-workers said that Stella had been using her work email for some personal correspondences."

"How did they know that?"

"Stella accidentally left the tab open. The co-worker doesn't remember what was written exactly, but it was enough for her to see it wasn't work-related. Apparently, Stella made some excuse, and they didn't talk about it."

The wheels in her brain spun fast. "We found nothing odd in Stella's emails, but we had only checked her personal one. Why was she using a work one for personal stuff?"

Austin's eyes lit up. "Exactly. I thought you should know. Maybe there's something there."

"Why wasn't this in the reports?" Mackenzie had diligently gone through every statement that was collected when Stella went missing.

"The officer didn't think it was important to make a note of it. I was talking to some of the guys, and it came up."

She wiped her brow. "Must be a new one. We tell them that every word spoken needs to go into the report, but, oh well."

The bell rang. She hopped over to the door, wondering who it was this time. When she opened the door, Nick filed inside. "I found something!" he announced and froze in the foyer, seeing Austin. "Austin?"

"Nick." He nodded.

Nick turned around to pin Mackenzie with an inquisitive look. His eyes drifted to the clock on the wall. "Did I interrupt anything?"

"No!" Mackenzie crossed her arms, appalled.

The corners of his mouth twitched, enjoying her reaction. Austin shifted on his feet and made a show of looking around her house casually.

The bell rang again. Mackenzie let out a growl of frustration. "Who the hell is it now?" She swung the door open, and her elderly, frail neighbor stepped back. "Mrs. McNeill!"

"I wanted to borrow a can opener, dear. Mine broke." She was a foot shorter than Mackenzie with a hunched back and thinning white hair crowning a bony face.

"Of course." She cleared her throat to sound more polite and let her in.

When Mrs. McNeill saw Nick and Austin, she looked at the clock. It was quarter past seven in the morning. An awkward silence descended again.

Blood roared in Mackenzie's ears when she finally declared, "Nobody spent the night here!"

"What a shame," Mrs. McNeill muttered, eyeing the two men. For someone in her eighties, she was full of energy.

"Mrs. McNeill!" Mackenzie chided, as the men looked away, anywhere but at the diminutive white-haired figure.

Mackenzie was in a foul mood as she gave her neighbor the can opener and ushered her out of the house. She turned to Nick. "Austin had a suggestion. Austin, why don't you tell him about it while I take a quick shower?"

She marched past them, flustered at having two too many people in her house early in the morning.

Mackenzie flew through her routine and tried hard not to think about the two men in her living room. She scrubbed her skin hard to wash out the thick paste of discomfort and quickly combed her hair and applied her makeup. Looking pristine and distant, she went back downstairs. "Where's Austin?"

"He left." Nick wolfed down a sandwich. "Sorry, I helped myself. I was starving."

She took a sharp breath and counted to ten. After lamenting how lonely it was to live alone, she hadn't realized that the habit had grown on her. Now watching another person in her space moving things around was odd. "Did Austin tell you?"

He nodded. "I told Jenna to contact the pharmacy. If they don't give permission to look at Stella's work email, then we'll prepare a warrant." He rinsed the plate and set it in the dishwasher.

"Okay. As much as I appreciate you being courteous

enough to clean my kitchen, this is getting weird," she moaned, forcing him to sit on the kitchen stool. "What did you find?"

"Ah. Yes. I'm sure you've been watching the news, right? Jonathan is putting up his own money."

"Twenty-five grand." She whistled. "That's a lot. But he did mention that Stella came into money when she was at university and a grandparent died."

"Yeah, and then I kept thinking about what possible reason it could be that Glenn Solomon was let go from his job since he had a squeaky-clean record." He was talking fast, eager to get the point.

"Are those two things related?" She scratched her head.

"They might be. I looked into Stella's finances." A sly smile coiled up his lips. "Back in university, she received a payment of *two hundred grand*, and it wasn't inheritance. It was a wire transfer from Acorn Metals."

"*What?*" she gasped. The synapses in her brain fired in all directions. Little electrical bombs going off in her head. "Why would that company pay such a large amount to a university student?"

"Since Glenn was the head of accounting, he must have had to approve of this. And he was let go within three months of the payment."

The only reason that Mackenzie believed could explain such a significant transaction was hush money. But what could Stella have possibly known that the Wildmans paid her two hundred grand over twenty years ago? Was that the reason she was taken as well?

THIRTY-SIX

"This is exactly what I was warning everybody about!" Captain Murphy roared, filing inside Sully's office.

Sully wobbled into a standing position, his art book sliding off his lap onto the floor. "Captain, I—"

"Sit the hell down, Sully. This isn't the military," Murphy sulked, glaring at Mackenzie. He was an old and grouchy man, his wrinkled face and bulbous nose perpetually morphed into irritation. When he regarded Nick, he tried to play nice. "Detective Blackwood, why don't you try to teach your partner not to piss people off? Especially the important ones?"

Mackenzie's eyes went wide, and her jaw hung open. She was ready to jump to her defense, but Sully shook his head.

"What happened?" Sully asked.

Murphy's hand curled into fists. "I just got a call from the mayor. Walter Cristane was supposed to meet with him to sell lumber to Lakemore, but he canceled last minute, giving no reason, and the mayor is worried you have pissed him off."

"Why do *we* need to buy lumber? Lakemore has trees everywhere," Mackenzie asked.

"Detective Price, *you—*!" Murphy waggled his finger, spit flying out of his mouth.

"Cristane is just throwing his weight around," Nick tried to placate him. The room was charged. Despite Mackenzie being the focus of Murphy's wrath and glowers, she had no urge to blend into her surroundings. "He just wants to send us a message. He won't go through with it."

"How do you know?"

"Are we not supposed to question persons of interest in a double homicide and abduction case now?" Mackenzie challenged.

"I'm sure something was wrong with your approach. It won't be long before the Wildmans decide to sever their contracts with Lakemore." Murphy glowered and turned to Sully. "I told you, always hire women with soft faces."

"Oh, that's a lawsuit waiting to happen," Nick blurted, resigned.

Mackenzie's gut was torched with rage. She gritted her teeth and clenched her muscles. Before storming out of the office, she gave a piece of her mind and her fist. Nick was at her heels. The loud voices of Murphy and Sully arguing continued behind the closed door. She walked past the cubicles, feeling the eyes of her co-workers, Ned and Dennis, on her.

"Murphy is an asshole." Nick kept up with her furious pace.

She had no idea where she was going. "He didn't have a problem with my face when he *forced* me to become a part of that stupid documentary."

"I think the trailer looked great. Especially that suplex with the *Top Gun* music playing in the background."

She halted. "What are you doing?"

"Trying to bring down your temper, especially before we go talk to the Wildmans," he confessed, looking worried. "We know what Bobby does to you."

"Oh my God," she cried and rubbed her eyes. The ache behind her eyelids returned and pooled to the center of her forehead.

"Are you getting headaches again?"

"No," she lied and attempted to redirect her energy. Murphy didn't matter. Stella DeRossi did. She saw Stella's picture appearing on the television in the lounge. That was the victim they knew about. There was someone else out there who was going to be chosen, if not already, to kill Stella. Glenn couldn't live with himself after killing Mia. Dominic's guilt was bottomless and spiraling. He had swallowed it all down to put a brave face for the world. But now he was facing the music.

"Mack! Nick!" Sully came up behind them. "Mack, I apologize on behalf of Murphy. None of us share his views on women—"

Mackenzie sighed. "I won't sue you, Sully. Anyway, what do you think about the Acorn Metals link?"

"It's a good one. But you need more before going to the Wildmans."

"What? Why?" Mackenzie asked.

"You questioned Cristane and he's threatening his city contracts. Murphy is a jerk, but I think his fear is justified," he said. "Make sure you have something more solid."

"Two hundred thousand dollars transaction is pretty solid to me," she argued.

Sully was adamant. "But it was twenty years ago, from a now dissolved incorporation that isn't under the direct supervision of Baron Wildman. He'll deny knowledge of this."

Mackenzie and Nick looked at each other, knowing Sully had a point. Moreover, it was Baron's first line of defense. His lawyer would repeat *my client has no knowledge* like a broken tape recorder.

"How the hell are we supposed to establish a direct link between Baron and the two hundred grand when we don't have access to the financial records of the Wildman Group?" Nick demanded.

"Get creative!" Sully sounded exasperated. He spotted trays of cookies and donuts lying in the conference room and rushed inside and piled them in his hands to carry them back to his office.

"You know Baron." Mackenzie crossed her arms and turned to Nick. "Do you think we can bluff him? Or scare him into divulging something?"

"He's too smart, Mack. He's a loaded guy and has been trained well by his lawyers. His only weakness is Bobby and his kids. If we catch him off guard and threaten his family, then he could slip."

She sank her teeth into the cushion of her lower lip. "Sully is right then. We need more."

It was that moment Clint found them, edging his way past the much shorter colleagues, and interrupted them. "You guys got a minute?"

"Please. Do you have anything?" Mackenzie begged.

"Not a lot, but..." Clint opened the laptop in his arms and perched the pen in between his lips. "I was able to clear up the video of that man making the drop."

The screen displayed the video shot by shot in slow motion. The frame of the man was enhanced in contrast to the blurry and colorless surroundings, but even his hands were in his pockets and his face was concealed in the shadow of his hoodie.

"He's above five feet, nine inches," Clint said, his lips moving around the pen. "Since he's slouching a bit, I can't be more accurate than that. His skin isn't visible so I can't pinpoint any identifying markers. But look at his hoodie."

Mackenzie narrowed her eyes. The man's body was at an angle, but there was a letter visible on the black sweatshirt. It was the letter "A" emblazoned in gold. "Is that a brand?"

Clint showed them another program that compared that

letter "A" to a database of known logos. But the program yielded no positive match. "Nope. But at least you know your guy owns a sweatshirt with something written across the chest starting with the letter A."

Mackenzie burned the information in her brain. It was only a little piece of him, but at this point she was hungrily taking whatever crumbs were thrown at her.

Back at her desk, she opened the email they had received from Anthony at the crime lab. There were deposits found under Veronica's shoes that didn't match the Red Pond or anything around it. Other than the dark-brown gravelly loam soil, typical of Washington State, some seeds and plants, *Polystichum munitum* (western sword fern), *Betula occidentalis* (water birch), and *Taxus brevifolia* (Pacific yew). None of these were found at, or in close vicinity to, the factory site.

"There are also some chemicals," Nick frowned. "Bleach and laundry starch. And one more they haven't identified yet."

"Some of them are cleaning reagents, right?"

"There's also titanium dioxide, barium sulfate, butane, ethylbenzene, and some hydrocarbon solvent, which are ingredients found in—"

"Spray paint." Mackenzie read a lot.

Nick blinked. "Of course you know that."

"She was held at an industrial building?"

Mackenzie opened the crime lab report for Mia Gallagher. Her tattered clothes and shoes had been sent to the crime lab to pick up any traces. Unfortunately, with her remains being pressed and wiped against the elevator shaft, some of the evidence had been lost. However mass spectrometry was able to pick up traces of the same flora on her shoes. Her clothes had traces of silver chloride, bleach, laundry starch, spray paint, and an unknown compound.

"At least we know they were held at the same place before being presented for the kill." Mackenzie's own words haunted her. "I'll contact the sheriff's department. They know Washington woods well. Maybe they can narrow down the areas where this kind of flora is found."

"And some industrial building in vicinity," Nick agreed.

Mackenzie was determined when she began typing the email and attaching the reports. *At least we're moving.*

She heard Jenna's boots clack on the floor before hearing her voice. Her raven black hair was pinned in a bun, and her face held the usual disdain when she regarded Mackenzie that disappeared when she looked at Nick. "The pharmacy cooperated to give me access to Stella's work email."

"Really?" Nick asked in disbelief. "I thought they have proprietary information in there."

"They do, but they all really loved Stella, so they want to help out. They printed out her emails and redacted customer names to preserve privacy, which was fair." Jenna handed him a thick stack of papers. "I went back at least three months and discovered around a month ago, she started emailing with someone." She directed them to a few papers with yellow Post-its attached.

Mackenzie looked at the email address. Unfortunately, it was all random letters and numbers, not conveying the name of the person. "What were they talking about?"

"They barely exchanged three emails. Stella said she had very important information. And in the last email said she'd like to meet at Twist bar a day after she went missing."

"Who was she talking to? There's no name?" Nick skimmed through the emails.

Mackenzie snatched them from him and read them aloud one by one.

Hello, I have an offer for you. I have some very important information that you'd be interested in. I hope we can meet to discuss further.

How do I know this is worth my time? I don't just meet anyone.

It is, Mr. Hawkins. If you aren't interested in meeting me, then I'll find someone else, and you can regret not knowing what really went down twenty-one years ago in the case that has forever haunted you.

Okay, you got my attention. Where do you want to meet?

Twist Bar. 9 p.m. October 19

I will be there. Here's my number for further correspondences.

"Mr. Hawkins?" Nick repeated, blinking in confusion. "Who's he?"

Jenna shrugged. "Is he a retired cop? She mentioned an old case has haunted him."

But a possibility had staunchly planted itself inside Mackenzie. She zoned out on Nick and Jenna's plans for tracking down who the phone number belonged to. Only listening to her uneven breath, she keyed the number in the email into her phone.

Her belief was confirmed. She had that number saved in her contacts.

"I know who it belongs to," she said, drawing their attention.

Nick waited for her to continue.

"Vincent Hawkins."

A famed journalist. The one whose career had almost been destroyed before Mackenzie and Nick's case catapulted him back to prominence and redeemed his unfairly destroyed reputation. It was a tip from him that had helped Mackenzie crack a case over a year ago.

Stella DeRossi had plans to meet the most important journalist in Lakemore. She had crucial information for him about something that went down twenty-one years ago. But before she was supposed to meet him, she had been abducted.

THIRTY-SEVEN

Spots of color appeared on the waitress's cheeks when she asked Nick: "And what can I get you?"

His thick eyebrows were dipped low, looking at the menu. "Just fries."

Mackenzie watched her lips open and close like a fish underwater. But when the waitress realized Mackenzie was shooting her a death glare, she fumbled an excuse and clipped away on high heels. "I never realized women pay attention to you."

"Jeez. Thanks, Mack," he said dryly.

She eyed him curiously. Like he was a specimen under a microscope. He was taller than six feet, with broad shoulders, lean muscles, thick eyebrows, dark hair and a chiseled jawline. "I guess you have all the traits of an attractive mate."

He almost spat out his water. "*What?*"

"Why don't you ever talk about your dating life with me?"

"It's tough to have a dating life when every other day someone gets murdered in Lakemore," he retorted.

They were seated at a bougie restaurant where they were supposed to meet with Vincent Hawkins. An Edith Piaf song played. The walls were exposed brick with posters of quotes from famous musicians hanging on them. It was lunchtime, with mostly professionals working close by dropping in to grab sandwiches and coffee. A few of them milled about the front waiting for takeout.

"I'm sure it can't be that bad. I managed a relationship for six years. Even though it ended with me getting cheated on."

His features tightened. "Yeah, and him getting a black eye."

She grinned. It was over a year ago when Nick had punched Sterling in the face after realizing that Sterling had never confided in Mackenzie about his affair despite Nick giving him a chance to come clean.

"You've changed," he noted, playing with a straw. "You used to be a lot more uptight."

"Yeah, well. Just a twig up my ass now. Not a thick stick."

He smiled, but his gaze was still scrutinizing.

Her eyes darted uncomfortably around. She still didn't like being read, being cut open for those around to see just how much she had carried, just how much she had spent all those years hating herself. But her past had been resolved. She touched her watch. She had closure.

Then why was happiness still eluding her? There was peace, but there was no joy. There was *nothing*. She'd escaped all that self-loathing and guilt only to end up in a vacuum.

"Why aren't you happy, Mack?" Nick asked, like he could read her thoughts. "You sometimes space out with this sad look."

Her eyes pricked with unshed tears. All her instincts reared their heads to tell her to shut down the conversation, to raise her guard. But she battled them. "You know, this person blackmailing people to kill others has nothing on me. I can't think about what I would have done if I were Glenn or Dominic because I have nobody to protect. It makes you wonder why you do anything at all."

"If you were able to leave him without fearing for your life, would you?" Mackenzie had asked while combing her mother's hair.

Melody looked like a wraith. Her skin was too pale. The arches of her bones too visible. Her eyes too ghostly. *"No."*

"But why?"

"Loneliness can kill you without you realizing that you're dying, Mackenzie." Her voice was hoarse. *"And then one day, you are dead."*

The memory clogged Mackenzie's throat. It angered her that her mother thought she'd have no one else, that her child wasn't enough. But now she understood her words better.

"You always said your life's purpose was to fix this town, to lock up criminals," Nick said slowly.

"It still is. I don't know why, but it doesn't feel like it's enough anymore." She shifted in her seat. "I... I'm replaceable, Nick. I'm just a regular detective, despite those stupid articles and the documentary trying to glorify me. Shouldn't I have something more in my life than a job?"

It wasn't until she said the words that she gained clarity. This was her deep-rooted issue that had been festering inside her. Who would have thought that Mad Mack was lonely? She felt like she had just been dunked in ice water. Her steely and unemotional image in tatters.

Nick leaned forward and placed his elbows on the table. "You don't need another person to have purpose in your life. You can if you want to. But you can live for yourself too."

They were meant to be words of strength, but they felt debilitating. Like instead of trying to escape the vacuum in her life, she was justifying it.

A grating laughter sliced through their bubble. Vincent Hawkins had arrived at the restaurant, dressed in his jeans and baggy T-shirt like a college student. His shoes were scuffed. His gray hair buzzed on the sides. A pen was stuck between his temple and ear, and a thin mustache capped his lips. The fact that he was loaded, making ten times Mackenzie did, had no bearing on how he dressed.

"Detective Price," he smiled, "looks like our fates are intertwined."

"That's not a good thing. This is Detective Blackwood. You know him."

Hawkins shook his hand. "Nice to see ya."

"Why didn't you want to come to the station to talk?" Nick asked.

"I'm working on a story with some big names. I don't want them thinking I'm talking to the cops." He raised his hands. "Not obstructing justice, detectives. Just some investigative journalism."

Mackenzie took out the copies of the emails. "That's you?"

Hawkins put on his reading glasses and flipped through them. "That's correct. This email ID isn't available online. You can only find it through word of mouth."

"Do you know who you were talking to?"

He jutted his lower lip. "The email just says admin of this pharmacy. No name."

The waitress returned with fries. Nick plopped one in his mouth. "Stella DeRossi."

Hawkins's face was ashen. "I see."

"There's no way you didn't know." Mackenzie crossed her arms, her gaze traveling all over his face. "When Stella didn't show up at the bar, didn't you research everyone who worked at the pharmacy?"

Hawkins was sharp and dedicated. He had crafted an impressive career over the years because of his attention to detail. She knew intimately how meticulous and good at connecting the dots he was; after all, it was him who had given her a vital clue last year that had been missed by the entire Investigations Division.

He sighed. "I had a feeling it could be her when I realized that the missing woman was a pharmacist, though I thought that it was probably too much of a coincidence. But I had no way to confirm and, frankly, I'm working on a big story. I've been busy. And since I never met with her or talked to her beyond those two emails, I didn't think I'd be of help."

"What case was Stella referring to in her email?" Nick asked.

There was silence at the table. Hawkins's typical cheerful persona veiled a hungry reporter fishing for vulnerability. His nostrils flared and he wiped his mouth, having a drink of water. "Ever heard of Hayley Walsh?"

Mackenzie and Nick looked at each other, baffled.

"It was twenty-one years ago," he said. "I was fresh out of college, looking for my first story, when Hayley Walsh, a nine-teen-year-old sophomore at the University of Washington, disappeared on a Friday night after going out with her friends."

It was the same university Stella and Bobby had attended, around the same time frame.

"The case is unsolved?" Mackenzie guessed. "Is that why it's been haunting you?"

"The case went to the FBI, but it was a bust. No leads. No evidence. I'd started working on that story." He stared into empty space. "I was eager to prove myself. But I got nothing. Eventually, I moved on, but it always bothered me that I never found out what happened to her. Almost felt guilty for giving up on her, you know."

For a journalist who had hardened with age and the horrific stories he had delved into, the memory of Hayley stirred some-thing in him. Somewhere that newly anointed journalist still resided inside him. This was his unfinished business.

"Truth be told, detectives, I've had breakdowns from that case." He blinked hard.

"How did Stella know that this case affected you so much?" Mackenzie asked.

He looked at them wryly. "Because she remembered me. Twenty-one years ago, I interviewed her. Except back then she wasn't Stella DeRossi, her maiden name was Stella Ambrose. She was Hayley's roommate."

THIRTY-EIGHT

Hayley Walsh was a mixed-race woman born and raised in Bellingham until her family moved to Tacoma when she was thirteen years old. She had a little gap between her teeth. Her skin was light brown with a splash of freckles on her cheeks. Her hair was dark and curly, messy and uncombed. She had an ethereal quality about her. None of her features were solid or striking, but she had a glow.

"Will the FBI share her case file with us?" Mackenzie asked Nick, who was sipping on his bourbon in a fancy, sculpted glass.

They were in his lair—the den in his house that he had converted to an office. It was a cozy space, devoid of any windows, just a yellow, worn-out rug that Nick's mother had knitted before she'd died, a table, and a bulletin board covering one of the wood-paneled walls. The room had a distinct incense smell—woody and smoky with hints of spices. Mackenzie always felt like she was trapped inside a cigar box when she came to this room.

"Yeah, I've filed a request. I'm sure we'll get it considering the urgency."

"They'll see your name and hurry up."

His mouth tightened. "Mack."

They were sitting on the floor surrounded by paperwork. Hawkins had sent them his research on the case. It was a thick stack of yellowing paper and fading ink. Even though it was a decades old case, he hadn't found it in him to send all the paper for recycling. Hope inside him still flickered all this time that perhaps one day the first story he had tried chasing would reach a conclusion. And as Mackenzie sifted through the collection of Hayley's photographs from university, she found herself hoping for the same.

"Why do all our cases end up involving some cold case?" she muttered.

Nick turned the glass in his hands, the dips and ridges catching the light from the lamp and casting a checked pattern behind him on the wall. "If only people did their jobs correctly the first time around."

Mackenzie found Stella's interview scribbled on a page in Hawkins's childlike handwriting. "Look. He talked to her twice."

Nick leaned forward, reading the page. "Stella said she wasn't out with Hayley that night."

"Hayley was attending her friend's birthday party, but she left around eight thirty saying she was going home."

"Except she never made it home. Stella said when she woke up, Hayley's bed was still made."

Mackenzie hunted through the papers to find the name of the place where the party was. It was in Mercer Island, around a twenty-minute drive from the city. Hawkins had taken a picture of the house where Hayley was last seen having fun with her friends. She traced the jagged edge of the picture, trying to smoothen all the impressions in it from being folded for years. The house was a regular one. But in a faded, old picture, it looked haunted and rackety.

"She told her friends she'd take a bus back," Nick said.

"According to Hawkins, the police couldn't confirm if she ever boarded any bus."

"We don't know if she even left Mercer Island."

Mackenzie went back to reading Stella's statement. Hawkins had scribbled some of his own observations in the margins. He had described Stella being in shock and confused when he first spoke with her. The second time, she was cagey and impatient, trying to cut short the interview. She had been constantly biting her nails and rocking back and forth. It was the last time he'd talked to her.

Until twenty-one years later when Stella decided to get in touch again through her work email.

"What made Stella decide to talk to him *now*? After all these years?"

"The hush money from the Wildmans probably ran out. Sounds like this was her ticket to get out of the rut she was in," Nick said, disapproval dripping from his voice. "She made a lot of money out of her roommate disappearing, didn't she?"

"It doesn't matter what she did. We still have to find her," Mackenzie replied coolly. "And we don't know the full story."

"Sully is right. If we go to Baron with this, he'll deny everything."

The Wildmans were close to untouchable. But Hayley Walsh could be the chink in their strong, steely armor. A name that caused ripples. But they were walking on eggshells. With Murphy breathing down their neck and the Wildmans close to icing them out, Mackenzie knew they needed something more.

She clicked a pen; the repetitive sound helped her focus. "How about Dominic?"

"Dominic?" Nick mused. "He's under house arrest until his trial."

"Do you think he'll talk to us in exchange for a sweeter deal?" Trapping the Wildmans was like cornering a stealthy prey. The last time Mackenzie had gone after powerful people, the town had paid the price. Not that everything was under her control, but she knew that she couldn't just barge in with accusations and coax admissions by intimidation.

This was a game of chess—attached to a ticking time bomb.

"Dominic has been the Wildmans' personal lawyer for over twenty years. If they indeed paid off Stella using Glenn, there is no way Dominic wouldn't know about it," Nick said darkly.

Less than an hour later, Mackenzie and Nick were ringing the bell to Dominic's plush mansion at Forrest Hill. The humidity had caused Mackenzie's red mane to fluff and frizz. Wisps of baby hair flayed in the light wind. Her usually poker-straight hair tied in a ponytail hung in curls. She looked over her shoulder at the winding driveway bordered by trees with branches almost as thick as the trunks. At the leaves that lay on the ground. She remembered how this past year this peace was fractured, how fear and unpredictability had become a part of the air. But fall was the season of leaves shedding along with the past. In that moment, she saw Lakemore throw off the mantle of its past, at the cusp of rebirth.

The door squeaked when it opened. Dominic appeared, his features taut with annoyance. "Now what do you want?"

Mackenzie noticed his ankle monitor. "Just a few more questions."

He sighed and held the door open for them. They were led inside a lavish house with a sweeping staircase, large fireplace, and a dining table enough to accommodate over ten people. There was no sound in the house, no feet padding on the floor, no whispers behind rooms, no doors opening or closing.

"My wife took our girls and left." Dominic gave them a sour smile, but his voice was thick. "Said she didn't want a murderer to raise them."

"I'm sorry," Nick said gently.

Mackenzie's heart skittered despite herself at the sight of Dominic rummaging through the house alone with a leash. He looked like he had lost almost half his body weight within a few days.

He dragged his feet on floor covered in dust and crumbs of chips. "She's not wrong. I did kill an innocent woman." He fell on a chair. "I did it to save my girls, but I still lost them. At least they're alive. I can watch them grow up from afar."

"The good news is that the DA is sympathetic toward you," Nick said. "We have his ear, and we can encourage a lenient sentencing."

Dominic was unaffected. "What else can I do for you? You already know what I did."

He was drinking coffee when Mackenzie spoke the words and he froze. "Does the name Hayley Walsh ring a bell?"

She watched blood retreat from his face, leaving behind a ghost. His hand trembled as he set the mug back on the table. "Hayley Walsh?"

"You know her."

The silence seemed to stretch, occasionally being snapped by the flicker of the fire and thudding of wood as chunks fell into the embers. "Yes. I mean, not personally. It was a big case. I watched the news."

"You recognized the name Glenn Solomon when we mentioned it the first time we met you?" Nick asked.

He closed his eyes in surrender. "No, but now that you said it. I was too preoccupied with my own anxiety to pay attention to the name of a man I last met decades ago."

"What happened?"

Dominic looked too frail and haggard, while he composed himself. "It was a very long time ago."

"I know you probably feel some sense of loyalty to Baron, but—" Mackenzie started, but Dominic's bark of laughter cut her off.

"That son of a bitch cut all ties with me when I was arrested. Hasn't even texted to check in on me. I should have known. Over the years, I've seen how ruthlessly he tossed people aside who were no use to him anymore. I was naïve to think that he wouldn't treat me the same. I owe him nothing."

"Then tell us," she pressed. "You have nothing to lose anymore, do you?"

He scoffed. "I suppose, you're right. Twenty-one years ago, Baron called me into a personal meeting. He looked... visibly shaken." He stared off into the distance, remembering the key details. "I'd never seen him so disturbed. He wasn't very vocal. He never is. But his face was... Anyway, he told me that a girl from Bobby's university had gone missing. I had been keeping up with the news. I'd heard of Hayley Walsh. It was only two or three days after she was last seen. He told me he needed my legal advice on paying off some people."

"Go on."

"They weren't law-enforcement officers, he assured me. Though he may have been lying, who knows. He told me that he felt bad for Hayley's father, a single parent, and her roommate. He wanted to help them out, but not too visibly, considering the ongoing investigation."

"And you believed him?" Nick asked. "That he just wanted to help strangers?"

"No," he said firmly. "But I was a young lawyer who had somehow impressed an American blue blood and was close to getting promoted at work for the same reason. I toed the line carefully. I never asked too many questions."

"It was your idea to use Glenn and Acorn Metals?"

"I took care of everything. And since I had no knowledge that this was a bribe, I was just helping my client with... charity."

Mackenzie suppressed the urge to roll her eyes. She respected how clever it was. But lawyers always made her job difficult. "And then Glenn Solomon got fired a few months later never to be employed again?"

"I had no idea," he admitted. "Baron told me he fired Glenn and didn't give him a good recommendation, which is why his career tanked. He never gave me a reason. But I heard that Glenn was getting cocky, even asking for money. Baron probably freaked out and wanted to tie up any loose ends."

"Why do you think he went out of his way to pay off Hayley's father and her roommate?"

"He never told me, but he didn't have to," Dominic replied curtly. "You might not guess it, but Baron loves Bobby to death. And the word going around was that Bobby was a person of interest in Hayley's disappearance."

Mackenzie's breath spiraled out of her lungs, hissing out of her nose with a sharp, ruffling sound. She glanced at Nick, who had a deep frown on his face. "Why?"

"Because Bobby was after Hayley. He had been asking her out for weeks, but she kept rejecting him. And then she disappeared."

THIRTY-NINE

The entire room flashed as lightning forked the sky outside. The sound of thunder followed soon after. Mackenzie's boots made a squelching sound on the carpet. The butler walking ahead of her sneakily looked over his shoulder, making faces at the mess she was making. The sky was inky black, only illuminated by the occasional bolt of lightning. As Mackenzie walked through a hallway, the shadows of swinging trees and creaking swing sets danced on the opposite wall.

The butler opened the double doors. A long dining table was set in the middle, laden with a feast, from chili fig spread and coq au vin to tarte tatin. Baron sat at the head, with Bobby and Linda flanking him on either side.

"What now, Nick?" Baron didn't even look up as he cut open his meat. "It's late."

Nick's hair was wet and sticking to his forehead. "We need to talk."

"Please have a seat." Linda was on her feet, immediately playing the perfect hostess. "Would you like to eat anything?"

"That won't be necessary—"

"I insist."

"Don't push them, Linda," Baron said from behind her.

Linda gave them a tight smile and clutched her string of pearls before sitting back down.

Mackenzie glanced at Bobby, who was scrolling on his phone, uninterested. The three of them were surrounded by so much opulence, but the atmosphere was dreary.

Nick drummed his fingers on the table. "Remember Acorn Metals?"

Baron's fork paused in midair, but he composed himself quickly. "What about it?"

"It went under around fifteen years ago."

"As a lot of companies do, Nick." His voice had a nervous edge to it. Everyone in the room noticed.

Bobby dropped his phone, casting a sharp glare at Mackenzie and Nick. It was the first time Mackenzie had seen him serious, not drowning his insecurities behind acts of vulgarity.

"Your company paid two hundred thousand dollars to Stella DeRossi—or Stella Ambrose as she was then—over twenty years ago. I'm sure you have seen her face on the news," Mackenzie said.

Baron's lips curled in a sneer. He dropped his cutlery and wiped his mouth with a napkin. "Detective Price, I own an empire worth six hundred million dollars, with more companies and investments I can count. I don't remember transactions dating back twenty years. Nor do I manage such things. I hire people."

"Yes. You hired Glenn Solomon to arrange that payment. The man who killed your mistress, Ms. Gallagher." She watched a tide of panic rising inside him. "You see why we keep coming back to you? How all roads in this case lead to you?"

Bobby sprang to his feet, knocking his chair back. "My brother has a lot of enemies. I didn't know you were one of them, Nick. Our families have known each other for thirty years."

"Bobby!" Baron snarled. "Stay out of it."

His face was crimson red. "Oh, come on, Baron. This is harassment! They keep showing up at our home whenever some woman in their grimy little town goes missing."

Earlier the air in the room had been bursting with tension, but Bobby's outburst had unleashed it. Mackenzie knew that this was the time to strike, the small opening they had when emotions were running high, and people could slip. "How about when Hayley Walsh went missing?"

Her name was like kryptonite for Bobby. His chest deflated. His anger evaporated, replaced by horror. He was a tall and strapping man, but the expression on his face reduced him to a child. Baron was on his feet and extending an arm over his shoulder. All his harsh words and glares were gone. Mackenzie finally got a glimpse of the protective older brother.

"Who's Hayley Walsh?" Linda's voice pierced through the silence. "Is she another mistress of yours, Baron?"

"Why don't you leave us alone, Linda?" he said in a tight voice.

"Absolutely not." She scoffed, like it was ridiculous. "What is going on?"

"Hayley Walsh wasn't a mistress of your husband," Mackenzie corrected. "She was in university with Bobby."

"I don't understand." Linda looked at them all like they were speaking a different language. "Bobby?"

He whirled to pour himself a drink. "She disappeared. That's it."

"Then why did your brother pay her roommate and her father all that money?" Nick demanded.

Baron sighed. "You talked to Dominic?"

Nick nodded.

"I see." He paced the room, lighting up a cigar. The smoke

plumes zigzagged out his mouth. "Bobby and Hayley knew each other. They had a class together."

"We weren't friends. Just friendly." Bobby didn't turn around, giving them his back. Occasionally, a bolt of lightning caused the light to bend and light up that large, symmetrical tree that Baron and Bobby used to climb as kids. But Mackenzie could see the reflection of his face, looking into the pressing darkness outside the window. His expression was passive and thoughtful.

"You were a person of interest in her disappearance," Nick said. "Some of your old classmates reported that you had asked her out a bunch of times, but she refused your advances."

"What are you implying?" Baron asked.

"I think it's obvious," Mackenzie snapped. "Under your orders, Glenn arranged a large sum of money to be transferred to Joe Walsh and Stella Ambrose, now Stella DeRossi, aka the missing woman. It was hush money because you believe that Stella knew something that could hurt Bobby. Maybe she knew what Bobby did to Hayley."

Linda made a mousy sound in the back of her throat. She looked like she could disappear into the velvet chair. She kept clutching her string of pearls.

"We gave them the money out of pity," Baron said. "Hayley's father was a middle-class man with no other children. We felt bad for him and decided to make his life easier. Same for Stella. She was Hayley's roommate."

"Two hundred grand because you felt bad for them?" Mackenzie asked in disbelief.

"Two hundred grand to us is like two hundred dollars to you," Bobby gloated with a bitter smile, which made Baron flinch. "I would never hurt Hayley. Or anyone. Why should I?"

"Because she rejected you—"

He rolled his eyes. "Oh, the same old excuse you gave when you thought I hurt Veronica."

"Why did you pay them off discreetly?" Nick asked.

"Because it was unethical," Baron replied. "Bobby was a person of interest, and we know it would have looked like a bribe." He fixed his tie, a tinge of finality creeping into his tone. "We have no knowledge of what happened to Hayley, or to any of these missing and murdered women."

Mackenzie's eyes were fixated on Bobby. Whenever Hayley's name was mentioned, his features changed. The corners of his eyes wrinkled. The corners of his mouth dipped. There was a slight tug between his brows. The boorish apathy in his eyes was replaced by pain. "How close were you to her?"

He swallowed hard. "Not much at all. We just talked a few times."

"Where were you the night she disappeared?" she asked.

"I..." He closed his eyes and rubbed his forehead. "I was at a party at my frat. Alpha Sigma Tau."

"Did you see her at all that day? Talk to her?"

"I don't remember anymore. If I did, it wasn't important."

Baron placed a hand on Bobby's shoulder. "Nick, we value our relationship with your father, which is why we didn't call our lawyer and shut down this interview right away. We don't have anything to do with this. Someone is out to get us." He was definitive in his statement. No fear or uncertainty leaking. Either he was an excellent liar, or he was telling the truth. But it was the younger Wildman who was more transparent tonight, the one who showed an emotion beside arrogance. It made Mackenzie wonder if it could be guilt. If Bobby Wildman really did kill Hayley Walsh for rejecting his advances. But one thing was certain, something inside him had cracked.

FORTY

OCTOBER 23

Debbie's face occupied the whole screen. Each time Mackenzie saw Debbie in the news, the latter looked brighter and larger than life. Like an actress on stage on a shooting-star trajectory. She didn't just read the news, she appealed to the people.

"Construction on the new mall—the Plaza—has been halted one week before the work was about to begin," she announced. *"The Plaza was touted to be the tallest building in town, housing all the big brands so that shoppers didn't have to travel to Olympia. On top of the business, it was supposed to bring hundreds of jobs to Lakemore. Our sources have confirmed that the project was being funded by the Wildman Group, the president of which, Baron Wildman, is now under investigation by the FBI."* She rambled more about Baron before she finished with a statement that was sure to ruin Mackenzie's day. *"For how much longer will Lakemore suffer because of the tactless investigation of the Lakemore PD? Baron Wildman is accused of extortion and blackmail. But who is paying the price? The honest blue-collar workers of our town."*

There it was.

Mackenzie turned off the television and went to the bathroom and stared at her pallid reflection in the mirror. She had her mother's eyes. Her mother's cheekbones. Her mother's chin. The only thing different was her hair. Melody had had curly, raven-black hair. Mackenzie pinched her cheeks, lifting them. She moved her eyebrows and pulled down her eyelids. Pathetic attempts to separate her and Melody. She did her makeup differently that morning—focusing on not highlighting her sharp cheekbones and contouring her nose. It was the only weapon she had against the world and her mother.

"I love you, Mackenzie," Melody whispered, tucking her into bed.

"I love you too, Mommy."

Mackenzie's heart twisted at the memory. There was a time it was easy to say those words. Now she didn't have anyone to say it to. And she didn't have anyone who would say it to her.

"The sheriff's office got back to us," Nick greeted her when she reached work. He was living on coffee now and obsessively popped breath mints in between his next dose.

Mackenzie unrolled the map he handed to her on her desk. Hers was the only organized one, devoid of food stains, ruined Post-its, and empty cups. It was a map of the state of Washington with many red circles.

"These are the places where the flora matches what we found under Veronica's shoes."

Her eyes made a quick work of the marked territories. Unfortunately for them, Washington was a large state with a lot of greenery.

"We don't even know if the women were held in Lakemore." Nick ran a hand through his unkempt hair. "Though I don't think he took them too far, since they had to be made available for Glenn and Dominic."

"But he takes a few days," Mackenzie noted. "It could

account for the time it takes to transport the women. Hopefully he's not venturing out of state."

Nick's hand mindlessly tapped for a pack of cigarettes. He took one out and popped it between his lips, taking empty drags.

"What happened to you?" she asked.

He blinked uncomfortably. "Just, my father called. People are asking him questions."

"What questions?"

It was Sully who answered from behind. "Baron Wildman is one of the biggest donors of the man Senator Blackwood was up against." His hand was dunked in a bag of potato chips and his mustache was peppered with yellow flakes. He rubbed his drum of a belly and swallowed a burp. "It looks personal."

Mackenzie wanted to roll her eyes, but a terrible thought made her skin crawl. "Would Nick have to be taken off the case?"

"Not yet." Sully stuffed his mouth with chips. The sound of them crunching between his teeth irked Mackenzie. "You two aren't investigating the Wildmans. You are looking into two homicides and one missing person. Anyway, where are you with Stella?"

"The sheriff's office sent us all these places that match the samples found under Veronica's shoes," Mackenzie updated him. "But none of them have an industrial building in the vicinity that I know of." Her shoulders fell. What if they had to expand their search to Oregon? She felt the distance between them and Stella stretching thin. It wouldn't be too long before it would snap, and she'd be lost forever.

"Why are you looking for an industrial building?" Sully inquired.

"We found chemicals on her which aren't part of a regular household and more common on an industrial site," Nick said.

"I'll double-check if there's anything nearby, but I think Mack is right."

"It's already hard to catch this guy," Sully said, wiping his hands on his pants. "The killing is done by someone else, so that forensic evidence doesn't help us much. And the envelopes he sends to blackmail don't have any prints or identifiable marks."

It was like someone had cracked the code to commit the perfect crime. They knew how to find someone's weakness and use it against them.

Justin came into the office, catching his breath, his cheeks pink. "Remember we had tagged the taser guns Murray had illegally sold?"

It took Mackenzie a moment to reacquaint herself with that information. Once the weapons reached the streets, they were essentially lost. She had given up hope of finding anything there, but renewed determination swam in Justin's eyes.

"What about them?" Nick was faster.

"The FBI has been keeping a close eye on a gang they traced to Riverview," Justin informed. "A Taser was fired two days ago in a confrontation. The AFID tags picked up at the scene alerted our system."

"Murray sold a lot of those guns," Sully grumbled, diluting the brimming excitement of the moment. "What are the chances it has anything to do with Stella?"

Mackenzie's nerves sang with anticipation. She was already wearing her leather jacket. "We're in no position to ignore even the flimsiest of leads."

FORTY-ONE

Mackenzie's knee bobbed and she checked her gun in the holster again. The sun was beating down on an unusually dry day. Plucking at her collar, she winced at the sweat beading on her hairline.

"Gum?" Special Agent Daniel St. Clair asked at her side.

"I'm good."

When Mackenzie and Nick had reached Riverview PD, an FBI team was waiting for them, led by Special Agent St. Clair. A slender man of average height, thick dark curly hair, and a kind, amiable face. A Mark Ruffalo lookalike. Mackenzie had first met him a year ago, when he had arrived to consult on another case in Lakemore.

"We didn't get a chance to catch up back at the station." He munched on Skittles. "How have you been?"

"Good." She answered on autopilot and then looked at him, remembering how her old case had devastated him. "How are you?"

"I got married."

"You did?"

He showed his wedding ring. "We met eight months ago, but it felt like it was meant to be. How's Lakemore? Still messed up?"

Mackenzie gave him a tight smile. She felt a fierce loyalty toward her dwindling town. No matter how glaring its flaws were, she didn't like an outsider pointing them out. "How long has your guy been undercover for?"

"Six months. The coastguard discovered a ship with animals imported from overseas illegally around two years ago. The operation is huge and has birthed smaller ones like this. A few months back, I was told to lead a team to track down dogfighting rings on the West Coast. This is one of the gangs we've been watching."

And now they were seated in a car behind a dumpster by an abandoned warehouse where the undercover FBI agent had informed them some deal was going to go down. Mackenzie looked at the homeless man digging through the trash and another woman taking a smoke break around the corner. Both were undercover agents wearing wires under their clothes.

The warehouse was situated on an empty lot that had collected garbage and litter along the years. The walls were painted with graffiti. The windows were cracked. Two more cars were parked in front of it. She stared at the building, wondering what the hell was going on inside.

"How do you think this is related to your case?" Daniel asked. "Got a suspect involved in dogfighting?"

"I suppose we'll find out." Her phone lit up with a message from Nick, who was in another car parked a few miles away. "A car just turned and is approaching."

Daniel straightened, shooting orders over the phone. The two undercover agents continued playing their part while casually scoping the area. Mackenzie's stomach clenched and a grating sensation pulsed through her as a red car came into view. Three men climbed out of the car, their skin covered in tattoos; they chewed on something while glancing at their surroundings, not taking much notice of the homeless man or the woman smoking. Mackenzie saw a gun tucked into the waistband of one of the men as they made their way inside.

"We wait five minutes and leave." Daniel checked his watch and confirmed if everyone else was in position.

"Thanks for taking me along. You didn't have to."

He gave her a small smile. "I told you I owe you one. And I know how much you hate sitting back and waiting for someone else to do the work."

When it was time, Daniel just nodded at her as they climbed out of the vehicle. The bulletproof vest held Mackenzie's chest and abdomen like a prisoner. But her initial discomfort evaporated as her training kicked in. Operating purely on instincts cultivated over hundreds of drills and then real-life scenarios, she knew how to control her racing heart and silence her loud thoughts. She trod carefully and soundlessly like a panther behind Daniel, the Glock in her hand. Drops of sweat hung from her eyelashes. She kept inspecting her surroundings, even though the FBI had assured her that the area was marked and under constant surveillance. Backup would be seconds away.

Daniel propped open a back door that had been left open by his undercover agent. He gestured her to follow him. They entered the warehouse, walking up a flight of stairs into a dark and dusty hallway with a door at the other end. The sounds of laughter trickled down the hall. They gave each other a look and nodded, slowing down their pace.

Mackenzie wasn't scared. There was no pit of fear growing larger in her belly. There was only excitement. She was in the enemy's territory, feet away from armed and dangerous men.

Then another sound came.

Dogs barking and growling.

They were getting closer.

Daniel and Mackenzie stood on either side of the door at the end of the hallway, catching a breath and scanning behind them to make sure they weren't followed. Daniel signalled her to wait, while he pushed the door open slightly. If it made any noise, it was drowned by the dogs barking and men talking. He peeked and beckoned her to follow him in. A tall wooden rack, stacked with bottles of alcohol, was directly ahead of them, protecting them. They knelt on the floor and peered through the space between wood brackets and bottles. A group of men sat around a large table playing poker and smoking. A cage covered by a tarp was next to them, rattling with movement.

"Shut their fucking mouths!" a man growled and slammed a card on the table.

Another man stood up and walked over to the cage, lifting the tarp to reveal barking and writhing dogs inside. It made Mackenzie's ears ache, the sounds they were making, whining and struggling, scratching and clawing.

"What should I do?" the man by the cage asked dumbly. "They won't listen."

Another one snickered. "Shoot one and the rest will shut up."

He scratched his head. "Which one?"

Mackenzie recognized him as the undercover agent Daniel had showed her a picture of at the station.

"Maybe the Labrador. It's the laziest one. Fucking useless."

"Uhhh." The undercover agent scrambled for an excuse. "Maybe we should wait before the auction—"

"Who the hell would pay money for *that*?"

"I don't know, man. Some turd with a kid? They go all mushy for charity cases."

Mackenzie couldn't see the face of the man he was talking

to. The angle kept his face hidden. She could only make out his dark hair. But it didn't matter because she felt the air grow colder. Something had shifted. The cackling and easy camaraderie between the men collapsed into silence. It was because the man was glaring at their undercover agent.

"Why do you care so much?" he asked. "Really thought about everything, haven't you?"

"Shit." Daniel's voice was low. "He's on to him."

The man pushed back his chair and sauntered to him, giving Mackenzie his back. "I've been watching you. You disappear, act suspiciously, hide your phone... what's up with you?"

The agent chuckled lightly, but it was faltering. "You sound paranoid. What's crawled up your ass? Your boss?"

Someone howled. But the situation escalated. The man grabbed the agent by the collar and shoved him against the wall. They began bickering between themselves and the others noticed, stopping their game and watching the pair. A trail of sweat roped down Mackenzie's back. She felt the air tighten with tension. Even the dogs in the cage stopped barking.

"Be ready." Daniel pressed her with a warning look.

Mackenzie was puzzled for a second, but then she saw the gangster take out his gun and point it at the agent. The agent's face was white as a ghost. The man clicked the safety off just like Mackenzie did.

"FBI! Freeze!" Daniel roared, revealing himself.

Then everything happened too quickly.

Two more agents burst into the scene from the front door. The undercover agent used the distraction to shove the man away, but a shot rang out. Then everyone was on their feet and bullets rained down in the warehouse.

Mackenzie hid behind the bottle rack as cover as shots fired in her direction, hitting the wall behind her. She leaned across and fired. Her eardrums were already ringing, each pop louder than the other. There was smoke and blood and curses exchanged. There was a loud cry, and she knew she had shot her target right in the kneecap.

"Release them!" one of the men cried.

"Fuck!" Daniel growled as someone opened the cage and the dogs were set free. It was chaos. Daniel began to throw orders around at Mackenzie, but over the sound of the dogs barking and bullets firing, she couldn't hear anything. The animals threw everything off balance, growling and attacking everyone in the room; loyal to nobody, only trained to fight.

Mackenzie breathed hard. She felt something sticky on her skin and realized a bullet had grazed her arm, leaving her skin sliced open. Amid the chaos, she saw someone running out the back. It was the same man who had threatened the agent. She zipped through the scene, dodging the stray bullets and the clawing dogs. One of them came after her and sank its teeth into her leg.

"Ah!" She almost toppled and grabbed a chair, swinging it at the animal, but not enough to seriously injure it. Then she followed the man out the door that led into an empty parking lot. "Lakemore PD! Stop!"

The criminal kept running, ditching his gun, which was out of bullets. He was fast; Mackenzie was faster, but a burning pain had bloomed where she was bitten, coiling around her calf muscle and rendering her slow. "Stop! Or I will shoot!"

He didn't listen.

"Damn it." She couldn't chase after him anymore. She ducked and took position, aiming at the man's leg. Tuning out all the muffled sounds from inside and the receding adrenaline leaving sour jitters, she took aim. She pulled the trigger. All that target practice had kept her sharp. The man dropped on the ground, moaning and rolling around, clutching his leg.

He wasn't going anywhere.

Mackenzie took a moment to catch her breath and then limped closer. The sun had reached its peak now. Cupping a hand over her eyes, she finally saw the man's face crunched in pain, his blood soaking the concrete underneath.

She recognized him immediately. It was Romero. Walter Cristane's muscle.

FORTY-TWO

The last thing Mackenzie remembered was removing Romero's jacket and tying it around his gushing wound. The heat had been excruciating. And so was the surprise of seeing him. She was waiting for backup when she began fading. Her surroundings had melted away and darkness rose instead as she fell on the ground.

Now she felt a hand holding hers. A strong, thick hand with hair sprinkling the knuckles. It belonged to a man. His grip was firm. Mackenzie felt warm and fuzzy from his touch; a sense of surety that seeped down to her molecules. It was a touch she knew from a very long time ago.

Suddenly, she opened her eyes and gasped for breath.

"Detective Price?" A doctor's face appeared, blocking the overhead light. "Welcome back."

"Huh?" Bewildered, she sat up slowly, realizing she was in a hospital. Her leg and arm were sore and bandaged. "Were you just holding my hand?"

The doctor was an old man with twinkling eyes and a foxy smile. "No."

"Oh, okay. What happened?" Her fingers touched her

watch of their own accord. A small smile played on her lips. She knew who she had remembered. She had remembered Robert.

"Your injuries aren't serious. The arm is a flesh wound. The dog bite wasn't deep," he rattled off. "Luckily, the dog that bit you doesn't have rabies, so you won't need any injections. And you are up with your tetanus shots as well. You will be on antibiotics for about a week." He sat on a stool with a grim face. "What concerned me was how long you were out for?"

She sighed. "Yeah. It was really hot and all that adrenaline..."

"You were out for almost an hour."

"*What?*"

He flattened his mouth and nodded. "We did some emergency imaging scans and the good news is that you have no signs of contusion or hematoma in your brain. How is your health otherwise? Any lapses in memory? Unexplained headaches?"

"Headaches. A lot of them. And not memory lapses..." She didn't know how to put it, but lately she had been thinking about Melody a lot. "Um, I get a lot of flashes... from the past. Only a few seconds, but they've gotten more vivid lately."

He nodded, understanding. "Have you hurt your head lately?"

She was about to deny it, but then she remembered. How on patrol she had fallen, and the back of her head had struck the concrete. "Yeah. I hit my head badly few days ago. But I didn't show any signs of a concussion."

"That's for a doctor to decide," he reprimanded her. "Next time you hurt your head, you come straight here. We'll run some tests, but it looks to me that you had a concussion. Frequent headaches are a common symptom. Even the flashes you are talking about. An undiagnosed concussion can cause hallucinations in rare cases. Any changes in your behavior or thinking pattern can be from a concussion."

"I see."

There was a knock on the door and the doctor asked Mackenzie if it was okay to have visitors. She nodded, without thinking, and felt self-conscious lying on a bed bandaged and bruised—completely opposite to her pristine and collected self. She hugged the blanket tighter when Nick waltzed in with a loose tie and shirt tucked out.

"Are you okay?" he asked.

"Yeah. An undiagnosed concussion apparently."

He released a frustrated breath. "Told you, you should have seen a doctor before."

"Since her scans were fine, I'm not worried about anything serious." The doctor stood up. "But have you noticed anything different from normal since she hit her head?"

The doctor had obviously assumed that she and Nick were together. Mackenzie hid her face in her hands, suppressing a groan. Nick didn't bother correcting the doctor. He was the one she spent most of her time with anyway.

Nick glanced at her all serious. "You killed that dog at the warehouse."

"Oh." Mackenzie frowned. "I didn't mean to."

He smiled at the doctor. "She's perfectly fine."

The doctor stammered, not understanding. "I'll leave you to it. By the way, Detective Price, I'm a fan. Looking forward to you representing Lakemore in that documentary."

Mackenzie was dumbfounded by the time they were left alone. "*You killed that dog?*"

"You didn't. I wanted to check if anything's changed." He shrugged innocently. "You didn't have an emotional reaction. Still Mad Mack."

Her eyes darted all over him, realizing that his usually crisp white shirt was smudged with dirt. Other than a gash on his elbow, though, he didn't look too bad. "What happened?"

"I found you by Romero, who is fine by the way. We closed in when we heard the gunfire, but it was so chaotic. I didn't even see where you were until I spotted red hair through the smoke disappearing behind a door. By the time I made it out after you, you had already shot the bastard and were passing out yourself."

"It wouldn't have been so bad if those dogs weren't there."

"Daniel didn't know. The undercover agent told him that a shipment would arrive later, but the schedule changed last minute."

"It's Walter Cristane's guy. What are the chances?"

"Romero's going to be out of surgery in two hours and Cristane's flying in from Vegas."

"Think it was Romero acting on Cristane's orders to abduct women?"

"Baron did say that someone was out to get him."

And who better than a man he had blackmailed into giving him money?

Mackenzie held an ice pack to her arm and looked over Romero's rap sheet in the station. It was quite extensive. From a few DUIs and misdemeanors to check washing and battery. He had been in and out of prison, though in the last three years, he had mostly managed to stay out. However, each time, he had savvy lawyers, ensuring lenient sentencing and an influx of cash that paid for his bail.

"There are perks of doing dirty work for a multimillionaire." Austin's voice came from behind. "Sorry, I didn't mean to pry. Old habit."

"No problem."

He lingered. "You got shot in the arm?"

"Barely. Got bitten by a dog. That hurt more." Her leg still throbbed; it would be a while before the medicine kicked in. "Burning the midnight oil?"

"Aren't I always?" He rubbed the back of his neck.

Mackenzie had a feeling Austin was lonely. New to a small town from a big city like Port Angeles, the move had been drastic enough, without his obsessive hunt for his missing fiancée. But now he looked dispirited. A man strung together with skin and bones without a purpose. "Do you have any family, Austin?"

He shook his head. His eyes were pools of blue, looking so vulnerable that it terrified Mackenzie. They were alike, adrift after losing the one person they had formed an attachment to. "When things get better, we should all hang out." She cleared her throat, injecting some casualness. "We usually hit the Oaktree Pub."

"Yeah. Thanks." He nodded and wandered off.

Mackenzie sighed and clasped her head in her hands. It was clear Austin wanted to talk about something. He had taken a step forward and Mackenzie had shut the door, not ready to allow intimacy and keeping things distant and casual. She felt like a failure in that moment. How after spending the last few months rebuilding herself and trying to remove the remnants of her past, she still dragged it behind her like shackles.

FORTY-THREE

Lakemore was almost drowning in rain. Water had collected
ankle-deep, running down streets and soiling everything. A
train was stuck and flooded. All patrol and available law-
enforcement officials were dispatched to help the rescue team.
The downpour was so fierce, she thought gravity had become
stronger, pulling every drop from the clouds. Puddles pooled on
the tarmac sidewalks. Soil was being wicked away by the torrid
rain. Driving home would be unwise. But she didn't feel like
going home anyway. Everything she knew and was good at was
right here. And every time she had pressed her head into a
pillow lately, Stella's image had come to her: floating with hair
whipping around like seaweed and milky white eyes.

The door creaked open, and Romero was brought into the
interrogation room, followed by a stout, bald, chirpy man
Mackenzie instantly recognized as Tom Cromwell of Cromwell
and Haskin. The seemingly friendly but secretly ruthless
lawyer—a favorite of the mob.

"Detective Price. Blackwood." He eagerly shook their
hands.

Romero had a toothpick between his lips. He limped

toward a chair in defiance, with no expression in his eyes, almost like it was inconvenient for him to be here.

"I thought we'd be dealing with the FBI," Cromwell said.

"The dogfighting is their case, but we are interested in the disappearance of Stella DeRossi." Nick placed a picture of Stella in front of Romero.

Romero's eye twitched, but he looked away, disinterested.

It was Cromwell, the paid mouthpiece, who spoke. "My client has no knowledge of this woman."

Mackenzie crossed her arms and watched Romero like a hawk. She had already anticipated how this was going to go.

"How did you get the taser gun?" Nick pressed.

Cromwell chuckled. "Come on, Nick. You know how guns and other weapons are distributed on the streets."

"Look, Romero," Nick tried reasoning with him. "You're in deep trouble with the FBI, but if you help us in our investigation, then we'll put in a good word for you. The FBI isn't even after you. We all know you're just the muscle of this operation. It's your boss, Walter Cristane, behind it, isn't it?"

Romero remained silent.

"Do you think he cares about you?" Mackenzie mocked him. "All his talk of brotherhood is bullshit. He's using you. And the minute it becomes too inconvenient for him, he'll cut you loose."

Romero's nostrils flared, as he stared at Mackenzie. There was a deep cut on his eyelid, making it droop. His jaw was held tight. He looked like he was close to snapping.

"Ah, so we have an agenda here," Cromwell exclaimed, feigning surprise. "It's Cristane you're after, but let me guess. You don't have a shred of evidence against him."

"Walter Cristane has been blackmailed repeatedly to invest in Baron Wildman's company," Nick said. "I can imagine he got sick of it and decided to do something about it. We'll get to him, but you can cut a deal and save your ass."

"I'm not worried about you getting to Cristane," Romero spoke for the first time in his distinctive drawl. "You can't touch anyone. You don't even know what goes on in your town. Everyone has a price. And from what I see, the price of people in Lakemore is a lot lower."

"Are you implying your boss has been paying people off?" Mackenzie demanded. Her blood raged in her veins, hot and heavy at his words, at the truth of them.

Cromwell touched Romero's arm. "He's just pointing out how corrupt your town is. But that is no secret."

"Give us names of who you were talking about."

There was a sharp knock on the glass behind them, puncturing a hole through the tightening atmosphere in the room.

"I'll go." Mackenzie pursed her lips and went out of the room, pissed off at whoever had interrupted them. When she reached the other side, she found Lieutenant Rivera with Walter Cristane.

Cristane's face was swollen with anger. The tinge of red darker when he looked at Mackenzie. "Who the hell do you think you are?" He marched toward her, standing nose to nose.

But she was the last woman on the planet to recoil. She stood her ground, shooting daggers at him.

Rivera interjected. "They're just doing their jobs, Mr. Cristane. It's protocol."

Cristane's eyes didn't budge from Mackenzie. "You're barking up the wrong tree. You'll get nothing from us."

"Did you just admit you're hiding something?" Mackenzie threw back. Even if Romero's connection to the case was purely coincidental, they had to confirm it. But their hands were tied. With uncooperative persons of interest who could throw money around and weasel their way out of anything, Mackenzie hadn't felt this kind of helplessness in a long time.

"You will cooperate." Rivera's stern voice came from behind. She raised a stiff eyebrow, and all her appeasing mannerisms dropped. "You will tell Romero to give us access to his house and belongings so that we can circumvent a court order and save time."

Cristane was appalled. "*Excuse me?*"

"You heard me."

"Why would I do that?" His laugh was sardonic, but his eyes were curious.

"If the information is leaked that Walter Cristane is a person of interest in the illegal import and export of animals and dogfighting, what will your board do? How will your share prices be affected?"

"Are you threatening me?" he growled low.

"No. I'm just asking a hypothetical question." Rivera kept her face blank.

There was a beat of silence. In the background, the sound of washing rain amplified. Mackenzie's feet were rooted to the ground. She couldn't believe what she was hearing.

Cristane grunted, seemingly giving in, and then stormed past her out of the room. His movement was so sharp that the air whooshed around her, lifting the stray strands on her head.

Rivera released a breath and rubbed her forehead. "Don't judge me, Detective Price. Apparently, this is how you get stuff done in this town. Or everywhere, really. You just hope that you find something at Romero's. Hopefully that hoodie you caught in that security tape."

Mackenzie was in no position to argue how good intentions weren't an excuse. The deeper she dug into her past and into others, the muddier everything became. "Yeah."

Nick came up behind her with panic in his eyes. "Mack, we need to go."

"Where?"

"I just got a call from Baron. Linda got a letter, threatening her sister."

FORTY-FOUR

In the car, Mackenzie drew geometrical shapes on the window. The rain had subsided, giving way to a cold mist. Condensation pressed against the glass. Tires sloshed through the buckets of water that had collected on the streets.

"Finally, someone came to the police when they were threatened," Nick commented after a while. "This is a good thing. It means Stella is still alive."

"It took him a long time to threaten someone else, didn't it?" Mackenzie wondered aloud. "He's probably spooked that Stella's disappearance has been making headlines. He's correctly assumed that we've made some progress. He's being slower, more cautious, taking his time."

"Making him harder to catch." Nick scowled at another roadblock and turned the car around. The sky was inky black. Houses and buildings had lost power. Sections of Lakemore were doused in darkness. It was like driving through the bottom of a lake. "What happened to you?" Nick asked.

She updated him on how Rivera had arm-twisted Cristane into getting Romero to cooperate.

He whistled. "She's not wrong. I grew up surrounded by this kind of shit."

"I don't get it." She shook her head. "I should, but I... I like clarity. Black and white."

"Even after the profession we're in and the things we've seen?"

"Because of that. If I acknowledge how complicated everything is, I'll have a permanent headache." She rested her head against the leather, enjoying the new smell in his car.

"I see your OCD is spreading to other areas in your life." He smirked. "I'm just teasing," he added, seeing her face. "You're probably compensating for your past."

"What do you mean?"

"You buried a body when you were twelve years old, Mack," he said carefully. After twenty years of guarding her secret close to her chest, Mackenzie had leaned on someone else. But it was still a sore subject that they hadn't spoken about. An inflammable topic that would catch fire if touched upon. "If you go to therapy, you could dig deeper into this."

"Why should I pay someone two hundred dollars an hour when I have you for free?" She clapped his shoulder.

They reached the Wildmans' house. The first time Mackenzie had seen it, she had been enamored by its opulence. But now, it looked like a haunted mansion long abandoned by its owners, situated in a secluded area where soon the woods and vines would swallow it whole.

One of the staff opened the door and ushered them in, leading them to one of the many rooms.

Linda sat on a chaise lounge, with a handkerchief balled in her trembling fist. Mackenzie couldn't imagine her in this state: utterly disheveled and falling apart. Her eyes were bloodshot; mascara was running down her tear-stained cheeks; snot dribbled its way down to her lip. Childlike whimpers escaped from her dainty throat.

Baron stood by the fireplace, the light from the fire dancing on his hard features. "Here you are!" He picked up a crumpled piece of paper and pushed it into Nick's chest. "Now do you believe me when I tell you someone's after us?"

Nick opened the paper and Mackenzie peeked.

Let's play a game. Kill Stella DeRossi or I kill your sister. If you choose the former, come to the Farmers Market at 5 p.m. tomorrow for further instructions. If you do not come or tell the police or anyone, I know who to kill instead. The choice is yours.

"When did you receive this?" Mackenzie asked.

A sob caught in Linda's throat as she opened her mouth.

Baron clicked his tongue, disgusted by his wife. "She got it this afternoon and tried—"

Mackenzie shot him down. "I'm not talking to you. She can speak for herself."

Linda spoke up, taking steadying breaths. "This red envelope was on my car when I came out of a boutique. I opened it... and I... I don't even know how I drove back home." The dam of tears burst again.

"Was there anything else with the letter?" Nick asked.

"Pictures of my sister."

"Where are they?"

She clenched her teeth. "I destroyed them."

"Why did you do that?"

"Because she was naked in them!" she cried aloud, her shrill voice ringing in the room. Her scorching, teary gaze was imploring. "They were taken while she was in the shower. I had no intention of leaving them around and risking *anyone* seeing them."

"She was going to go!" Baron's laugh was bordering on

manic. "Can you believe how stupid she is? Luckily, I caught her looking for my revolver in our safe."

Linda was on her feet and continued in her rasping voice, "You called the police! How dare you call the police!"

"What were you going to do, Linda? Kill that woman?" he retorted.

"Now they'll kill my sister!"

"No one will kill your sister." He grabbed her shoulders. "We've called the police and they'll protect her."

"He got inside her shower!"

"Okay, everyone needs to calm down," Nick said. "Mrs. Wildman, your sister is here, right?"

"Yeah, she's in the guesthouse. But she doesn't know anything."

Mackenzie was already taking out her phone. "We'll have a round-the-clock team for her. Patrol car will always be sitting outside. In the meantime, tell her not to leave the house."

"How long is she to stay a prisoner? When will you catch this person? This is ridiculous," Linda snapped.

"As ridiculous as you agreeing to this?" Baron pointed at the red envelope.

"It's easy for you to say, Baron. You don't care about her."

Their bickering ensued, as Mackenzie fished out an evidence bag from her jacket and put the envelope and the letter inside to send to the crime lab.

Mackenzie whispered to Nick, "There's no way he'll get to Linda's sister if we provide security."

"And I'm sure Baron will beef up security with his own staff. But he could retaliate by hurting anyone. They've got kids, friends, relatives... how many people can you protect?"

"The previous ones blackmailed never went to the police. He might have not been expecting this."

Nick's eyebrows crashed together. "He relies on his target to cave."

"So, he could be bluffing. Relying on his target to cave."
Mackenzie nodded, her blood running cold. "Which means if
Linda didn't listen, then he'll find someone else to blackmail."

FORTY-FIVE

OCTOBER 24

The thing with something unfinished was that it didn't just exist inside you, it grew and blossomed and flourished until every tiny nook in your brain, every beat of silence during your day, was consumed by that. It returned with full force, fresh and raw, never getting old. The feeling never waned. That was what lack of closure did. You weren't just stuck; you were slowly wrecked—one awful feeling at a time.

Joe Walsh emanated that from afar.

Mackenzie recognized it immediately. She had seen it in many people she had dealt with, including her own uncle Damien, who had never found out what had happened to his brother, Robert, until a few months ago.

The house was next to a strip mall that had shut down a long time ago. Joe raised an axe in the air and swung it downward, chopping the wood into two halves that fell on either side, joining a growing pile. It was a destitute place. Just a father with no answers living all alone.

Hayley's father in his seventies, still working at an electronics repair company TechKnow, to make ends meet.

"Joe Walsh?" Mackenzie flashed her badge, approaching him.

He looked up. His gray eyebrows were as thick as his mustache. He wore a cowboy hat and coveralls with combat boots. The sleeves were rolled up, exposing his muscular arms. For a man in his seventies, he was fit and imposing. "What do you want?"

"We're here to talk to you about your daughter," Nick said gently.

Silence. Joe's arms froze. Birds chirped. Leaves rustled in the wind.

"Did you find her?" he whispered.

It tore something inside Mackenzie's chest. She opened and closed her mouth gormlessly. She looked at Nick, who also struggled to answer.

"No, we haven't."

Joe dropped the axe on the ground, blankness seeping into his face again. "Why are you here?" He wiped his hands. "I'm a busy man."

"We're looking into your daughter's disappearance again," Mackenzie said. "We were hoping you'd talk to us."

"Why? Are there any new leads?"

"Stella DeRossi is missing. You knew her as Stella Ambrose? Hayley's roommate?" Nick explained.

Joe crossed his arms, his jaw ticking. "Of course. How can I forget her?"

"You must have seen the news."

"Yes, I have." There was not an ounce of sympathy in his tone for the missing woman.

"We have reason to believe that the cases might be linked," Mackenzie said. "We discovered a significant transaction to you from a company that was traced to Baron Wildman."

Joe's face contorted like he had tasted something bitter. "I never touched that money for myself. I spent every penny of it to set up scholarships under Hayley's name in different schools and universities." His hand did a sweeping gesture of his surroundings. "Think I'd be living in this dump still if I'd used that money?"

"Why didn't you use that money?"

"Because it was from Baron Wildman." His voice broke. "His brother hurt my child. I know it. Hayley used to complain about Bobby all the time over the phone. How he wouldn't take no for an answer. I should have taken her more seriously..."

"Did you tell the police about this? About Bobby?" Nick asked.

"What do you think? Of course I did. I begged and pleaded and all they said was that there was no evidence, no witnesses, nothing." He wiped a stray tear and sniffled. A proud man not wanting to show his emotions. "They're rich and we're poor." He picked up logs of wood under his arm and carried them to a shed with Mackenzie and Nick tailing him. "Doesn't matter what you look like or who you are or where you're from. It always boils down to economics. It was obvious that Bobby was protected throughout. The cops never took my claims seriously. Baron must have paid off the right people."

"And what about Stella? She was paid too."

Joe stacked the logs in a shelf and began sorting the hay. "Oh, she knew something. She must have, which is why they paid her off. That one will burn in hell for betraying my Hayley like that."

Mackenzie and Nick exchanged a loaded glance.

"Do you have any idea what Stella could have known?" Mackenzie asked.

He shrugged. "Probably something that could lead to Bobby's arrest. Can you believe that?" His eyes twinkled with tears. "A young girl goes missing after being harassed by a guy on campus. And her *friend* betrays her for money."

"You never tried contacting her?"

"I did back in the day, but she always acted evasive."

"Why are you so convinced that Bobby is the one behind what happened to Hayley?" Nick asked.

"The same damn question the police asked me all those years ago." Joe almost looked offended. "But my answer didn't mean anything to them now. Why does it matter today?"

Nick looked so unsure in the moment. Mackenzie only saw that side of him when it came to Luna. "I have a daughter too. And I know that doesn't mean much since a lot of assholes you dealt with back then were also parents and did nothing. But all it takes is one person to give a shit. And I do. Take that chance for Hayley and cooperate with us. Please."

Joe scrutinized him from head to toe. "Hayley told me that Bobby had called her that evening. He said he was going to some show that night at Mercer Island and wanted to know if she was down to meet up with him. She said she'd think about it."

"Bobby said he was at a frat party that night," Mackenzie remembered aloud. "Did the police check his alibi? Phone records?"

"Hayley didn't have a cell phone. He had called her dorm room. And they didn't check Bobby's cell phone records. They asked a few people at the frat party and they said they'd seen Bobby around."

Mackenzie frowned. Bobby's alibi was flimsy. It was no secret that he had been after Hayley. Statements of drunk students weren't solid enough. He could have easily slipped out of the party and back in. The police should have tried harder to confirm his alibi.

"Like I said," Joe replied to Mackenzie's puzzled face. "The Wildmans bribed everyone important."

"Did Hayley mention what show it was?" Nick asked.

"No." There was ice in his voice. "Whenever I see that family, I see pure evil. Bobby is the reason I haven't heard my daughter's voice in over twenty years. And Baron... that entitled son of a bitch has always saved his brother's ass. First, he spoiled him and now he looks away. If it were up to me, every single one of them would be in prison for life for what they did to my family." He strutted away, carrying the raw pain that hadn't dimmed in all these years. Time had magnified it.

Mackenzie and Nick walked back to the car, leaving a lonely man whipping arcs in the air with his axe.

"Are you thinking what I'm thinking?" Nick asked in a low voice.

Mackenzie nodded. "Looks like we have another suspect."

FORTY-SIX

During lunchtime, Mackenzie slipped away and found herself returning to Hidden Lake. Everything had been moving too fast. After the visit to Joe, she had spent the morning at the hospital undergoing further tests to confirm that there was no brain damage from her concussion before popping mild painkillers to help control her random bursts of headache.

Take it easy. The most important thing after a concussion is to not take on stress, the doctor had repeated sternly.

Not take on stress? Easier said than done when there was a woman's life hanging in the balance and the deadline the black-mailer had set was today. At least they had blocked Linda from succumbing to the blackmailer's manipulation, thanks to Baron catching her and calling for help. Mackenzie hoped that they bought Stella more time. That their blackmailer was scrambling to find someone else to trap.

A prickle of fear knocked the back of her neck.

She stood at the edge of the shore, watching the water gently lap from the wind. The lake looked gloomy. The mist lurking above it looked smoky, dark swirling tendrils teasing secrets that were buried deep below. The trees on the other side had lost all their leaves. They were tall sticks with arms poking out at different angles. Except they looked burnt from this far. Like a fire had ripped through the woods, leaving stubborn and charred trees still standing.

Mackenzie's phone rang. "Detective Price."

"The CSI and FBI have been going through Romero's house," Nick said. "I just heard back that they didn't find any sweatshirt resembling the one we saw on the video from Lakemore Gardens."

Mackenzie felt a sting of disappointment. "He could have ditched it. Is he under arrest?"

"Out on bail."

"*What?*"

"His bail was set at five hundred grand, which Cristane paid immediately. His passport has been seized though," Nick said dryly. "But the FBI is already planning on bringing more charges that will keep him behind bars for good. He's on borrowed time."

"Good." She flexed her fingers turning stiff in the cold.

A pause. "Where are you?"

"Just taking a walk." Her eyes swept across her void surroundings. The sky was too dark for this early in the day. Made her feel like she was in a cave with rising smoke. "Wanted a change of scenery."

"Can you believe that Stella took money to shut up about Bobby?" Nick scoffed. "I've never met the woman, but this is disappointing as hell."

"When we find her, maybe she'll tell us a different story. There could be another side to this."

"What if there isn't?"

Whenever they had a victim, they tended to see them in a positive light. Perhaps to have a stronger motivation to find them, so that deep down they were always rooting for the case to be solved. But not every victim was innocent.

"Then we'll leave her fate up to the court, I suppose. Our job is to find her," she said firmly, remembering Jonathan. He was sitting every day at the station looking bonier and more tired with dark circles that grew larger and darker.

"Do you want to meet me at the school?" Nick asked.

"School?"

"Luna's school. Remember you agreed to meet her class?"

The promise had flown out of Mackenzie's head. "Of course. I'll be there in thirty."

"Thanks a lot for doing this. I know you hate this kind of—"

"Shut up," she groaned. "See you there."

She removed one of her boots and socks and gingerly tipped her foot into the water. Cold zings pierced her skin, seeping into her bones. Her toes wiggled rigidly. She withdrew her foot from the freezing water.

She wasn't ready yet.

Children scurried around them. They chased and giggled, running wildly with messy hair. Mackenzie and Nick were waiting in the hallway to be called inside to Luna's class. "I've told uniform to keep an eye on Joe," Mackenzie said.

Nick was looking at the artwork framed on the walls, sincere drawings made by kids who couldn't color between the lines. "I wonder why Joe wouldn't just put a bullet through Bobby's head."

"Nick!"

He rolled his eyes. "I'm not saying he should. But you saw what that man is going through. He's got nothing to lose."

Mackenzie ignored the thundering of her heart against her ribs. Her life had become just as vapid. "Maybe he's being strategic about it. Planning a slow and painful destruction of the Wildmans. Lord knows he's had all the time to prepare."

The teacher came out of the room and ushered them inside, expressing her gratitude for the millionth time.

When Mackenzie entered the classroom, she was greeted by a crowd of beaming faces small enough to fit in her hand. "Hello, everyone."

"Hello, Mad Mack!" they chorused. It was the only time she didn't mind being called that name.

She gave a little wave to Luna, who was sitting in the front and had just recently lost a front tooth.

"So, what questions do you have for me?" she asked the room hesitantly.

When every hand in the class shot up, Mackenzie shrugged off her leather jacket and perched on the table.

"We'll get to everyone. Let's start with you."

Mackenzie spent an entire hour answering questions she never thought she would. From *"Is liking donuts a requirement to join the police?"* to *"Why don't the police have capes?"*

And there were some other interesting asides.

"We should plant chips inside everyone that sends an alert to the police when they're planning to commit a crime."

"Why don't the police hire someone like Batman to do the things they can't because of protocol?"

"Can we meet serial killers so that we know how not to think like them?"

The last question came from Luna, which made Nick face-palm. Nothing fazed Nick more than Luna's fascination with serial killers and cemeteries.

Once the session was over, everyone clapped and some even asked Mackenzie for her autograph, making a flush rise in her cheeks.

Luna held Mackenzie's hand and decided to show her the school, showing off to her friends how Mad Mack was her aunt.

"We only have twenty minutes, Luna." Nick walked behind them with his hands in his pockets.

"It won't take long, Daddy." Luna raised her chin in defiance, looking too serious for a nine-year-old with pigtails. "You'll find your missing woman." When Mackenzie's eyes went wide, she said, "I like to stay in the loop and give suggestions."

Holding Luna's tiny hand in a tight clasp, Mackenzie's heart felt full. Relief washed over her that she was at least capable of a positive, meaningful emotion. She hadn't turned too cold.

"And this is the last stop. The science lab." Luna led them inside a white room with instruments and chemicals.

"Are you allowed to be in here?" Nick frowned. "This doesn't look safe."

"We don't touch anything. We just watch Mrs. Goodman perform experiments and take notes," Luna explained. "But I know the theory behind all these chemicals." She pointed proudly at a shelf of them with clear labels. She began reciting the chemical names and their uses. "And this is acetone. Used to clean paint, grease, oil, permanent ink, resin—"

"Permanent ink?"

"Yes. It's highly flammable and evaporates easily."

"How does this little head have so much space for all this information?" Nick ruffled her hair.

"Acetone was at Romero's place," Mackenzie mumbled to Nick. "Along with a few blank checks."

Mackenzie's phone buzzed with an update from Anthony at the crime lab. They had identified the third compound under Veronica's shoes. It was carbon tetrachloride. Since it evaporated easily, there was only a small amount of it left, making it harder to identify.

"The traces we found under Veronica's shoes. The last compound was just identified." Mackenzie's mind was working fast.

"What is it?" Nick asked, handing Luna his phone to distract her.

Mackenzie began searching on her phone. Carbon tetrachloride, spray paint, and laundry starch yielded one use. Printing counterfeit money.

"All this is used to make counterfeit money." Her eyes widened. "Romero has been convicted of check washing before so that doesn't seem too far off."

Nick rubbed his jaw. "But we found no equipment or other materials required at his house. No stash of counterfeit bills. Which means he must have the whole thing set up someplace else."

"Probably an isolated place, hidden from easy access." She looked at him pointedly.

"A place you could hold someone captive," Nick muttered. "Surrounded by foliage that matches the deposits found under Veronica's shoes."

"All this time we were looking for an industrial complex in the vicinity. But this operation is off the grid."

He blew out a breath. "A remote cabin surrounded by woods? A hell of a lot of places in Washington."

"Romero won't help us. Not when it could lead us to Stella, which is a far bigger charge than what he's facing right now."

"Looks like we're on our own to figure this one out."

Mackenzie grimaced, but at least dim light had dappled across the dark path ahead. Her only hope was that Stella was alive at the end of it.

FORTY-SEVEN

Mackenzie rolled up her sleeves and held her breath. The pungent smell of rotten eggs and expired milk hit her like a punch in the face. She picked up the garbage bag and spilled the contents on the floor. She and Nick had been dispatched to a room in the basement of the police building to dig through Romero's trash, to contain the smell and unseemly sight.

"Christ, I didn't sign up for this." Nick scowled at the buzzing fruit flies. "Haven't done this since I was uniform."

"Those were the days." Mackenzie almost gagged at the banana peels covered in milk. "What are we looking for exactly?"

"Receipts or anything similar. Romero's phone records show nothing. And it's going to take some time for his bank statements to come out." Nick passed her a pair of latex gloves and sat on the grimy floor. "And I'm certain that he isn't using his credit card to purchase the stuff he needs for his illegal operations."

Mackenzie sneakily cleaned a little spot on the floor and then sat on it, wondering what stain it would leave on her ironed black pantsuit. The putrid pile between them mostly consisted of rotting leftovers. She was half-expecting a ripple of movement from a rat. "I'm waiting to get used to the smell."

Nick took out a cigarette, lit the end and put it on a makeshift ashtray on the floor next to him.

"That won't help the smell."

"It helps me." He rummaged in the pile again and pulled out a used condom before dropping it, horrified. "This is the worst day of my life."

"Check this out." She waved a clot of hair. "What's worse? This or the condom?"

"This." Nick picked out the winner. It was a purple-colored used condom with hair.

"Okay. I'm officially scarred for life."

Mackenzie focused on the task at hand, hoping the smell wouldn't permanently damage the inside of her nose. Being in the basement, there was no window they could open. They were trapped inside a gas chamber. The room had bright and clean white walls. It was supposed to be the new janitor's closet, but much like everything else at the Lakemore PD, there was no rush to transition.

"Why would Romero kidnap and get these women killed?" Nick asked.

"Cristane is a resourceful man. He could have hired a PI to dig into the Wildmans' past and discovered this Walsh incident on their otherwise perfect record."

The Wildmans weren't prone to controversy. They were old money, enjoying unimaginable luxuries without any desire for publicity. The disappearance of Mia Gallagher was the starting point of Baron's doom. One by one, the bricks of his carefully constructed life were falling and revealing all the gruesome secrets he had worked hard to hide.

"Why go through all this to exact revenge?"

Mackenzie shrugged. "Cristane can't be too obvious. Especially with the dirt Baron has on him. I would say Cristane found a way to go after him without rousing any suspicion."

Mackenzie found a crumpled piece of paper. Believing it to be another unpaid parking ticket, she was ready to discard it with no hope. But when she opened it, it was a receipt for laundry starch and acetone. It wasn't from a major retailer, such as Home Depot, but from a shop she had never heard of. The paper was wet with smudged ink and yellow stains. But she was able to make out the date. It was purchased just over two weeks ago. "What do you think?"

Nick inspected it and nodded. "I think I also found something."

She saw the crinkled paper with brown spots on it. It wasn't a receipt; it was a safety data sheet of a product —trichloromethane.

"That's another name for chloroform!" Mackenzie exclaimed.

"Which was used on Mia."

Sully grumbled on the phone for the hundredth time, his expression unchanged. Mackenzie looked at the little fishbowl sitting on his table. Apparently, the sergeant's new hobby was watching a goldfish blow bubbles out of its mouth.

"Are we allowed to keep a pet inside?" Nick asked.

Sully pressed a finger to his lips and hung up. "Cristane doesn't know where Romero is."

"He's lying," Mackenzie said crossly. "He's protecting Romero."

"He said Romero went out to run an errand." He waved his hand dismissively. "But now he isn't answering his phone."

Mackenzie chewed the inside of her cheek. "He's out on bail. He can't just disappear!"

Sully knocked on the fishbowl gleefully, his eyes filling with warmth like he was playing with a baby. When he looked up at them, he straightened his face and his tie. "I will take care of this. You try to find out where he bought those items from and where he's set up his operation."

"The foliage we are looking for is nowhere around Romero's house," Nick said.

"It could be around this shop." Sully's eyes narrowed and fingers interlaced. "I doubt wherever he's running this operation from is too far. It's a bitch to drive far so frequently and haul containers around."

"We have that list of places in Washington from the sheriff's department so we can check for any structures around."

"Get on it. Oh, and Mack? Good job," Sully said.

Mackenzie fled the office to go to her desk and opened Google. Her foot kept tapping and her nerves were singing. She typed the name of the hardware shop; luckily, it only had three locations in the state.

Nick leaned over her cubicle, placing a hand on her desk. "Now we cross-reference it to that soil document from the sheriff's department."

Mackenzie opened that too with the red circles marked on the PDF file. Comparing them, there was one branch of the shop which lay on the outskirts of woods with matching foliage to the report. It was right here in Lakemore.

"We found it," Mackenzie whispered, trying to get a street view of the woods, but they seemed out of luck. "We need Clint."

The next hour went by swiftly. With Sully busy with the DA's office trying to track down Romero and Nick getting the paperwork ready to charge Romero with abduction once they found Stella. Mackenzie was left alone, pacing, while Clint clacked on the keyboard and worked his magic.

"I'll look for utility bills in the area. If there's a counterfeit scam set up, they must be using electricity," he explained.

The next few minutes were agonizingly slow. Finally, they had a solid lead that could lead them to a place, not a person who would just stonewall them. Mackenzie had been brimming with anticipation, heart racing, when Clint arched his neck above the monitor.

"I think I found it. I'm sending you the coordinates. There is a property there registered to some company called Aztra Inc."

FORTY-EIGHT

Mackenzie and Nick had to wade through the thickets and bushes. Trees stood too close, tall stick figures without leaves, guardians of the woods, watching the choppy terrain speckled with dips and bumps. Autumn leaves and pine needles carpeted the ground. Her hands grazed the blistered barks of trees, while Nick guided them towards their destination. The sky above carried a tinge of green, almost emerald. A storm was coming, or at least passing over.

"Did Sully locate Romero?" Mackenzie asked, climbing over a toppled tree.

"They tracked his phone, but he left it at home." Nick paused, deciding which direction to venture into. "This way."

The trees eventually thinned into a clearing. They had been climbing uphill and now Mackenzie batted away a branch blocking her view and hitched her breath at the red cabin that came into view further up the slope. The clearing was wild, with tall yellow grass gathered around the cabin, hemming it in. Near it was a pond in a slight depression of the ground. Tiers of rocks, brown and glistening, surrounded it. Clouds overhead were gliding and, for a moment, the house and its reflection in the water were stark, but the trees surrounding it were hazy in green mist. It looked like a dark fairy tale.

"What's Aztra Inc?" Nick asked. "Some company belonging to Cristane?"

"I think so. Justin is running it, but I wanted to get here first." She checked her gun strapped to the holster. "The shop where Romero purchased the chemicals from is just a mile from the edge of these woods."

He nodded. "No footprints."

"On this side."

They inched closer to the cabin. A jarring presence in the middle of the forest. There were no visible hiking trails fanning out of here. Getting a closer look at the muddy water in the pond, Mackenzie doubted anything was alive inside.

Reaching the red door with peeling paint, she gave it a firm knock. "Lakemore PD! Open up!"

Silence.

It was too quiet. No wind. No birds. Just this ominous clearing carved into the earth out of nowhere.

Nick shoved his shoulder into the door. It broke open without a fight. Inside was roaring black. Mackenzie stared into the darkness, looking for any changes in the pattern. But it was thick and emanating something she couldn't put a finger on. Her hand blindly searched for any switches, but there was nothing. They used the flashlights on their phones. A sweep of light showed a long, narrow room with rusty walls. The windows had been boarded up to keep the light out.

"Is anyone here?" Mackenzie shouted. Her voice bounced back to her. They trod carefully in the darkness, the treacherous cabin looking for ways to maim them. Her foot bumped into something, making her jump, only for it to be another container.

"I see bleach, starch, spray paint, some other word I don't want to pronounce," Nick recited.

"They all match what we found under Veronica's shoes." Mackenzie focused hard. "Oh, there's carbon tetrachloride."

"And the printer." It sat at the other end of the room.

"I don't see any bills. He probably moved them already."

There was another door on their right. Mackenzie opened it with a creak. More darkness. She shivered, suddenly feeling cold. The fading light from outside had died. She was never afraid of the dark, but no one could feel comfortable in this level of opaqueness. It was against human nature, against evolution to be unable to spot prey and predator. The only reason her knees didn't buckle was because she felt Nick behind her.

She hazarded a step and then another. The light from her phone showed an empty washroom with cracked sink, spotty mirror, and a toilet. There was a bathtub behind a shower curtain.

"I got a bad feeling," Nick blurted.

With a stiff hand, Mackenzie ripped open the shower curtain.

Stella DeRossi lay in the bathtub. Her was body contorted to fit in, wearing the same clothes as the day she had disappeared. Her skin was matted with dirt, her hair greasy.

"Oh my God." Mackenzie kneeled to check her pulse. When the light was too close to her face, her eyelids fluttered. "She's alive."

"Damn it. I got no reception," Nick cursed.

"Stella? Can you hear me? I'm from the Lakemore PD."

Stella's gaze was hazy and neck lolling, but her eyes soon became sharp. Like she was waking up from a slumber. Her breathing turned erratic.

"It's okay. Stay calm. We'll help you out of here."

She was only skin and bones, but she managed to grip Mackenzie's hand.

Stella's voice was hoarse. "Behind you."

FORTY-NINE

Mackenzie's heart climbed up her throat and stayed there, making it difficult to breathe.

And then everything happened in a flash.

A gun went off, loud and booming, making the entire structure shake.

Someone screamed. It was Mackenzie herself.

She ducked on instinct, covering Stella with her body. Her phone left her grip and fell into the darkness on the floor.

Another loud pop. A resounding sound that made her ears ring. Someone grunted—male and ferocious.

"Nick!" she cried. Her hand went to her Glock, pulling it out, but where should she aim? There were two enemies: the unknown assailant and the darkness. They were shrouded in darkness so thick that she felt it pressed against her skin.

Something clanged and clattered; a door opened and closed; furniture toppled. Next thing, Mackenzie felt Nick knocking into her shoulder as he sprinted past her.

"Nick!" she yelled after him. But all she heard were footsteps running away. He must have gone after whoever had attacked them.

Mackenzie's breath was sharp and loud in her ears as she fumbled under the tub, looking for the phone she had dropped in the mayhem. She turned on the light and glanced over at Stella, making sure no bullet had struck her.

"Stella? Can you hear me?"

Stella gave a feeble nod.

"Okay, we need to get you out of here." Mackenzie's mind spun and stretched in all directions. Where was Nick? Who had shot at them?

Gently, she helped Stella out of the tub, draping her arm over her shoulders to carry her weight. An awful feeling bloomed inside Mackenzie as she guided Stella out of the room using the light from her phone. Her breath stuck in her throat when she saw fresh blood on the floor by the door. Whose was it? Was Nick hit?

"Jo-Jonathan," Stella's hot breath was in her ear.

"Yes. He's fine. He's waiting for you." Mackenzie reached the front door and swung it open. The sun was setting, the blazing light dipping away and giving way to softer hues of golden and red. It looked like the color of blood.

She decided to call for backup, but the screen was frozen. A crack ran through the middle of it. "Damn it." She wiped the sweat beading on her brow, scanning the darkening woods for Nick.

Stella was fading in her arms. Mackenzie set her on the ground, resting her back against the cabin wall.

"W-water."

Mackenzie rushed back inside the cabin, not wanting to leave Stella alone for long. The light from her phone was still on, guiding her to the washroom. There was a dirty glass on a cracked sink. The thought of how many infections Stella must have caught here floated through her mind as she filled it with water. Her brain was too frazzled to formulate a plan. She couldn't leave Stella alone, not when she didn't know how many accomplices the person who had shot at them had, not when she hadn't had a chance to contact anyone back at the station. Going over her options, she carried the glass outside to Stella and stopped dead in her tracks.

Stella wasn't where Mackenzie had left her.

Twigs crunched behind her. A whimper singed the air. Mackenzie dropped the glass; her hand went to her Glock as she spun around.

Her stomach turned somersaults.

Romero held a gun to Stella's head. "I'll blow her brains out. Lose the gun."

Mackenzie licked her lips and considered her options. But when Romero pressed the barrel into Stella's temple, she slowly placed the gun by her feet and kicked it away.

She could taste the fragility of this moment. Those dreaded seconds before the vase, diving down, finally crashes into the ground.

"Romero, you're out on bail," Mackenzie reminded him firmly. "There are people looking for you. You're only making things worse for yourself."

"Shut up!" he growled. There was an open gash on his forehead. His face was smeared in fresh blood.

Where was Nick?

"Please," Stella sobbed uncontrollably. "Please don't hurt me. I can't—"

"Shut up! Let me think!" Romero tightened his hold around her ribs.

"Why don't you leave Stella alone?" Mackenzie said.

"I need the police to stay out of my business. Looks like this one will be stuck with me while I make my way out of here."

Mackenzie made a quick study of the jittery man in front of her. He blinked rapidly and shuffled on his feet a lot, perhaps still reeling from his head injury. But he lacked focus and precision. He was acting purely on his spirit to fight. She knew to take advantage of her surroundings because he wasn't paying attention. But it was getting darker.

As she inched closer, a loosely hanging sconce on the wall of the cabin caught her attention. It was drooping low, right over Romero's head.

"Where is Detective Blackwood, Romero?" she asked.

"I don't fucking know. Stay back!"

She made a show of cowering against the cabin. There was a shovel against it. The walls were flimsy. A loose enough structure that had vibrated when it had rained bullets inside. All she had to do was take the shovel and whack it against the sconce, making it fall.

"Her name is Stella DeRossi," she continued. "She has a husband waiting at home for her. You must have seen the news."

"Save your psychobabble, lady." He waved the hand holding the gun in the air.

Just the tiny window Mackenzie needed. She picked up the shovel and swung it high, over the sconce, severing its loose connection. The sconce fell on Romero. The gun went off in the air.

"Fuck!" he bellowed; his grip on Stella loosened enough for her to fall on the ground and crawl away.

Romero was on his knees, clutching his head when Mackenzie swung the shovel against his arm. The gun fell out of his hands. He scrambled to get it back, but she whacked him with the shovel again. Mackenzie went for the gun, but his hand wrapped around her ankle. He pulled her to the ground, knocking her down on her ass. They wrestled for the shovel. He was injured, but he was much stronger. A burly man. A street fighter. A goon hired by Walter Cristane.

He rolled on top of her, digging his leg into her knee at an angle that made a scream rip out of her throat. His furious face was inches above hers. The shovel was lodged between them. He moved it further up, to press it against her throat.

Mackenzie could smell his dank breath. She felt the wet mud against the back of her neck. She felt the cool shovel sinking into her throat, making her eyes bulge. A manic look clouded Romero's eyes.

It was then that she used her other leg to kick him between the legs.

"Ah!" His face twisted in pain.

She slammed him in the nose with her elbow, his weight finally off her. She grabbed the shovel and stood up, while he rolled on the floor grabbing his junk, his nose at an unnatural angle.

Mackenzie limped toward Stella. Her knee was sore and heavy. Pain shot up in hot strings every time she put her weight on it.

"Mack!" Nick emerged from the trees.

"Nick!" she sighed. "Thank God. Were you shot?"

"No, I think I dislocated my shoulder when I ducked." He shook his head. "I lost him. Took me a while to find my way back. Heard a gunshot. Are you okay?"

"Yeah." She scowled at her leg. "I hurt my knee. My phone isn't working. We need backup."

Nick nodded, panting and took out his phone from his back pocket. "Where is he?"

"What?" She followed his eyes over her shoulder.

Romero was no longer there. And neither was the gun he had dropped. But the trees behind swayed like someone had just gone through them.

"Shit!" Mackenzie cried. "I didn't..."

"Call for backup. I got some bars now. I'll go after him," Nick instructed.

"But you're hurt. I'll go—"

"You can't even walk without limping. It's just my arm. I'll be fine." His dark eyes looked brighter than ever. For some reason, that scared the hell out of her.

And then he was gone.

Mackenzie swallowed the tears in the base of her throat and called for help. She related her badge number and gave her location. Luckily, Stella didn't have any external injuries. Her ordeal was purely from a muddled brain due to drugs.

Mackenzie waited in agony. Was Nick able to catch Romero? She stayed on the line, while uniform was dispatched to the woods along with the sheriff's deputies. But it would take them a while to find the cabin.

The silence was blaring. The birds stopped singing long ago. And now there was no light in the sky. Just a shroud of darkness over this wretched place.

But then a gun was fired somewhere in the woods. Mackenzie handed the phone to Stella, instructing the operator to stay on the line.

"Nick!" she screeched, her voice cracking.

And off Mackenzie went into the belly of the woods.

FIFTY

Mackenzie didn't know how she got there. She didn't even know exactly where she was. She had just run. But she knew what she saw. She saw a man lying on his stomach. He was too still. Was he alive?

Next thing she knew, she was on her knees. She was crying. She was praying. She was reduced to a new level of desperation. With a shaking hand, she reached out to find out who it was.

A hand came on her shoulder. Mackenzie's hand went to her gun. She turned around.

"Mack."

"Nick." Her eyes widened. "Oh, thank God." She released a breath she wasn't holding. Relief flooded her so hard that she fell on her ass. "Damn you."

"What did I do?" He looked confused.

"What happened?"

"He was about to take a shot at me, but I got there first. I'll go back to Stella. One of us should stay here with him." When Mackenzie began standing up, he rolled his eyes. "I'll go. Of all the times for you to injure your leg. Jesus."

Mackenzie was catching her breath and checking Romero's

vitals when a beacon of light swept in arcs around her. "Over here!"

Justin led the pack of rescuers. "Ma'am!"

"I'm fine." She hitched her thumb over her shoulder. "Nick is with Stella."

Justin hesitated, but when Mackenzie glared at him, he headed to the cabin. The deputies helped Mackenzie up and carried Romero, who still had a faint pulse. At the edge of the woods, a swarm of squad cars, ambulances and the crime scene unit van were parked.

"The cavalry's here," she muttered as she was helped into an ambulance by uniform. Anthony was grumbling about having to venture into the woods to get to the crime scene. When he spotted Mackenzie, he gave her a dismissive wave. Soon, Nick and Stella were escorted out and surrounded by paramedics. The ambulance carrying Romero had already taken off.

"Think he'll make it?" Mackenzie asked Justin, who gave her water.

"He better. He has some questions to answer about that cabin."

"What do you mean?"

"It's owned by Aztra Inc," Justin informed. "We tracked down the parent company. It belongs to the Wildmans."

"But Romero doesn't work for the Wildmans."

"Or so we thought."

Sirens rang and splashed color in the dark night. A paramedic came to Mackenzie's aid to check on her leg. But she was too absorbed by the thought of who Romero was exactly working for.

Back at the station, Mackenzie held an ice pack to her knee. After being subjected to X-rays and CT scans, she was finally given a clean chit that she had no broken bones or torn ligaments, just some swelling that would die down in a few hours. She limped to her desk and perched on it, sighing in relief, waiting for the stiffness that had left her leg woody to melt away.

"You found Stella?" Austin came up to her urgently.

"Yeah." Her throat was dry and tongue sticky. "She's at the hospital. Her husband's also there."

He sighed. "Thank God." His worried eyes raked all over her. "There was chatter that someone got shot?"

"No. Just Nick dislocated his shoulder."

The events of the last few hours had left her numb and wrung out. She tasted blood and earth and grit. Her frayed appearance was a glimpse into what she had been through.

"Don't you want to go home and take a shower?" Austin asked.

"I got called in by the boss. How are things with you and Rivera?"

He shrugged, his lips twisting in a frown. "Still walking the tightrope. I hope things aren't awkward for you. Hate for you to get into trouble because of me."

Sully emerged from his office. "Mack!"

"Don't worry about it," Mackenzie assured Austin, leaving him standing again.

The sight of him always filled her with a strange turmoil. She threw him a glance over her shoulder. He stood in solitude by his desk. A man trying to cut the strings of his past that still held him. It was a place where Mackenzie had been stuck in for years. But did finding closure really help her? Her heart sank, realizing she was still unhappy. Her fingers touched Robert's watch.

"Romero didn't make it." Sully crossed his arms.

She dropped her head back and threaded her red hair. "Shit."

"Justin's at the scene with the CSI. He said there's no red envelopes there."

"What about at his apartment?"

"Nope," he said flatly.

"Well, that doesn't mean anything. He could be keeping that stuff anywhere."

"Cristane is heading back to Lakemore. Baron will be in tomorrow. I highly doubt Romero was the mastermind." He went back to his office and began packing his things, stifling a yawn. "Did you see that brutish man? No way he's got a brain in there."

"I'll take Stella's statement at the hospital."

"Weren't you just there?" He picked up the fishbowl. Through the glass, his mouth was magnified, and Mackenzie noticed the breadcrumbs lodged in his bushy mustache.

"I was at Lakemore General." She cleared her throat. "They took her to the hospital in Olympia."

"Get there." Sully put on his coat. "If Romero was just the hired help, that means he's replaceable. With the person orchestrating this still out there, this might not end with Stella."

Mackenzie had lost track of time when she finally reached the hospital where Stella was being treated. She tightened her hold on the steering wheel, thinking of Romero dying in those woods following the frenzy that had left her nerves raw. Romero didn't have any personal connection with the victims that they knew of. If he were hired by someone, then they could easily hire someone else. Especially wealthy people like Cristane and the Wildmans, who had plenty of resources. When was this going to stop?

She entered the hospital and was directed to the room by one of the administrators. She passed by a young couple sitting on chairs. The woman was pregnant, ready to pop out a baby anytime. The husband pressed a kiss on her wedding ring and rubbed her belly. Both were beaming and bursting with joy and nervousness. A blush spread on the woman's face that was glistening with sweat. Her contractions were starting, but Mackenzie hadn't seen anyone look happier.

A sob caught in her throat. She rushed past them quickly toward Stella.

A hot spurt of shame conquered her when she found Stella and Jonathan. Here she was coveting more when Stella was just happy to be alive.

Stella was sitting on a bed wearing a hospital gown. Jonathan sat on a stool, his large hands enveloping hers, his eyes teary. Two uniforms hovered close, nodding at Mackenzie.

"Stella? How are you doing?"

Stella smiled weakly. She didn't have any bruises, but her face was gaunt, and her bones had sharp edges under her pale skin. "I'll be fine now that I'm home."

"You're never leaving my sight ever again." Jonathan kissed her hand.

"I was wondering if you could answer some questions?"

"Seriously?" He frowned. "My wife has been through a lot. We haven't been home yet. She needs to eat and have a good night's sleep at least."

"I completely agree." Mackenzie raised her hands. "This is not an interview. It's just that sometimes some memories or information become blurry the longer the victims spend time away from where they were being held. So we try to have a quick conversation as soon as possible."

Jonathan opened his mouth to argue, but Stella interjected. "It's all right, Detective Price. You and your partner saved my life."

"Do you remember anything from the time of your abduction?"

Stella shook her head, a shiver running through her. "I was

running one minute in the woods and the next I woke up in that tub."

"You never talked to the man who took you?"

"No. Never. I barely remember my time there." Stella's voice grew soft. "There was food every now and then. I don't know... I had no idea who he was."

"It's okay. Based on your bloodwork, it looks like Romero kept you on chloroform throughout. Probably slipped it into your system through the food."

"Romero?" Stella made a face.

"Yes. The man today? His name is Romero."

Her eyes flitted, like she was doing a calculation in her head. She pulled her hand away from Jonathan and tucked her hair behind her ear. "He wasn't the one who held me there."

Mackenzie froze. "Excuse me?"

"It wasn't him," she insisted.

"How do you know that?"

"Because Romero has a distinct Texan accent."

"But you just said that you never talked to or saw your abductor," Mackenzie countered.

Stella pinned her with a hard look. "I never did. But one time I heard him talking. Maybe to someone else, or on the phone. It was a man's voice, and he definitely didn't have a Texan accent."

"Did you hear what he said? Any name? Any place?"

"It was something general. Nothing in particular. I was just passing out when I heard him through the wall," Stella pled with a firm resolve. "But I'm one hundred percent sure that he sounded nothing like Romero."

Mackenzie tapped a pen against her pocket diary. Romero had an accomplice who was still at large. The game was far from over.

FIFTY-ONE
OCTOBER 25

When the morning light spilled in the room, Mackenzie was already awake. The bed was comfortable. The temperature set to her liking. But as her eyes drilled into the ceiling above, hollowness expanded inside her. She woke up feeling like someone had scooped out a piece of her chest. She forced herself to get up and pressed her palms into her splotchy, bloated face. Dragging herself to the bathroom, she analyzed her reflection. Her faint bruises and cuts from yesterday were eclipsed by her eyes. Her red, dull, terrified eyes.

She turned on the faucet and splashed cold water on her face over and over and over again. Until this wretched emptiness left her. Until tears didn't prick her eyes. Until her chest didn't feel like it was brimming with icicles. When her skin was raw, she stopped. But those feelings hadn't ebbed.

Even touching the watch didn't help. Her talisman that reminded her that there was a time when she was loved. A time when she had a normal family. A time when numbness wasn't a constant companion.

Mackenzie didn't know what she was thinking. The razor-sharp focus came out of nowhere and then she was out the door in her pajamas, racing in her car to Hidden Lake. As if the solution lay there.

She reached her destination and got out of the car. She was burning hot inside, the cold a long-forgotten sensation. Her damp hair stuck to her forehead. It was early in the morning. And this area wasn't popular with the morning runners. The sun might have been rising, but the place was shadowed by a cloud, as dark and cryptic as the time before. The mist rising above the lake. The barren trees looking charred, like there was a forest fire.

Mackenzie took off her shoes and dipped her foot in. It was cold. But today it didn't sting her as much. It was almost comforting. As she walked into the lake, water gathered around her almost lovingly, like it was taking care of her. She smiled, ready to take a swim, still in her pajamas. She did a few strokes, going further in, but not too much. The lake was vast and got deeper. She stopped and floated, the water just under her chin. It was ice-cold, rattling her bones. But in an invigorating way. She bobbed in the water for a while, finally not running away or denying her past, but basking in it, looking at the woods that took so much from her, without any fear and bitterness. It was almost like she was washing away something hardened and calcified inside her.

She sucked in a sharp breath and ducked under the water. She could hold her breath for an impressive amount of time. Few bubbles escaped her lips. She twirled underwater, her red hair like strands of fire dragging in the current, her skin glistening, looking whiter and sparkly. She looked to the surface and saw herself.

It made her pause.

A young Mackenzie, only twelve years old, swimming in the water, giggling. It wasn't a memory. She had never swum here before. She definitely didn't laugh like that when she was twelve.

It was a fantasy. Because she saw Robert swimming with her, showing her how to do butterfly strokes, keeping a close eye on her. The little Mackenzie laughed and danced freely, splashing water around. It was the life she could have had. It was the life she was denied.

Mackenzie raised her hand to touch the fantasy, to be a part of that happiness, when someone jerked on her other arm, dragging her back up. As she was pulled away, her vision dissolved in the currents. When she broke the surface, she took in a huge gulp of air. Her lungs had been starving for it and she hadn't even realized.

"What the hell?" she screamed at the arm pulling her toward the shore.

It was Nick. He was in his shirt and pants, a sling on his arm and soaking wet from head to toe.

"Nick!" She wrenched her arm away when they were on the shore again. "What are you doing?"

He turned around, water dripping from his hair, eyelashes and nose. "What am I doing?" he hollered, his voice bouncing. "What the fuck were you doing?"

She hadn't seen this kind of rage emanating from him before. He didn't frighten her, but for the first time he intimidated her. Breathing hard, he towered over her, his broad frame engulfing her.

"How are you here?" She rubbed her eyes.

"You didn't answer me."

"I came out for a swim."

He blinked in disbelief. "In your pajamas? And what kind of swimming involves you being underwater?"

"It was an impromptu decision," she said honestly. "And I can hold my breath for a very long time."

He scoffed, turning away from her again. "I can't even." He narrowed his eyes. "Mack, were you trying to kill yourself?"

"No! Of course, not!"

"Then what the fuck was that?" he shouted with panic and anger in his eyes. "What were you doing? And I don't buy your 'impromptu' excuse. I've known you for almost a decade. That's not you."

A breeze brushed past them, causing Mackenzie to shiver. She wrapped her arms around herself, her back teeth chattering.

Nick scowled and gestured her to get in the car. "You'll catch a cold."

She followed him, like she was a child being scolded. "I really was fine, Nick. It isn't a big deal."

He slammed his fist on the hood of the car. "The hell it was. If you actually believe that this was nothing, then you're lying to yourself."

Mackenzie was rooted to the spot on the ground. Did she need help? She had had no intention to end her life. But something was missing inside her, like an organ. Like her heart had grown heavy and lungs weaker.

Nick was opening the door when he stopped. "Mack?"

"I just... wanted to feel different," she confessed.

"Different?"

"More." She scoffed at her stupidity. "I wanted to feel more. God, I sound dramatic, so let's just forget any of this happened."

"Help me understand," he begged.

She hesitated.

He'd swum with one arm in a sling to get to her, thinking she needed help. The temptation to unload won out. "I feel nothing. I don't know why. And, frankly, having nothing beyond this job in my life is... lonely."

"Look, you've gone through some seriously messed-up shit in the past—"

"But I was fine all summer. I dealt with it!"

"What if you didn't? You've spent your whole life suppressing. Maybe you did that again." His face softened. "Maybe you need to talk to someone. Like a professional—"

She felt blood rush to her face. "Absolutely not."

"Why are you so stubborn? It's not a sign of weakness—"

"I know, it isn't. It's just not for me. Please accept that." She wiped her face, trying to compose herself and bring her mask back. Her outbursts irked her. "Anyway, how did you find me?"

"I was driving to work and saw your car parked on the side. I waited, but then realized you were nowhere to be seen and had a bad feeling."

"You don't take this route."

He shrugged. "I don't know. I just did today."

"Why?"

"There was an accident on my normal route, and I was too impatient to wait." He was still annoyed. "Guess you got lucky."

Mackenzie climbed back in the car, the hot air blasting in her rigid face. Her phone rang. "Detective Price."

"Ma'am," Justin said in his robotic tone. "The CSI found that sweatshirt we saw on the security tape at Lakemore Gardens at Romero's cabin."

"Good work."

"That A on the sweatshirt? It was actually capital alpha. Alpha Sigma Phi is written across in gold."

Her mind ticked over his words. "A frat? Did Romero even go to college? I don't remember from his background check."

"He didn't," Justin replied. "But I was going over everyone's statements and caught something. Bobby Wildman was part of that frat when he was at UW."

Mackenzie's eyes spelled surprise. "Bobby Wildman."

FIFTY-TWO

To Mackenzie's mortification, they had driven straight to the station without giving her a chance to change. When she arrived at the office, her fellow detectives gazed at her from their desks, frozen and stunned. Jenna reined in her laughter. A pen slipped from between Ned's lips. Austin went still, the handset almost slipping from his grip. Mad Mack never showed up without her makeup, hair straight as an arrow, and wrinkle-free pantsuit. They all looked at the spectacle, at the woman behind the glamor.

Troy waggled his eyebrows, swaying on his chair. "Did Mom and Dad go for a swim?"

"She drove the car into a lake," Nick announced.

Mackenzie's mouth hung open, while everyone chuckled and went back to work. Nick gave her a wink.

"Sure, you did." Troy didn't believe a word but didn't press them.

Nick opened a gym bag he kept under his desk and handed Mackenzie a dry hoodie. "It's clean. I keep a spare on me. I'll just wear my old gym clothes."

She sniffed it when he left to change. If something didn't

smell like laundry detergent, she didn't wear it. The hoodie passed the test and she slipped it around her after drying off in the restroom.

"Bobby's here," Sully announced and glared at Mackenzie. "Do I need to know?"

"Nope."

The good thing about Sully was that he liked keeping to himself. His bandwidth could only accommodate cases and hobbies, which was currently a goldfish. "Wrap this up, will you?" he grumbled irritably. "He's in the conference room."

"Why isn't he in the interrogation room? He's a suspect, not a person of interest," Mackenzie asked as Nick returned.

"Because he's Bobby Wildman. Ask Murphy." Sully rolled his eyes and ambled away.

Mackenzie snorted. "You've got to be kidding me."

Nick's jaw was locked tight as he gathered his notes. Together, they headed to the conference room, where Bobby was in a frantic conversation with Captain Murphy who seemed to be placating him.

Mackenzie whipped the door open, not hiding her disdain for Murphy. "Mr. Wildman, let's head to the interrogation room."

Bobby fidgeted, but it was Captain Murphy who jerked his head to pull Mackenzie and Nick back outside. "Detective Price, you can talk to the man here."

"He's a suspect in a murder investigation." She spelled it out for him like he was a child. "Are you telling me to break protocol because he was born with a silver spoon in his mouth?"

He fisted his hands and gritted his teeth. "Our town cannot afford to lose more business."

She opened her mouth to reply, but Nick pitched in. "All right. We'll take it from here."

Murphy nodded, throwing Mackenzie a look of scorn before leaving.

"Thanks for having my back," she hissed to him.

"Murphy can't stop his arrest, Mack." He tipped his chin at Bobby who sat alone. "And he showed up without a lawyer."

"Why?"

"I don't know. Arrogance? All right, let's go in."

When Mackenzie stepped back in the room, Bobby's nervous eyes found hers. For the first time, she saw palpable fear. His clammy palms rubbed together. He kept cracking his knuckles. His cheeks were sunken. All the obscene sense of humor and naughty glint in his eyes vanished.

"You're here without a lawyer?" Mackenzie asked.

"My brother couldn't afford to spare me one." His mouth flattened. "What is this about?"

She opened the file and showed him a picture of the hoodie found in the cabin. It had been stuffed in a corner, covered in dust and cobwebs. But the letters in gold stood out boorishly.

Bobby's eye twitched. "I don't recognize this."

"Really, Bobby?" Nick sighed, showing him another picture from one year ago. Bobby had been wearing the same hoodie at a reunion party with his fraternity brothers.

A shudder raked through him. He leaned away, crossing his arms. "That hoodie could belong to anyone. A lot of people have it."

"Which is why we're testing it right now for your DNA. There are some hair fibers on it. Do you want to come clean now or wait for us to get the call?"

Bobby let out a hysterical laugh. It was almost birdlike. "This is insane! You can't take my DNA without my consent. And I'm not under arrest."

"We have your DNA on file," Mackenzie said. "From the time that you were arrested for a white-collar crime."

"And since you claim you are innocent, why don't you tell us where you were during the time Stella, Mia, and Veronica were abducted?" Nick asked. "I'm sure you'd have a strong alibi."

Bobby ran a hand through his hair; there was sweat patch in his underarm. "I'm sure I do, but I don't remember off the top of my head."

"We actually checked." Mackenzie pulled out the statements Justin had collected. "You were supposed to attend a bachelor party the night Mia was taken, but you never showed. And that hooker you had booked for when Veronica was abducted said that you paid her but didn't come to the hotel."

"We're in the process of checking your alibi during Stella's abduction." Nick smiled mirthlessly.

"There are just coincidences." Bobby's face paled. "Why would I hurt them?"

"You can tell us now or we can wait until we get DNA confirmation from the hoodie and arrest you," Mackenzie warned.

Taking loud breaths, Bobby finally said, "I did it."

"What?" she blurted.

"I... I took Mia Gallagher, Veronica Fang, and Stella DeRossi." He blabbered too fast. "I sent those letters. I left the girls for them to... kill."

Mackenzie was flustered at his eager confession. "Why?"

"Have you seen how my brother treats me? I've been hauled in for questioning and he couldn't even bother to send me one of his many, many, *many* lawyers."

Mackenzie and Nick looked at each other. She scrutinized him closely. Bobby's frantic eyes bounced between them.

"Um, what was Romero's role?" Nick drummed his fingers on the table.

"Romero and I have known each other for years. We ran that check-washing scam together all those years ago," he explained casually. "Baron was able to save me, but Romero ended up doing some prison time. I felt like I owed him."

"So you let him use your cabin for counterfeiting?"

"It was just sitting there, collecting dust, in the middle of nowhere. I wanted it to be a hunting cabin, but my brother decided to not blow his money to renovate it." His thin lips pressed in a line. "I'm forty years old and still have to ask my brother for money, despite having a stake in the company."

"Did Romero help you abduct them?" Mackenzie asked.

Bobby shook his head. "All he did was supply with me with the taser guns. When I was following Mia, I found out about Wren Murray and his side hustle. Romero was looking for a supplier, so I pointed him in this direction and asked for some Tasers. Beyond that, believe it or not, Romero didn't want anything to do with it. But I had no other place to keep the girls. I told him if we wanted to continue using my cabin, then to keep his mouth shut. You scratch my back, I'll scratch yours."

"All this to torture your brother?" Nick's eyebrows shot up. "I know there's some sibling rivalry but—"

"Come on, Nick. You know what he's always been like." He leaned back, malice dripping from his voice. "Condescending and arrogant. Always making me feel like I'm nothing without him."

"He has saved your ass so many times—"

"Not because he loves me. He's a megalomaniac," he bit out. "He always wants to be the bigger person in any room. Remind me of the favors he's done. How I should always be indebted to him? Screw him."

"Of all the ways to torture him... why this *game*?" Mackenzie asked.

Bobby looked unsure for a moment before resolve tightened his features. "I didn't want to get my hands dirty. I figured the chances of me getting caught would be less if I involved more people. The clues would lead you in all directions."

Mackenzie sighed impatiently. "But the people you targeted

can be tied to what happened with Hayley. That implicates you too."

His smile was self-deprecating. "That wouldn't make me a good suspect, would it? But I suppose you figured it out either way. Was it Romero? Is that how you found out?"

She didn't answer his question and instead displayed pictures of Mia Gallagher and Veronica Fang, and he couldn't stomach the view. "Is there anything else you want to tell us, Mr. Wildman?"

Bobby opened his mouth as if to say something, but then changed his mind and shook his head stiffly. "Nope. This was me. I *am* sorry. I... Never mind."

"Come with me." Nick stood up. "We have to take your official statement."

Bobby followed Nick out, with tense shoulders and raggedy breaths. Mackenzie watched them go, alarm bells ringing in her head. She couldn't place a finger on it, but something was very wrong.

FIFTY-THREE

"Prominent tycoon Walter Cristane has been in the news lately for all the wrong reasons," Debbie announced to her viewers. *"It was only recently we reported that relations between Cristane and Mayor Rathbone were strained and now an FBI investigation into Cristane has led to multiple arrests within his company."* The screen switched to a blurry image of Walter Cristane climbing out of his car and being escorted into a glass building. Cameras flashed in his face. Microphones were thrust closer to his mouth. His private security flicked hands away, while Cristane sulked behind his sunglasses and hurried inside the building. *"Our sources indicate that the FBI has been looking into wildlife smuggling, the penalty for which—"*

Mackenzie slammed her laptop shut, unwilling to listen to more. Nick was still taking Bobby's final confession and getting him to sign the papers. But something didn't sit well with her. Wincing at her wet hair from the lake, she made her way to the restroom, only to freeze at her reflection.

She didn't recognize herself. Her uneven pale skin and a spatter of freckles on the nose. Her eyes looked baggy and smaller without the mascara. It had been a while since she had allowed to see herself like this. Exposed. Raw. Vulnerable.

She touched her face lightly, wondering what woman she was becoming, if there was another version of her hidden all this while, just waiting to come out.

"Don't cry, Mommy," Mackenzie said to a whimpering Melody, who lay on the bed with an arm over her face. Tears rolled down the sides of her face, wetting the pillowcase.

"I'll be okay in a bit, honey. Just give me a minute, okay?"

Mackenzie rested her chin on Melody's knees, wanting to go out and play. "When will you be okay?"

Melody removed her arm. Her red eyes settled on Mackenzie, and despite the pain they held, a smile broke across her face. "As long as I have you, I'll be okay."

Her ringing phone pulled her out of her stupor.

"Hello?"

"Mackenzie?" a deep voice said on the line. Mackenzie recognized the voice belonging to her Uncle Damien.

"Oh, hi." She wiped her tears. "How was your trip? Hawaii was it?"

"It was great. I'll tell you all about it. Do you want to come over next weekend for dinner?"

"I'll get back to you on that? There's this case..." She trailed off.

"Oh, of course. Let me know."

He clearly didn't think much of it. And soon they hung up. Deciding her problems were too difficult to ponder over, her mind wandered to Bobby's eager confession. She patted her hair dry as Bobby's words percolated.

Would Bobby go to such extreme lengths to punish his brother? And why did he confess so eagerly? For someone who had weaved a web to not get his hands dirty, he didn't even deny it once. He even showed up without a lawyer, as if he wanted to surrender.

When she returned to her desk, she found Lieutenant Rivera looking at Mackenzie's disorganized workspace with her hand resting over the edge of the cubicle wall. "I have never seen your desk so messy," she commented and then stopped, eyeing her. "Or you."

Mackenzie looked down at her bedraggled state, Nick's sweatshirt dwarfing her frame. "Had a bit of an accident. What's up?"

Rivera jerked her head to a room. "I heard Bobby's confessed to the whole thing. What does your gut tell you?"

"That something's amiss. He put so much planning into this and then he confesses so easily?"

"I agree. Talk to Stella. She has a connection with Bobby," she instructed.

"You think Stella might know something?"

"It all boils down to the Hayley Walsh case," Rivera said, matter-of-fact. "But do change before you go see her, detective."

Mackenzie blushed furiously and picked up her keys.

An hour later, Mackenzie climbed out of her car, feeling more comfortable in her skin. She had taken Rivera's advice and gone home to change and take a shower to wash away the lake water. Combing her hair and covering her face, her spine automatically straightened, and her strides felt more confident.

Jonathan DeRossi opened the door, sighing deeply. "Like I told you before, I'm grateful you got her back. But we need a break from the police. She needs some space to heal."

"Let her in, babe." Stella's voice filtered from inside.

With a clenched jaw, Jonathan moved aside, letting Mackenzie in. The house looked cleaner now, with no dirty dishes piling in the sink or clothes lying around. It lacked staleness; a light perfume infused in the air. Stella was curled on a couch with her feet underneath her. A blanket was wrapped around her, and her hands nursed a steaming cup of coffee and a fruit tray on her lap. Despite looking shockingly frail with tired eyes and a purple bruise marring her neck, there was color in her cheeks and sparkle in her eyes.

"How are you feeling?" Mackenzie asked, taking a seat.

"I'm home." Stella's chest deflated. "Thanks to you." Jonathan came from the kitchen with freshly cut fruit and took away her cup. "And thanks to my husband, who is on a mission to make sure I heal quickly."

"I just needed to ask a few follow-up questions. Before that, you should know that Bobby Wildman has confessed to your abduction."

Stella froze; her lips parted. "W-what?" she stammered.

"Stella? Who's Bobby Wildman?"

Mackenzie watched Stella process closely. Her twitchy fingers lingered over her lips. Her eyes clouded with a memory of the past. "I... Why?"

"You weren't the only victim, Stella," Mackenzie explained. "Two other women were abducted before you and were killed."

"But who is this guy?" Jonathan pressed.

Stella held his hand. "H-he went to university with me. But I hadn't spoken to him in almost twenty years."

"What happened with Hayley?" Mackenzie asked point-blank. "Do you know anything?"

A ripple went over Stella's body at the mention of Hayley's name. The peace in her eyes from finally being home was displaced. Her forehead bunched, and she put down the fruit tray and the blanket. "I'm so sorry for what happened. I swear... I... God, I'm horrible. That's why this happened to me."

"You're scaring me." Jonathan's gaze pierced into hers.

Stella hesitated to meet his eyes, her face turning red. "You have to understand, Detective Price. My father was sick. He had cancer. The hospital bills were piling up. And I wasn't on a full scholarship. My life was falling *apart*. I couldn't even afford residence after that semester."

"That's why you accepted money from the Wildmans after Hayley disappeared?"

"It wasn't greed!" she pleaded. "It was desperation. And I felt horrible."

"Why did the Wildmans pay you off?"

Stella took a shuddering breath and cleared her hair away from her face. "I saw Bobby and Baron that night."

Mackenzie couldn't hide her surprise. "Baron?"

She nodded. "I saw them in a car outside my dorm. They saw me watching. Two days later, they found me and offered me money to keep that information from the police."

"Bobby's alibi was that he was at the frat party the entire night."

"He lied," she emphasized. "His brother too."

"What were they doing? Do you remember?"

"They were just talking... arguing. Baron climbed out of the car, and it looked like he wanted to go into our dorm building, but Bobby came out and stopped him. Then they got back in the car and drove away."

It was hardly suspicious activity. Baron could have been visiting his brother. But they had lied to the police. Bobby had been ruled out of the investigations because he had an alibi.

"When you were offered money, did they say anything?"

"No. It was clear that they thought my statement could change the direction of the investigation. Maybe they'd assumed that I'd seen something more. But I didn't correct them." She bit her lip. "It's not like I'd seen Bobby hurt Hayley..."

"Why did you decide to tell your story to Vincent Hawkins after all these years?" Mackenzie asked.

"I'm not a monster, detective." Stella's eyes welled with tears. "I've thought about Hayley and how I failed her every single day. A few weeks ago, a colleague of mine told me his kid is sick. She's undergoing chemo. She's only eleven. She comes over and sits at the pharmacy while her dad works, and we've bonded. Her name is Hayley." Her voice broke. She picked up a handkerchief and blew her nose. "I know it's stupid, but I see her sitting there almost every single day and it was like my past was being shoved in my face again. Like it was a sign from the universe that I needed to do something."

Mackenzie gave her a moment to compose herself. Jonathan ran his hand over her back, looking conflicted. Her silence over Hayley's disappearance was a dark stain in her life. Something that had slowly bitten into her soul without her realizing until a little girl with the same name showed up at her workplace. A not-so-subtle reminder.

"It can't be a coincidence, can it?" Jonathan asked. "That this Bobby decided to abduct Stella when she was going to come clean?"

Mackenzie nodded faintly. Did Bobby's bitterness toward his brother run that deep that he was willing to jeopardize himself in the process?

"I do feel awful," Stella repeated, seeing Mackenzie out. "I've thought about reaching out to Hayley's father. Begging forgiveness. But I don't have the courage."

"I saw him a few days ago," Mackenzie said.

Her eyes widened. "How is he?"

Seeing Stella's bony frame and sunken face, Mackenzie toed the line between honesty and diplomacy. "He's angry and upset. Understandably, he hasn't let it go."

Stella swallowed hard. "Can't blame him. But maybe Hayley can get justice now?" she asked hopefully. "That family lied. You have to find out what exactly happened that night."

"Trust me. I plan to."

FIFTY-FOUR

When Baron Wildman marched into the Lakemore PD station, Mackenzie realized why storms were named after people. He came with ammunition. A puffed chest and ticking jaw. He barreled down the hall, flanked by an army of suits. Everyone at the station took notice, parting and making way for him until he reached the office of Investigations Division.

"Where is he?" he demanded from Rivera, who was instantly by his side.

"He's in the interrogation room with Detective Blackwood," Rivera said.

Baron jerked his head, and some of the lawyers scampered to the room. His nostrils ballooned like a raging bull, while he conversed with Rivera in a frenzy. Mackenzie stayed put by her desk, her feet rooted to the ground and arms crossed.

"Who is that?" Troy whistled. "He looks close to losing it."

"Baron Wildman. His brother confessed to the whole thing without a lawyer."

He snorted. "That's dumb."

She agreed. "Yes. It *is* dumb. Especially for someone who had seemingly thought of everything."

Troy clicked his pen, searching her eyes. "You think Bobby's protecting someone?"

She nodded. "The only person I can imagine Bobby would protect is standing right there." Her eyes never left Baron and his blotchy face. Stella's words swirled inside her. How Baron had been on campus that night with Bobby. She picked up Hayley's picture that was pinned to her desk and positioned it on top of a file to test out a theory. She went to Rivera and Baron, holding the file against her chest, Hayley's picture staring Baron right in the face.

"Mr. Wildman, if you have any questions, I'll be happy to answer them."

Baron was irritated at being interrupted. He opened his mouth to dismiss her, but a strangled breath escaped his throat when he saw Hayley's picture. Without realizing, he took a step back and looked away, covering his mouth with his hand.

"It's all right, Detective Price." Rivera glared at her. "I'll handle it."

But Mackenzie was already walking away. For the first time, she had seen Baron's reaction to seeing Hayley, as opposed to just talking about her. This was a more effective blow. A test. And he had failed. It solidified what Joe Walsh had strongly believed and what Stella had suspected.

Popping a mint in her mouth, she hastened to the drafty basement. The musty smell greeted her, dangling bare bulbs casting her shadow on the drywall. She signed in the register with the evidence room clerk and followed Sean, the clerk, to the locker room.

Austin was sitting at the large table in the middle of the room, sifting through a jewelry box with latex gloves. "Hi."

"Hey." She nodded, while Sean opened the locker and left. "What are you up to?"

"Woman killed in 1989." Austin brushed away his long,

golden locks falling over his forehead. "You can imagine the sense of urgency."

Mackenzie took out the bag the FBI had sent over in the case of Hayley Walsh and opened it. "I'm sure the woman has family who wants answers."

He shrugged. "Heard you caught your guy."

"I thought so too." Mackenzie poured the contents out on the table. Being a missing person's case with no known site of abduction, the evidence collected had been sparse. Only a few items collected from Hayley's bedroom. She could feel hope flying away when she realized how little she had to work with. "Damn."

Austin looked up. "Couldn't find what you're looking for?"

"I'm not sure what I'm looking for." She sighed and flipped the pages of Hayley's journal and homework that had been left on her bed. "No wonder the FBI sent over the case file for this so happily. This is nothing."

There was a small evidence pouch with the label showing the contents were lifted from the trashcan on Hayley's side of the room.

"Why do you think you have the wrong guy?" Austin asked curiously.

"Because he did something very dumb for someone who planned every detail of this game so meticulously. He confessed without a lawyer before we even presented him with hard evidence." There was a pack of gum, an old wrapper for some stationery, a university brochure, and a small piece of paper too faded to make out anything.

"And you think you'll find your real killer like this?"

She ground her jaw. "No, but I think he's protecting his brother. And the least I can do is go after him. But there's nothing here."

Austin pushed away his tray and reached across the table to grab the bag. He inspected the little things Hayley had left behind, never imagining that years later two strangers in a sterile, cold room would be turning them over in their hands, wondering what had happened to her.

"This..." He leaned forward, opening the piece of paper. "It looks like a ticket."

Mackenzie borrowed his magnifying glass and peered through. The paper was too faded and stained to make much out. But the words "seat 34D" were clear. And there was a date. It matched the date Hayley went missing. If Mackenzie's memory served her right, then Hayley had gone to a house party that night. "Ticket for what?"

Austin shrugged. "You should send it to the crime lab," he suggested. "Back then they didn't have the kind of technology we have now. Anthony could clear this up for you."

"I will. Thanks."

She opened the door to leave and bumped into what felt like a hard wall.

"Sorry." Nick stepped back. "I was looking for you."

"How did it go with Bobby?"

He shoved his hands in his pocket. "The lawyers stonewalled me as expected. I wasn't even done fully interrogating him."

"The sweatshirt will come back with his DNA."

"Yeah, but also..." He stroked his chin. "I don't think he did it."

"You think so too?" Her eyes widened, relief surging through her. They had always been so in sync that not thinking alike felt like an anomaly, a source of annoyance. Like a pebble in a shoe.

"We should check out his place. Find out why he's lying."

FIFTY-FIVE

Crickets chirped. Stars popped into the midnight sky. The thick carpet of moss on the ground looked black. The lights in the Wildman house lit up one by one. Mackenzie and Nick had arrived with a court order and a team of uniform. One of the staff opened the door and looked like a deer in headlights at seeing the caravan.

"Is Linda Wildman in there?" Nick asked.

The woman skittered away, and Linda appeared at the door dressed in a robe with curlers in her hair. "What now?"

Nick handed her the court order. "Sorry, Linda. But your brother-in-law was arrested today for the abductions of Mia Gallagher, Veronica Fang, and Stella DeRossi."

She squinted at the paper, moving aside as the officers filtered inside. "I don't understand. Where's Baron?"

"At the station."

They moved past her, going straight for the east wing where Bobby resided as they'd been told.

"Can you please be quiet? My kids are asleep," Linda begged, struggling to keep up with their brisk pace. "Is Baron in trouble too?"

"No. He's just there with Bobby," Mackenzie said.

"Oh, thank God." Her shoulders sagged in relief. "I don't know what I'd do without him. Do you need anything from me? Can I get you a water?"

Mackenzie stared at Linda's bright eyes, mildly shocked. It was like Linda was incapable of grasping the gravity of the situation. Her world had tapered to only entertaining guests and displaying etiquette, so oblivious to everything happening right under her nose.

Linda turned away, fixing her curls and humming a song.

"We just told her that her brother-in-law kidnapped women and she had no reaction," Mackenzie whispered to Nick, as they climbed the sweeping staircase.

He scoffed. "She'll probably pop a few Xanax and go to sleep. She's always been like this."

"But why was *she* sent a letter?" Mackenzie asked. "Did Bobby tell you?"

"We never got to that. We were still on Veronica when the suits walked in and told him to shut up," he said disapprovingly. "So, Stella saw Bobby and Baron that night outside her dorm?"

"Yeah. They were arguing. I have sent a ticket from Hayley's bedroom to the crime lab. It's dated for when she disappeared." She put on her gloves, entering Bobby's massive suite with a balcony that had a hot tub overlooking the woods. "That's nice."

"Look for red envelopes and anything that could have belonged to the victims or could be tied to the cabin," Nick instructed uniform, who began surveying Bobby's bathroom cabinets and chest of drawers.

"If he's lying, then why was his sweatshirt at the cabin?" Mackenzie asked. "I'm assuming we'll find his DNA on it."

"Baron also has access to the sweatshirt. Or anyone really."

She half-heartedly dug through Bobby's sock drawer.

"Baron wouldn't do anything on his own. He'd hire someone. And we still don't have access to his finances."

"He's almost a billionaire, Mack. No way we're getting easy access to those. And even if we did, these guys are smart with money."

She crossed her arms. "You're saying that there's no hope? That rich people like Baron are so resourceful that it's pointless."

"No." He gave her a flat look. "We just have to be creative. Otherwise, trust me, we'll be up to our eyeballs with paperwork for years."

It nagged Mackenzie, but Nick had a point.

She picked up a pouch of hash and some other drugs from Bobby's bedside drawer and gave it to one of the cops. Bobby's room was a museum of everything a man didn't need, from a crystal dog bathtub to luxury ice cubes.

There was a laptop sitting on a desk, where she was sure no work was ever done. She opened the drawer under it and withdrew a stash of papers and envelopes. Most of them were party invitations, a few postcards, and some letters from hospitals and organizations asking or thanking him for donations.

Then four words caught her attention. They zapped her like she had been electrocuted, leaving her mind temporarily foggy.

Let's play a game.

"Nick!" she called out to him from the other side of the room.

He had been kneeling under the bed and straightened with a frown. "What did you find?"

She was left tongue-tied as she held the scrap sheet of paper closer. A shiver skated down the length of her spine like a lit match.

I know what you did to Hayley Walsh twenty-one years ago.
Let's play a game. Do as I say. If you refuse or tell anyone, I go
to the police with evidence.

Below the words was a little symbol resembling a reverse S
below a cross drawn in ballpoint pen.

FIFTY-SIX

OCTOBER 26

When Mackenzie stepped out of her house in the cool morning, she felt something different. The sharp edges of the air cut into her skin. Her eyes slid over the front yard that she had meticulously tended to all summer but had neglected in the last two months. The crown of leaves of the weeping willow brushed the tips of wild overgrown grass. The tree was bent lower than before, like it was carrying a heavier weight. It almost looked exhausted, devoid of all the sturdiness and mystique that Mackenzie had loved about it. She walked past it toward her car but stopped in front of the light pole, noting a printed ad for a friendly football game the Lakemore Sharks were having against some kids in rehabilitation programs. The fact that they were having it mid-season meant more positive publicity. The sales from tickets were being funneled to a school for children with special needs.

Mackenzie stared at the advertisement, trying to decrypt her feelings. Football had been the pulse of the town ever since she could remember. All this was an aggressive campaign to rehabilitate football culture following the events of last year. But as Lakemore began to seal the cracks in its foundation, new splinters were appearing in other places. It was at the mercy of corrupt and powerful people. People who held the strings to control a bleak town. Lakemore had become a punching bag, perfectly ripe for exploitation. It was surrounded by cities far more interesting.

But Lakemore was turning from dull to putrid. It wasn't being taken care of enough and it was attracting everything rotten. And now another danger had arrived. Someone smart enough to create a web of guilty and frightened minds to do their dirty work for them while remaining anonymous. It didn't just take planning and clever fiendishness to devise an operation like this. It required burning passion.

And as long as anyone out there had something to lose, no one was safe.

Mackenzie watched Bobby in the holding cell. He rested his elbows on his knees; his hands knotted in front of him; the lines of his forehead deeper than ever. She leaned against the cold metal bars and clicked her fingers to get his attention. He looked up, his eyes weary. She offered him a strip of mint. His gaze narrowed with suspicion, but he walked up to her and accepted the gum.

"Your charges are being negotiated."

Surprise flickered on his face. "What?"

"Nick and your lawyers are talking to the DA." She angled her head, noting his lack of relief.

Bobby's lips quivered. "I-I... What happened?"

She took out her phone and showed him a picture of the letter. "We found the letters."

"Shit." He turned away and yanked his hair.

"There was more than one." She swiped over the pictures. "You got instructions on whom to abduct, where to keep them, whom to leave the blackmail letters for, and then where to leave

Mia and Veronica." Justin and Jenna had been closely going over the letters to search for any clues that could point to the sender.

"I didn't know what to do." He curled his hands around the bars; his eyebrows knitted.

"Because they knew what you did to Hayley. You killed her?"

He hung his head low at half-mast. "I know you don't have the best opinion of me and rightfully so. I'm a jackass. But I'm not a murderer."

"If you didn't kill Hayley, then why did you agree to this? What *evidence* do they have on you?"

Bobby looked torn, fidgeting and squirming, trapped like a fly in a cage under Mackenzie's unforgiving gaze. "I'm glad you saved Stella. Mia and Veronica's deaths are on my conscience."

"And they will continue to be."

Bitterness leached his voice. "I don't expect you to understand. I don't imagine you've had to do something horrible to save your ass."

You have to help me bury him. Melody's whisper was cruel and cutting. Mackenzie had lived with her actions for years, suppressed her guilt as it continued growing inside her, eating her alive. But she had never hurt an innocent person. She had played no part in killing anyone.

"The DA is considering the fact you were blackmailed and aren't the mastermind of this twisted game. But if you cooperate, you can cut a deal."

"Cooperate?"

"Tell us what happened to Hayley," she enunciated. "Clearly, it has been bothering you for years. Even I can see it."

Bobby ran a frustrated hand through his hair. "I don't know anything. I want my lawyer."

Mackenzie rooted her jaw, biting down hard and shook her head, almost disappointed. He was stubborn, still holding it together like a cracked vase. She just had to push him hard enough. But her plans were thwarted when Bobby's lawyers arrived, wanting to speak to their client alone.

She went back to the conference room.

Nick approached her, unbuttoning his cufflinks and rolling up his sleeves. "We're looking into Bobby's phone and laptop. And look what we found." He gave her a hard copy of an email.

Tell anyone and you go to jail for murder.

"When was this sent to him?" Mackenzie asked.

"A few days back. During our investigation. Whoever it is has been keeping tabs."

"The victims have been in the news. What was the email address?"

He shrugged. "A generic combination of random letters and numbers. You talked to Bobby. Did he say anything?"

"He's just spooked. Gave away nothing. What did the DA say?"

"Until our guy is caught, Bobby stays under custody, though he faces lesser charges now." He looked contemplative. "I suppose that's why he did this. Better to have an abduction charge than a first-degree murder one."

"So he did it. He must have killed Hayley."

Nick pulled out his cigarette case, a gift from Mackenzie years ago, and took out a tube to suck on. "I've known the guy all my life, Mack. He's slimy as hell, but he's not a murderer."

"A lot of people are capable of murder if pushed enough."

"I know." His lips moved around the cigarette. "But based on my experience, it's hard for me to believe he's capable of actively taking a life. You heard back from Anthony on that ticket you found?"

"Not yet. If we can actually track Hayley's movements that night, then we might get somewhere." They were grasping at straws, relying on footprints that had faded in the last two decades to lead them to answers. "Was Clint able to track the IP address of the sender of the email?"

"I guess he did." Nick looked past her to Clint hurrying up to them, his glasses sitting crooked atop his slim nose.

"Luckily for us, VPN wasn't used. That would have been a nightmare," Clint informed. "I sent that IP address to the ISP along with the timestamp and they just got back to me with the name and address." He gave a slip to Mackenzie.

Mackenzie's heart jackknifed in her chest. "You've got to be kidding me."

Nick looked over her shoulder at the name and address. It was a computer at the Wildman Group office and the name registered to it was Baron.

FIFTY-SEVEN

Sully's goldfish was dead. He sighed, with his chin resting in his hand, as he stared at the floating body in the fishbowl. Through the glass, Mackenzie could see crumbs of cookie hanging in the hair of his mustache.

"Why would Baron blackmail his brother?" Mackenzie leaned against the wall. "This makes no sense."

Sully glowered at the information from the ISP. "And yet."

"Baron has sent his entire team of lawyers to help Bobby," she argued. "What's his motive?"

Doubt reared its ugly head. Mackenzie chewed the inside of her cheek, trying to piece it all together.

"I might be able to answer that," Nick said with a somber look. "As you know, our families were close for many years. I think it has to do with the will."

"The will?" Mackenzie asked.

"Bobby inherited half the estate when their father died and he has shares in the company," he explained. "Not that he cares or knows anything, but any decision the Wildman Group makes requires his signature. But he has always been a troublemaker. There was a provision that says that if he is convicted of a crime, then his shares and inheritance revert to Baron."

Mackenzie recalled it being mentioned in passing when she had first met them. "Baron turned on his own brother for money and control over the company? After spending years taking care of him?"

"Last year, Baron dished out more than one million dollars in an out-of-court settlement with a man who Bobby had beaten up following a drunken altercation," Sully added, interlacing his fingers. "It was in the news."

"And that's just one," Nick said gravely. "Can you imagine the money he spent buying off everyone investigating Hayley's disappearance?"

"But why would he use Hayley against Bobby? Stella said that Baron was there with him. He isn't completely innocent. The least he's been involved in is a cover-up," Mackenzie countered.

"It's the perfect cover." Nick let out a humorless laugh. "Bobby would *never* imagine his brother being behind all this. We wouldn't for the same reason. But think about it, Baron is the only one who had to gain from all this. Everyone who could have put him in jail was targeted. And even his mistress and wife, who had been creating havoc in his home life."

"Bobby gets the blame for everything and goes to jail, along with everyone who could have hurt Baron. While Baron gets full control of the company and an extra forty million in the bank." Sully took out a newspaper and sharpened a pencil. "Money and self-preservation are strong motivators."

"Blackmail has been Baron's weapon of choice in the past," Mackenzie conceded. "And he is strategic. Unlike Cristane, who is too brash."

"Don't know if you heard but there was this piece of land Cristane and Baron were bidding on in Lakemore." Sully began filling out a crossword puzzle. The beefy sergeant worked best when he was multitasking. "The land went to Baron since Cristane is now being investigated by the FBI."

"That's fortunate timing," she muttered.

He scoffed. "Luck has nothing to do with it, Mack. Who do you think tipped the FBI about Cristane's illegal activities? The email was traced to Baron's computer." Sully flattened his mouth, his gaze slicing to Mackenzie and Nick. "You know what to do."

The game was finally up.

The double glass doors to the Wildman Group building whooshed open as Mackenzie and Nick waltzed in with a team. They drew everyone's curious glances. Impeccably dressed professionals froze in their spots to find out what the commotion was about. Bobby's arrest hadn't been made public, but the rumors were rife.

"Ready to end this nightmare?" Nick asked in the elevator.

"You bet," Mackenzie said when the doors opened.

Baron's office was a giant glass box occupying almost half a floor. On the other half of the floor were smaller cubicles. Construction was ongoing. Some men bumped into her on their way out.

"Sorry."

"No problem," she replied distractedly, focusing on Baron inside his office. He was sitting on an armchair and chatting with a middle-aged woman with a bob cut. His raucous laughter rang out loud. His shoulders shook. His hand slapped his knee.

When his assistant knocked on his door to catch his attention, Baron's face fell. He stood up, and Mackenzie heard him stammer vague excuses to get the woman to leave.

"What is this about?" Baron asked, puzzled, as uniform filtered in and checked the notepad on his desk.

"It's a match," Officer Peterson confirmed to Mackenzie and Nick.

"Bag the computer," Nick ordered. When Baron opened his mouth to protest, he showed him the warrant. "Court order, Baron."

Baron slouched on a chair, worry now lining his face. Chaos engulfed him. Outside, his employees watched and whispered amongst each other. A slate of lawyers filtered in to check if Nick had the right paperwork. But Baron looked like he had seen a ghost. Like everything unfurling around him was just the beginning.

"We traced the blackmail email to Bobby to your computer, Baron." Nick cocked his head. "And one of the letters."

Baron's eyes were scorching with truth or lies, Mackenzie couldn't tell. "I didn't do this."

"Baron, keep quiet," his lawyer snapped. "You don't have an arrest warrant."

"Not yet," Mackenzie replied coolly. "The external IP we traced could be any computer on this floor. Once we confirm that this computer was used to send out the email, we'll have cause to arrest him."

There was noise all around them. But Mackenzie could hear Baron's silence the loudest.

FIFTY-EIGHT

"Mack, are you coming out tonight?" Troy asked at her side.

"Nope," she replied, engrossed in paperwork, ignoring the flutter of activity around her.

"But it's my birthday," he pouted.

She shot him a look that said *try again*.

He sighed and divulged, "Finn's out of the hospital. We're taking him out."

Troy's partner, Finn, had been shot a month ago. Together they were in the business of lifting spirits and bringing some much-needed light into the otherwise monotonous atmosphere that plagued the Investigations Division, and Lakemore in general. Being smothered by crime, it was easy to crumble.

Mackenzie closed the file and smiled, now that the case was almost closed. "For Finn."

The Oaktree pub was pulsing with energy. By the time they reached it, it was filled with patrons—a few students, but mostly blue-collar workers and some fellow officers still in uniform. Mackenzie found herself wedged between Nick and Austin.

Finn sat across from her, glorifying his story of getting shot for Ella and Pam, Troy and Sully's wives respectively.

"Nick, how'd you hurt your arm?" Pam asked, once Finn had finished his story, expecting another riveting tale.

"Fell off the bed," he lied breezily, not wanting to steal Finn's thunder.

"Mackenzie, congratulations on the documentary!" Ella clapped her hands. "How exciting!"

"Aw, yeah. Mack is *so* excited about it." Troy plopped a fry in his mouth, grinning at Mackenzie.

"They featured a lot of female detectives. I'm sure I was barely in it," she protested.

Ella gasped. "You haven't watched it?"

She shook her head.

"You were in it *a lot*. You're going to have some fans now." She beamed.

"Kill me," Mackenzie muttered under her breath, bringing the wine glass to her mouth.

Austin heard her and chuckled.

When Becky arrived, there was another round of cheers.

"You made it!" Finn gave her a hug.

"Didn't have too many bodies to cut open today," she quipped. When others groaned and made faces, she sighed. "You guys don't have good taste. Scoot, would you, Nick?"

Nick shifted to accommodate Becky between him and Mackenzie.

"You close the case?" Becky asked Mackenzie.

"Just wrapping up some paperwork. We make the arrest tomorrow morning."

"I'll cheers to that." She poured herself a beer from the pitcher. "How is everything else going?"

Mackenzie shrugged. There was nothing *else*. Her life started and stopped within the walls of Lakemore PD. "Fine."

She noticed Nick's eyes darting to them, even though he

was speaking with Sully. Always paying attention, that one, she thought.

"You know Chad was asking about you again." Becky nudged her suggestively.

"Oh, Becky. Just when I had suppressed that memory." Mackenzie grinned, taking another sip.

"I'm just saying. He's good for a night. Just don't use your brain, and your other parts will sing."

Austin overheard and choked on his drink. Mackenzie gave up.

"Sorry, Austin, you'll get used to me." Becky laughed. "You know, I have a cousin who is looking for someone. Would you be interested in getting set up?"

Becky was unaware of Austin's story. Mackenzie saw his face falter. The pain of moving on slicing through his eyes. It had been over a year since his fiancée went missing, but he was clearly not over it. Mackenzie's divorce had happened less than a year ago, but that was a decision she'd made. Austin had had his fiancée ripped away from him.

"He's too busy," Mackenzie interrupted. "Are you changing careers, Becky? From coroner to matchmaker."

Austin smiled at Mackenzie in gratitude, and she returned it.

The conversation flowed easily all night. She had spent her entire life feeling alone in a crowd, her steely armor keeping everyone at bay, a defense mechanism that had developed and strengthened over years. But in the last few months, she felt like she was reborn. Finding that softness within her harsh edges.

Lakemore had been doing the same thing. Within the crime and poverty that defined its unremarkable contours, it searched for pride and peace.

. . .

Three hours later, everyone was calling it a night. Except for Mackenzie, they'd all had too much drink.

Nick swayed when he stood up. "Damn it."

"You forget how old you are when you were chugging that whiskey?" Mackenzie smiled sweetly.

"How could I when I have you reminding me every day?" He rolled his eyes, but a smile played on his lips.

"You're in no condition to drive," Becky told him. "Neither am I. But I called Garrett to pick me up."

Nick slapped his face to sober himself as they all stumbled out on the sidewalk into the humid night.

"I'll drive you home." Mackenzie steadied him as he almost leaned into her. "I only had one glass of wine."

"Didn't you drive?" He frowned; his eyes glazed.

"No, I came with Troy. My car's back at the station. I'll pick it up tomorrow and call a cab from your place." When he was losing his balance even more, she put his arm over her shoulder and wrapped hers around his narrow waist. "Where's your car?"

"End of the street." He pointed.

They broke away from the group, saying their goodbyes.

"I heard *Chad* is still interested."

"You know, I think *you* are more interested in Chad than he is in me." She helped him walk straight. "God, why did you drink this much?"

He laughed. "Why did you drink so little?"

"Consideration for my liver, among other things."

His black SUV came into view. And Mackenzie froze. Her blood ran cold. There was a red envelope on the windshield, under the wiper. Nick was too unfocused to pay attention. She gently untangled from him, mumbling something she didn't even remember.

Her feet weighed a hundred pounds each as she crept closer. Her fingers plucked out the envelope, the texture feeling a little too sharp and hot under her fingertips. Like it would scar her if she held it for too long. She opened it with her heart thundering in her chest. She feared the worst and when she realized what was inside it, the worst came true. She felt rattled to her core.

Let's play a game. Stop looking or Luna gets hurt.

FIFTY-NINE

Mackenzie couldn't breathe. She blinked. And blinked again. This wasn't real. She'd had too much to drink. Except she hadn't. She was one hundred percent sober and what she was holding in her shaking hands was real and concrete.

"What happened?" Nick asked from behind her, fiddling on his phone.

She couldn't answer. Shards of glass had blocked her throat.

When he finally looked up and saw her face, he registered her shock. He tried shaking off his drunken state and reached for what was in her hands. He snatched it from her and read the words under the glow from the streetlight.

All his drunken stupor melted like wax. His breathing turned ragged.

"Fuck!" He crumpled the paper and marched to the driver's seat.

Mackenzie pressed her hands into his chest, easing him away. "I'll drive. Call Shelly."

There was war on his face, but he grunted and headed to the passenger side.

Mackenzie took out a siren, turned it on and set it atop his car so that they didn't have to worry about the speed limit.

She pulled the car away, driving as fast as she could and got on the highway heading out of town.

Nick was on his phone, his nostrils flaring like he was struggling to draw breaths. "Shelly. Where's Luna?"

"Nick?" Mackenzie could hear Shelly's sleepy voice. "It's one in the morning."

He pinched the bridge of his nose. "Shelly, listen to me. Go check on Luna. *Now.*"

The terror in his voice was unmistakable as silence descended. Mackenzie assumed Shelly was checking in on Luna. A few seconds later, she said, "Luna's not here! Oh my God. Oh my God."

Mackenzie gripped the wheel tighter, flooring the accelerator, switching lanes. Her heart had jumped out of her body.

No. No. No.

Nick was hyperventilating on her side. He yanked at his seat belt, squirming in his seat. "I'm on my way. Call 911."

"Nick, where is she? I tucked her in few hours ago!" Shelly started crying hysterically.

He gritted his teeth. "I'm on a case and the culprit threatened Luna."

Mackenzie tried to maintain her cool.

Luna had been taken.

The reality sank in like a heavy rock falling into the pit of her stomach. The thought of Luna getting hurt made her heart career beat to beat. But she knew that Nick was not going to maintain perspective, so she had to. She had to hold on to the last thread of sanity. But it was hard when tears were at the verge of falling from her eyes.

When they reached Shelly's house, Nick climbed out of the car before they even came to a full stop. It had started raining at some point, but Mackenzie had been so lost that she hadn't registered the pounding water.

Shelly opened the door still in her night-robe, her pixie-like brown hair messy. Nick pushed past her heading to Luna's bedroom.

"Mackenzie?" Shelly's cheeks were streaked with tears, and more were flowing. "What's happening? Who took her?"

She didn't remember what she said, but Shelly drew breaths in gasps and plodded after Nick to Luna's bedroom. Mackenzie saw a picture of Luna in the living room above the fireplace, dressed as a ballerina, standing between Shelly and Nick.

She followed them into the bedroom, where Nick was on his knees with his head in his hands. The window to Luna's room was wide open. A harsh chill enveloped the space. It was cold, unforgiving, and dark.

Then the police were at the door, and Mackenzie took charge explaining the situation to them, while Nick was still trying to process what was happening. They took over the house, asking Shelly questions and inspecting Luna's room.

Stop looking. This was different. Luna was clearly an aberration. She had nothing to do with this. No one could be blackmailed into killing her. This wasn't strategy. This was desperation.

"I'm going to kill Baron." Nick came out, his eyes wild. "How dare he come after my kid?"

A uniform came up to Nick. "Does your daughter have a history of running away?"

Nick lost it. He fisted the cop's collar and slammed him against the wall. "No, she's *nine* years old. Quit being a waste of space and get an AMBER alert out."

"Nick!" Mackenzie pulled him away from the officer, who coughed and wilted under Nick's furious gaze.

Nick began barking orders to check the neighborhood and

traffic cams in the area. There was chaos everywhere, palpable tension in the air.

The detective in charge arrived. He knew them well, and Mackenzie found some relief that everyone was going to be taking this seriously.

"I'm going to go talk to Baron," Mackenzie told Nick, when she caught a moment where he wasn't yelling at someone.

"No, I will—" He was shouldering past her, but she yanked him back.

"No. I will. You'll just beat him up and the last thing we need is him using that as a defense. You need to stay here."

Nick didn't fight back. He almost looked like a scared young boy. It was unsettling for her to see him like this. He was always an absolute in her life. An unwavering pillar of strength. Her own fear about Luna was so monumental that knowing that she only felt a fraction of what Nick did made her realize something.

The thought came to her unbidden. She had someone to lose. She had someone to fight for.

SIXTY

It was nine years ago Mackenzie had met Luna for the first time. She was just a month old and wrapped in a red blanket. Mackenzie had never seen anyone so small. She was terrified of holding her. And when she had brushed her lightly on the cheek, Luna had grabbed her finger and began licking it. It was one of her most treasured memories.

Mackenzie blasted inside the Wildmans', ignoring the fumbling protests from whoever greeted her. Rage blinded her. She reached the extravagant foyer cloaked in darkness.

"Lakemore PD!" she yelled. "Mr. Wildman, we need to talk, now." The house had many ears, with all the staff trailing around.

One by one, the lights began turning on. Feet tapped on the floors above and, soon enough, Baron was winding down the staircase, fuming.

"What the hell is this?"

White-hot anger surged through her at his sight. "Did you take Luna?"

He looked at her like she had lost her mind. "What? Who?"

"Luna Blackwood. Nick's daughter. He received one of your notes on his car. *Stop looking or Luna gets hurt.*"

"I didn't do it," he said simply.

Mackenzie got in his face. "You're lucky I didn't allow Nick to come here. He will kill you if anything happens to his child."

"I have no idea what went down with his kid," Baron seethed. "I'm not stupid enough to abduct a senator's grandchild."

"I think you'll do anything to save your own ass. But this time you've crossed a line."

"I wouldn't hurt someone's kid!" He was clearly appalled at the idea.

Mackenzie didn't hold back this time. "Wouldn't be the first time for you. You and your brother did something to Hayley all those years ago. We have a witness that you and Bobby lied about what happened that night. You are capable of anything."

Baron stumbled back and turned away to face outside the window, overlooking the backyard. Lightning struck, illuminating the patch of darkness, revealing the decades old tree that stood in the middle. "I don't know how else to convince you, Detective Price."

"You know we are moving against you, and you made a desperate attempt." She accused him. "But it's going to backfire."

"I didn't do any of it!" He picked up a glass and flung it across the room. It smashed against the wall. "Why would I? My life was perfect."

"Your mistress was sick of you forcing her to sleep with men. Your assistant was collecting evidence against you to extort money. I bet you've been keeping tabs on Stella all these years and just when she began talking to a journalist, you had her taken too. You use your brother, whom you are tired of covering for. He gets the blame for it all, giving you control of the company. Do I go on?"

"You have it all figured out," he mocked her. "From my perspective, my brother is in jail, and I might be too. Our bank accounts will be frozen. My wife and children will have no support system. Life as they know it will be over. And God knows what will happen to the company I worked so hard to build."

Silence hung between them, imposing and fragile.

Baron fell on a chair and rubbed his chest. The paranoia written on him in huge block letters. "Have you even considered the possibility that I'm being framed? Or have you made up your mind against me?"

Mackenzie's breath came out like a sharp hiss. The email had come from his computer at the office. Then she blinked, and the image of Luna huddled on the floor in a dark room burned against her eyelids. For Luna, she had to consider everything.

SIXTY-ONE

No one was sleeping that night. It was three in the morning by the time Mackenzie caught a cab back to the Lakemore PD. There were some officers on the ghost shift, but the building was pretty much dead. The sound of her wet shoes squelching echoed in the walls. Her phone rang and she picked it up after the first ring.

"Did you hear anything?" she asked Nick.

"No, the CSI is in her room. I've called Anthony to make sure this is prioritized."

"Where are you?"

"Going on foot search with some guys." He sighed. "It's dark and raining. Have no idea if I'll find anything. What did Baron say?"

She was going to tell him that she was looking into his innocence again but stopped herself. It was the last thing Nick needed, especially when she didn't have anything solid. "Nothing. I'm back at the station to make a list of Baron's properties to see if he has her anywhere. I checked his house, every single room, and found nothing."

"Okay."

"Okay." She reached her desk. Nick stayed on the phone, not saying anything. She didn't know what to say either. After a few seconds, the line went dead.

Sitting alone in the office, she tried to keep the terrifying thoughts at bay. Separated from the scene, it almost felt surreal. But those thoughts were there, clawing at her feet, threatening to take her under if she looked down or strayed her focus.

Mackenzie checked Clint's report on tracking down that email, making sure no mistake had been made. There was none. She went over the contents of the letters and email again. They were direct, to the point, using no flowery language. The letters had told Bobby what to convey to Glenn, Dominic, and Linda verbatim. She played an old video of Baron giving an interview to CNN. The anchor asked him about his schooling in Britain. She had forgotten; it explained that minor British tinge to his accent. The IT department had gone through his computer and verified that the email was sent from it. She also had access to some other emails and was glancing through them when she noticed something.

Baron was still in the habit of using British spelling.

Analyse the data. Apply for a licence. Travelling tomorrow.

She opened the pictures of the letters sent to Bobby again, paying attention to the spelling this time.

Honor our agreement.

In gray hoodie.

Leave her at least ten meters away from the sign.

Mackenzie pored over Baron's old documents and some finance articles he had written. He never used American English. She sat back, her scalp prickling.

Could Baron be telling the truth?

Hours bled into each other. By the time dawn rolled around, Mackenzie was still at her desk. She dozed off for barely thirty minutes. Nick had messaged her; he had spent all night on foot tracking the nearby woods but to no avail. This morning he was with uniform, canvasing the neighborhood to ask if anyone had seen or heard anything.

"Mack!" Sully barreled into the office.

She gazed up at him with swollen eyes.

He frowned at her. "Were you crying?"

She looked down at a forensic report she was reading again. The ink was smeared by her tears. She must have been crying in her sleep.

Before she replied, understanding crossed Sully's face. "Of course, you are. I know you're close to Nick's kid."

"Who told you about Luna?"

"Got a call from Mulgrew at Olympia PD an hour ago. He updated me on everything. It's their jurisdiction, but we are officially helping them. This is family." He gestured her to follow him. "Now, you have a list of Baron's properties in the state?"

Mackenzie handed it to him, as they entered his office. "I

suggest dispatching the sheriff's office to check these places out."

Sully took it from her and called the sheriff's office immediately. It was the swiftest she had seen her sergeant act, with a previously unseen precision and efficiency. At least Luna had two entire police forces looking for her. Mackenzie would have cracked a smile if the situation hadn't been so precarious, if the worst-case scenario didn't raise bile in her throat.

Justin poked his head in. "We got the judge to sign the arrest warrant."

"You go and make the arrest," Sully ordered. "I need to talk to Mack."

Justin nodded and disappeared.

"When Baron gets in, you do the questioning," Sully said. "But I need you to compose yourself. You look like shit."

"I already talked to him." She conveyed her exchange to him, watching the frown on Sully's face deepen.

"He's lying. He made a huge mistake going after a kid like that."

Mackenzie shifted uncomfortably. "There is something that's bothering me."

"What?"

She showed him the letters and other emails and articles written by Baron. She had underlined all the words that didn't match. "Baron *always* uses British English spelling. He grew up in the UK. But all the letters are in American English."

Sully stared at them for the longest. "Maybe he did this to throw us off."

"Maybe. But going into this level of detail is hard to believe. Usually, people don't really pay attention to what spelling they use."

"He has planned everything to the T," he argued. "This entire game he's concocted is genius."

"But he used *his* computer to send Bobby that email,"

Mackenzie pointed out. "If he's been so careful to switch to American spelling to deflect suspicion, then why was he careless enough to send an email from his computer? That too without using VPN or an Onion site."

That made Sully think. He shrugged and scratched his head and fidgeted. Mackenzie noticed his mustache, that was usually always neatly combed, was unruly. Clearly, he too had hastened to work after getting the phone call about Luna. "That email was convenient," he admitted. "All the other correspondences were via letters, which are untraceable. Except for this one email, which said something that could have been said in a letter."

"And an email that was damned easy for us to trace," Mackenzie said. "I'm not giving Baron a clean chit at all, but I do think this needs to be looked at again."

"It's not inconceivable that Baron has been a mark too. Okay. If not him, then who?"

"Joe Walsh has hell of a motive to want Baron destroyed. But I don't see him gaining access to Baron's office."

"So someone who works for Baron? Go over the list of employees in that building. Get Peterson to check everyone's background and criminal record."

Mackenzie nodded and scurried to work. The bad thoughts kept creeping back in the silences or pauses. She looked like she had gone through hell. Her stress was leaking out, visible on her flushed skin, her scraggy hair, pinched eyebrows and restless movements. After relaying information to Peterson, she began coordinating with the patrol to secure all Lakemore borders and send out Luna's information to all nearby access ports. The MUPU had sent out posters, which were being put around. The Amber Alert had been issued. Things moved fast. The word had spread that Nick's daughter had been kidnapped and the atmosphere at the Lakemore PD had become dreadful.

Mackenzie felt all eyes on her. They all gave her space, but also shot her concerning looks, waiting to hear some news on Luna.

Mackenzie had just hung up with Olympia PD, asking if they needed any volunteers, when she was interrupted by Tom Cromwell.

"Detective Price!" he cried with a forced cheeriness.

Mackenzie stood up, towering over the short, bald man, but it was impossible to intimidate a confident man like him. "What are you doing here?"

"I'm Baron Wildman's new lawyer. He's been arrested so I thought we should talk."

She wanted to slap him away. Luna was somewhere out there at the verge of fatal danger. She almost snapped at him but decided to switch tactics. "Let's talk privately."

Cromwell was surprised but played along. Mackenzie took a few deep breaths to mask her annoyance. She couldn't afford to be direct when she had so much to lose. They found a corner outside the office by the water cooler.

"This is just between us." She dropped her voice and made a show of looking over her shoulder. "I'm not convinced that Baron did it."

"I'm listening."

"I suspect that someone else sent the email from his computer. But since I have no evidence, I couldn't stop the arrest warrant."

"Is that so?" He raised an eyebrow. "My client told me you barged into his house and accused him of kidnapping a child. And now you're on his side?"

"Yes, but the things he told me made me think. And I feel bad for the guy. His brother's going to prison after being black-mailed and he might be getting framed." She feigned sympathy. But she had to make it seem she was on Baron's side. Even if Baron were innocent of this it didn't make him an innocent person. There was a father out there who had spent the last twenty-one years with no idea what happened to his daughter.

Cromwell studied her. She kept the mask fixed. Finally, he sighed resignedly. "I'm sure my client will cooperate. He is eager to prove his innocence."

"If I tell you what day and time the email was sent from his computer, can you ask him who was, or could have been, in his office then?"

"Certainly."

She gave him the information and watched him leave with a bounce in his step and hoped that Baron would reveal something helpful.

Nick called over the phone again. "Anything?"

"Baron is in custody, talking to his lawyer," she said. "We have the sheriff's office checking off all his properties in the state."

"He's going to use Luna as hostage."

"He needs Luna." *If he has her*, she resisted adding. "He's already in deep shit. I highly doubt he'll actually hurt her and add more charges. But I'm working to make sure the case is airtight. Don't want anything to slip past us."

"You know when I held her for the first time, this was my biggest fear." He confessed after a beat of silence.

Mackenzie found a quiet corner and pressed the phone closer to her ear.

"I was so scared that my job would affect her," he continued. "It's messed up, but a small part of me was glad that Shelly and I weren't together so that there was some distance between me and Luna. Some father, aren't I?"

"Don't be silly, Nick. You've always been there for Luna. You never let her feel otherwise. And you were prioritizing her safety, like a good parent."

"And still this happened." He sighed.

"There was no way we could have seen this coming." Her

insides shuddered. "There was not even a hint that Luna could have been in danger. How's Shelly?"

"Can't stop crying. And there's that asshat of her boyfriend who can't even be bothered to be here." Mackenzie pictured Nick scowling at the thought. "Anyway, I got to get back."

"Yeah." The dim tone of his voice left a sour taste in her mouth.

She pressed the cold phone against her forehead, feeling feverish. She went back to the office and popped a Tylenol when Cromwell returned with a conspiratorial smile.

"Do you have any names?" she asked. He handed her a list of at least fifty names. "This many?"

"There was an office party that afternoon. An employee who'd worked for the company for over forty years was retiring."

"And any of these people could have gone to his computer? His office wasn't locked?"

"There was repair work going on in all offices on that floor. Including his. All doors were left open."

"I see..." Something clicked in Mackenzie's head. "What kind of repair work?"

"Electronics. Recycling some old monitors and installing new ones and printers." He frowned. "Why?"

Mackenzie was close to something. She felt it on her fingertips. "Do you know the company name by any chance?"

"Yes, it's TechKnow Repair."

TechKnow Repair was where Joe Walsh worked.

SIXTY-THREE

Mackenzie could feel the beats vibrate through the floor up to her legs. The bar was thumping with some pop song she didn't recognize. Edison lights were strung across the small space to compensate for the lack of windows. The walls were painted dark blue with red splashed in random shapes and patters like ink splat or bloodstains. The tables were the color of copper, and the wood on the back of the chairs were carved into teeth. The lavish bar was stocked with alcohol of all colors in flasks and bottles of sparkling crystal. The patrons weren't regular people; they smoked Cuban cigars and wore three-piece suits. They threw indignant looks at her, like she was someone in their way, ruining the delicate ambience.

She approached the bartender and flashed him her badge. "I'm looking for Joe Walsh."

The bartender pointed at a door at the back. She muttered a thanks and weaved across the room. The door opened to a busy kitchen with many cooks preparing meals in a hum of activity. Her eyes drifted, finally locking onto Joe in a corner, tinkering with a kitchen display screen.

"Joe?" She walked up to him. He turned around with a screwdriver tucked in his ear. "We need to talk."

Joe eyed her with caution. "How did you know where I was?"

"Called your company, TechKnow. The same company that services the electronics at Wildman Group." She didn't spend time easing into the inquiry.

He didn't flinch. "We're a big company. The Wildman Group is just one of our clients."

"Ever done a job there?"

"A few." He shrugged.

"Considering your hatred for that family, I'm surprised."

"I go wherever I'm needed. Hence here too." He made a sweeping gesture at the loud kitchen with sweltering heat. "Baron is a part owner of this restaurant. Did you know that?"

"When was the last time you were at the Wildman Group on a job?"

"I'll have to check, but not too long ago. They were replacing a whole fleet of monitors and printers." He paused. "Why?"

"Did you have access to Baron's personal office?"

"Maybe? I don't know. We were working three floors. Wasn't really paying attention which office belonged to who." He sounded annoyed. "What's this about?"

"An email was sent from Baron's computer the day you had access to it. It looks like someone's framing him for a crime."

"Yeah, me and another ten guys. But I see." He smirked and closed his toolbox. "Let me guess. Baron is innocent and you've decided to hound me instead. History does repeat itself."

Shame filled Mackenzie. She saw that tangible hopelessness on Joe's face. She'd seen it in victims and their relatives before. When despair ran so deep that it dripped from their faces. A dimness in their eyes. A looseness in their muscles. But she also knew that loss could pave the way for evil. "You have my sympathies, Joe, but my partner's little girl has been abducted," she said firmly. "And, trust me, if I find out that you had anything to do with this, then I will make sure you'll never be a free man again."

"I'm not a free man, detective." Joe's eyes watered, but there was also madness, a kind of fanaticism. "I'll never be free of the pain that family inflicted on me. Whatever Baron's going through, he deserves it. The person who is framing him is doing mankind a service." He slammed the receipt on the fixed scanner and pushed past Mackenzie.

One thing was clear to Mackenzie, that Joe was a man with nothing left to lose. His hatred knew no bounds. And she couldn't completely dismiss the possibility that in his quest to return the pain, he had chosen to ignore collateral damage.

She called Justin on her way out, who picked up immediately.

"Yes, ma'am."

"Contact Tacoma PD and ask them to visit Joe Walsh's house and do a quick check of the place. And I want eyes on him 24/7. I want to know where he goes and who he talks to."

SIXTY-FOUR

The clock was ticking. Hours went by quickly but painfully slowly at the same time. Mackenzie had been going over Peterson's report on everyone present at the Wildman Group party when the email was sent. A few of them had disorderly conducts or tax evasion charges, but nothing violent. There was one name that stood out, however. Walter Cristane had been present. But being an investor in Baron's company, his presence wasn't peculiar. Other than him, no other guest seemed to have a connection to the case.

Mackenzie's head felt like it was going to explode. She still hadn't fully absorbed what had happened. Luna's picture on Nick's desk was jarring. She purposefully avoided looking at it, knowing she would cry and stop being useful. That combined with lack of sleep was eating her alive inside. But she couldn't stop. Not for a single second. Even as her stomach growled in hunger and shivers left her body hot. She was popping another Tylenol when Justin barged in the office.

"Tacoma PD sent two officers to check Joe's property," he informed her. "Joe was cooperative and let them have a look around. No sign of Luna."

Mackenzie squeezed her eyes shut and smothered another wave of disappointment from consuming her. "Okay. Okay. Is there patrol keeping an eye on him?"

"All the time," he assured. "But Joe went straight home from that restaurant you called at and hasn't gone anywhere since."

"He probably knows he's being watched after I confronted him." She berated herself for not being more tactful. "But he could be keeping Luna elsewhere. Does he own any other place?"

"Not to our knowledge. I'll tell Clint to access the county's records of property and check if anything's registered under Joe's name."

"Do that. I'm assuming that the teams are still working their way through all of Baron's places?"

"Yes, ma'am. Nothing yet."

Her mind mulled over if there was anything else they could do. "Send uniform to speak with Joe's friends and colleagues. Ask them if there's a place Joe visits a lot and if his behavior has changed in the last few days. I don't care how insignificant it is, but if he's mentioned *anything* odd, then I want to know."

"Certainly."

"And don't send any rookie cops. I want to know every single thing about Joe Walsh."

He nodded and hurried away.

Mackenzie finally looked at Luna's picture. Tears didn't come. Rage did. It fueled her, evaporating her tiredness. She plucked away the picture, grabbed the case files and strode to the conference room with purpose. She gathered Jenna, Peterson, Sully, and Justin, when he returned, to join her. Luna's picture was inspiration. A source of infinitely renewable motivation. She clipped it to the whiteboard and faced everyone.

"I don't need to tell you what this means to us. You know it already. I'm not leaving this station until I find Luna, and neither are you," she instructed, knowing very well one of them was her boss. "There is reasonable doubt that Baron is being framed. We can prove that the email blackmailing Bobby came from his computer, but it was at a time many people had access to it. From Joe Walsh to Walter Cristane, they both could have planted that email."

"But Baron could still have been behind it," Jenna argued. "He's twisted enough to make it look like he's being framed."

"I'm not dismissing that possibility, which is why we have the sheriff's office looking into it and Lieutenant Rivera grilling Baron." She slid forward the case file. "Asking persons of interest isn't going to get us anywhere. The profile of this person is someone very shrewd and patient. Not a fool who would easily crack under pressure."

"We find hard evidence. We find Luna," Peterson agreed.

"Exactly. Anything picked up from a crime scene or the victim's body doesn't help us because the person behind this never had direct contact with either," she said. "There is only one thing that they've touched."

"The letters sent to Bobby," Justin said. "But the crime lab didn't find any prints."

"I know. But it's all we've got. We will review every piece of information and focus on the letters. And we're not leaving until we find a solid lead."

Everyone rolled up their sleeves and got to work. Mackenzie tried not to focus on how little they had to go on. She couldn't be bogged down. Not when it came to Luna. Coffees after coffees were poured and slurped. Pages were flicked. Confirmatory phone calls were made.

"I have a question." Peterson hesitated. "Why threaten Luna now? We were already in the process of building a case against Baron."

"To make Baron seem desperate. To further weaken his chances," Sully said. "Provided someone did frame Baron. We might find out it was him all along."

"Or someone who really hates him," Jenna muttered.

"How did Bobby receive these letters?" Justin asked.

"They were left on his car or in the mailbox with no stamp or sender information," Mackenzie said. "Just like with Dominic and Linda and I assume Glenn."

When Nick called her again, she excused herself.

"Anything?"

"No. Your side?" he asked hopefully.

It killed her to erase his hope. "No, but we are all working on it and we won't leave until we find something."

"Baron. I'll kill him."

The last thing she wanted to do was tell Nick they had doubts about Baron. It would only make him feel that they were back to square one and further away from finding Luna.

"I'll keep you in the loop," she told him and hung up.

Light was fading outside, and stars began to appear like snowflakes. The sky was a creamy pink, stuffed with clouds that looked like cotton candy. Some people were beginning to leave. Rivera appeared in the hallway, exhausted. Her eyes locked with Mackenzie, and she shook her head. She had been unable to get anything from Baron.

Mackenzie's throat closed.

No. No. No.

Sully had been staring at something on the blackmail letters for too long with a magnifying glass.

"Sully?" Mackenzie asked, knowing the sergeant's ticks. "What do you have?"

"These letters." He positioned two piles in front of Mackenzie. The first was the ones sent to Bobby. The other was the ones Bobby had sent out to Glenn, Dominic, and Linda.

"Bobby wrote his on a typewriter he had in the east wing of the Wildman house," Mackenzie recalled. "The crime lab was able to confirm that."

"That's right. Portions of the last message he sent to Linda were still on the ribbon," Sully said. "But the ones written to Bobby are different. You can see striations in the typeface." He showed them to Mackenzie.

"How did the crime lab miss this?" Jenna asked.

"Whoever was looking doesn't know much about typewriters, but I do, thanks to my hobby from a few years ago." He adjusted his belt buckle. "A vintage typewriter was used here. They use cloth ribbons as opposed to typewriters these days which have film ribbon."

"Cloth ribbon? Do they even sell those anywhere?" Peterson wondered.

"Some places do. But we can narrow down the model based on the abnormal spacing and some nicks on certain letters. I bet there aren't a lot of places selling that combination."

"We need Clint." Mackenzie wasn't finished with her sentence when Justin was already on his way out.

A giant ball of restlessness sat in Mackenzie's stomach like a heavy rock for the next hour as Clint tapped away on his computer. "I will work better if I can't smell coffee on everyone's breath."

The five of them had huddled around Clint. They broke apart, giving him space to breathe.

A few minutes later, he said, "I have a list of shops selling the ribbons. You were right, sergeant. The list is narrow. And you're lucky I couldn't find any online places."

Mackenzie looked at his screen. "Three in Olympia. One in Lakemore and one in Tacoma."

"Should I expand it to the entire state?" Clint asked.

"Yes. I don't want to take any chances. But we'll hit these five places first." She checked her watch. "We don't have much time. They'll close shop in an hour, and we can't afford to wait out the night."

"Mack, you take Tacoma. Peterson, check out the one in Lakemore. The three of us will drive to Olympia." Sully clapped his hands. "Chop! Chop!"

Mackenzie ran back to the office to get the keys and her jacket. Her throat was parched, so she swallowed a glass of water on the way, dunking the cup in the trash.

Tacoma was only a fifteen-minute drive away, but with traffic at this time it would take double that. She drove fast, not unhinged, maintaining her focus and level-headedness. Losing control would only affect her efficiency and hurt Luna. She reminded herself of that over and over again as the curves of the road became tighter and the greenery faded.

The shop was inside a mall in Tacoma. Not minding the ridiculous parking fees, she climbed up the escalator, pushing people aside. There were only ten minutes left before the shop closed. She got a message from Peterson.

Lakemore shop hasn't restocked on that typewriter since last year.

One down. Four more left.

The shop appeared, next to a salon and a shoe shop. It turned out to be a quaint, antique store named *Weird Things*. Inside was a maze of things Mackenzie hadn't seen. Christmas cards from the Victorian era. Tribal baskets. Old toys from the colonial era. Antique purses. Some pottery and chinaware. For a moment, she was lost before she finally saw a typewriter matching the model and description Clint had suggested. It was the only typewriter in the store.

"We're about to close soon..." a middle-aged woman said apologetically.

Mackenzie showed her the badge. "Does that typewriter use a cloth ribbon?"

"Yes!" the woman exclaimed. "It's from 1930. It was sold

for over $3,000 at an auction a while ago, but after the buyer passed away last year, his children donated it to us."

"There's only one? Do you have any other old typewriters? Have you sold any lately?"

"I'm afraid that's the only we have in our store or ever had. It's priced at $4,000, so it's difficult to sell. But we do invite people to use it for a fee. To get the experience of working on it."

Mackenzie's hands twitched as she took out her phone and showed her a picture of Joe Walsh. "Has this man ever come to use this?"

"No. It was—"

She swiped her finger to reveal the other picture. "This one?"

"Yes!" She smiled. "That's the one."

Mackenzie looked at the picture of Baron with his family. She gritted her teeth. He had lied to them and sent them on a wild goose chase just to waste their time.

"She said she couldn't afford it but was adamant about using it. She mentioned once she was working on a novel."

Mackenzie was dumbfounded. "Sorry? She?"

"Yes, the woman in the picture you just showed me."

The woman in the picture with Baron was his wife. Linda Wildman.

SIXTY-FIVE

The weather had become wild. Wind blew hard, threatening to strip the trees bare. There was no sign of rain or thunder. Just the eerie whistling of the wind, sending everything soaring away. Mackenzie climbed out of the car along with Justin. They struggled to walk up to the door, pushing against the mighty force that sent dirt flying into their eyes.

After she'd rung the bell many times, Linda finally opened the door, nursing a drink. "Oh, please come in!" her sweet voice cried out. "For goodness' sake, what are you doing out there in this weather?"

They stepped inside. It was still so loud outside, the sound of wind roughing up trees and slamming into objects, but when Linda shut the door, there was deadly silence. It was just them in an ostentatious and tacky house. A gilded cage.

Linda looked mildly intoxicated from the sway in her step and goofy smile. "Will you have something to eat or drink?"

Mackenzie's jaw was strained as she analyzed the woman in front of her. A perfected, crafted exterior, polished mannerisms, and a seemingly oblivious socialite hiding someone else entirely. "Where is Luna?"

Linda's smile fell. But only for a second. Then she put it back on, ready to fool the world again. "I'm sorry, what?"

"We know it was you," Mackenzie whispered. "We were able to trace the letters you sent to Bobby to a typewriter at a mall in Tacoma. Forensics have confiscated it and are running tests to confirm that that typewriter was used. The shop has you on surveillance typing away on it."

Linda gulped down her martini. Her face was rigid now, almost cold and cruel.

Mackenzie continued, "You often visit the salon next to the shop. That's how you got to know about that antique store. You planned everything meticulously. But even perfectionists make mistakes."

"I suppose you want to know why?" Linda scoffed.

"I want to know where Luna is first. Where is she?!" Mackenzie shouted in Linda's face.

Linda winced ever so slightly. With her steely composure intact, she slammed her drink on the table and turned on her heel, disappearing out of view. "Feel free to check the house. I'll be calling my lawyer."

"Justin, check upstairs," Mackenzie ordered and began going through the rooms on the first floor. Disappointment mounted with each room she inspected yielding no sign of Luna. She had checked the house the night Luna was taken. The chances of her being here were slim. It was then Mackenzie noticed the door going down to the basement was slightly ajar.

Linda still hadn't returned from her phone call.

Mackenzie ventured down the stairs to the cold basement. There was a large living space with a bar, kitchenette, a flat-screen television, a range of games, from a pool table and ping-pong table to a makeshift rink and putting greens. She threw open doors to bathrooms and guest bedrooms until only one was left. She clicked the door open, and light flooded the room.

It was the size of Mackenzie's bedroom with wine racks running in an arc in a climate-controlled room. There was an oak table in the middle and tiny feet on the other side.

"Luna!" Mackenzie crossed the room and froze.

Her blood ran cold.

Linda was crouched next to Luna, holding her against her chest with a frenzied look in her eyes.

"Don't come any closer!" she hissed, pressing a gun against Luna's temple.

Luna had never looked smaller to Mackenzie. Her head was almost as big as the gun. Dread swirled in the pit of her stomach. Time slowed and stretched before her. For a few painfully long seconds, it was so silent that all she could hear were Luna's ragged breaths.

"You're making a big mistake," Mackenzie warned.

Linda blinked. "It wasn't meant to go down like this. Drop your weapon."

"Aunty Mack..." Luna whimpered.

Fear rose inside her chest, pulling it in like an implosion. She had been in countless situations like these. But for the first time she struggled to go on autopilot. Her training wasn't kicking in as smoothly as it should. Instead, her throat was closing and her fingers shaking.

"Kid, you'll be okay." Mackenzie lowered the gun to the floor as slowly as possible, but her eyes never left Linda. Noting the glazed look in her eyes, she said softly, "You have a daughter around Luna's age, don't you?"

Linda sniffled and shook her head in defiance. "It won't work. I'm going to walk away, Detective Price. Don't follow me and I won't hurt Luna."

Mackenzie's options were limited. Especially when Luna's life was hanging at the end of a barrel.

Linda stood upright with a tremor in her step, pulling Luna

along with her. Luna's face was flushed pink. There was still sleep in her puffy eyes. She had been crying.

"I promise everything will be fine if you just let me go," Linda chanted over and over, retreating from the room.

As the distance between them increased, Mackenzie felt her heart was falling down her chest to her toes. Luna was slipping away. Helplessly, she racked her brain for a plan. When Linda was at least ten feet away, there was a sound.

A door opened and closed.

Heavy footsteps.

Linda looked over her shoulder, the gun still pressed against Luna's head.

"*Duck*," Mackenzie mouthed to Luna, who nodded.

Summoning all her strength and letting her instincts take over, Mackenzie launched herself into a distracted Linda, pushing Luna out of the way.

She pressed her body into Linda, who thrashed and flailed her arms and legs. But it wasn't only training but also strength she lacked. After all those years of starving herself, she was just skin and bones.

"No!" she growled, and Mackenzie smelled the alcohol on her breath.

She snatched the gun from her grip and slid it across the room.

"Freeze!" Justin pulled out his gun and aimed it at Linda, who was still struggling under Mackenzie.

"It's over!" Mackenzie pinned her wrists on either side of her face, glaring at Linda. "You are done."

Linda went limp. Her protests died in a heartbeat. The panic in her eyes gave way to that glazed look again.

With Justin still hovering over them, Mackenzie released her and stood up. "Don't let her out of your sight."

"Yes, ma'am."

Mackenzie was finally able to breathe without it hurting too much. "Luna..." she whimpered.

"Aunty Mack," she croaked.

Mackenzie crushed her into a hug, her tears falling atop Luna's head. Everything she had been holding back came tumbling out. "Thank God." She pulled away and inspected Luna, running her eyes over her face and arms. "Are you hurt?"

"No. You did hug me too hard though." She cracked a smile.

Mackenzie's heart came undone. "Kid, were you always this small?" She wiped away her tears and took out her phone. "I'm going to call your dad. We'll take you to the hospital to get checked."

"He must have gone crazy."

Nick picked up after two rings. "Yeah?"

"I have her. She's fine. She's not hurt."

"Let me talk to her." His voice was thick.

While Luna talked to Nick over the phone, Mackenzie realized how surreal it was. Like she had finally awoken from a nightmare, still feeling groggy. The last twenty-four hours were remnants of another life and another world, slowly fading away while leaving unpleasant tingles on her skin.

Luna handed the phone back to Mackenzie. "He wants to talk."

"Where was she?" Nick demanded.

"At the Wildmans'—"

"But we checked their house!"

"We did, that's why Linda moved her here afterwards, knowing we would have crossed this place off our list."

"Wait. Linda?"

"Now's not the time." Mackenzie checked Luna's eyes to make sure they weren't yellowing. "I'm taking Luna to Lakemore General."

She heard the car roar to life when Nick said, "I'll meet you there."

Mackenzie carried Luna in her arms. Despite being kidnapped and spending twenty-four hours away from her family, Luna was calm and collected. Mackenzie was amazed at her strength. She held on to her tightly, afraid she'd slip away again.

"Linda Wildman, you're under arrest for the abduction of Luna Blackwood," Mackenzie cited, and Justin gladly pulled out handcuffs. "You have the right to remain silent." As she recited her Miranda rights, Linda's expression was one of defiance.

The hospital had been a blur. Swiftly, Luna was surrounded by doctors and nurses doing a routine check-up and blood work. Despite being told to wait outside, Mackenzie had no intention of letting Luna out of her sight. She looked smaller than ever before. Her usual wit and sass had melted away, revealing her innocence, as she looked around a little confused and a little scared.

Nick and Shelly came running down the hall. When they saw Luna, they broke into tears. But Luna's lips curled into the brightest smile. Shelly held Luna's hand and kept kissing it, almost worshipping her. Nick fussed over her, checking her arms and legs and torso, touching her hair to make sure she was real, and releasing a volley of questions at the doctors.

Mackenzie turned away, not wanting to intrude on an intimate moment. She had work to do.

Peterson had been standing guard along with one other cop.

"Tell Nick that I'm at the station questioning Linda," she said. "He needs to be with Luna. And I need to get a confession."

SIXTY-SIX

Linda was in the interrogation room. She was a pristine splash of color against the white and gray. It was a room that had seen many kinds of minds: violent, entitled, and delusional. But Linda Wildman was none of those. She was a different kind of evil. Smarter, stealthier, and deliberate. She sat with a small smile on her lips and a slight tilt to her neck. Not looking like someone who had been arrested and was going to spend their life in prison.

"Her lawyer?" Rivera asked. She and Mackenzie watched Linda from the other side of the glass.

"She's refused one."

"That woman scares me." Rivera placed a hand on her hip. "Think we're dealing with an actual psychopath here?"

Mackenzie studied Linda, as if she could see her down to her molecules. "Let's find out."

She was brazen-faced when she entered the room. Linda's eyes tracked her, still holding that genial beam like they were friends meeting for coffee.

"Are you sure you don't want a lawyer, Mrs. Wildman?"

"Yes, I'm sure." She pressed her lips in a thin smile.

"Do you realize what kind of charges you're facing?" Mackenzie checked again. "It's not just abducting a minor. Blackmailing someone to commit murder makes you an accessory at the least."

"I know." She fixed her hair, paying attention to her reflection in the mirror as if this interview was all an inconvenience to her.

Mackenzie twirled a pen in between her fingers, beginning to think that Linda was dissociating to process getting caught.

But then she became serious. "You want to know why I did it?"

"Yes."

Her smile was pained this time. Her nostrils flared and she held back her tears. "People look down upon me a lot, Detective Price. Because I'm not like you. Because I don't represent the modern woman. I represent traditional values. I'm that woman who stands behind her husband and supports him, who always compromises and gives, whose purpose in life is to create a pleasant atmosphere at home for my hard-working husband, who is a society leader and a perfect host. I'm the woman who is expected to not create a scene even if her husband keeps cheating on her." Her lips quivered when she said the last sentence. She blinked away her tears and drew an uneven breath. "Because men will be men. Because a woman is supposed to be forgiving if he apologizes sweetly. Because our marriage will be stronger for it."

Mackenzie listened, remembering how she had felt when Sterling had cheated on her. The conflict between still loving him and realizing broken trust could never be repaired had torn her. Linda had housed a lot of negativity, and now everything was pouring out without Mackenzie having to try to pull it out of her.

"I'm a trophy wife." Linda giggled, but it never reached her eyes. "Have you seen how Baron treats me? Like I'm a fool who only knows how to swipe a credit card. Every day my husband belittled my intelligence, my potential and then he cheated..." She closed her eyes, her face contorting in pain. "...And cheated and cheated again to destroy my dignity."

"Why didn't you just leave him?"

"Why should I?" She leaned forward, spitting the words. Her sudden outburst almost made Mackenzie blanch. "Why should I be subjected to *years* of humiliation and insults and degradation and give him the easy way out? I did so much for him. I raised our children. I never complained about how he was feeding that man-child brother of his. Look at me! Look at the efforts I made to look young and beautiful. And what does he do? Dip it in the first young blond he meets?" Her breathing was labored. "I could walk away. But then he'd win. He would just love to get rid of me. I'm nothing but this old piece of rag in his life. I like balance. I like fairness. It's not fair for him to hurt me so much and then for me to act like the *bigger person*."

"This entire game was to destroy Baron? To frame him?" she asked incredulously.

Linda nodded, sniffling. "When I realized how little he thinks of me, at first I was angry. Extremely livid. But then I decided to use it against him. I played dumb and dumber, and he let his guard down. I overheard him and Bobby talking about Hayley Walsh one night."

"What were they saying?"

"Baron was scolding Bobby over how many people he had to bribe and what he had to do that night to cover up Hayley's death."

Mackenzie swallowed hard. It didn't come to her as a surprise that Hayley had been dead this entire time. But that ring of definitiveness was still daunting.

"And I knew what to do," she said with a sick smile. "Baron was so careless around me that I easily went over his finance statements and emails and discovered Glenn Solomon and Dominic's role."

"That's when you hatched the plan."

"Initially, I didn't intend for it to get this big. I just wanted Mia dead. She was sleeping with my husband and wasn't even embarrassed about it. But I'm not stupid enough to pull the trigger myself. I knew I would get caught with all the technology you guys have these days." She flicked her hand, sitting back and crossing her legs. "I needed an enforcer. And Bobby was the perfect lap dog. I had heard enough about Hayley to have leverage over him. At first, I thought I should just blackmail him to kill her. But I've known Bobby for over a decade. He's not capable of murder."

"So you decided to direct Bobby to Glenn," Mackenzie accused her. "Glenn had done absolutely nothing to you."

"He didn't. But he did to Hayley. He's not completely innocent. But I had started something." She was almost proud. "By involving Glenn, I realized I didn't have to stop at Mia. I had the opportunity to cause some very serious damage to my husband. One time when I was visiting Baron at work, I saw Veronica's diary sitting on her desk."

"You knew she was collecting evidence against Baron…"

She shrugged. "I'd heard that Veronica wasn't happy. I put two and two together and found someone for Dominic to take care of."

"It was through your snooping that you found out about the wire transfer to Stella. But why did you target her?"

"I knew she was going to go public with the story," Linda said. "I had been talking with Vincent Hawkins."

"Vincent knew about you?" Mackenzie raised her eyebrows in disbelief.

"Not in the way you think," she corrected. "I had approached him wanting him to do an intimate portfolio of our family. Everyone knows how opportunistic Hawkins is. Doing a profile isn't his forte, but he wouldn't have missed the opportunity to gain close access to a powerful family like ours. It was my intention for him to eventually discover Baron's corruption in building his empire, but I couldn't have been the source obviously. In one of our meetings, he hinted about someone who could have damning information about Baron. When I further investigated, I found out it was Stella."

"Giving you another prime victim to exploit as a weapon against Baron. She could have helped your agenda. Her cooperation with Vincent would have been destructive to Baron's image."

"Baron's *image*?" she repeated incredulously. "Do you think I give a damn about that? Everyone knows the guy is a jerk. I didn't trust Stella's story to cause *enough* damage. But another person with motive to hurt Baron abducted? That didn't bode well for him at all."

"But you sent yourself a letter? Baron had caught you snooping around for a gun."

"I was acting, and that fool bought it. I got Bobby to send me that letter to throw any suspicion off me. That evening, I waited for Baron to get home, and when he did, I put on the best performance of my life, pretending to look for a gun so that he would catch me."

Mackenzie sighed. "You had no intention of hurting Stella?"

"Absolutely not. I was going to instruct Bobby to let her go, but you got to her first." She licked her lips and widened her eyes earnestly. "I had no intention of hurting Luna either." Her voice was soft. "I swear. I was going to move her to one of Baron's storage lockers to further implicate him and send in a tip. I'm sure you've noticed that I didn't hurt a hair on that child. Please tell Nick how sorry I am."

Mackenzie was unaffected by Linda's assertion, even if it were genuine. There was no excuse for subjecting Nick and the rest of them with that soul-shredding terror. It had been the worst twenty-four hours of her life. "We were already building a case against Baron. Why did you go after Luna?"

"I thought you needed a push. I would never make the mistake of underestimating Baron's reach and influence. If I made it look like he'd threatened a senator's grandchild, then that would have sealed his fate."

Mackenzie set the pen down and cracked her neck, processing the twisted and grim consequences of Linda's indignation. "You made a big mistake. Because you took Luna, we reviewed everything again and caught you."

Linda's mouth twisted in a frown. "Well. At least Baron still goes to prison for his white-collar crimes. And my testimony will make sure he's punished for his role in Hayley's death. My package will reach Hawkins any time now."

"What package?"

"I had a failsafe. In case I got caught or Baron got away *again*. I collected every single piece of evidence against Baron, made copies and arranged for it to be delivered to Hawkins. If you can't trust authorities, go to the media, right?"

Mackenzie shook her head. Disappointment flooded her. That was what constant degradation could do. When every day the little words and actions scraped one to the point that they weren't themselves anymore, almost unrecognizable. They lost their compassion, hardened by the ridicule and driven to a frenzy when nothing else mattered but the need to return that pain. "You are the reason three people are *dead*. I can't believe you thought all this was worth it. And do you know who lost the most in your madness? Your children." Linda looked crestfallen. "Both their parents and their uncle are going to prison. Your retaliation against your husband made sure they lost their entire family in days. All your talk about the things you wanted especially for your daughter..."

"My sister will take care of them." Linda held back her tears. "She'll be a better mother to them without any of my bitterness rubbing off on them. And their money is secure in trust funds. In a way, they'll be better off without us."

Mackenzie was ready to leave. "I'll go and prepare your statement. You need to review it again carefully before you sign."

"Wait!" Linda reached forward, clasping Mackenzie's hand in hers. Her skin was cold and clammy and withered. "I have to tell you more."

"What is it?"

"Baron and Bobby know where Hayley is buried. I heard them talk, but they didn't mention the location in their conversation. Talk to Bobby. He's guilt-ridden. He'll crack under pressure. Baron is a cold son of a bitch."

Mackenzie withdrew her hand and felt the corners of her eyes tighten. "Why are you telling me this?"

"Our family owes Joe Walsh the truth, and I have no intention to be like Baron and Bobby. I'm not a monster. I would never put a parent through that. I do have one request."

"Okay..."

"Can you please make sure Baron knows that it was *me*? I need him to know that I was the one who ruined his life, the one he underestimated the most."

Mackenzie nodded in a haze and left the room armed with more information and a sense of closure. She took a deep breath away from Linda and her cut-throat bitterness. Just being in the same room with her had been grating for her nerves.

Rivera and Justin took over, getting Linda to sign her confession and then process her.

Mackenzie had just left a message for Anthony at the crime

lab to get an update on the ticket found at Hayley's when Nick stormed into the office in confident strides with his tie askew. "I need to talk to her. Where is she?"

"Getting processed. How is Luna?"

He pinched his eyes shut and opened them again. Peace returning in their midnight depths. "The doc said she just needs to rest. She's at home with Shelly right now. Why did Linda do all this?"

Mackenzie's phone rang. It was Anthony calling her back. "Hell hath no fury like a woman scorned," she said before answering. "Hello?"

"Mack, I was just going to call you," Anthony chirped. "I just got back the results on that old ticket."

"You figured out what it was?"

"I can tell you this piece of evidence wasn't bagged like it should have. But electron dispersion spectroscopy indicated ethylenically unsaturated monomers, so it didn't deteriorate. UV analysis revealed it was a receipt for two tickets to a play called *Miss Saigon* playing in a local theater at Mercer Island. I'm emailing you a copy now."

"Thanks." She disconnected and waited for the email, while updating Nick on everything Linda had divulged.

Nick fell on his chair and ran his hand through his hair. "They buried Hayley somewhere."

Mackenzie nodded. "I'm going to talk to Bobby after I get everything from Anthony. You go home. You look beat."

"So do you," he said, amused. "When did you sleep?"

"I don't remember." Her body was aching in protest, but she was so close to the finish line that she wanted to power through before being dead to the world. "But Joe has waited too long for answers. I don't want him to wait any longer. You should go home and be with Luna."

"I'll stay. I need to help." He cleared his throat. "And I didn't thank you for finding Luna."

She rolled her eyes and spun on her chair when a notification popped up. "Got it."

The image loaded. It was a receipt for the play at a local student-run theater. It was for nine in the evening. The names of the guests were printed in block letters.

Hayley Walsh. Bobby Wildman.

"We got him," Mackenzie whispered.

SIXTY-SEVEN

There was a loud sound like a ringing alarm. Metal clanged on metal. A guard yelled. Mackenzie shifted in the uncomfortable chair that dug into her tailbone. She rubbed her arms; goosebumps sprouting despite the leather jacket. The interrogation room was cold, impersonal, and intimidating.

"You didn't have to tag along," she mumbled to Nick, who was on his phone, checking with Shelly if Luna was okay.

His eyebrows bunched. "I did."

The door opened with a screech. Bobby was brought out in handcuffs. He slumped on a chair, avoiding their eyes and recoiling his body like he was a petulant child caught doing something wrong.

Tom Cromwell hurried into the room; energetic and muttering apologies for being late. He placed his briefcase on the table. "Why did you want to meet?"

"We know who blackmailed Bobby," Mackenzie said.

Bobby's eyes flitted to hers, waiting for an answer.

"Linda."

He stuttered. "W-what?"

"She hated your brother. It was all a ruse to frame him. You were just a means to an end. But we're here on another matter."

"And what's that?" Tom asked.

"The *death* of Hayley Walsh," she said, watching Bobby closely. His lips parted as he stared at her somewhere between disbelief and surrender. "Linda has testified that she overheard a conversation between you and Baron, in which you talked about burying Hayley." Cromwell opened his mouth to argue, but Mackenzie continued talking. "She has collected bank statements of Baron bribing authorities to look the other way. And we have this too." She placed a picture of the receipt. "Found in Hayley's bedroom. You two were supposed to watch a show that night. *Miss Saigon*. That's why that first letter frightened you into committing those crimes. That sign at the bottom is *Miss Saigon's* logo."

Bobby was unraveling. The threads entwining his composure were coming apart. He looked at Tom helplessly, who inspected the picture with a flat mouth.

"This doesn't prove anything. My client never left the frat party. Hayley might have bought two tickets, but that doesn't mean my client attended the show."

"Actually, we have a witness. Stella DeRossi saw you and your brother that night in a car having an argument right outside her dorm. That was why your brother paid her off. Because her testimony would prove you lied about your alibi."

Bobby held his head in his hands, his shoulders shaking as he drew choppy breaths.

"But we're here to make a deal," Nick said.

Bobby looked up. "What do you mean?"

"The DA has decided that it's more important for a father to get some closure," Mackenzie said. "If you tell us what transpired that night *and* where Hayley's buried, then you will be charged as an accessory. You can't avoid prison, Mr. Wildman. But an accessory does mean a reduced sentence."

Cromwell and Bobby talked in whispers to each other. Mackenzie didn't like it. But, technically, Bobby had been blackmailed into abducting the women. And if spending less time in prison meant that Joe would finally get peace, she couldn't complain.

"Okay." Bobby nodded, his face flushed as he narrated the events of that night. "What no one knew was that Hayley and I had been dating. Only three months, but she broke up with me. I wasn't harassing her. I was trying to get back together with her. The day before, I had asked her to watch that play with me. Going to the theater was kind of our thing when we were together." His lips quirked in a fond smile. "We usually went for underground shows or ones happening far away from Seattle. Not the mainstream ones. Initially, she said no. But I guess I wore her down. At the last minute, she bought two tickets on a whim."

The conversation in which Hayley told Joe she was invited to the show must have happened before she changed her mind.

"I met her that night at the theater. We watched the show and when it was over, she needed to use the restroom. I was waiting for her. Since it was the last show, almost everyone had left. When she came out, it was only the two of us." His chest quaked as his recall began to fringe on the devastation that had followed. "I'd had a lot to drink. I tried kissing her. She moved away and we kind of got into a fight. We were arguing, and she got really mad at me. She pushed me away and on reflex I pushed back. But she tripped and fell down the stairs." He paused, taking a few moments before continuing. "They were steep stairs. I watched, horrified, and chased after her. But she wasn't moving. She wasn't breathing. Didn't have a pulse. And I started panicking. Instead of 911, I called Baron."

Mackenzie could see it all happen. How a drunk and immature Bobby panic-dialed Baron after accidentally killing his ex-girlfriend. How Baron, who always protected his brother and the Wildman name, denied Hayley dignity.

"We loaded Hayley into the trunk of the car and drove around trying to figure out what to do. We came back to campus but realized it wasn't the best place. Truth be told, both of us were rattled. I suppose that's when Stella saw us on campus. I swear I didn't *murder* her. Her heel got caught into the carpet… it was an accident! I'm sorry."

"Where did you bury her?" Mackenzie asked.

"At our house. Under that tree Baron and I used to climb. That's where you'll find Hayley. She's been with us all these years."

The events that followed were a blur. Like Mackenzie was underwater and watching everything unfold above the surface. There was a sense of detachment but also tranquility. Following Bobby's revelation, Mackenzie and Nick descended on the Wildmans' house once more with the CSI and coroner's team. The technicians dug sticks into the yard and rolled out the crime-scene tape. They began digging. Mackenzie planted her butt on the ground, watching the hole get deeper and deeper, until finally one of the technicians cried out, "We got bones."

SIXTY-EIGHT
OCTOBER 28

Becky was done with the analysis of the bones. Her voice sounded like a fading echo. "Based on the exfoliation of the cortical bone, the time of death was around twenty years ago. Osteon age from the bone puts the victim in her early twenties. DNA testing confirmed this is Hayley Walsh. The cause of death was cranio-cerebral trauma, and the skull injuries were above the hat brim line, consistent with falling down stairs. She fell backward because her occipital bone was severely impacted. There were no signs of assault or defensive wounds. I'd say that Bobby's version of events is true. I didn't find any evidence that suggests otherwise."

Later that day, Mackenzie drove to Tacoma with Nick to visit Joe. She would never forget that memory, it was burned in her brain. Joe had opened the door; his face pinched in annoyance. But before Mackenzie could even open her mouth, there was a shift in his face.

"You found her," Joe had whispered, tears swimming in his ghostly eyes.

It was the hardest thing Mackenzie ever had to do. She didn't remember saying the words. But she remembered Joe falling on his knees and crying hysterically. She'd killed his hope. Hope was sticky and stubborn, refusing to die, somehow burning in a small corner. Losing hope was worse than losing love. But at least he knew.

A few days later, Joe was handed over Hayley's remains so that she could finally be buried with dignity and respect. The funeral was held on a beautiful morning. The air smelled like spring. The sun decided to shine brightly. Mackenzie and Nick attended and so did Stella, Jonathan and Hawkins. Joe sat next to the closed casket with his hand draped over it protectively. The rest of them stood silently at a respectful distance. When Hayley was finally put into the ground, Mackenzie wiped away her tears.

Then, two days later, Joe passed away peacefully in his sleep. He had been holding on just so that he could send his child off with love and care. His purpose was fulfilled. When Mackenzie heard, her heart sank. But she thought at least they were finally together in some other world out there. She went home that night, drained and disturbed at the thought of how at the end of this case, two families were destroyed.

EPILOGUE
NOVEMBER 2

"I'm surprised you called." Austin returned to the table, holding a glass of wine for Mackenzie and glass of beer for himself.

They clinked their glasses and took polite sips. "Usually, Nick and I celebrate the end of a case together. But he's with Luna."

"Yeah, I imagine he'll be spending every free moment with her for a long time."

The bar was thumping with the beats of a slow rhythm. Fairy lights were strung on the ceiling. The space was littered with plastic tables and chairs covered in tablecloth. The crowd were mostly college seniors or juniors with fake IDs.

"I don't usually come here." Mackenzie was almost embarrassed by her choice. "But with the documentary, a lot of people are recognizing me at Oaktree."

"Not enjoying the fame?"

"Absolutely not."

He laughed at her mortified expression. "I'm sure people will move on eventually."

"Fingers crossed."

The evening began fraught with silence and awkwardness.

It was evident neither of them were talkers. Mackenzie was freshly jaded from recent events. Austin was still learning to open up to new people in a new place.

"Is Rivera still giving you a hard time?"

His eyes twinkled in mischief. "Still on thin ice. I was such a straight arrow back in Port Angeles. It's kind of nice being the bad boy of Lakemore PD."

She sputtered out a giggle. "That's an ambitious reputation to maintain. Now that Finn's back, will you go back to working alone?"

"Actually, no. I'm being paired up with Justin."

"Finally. He should have been promoted a long time ago." She tapped her chin. "That will be a good team. The bad boy and the biggest rule stickler in the department."

Her phone trilled with a notification. Vincent Hawkins had published his story. An exposé on the exploits of the Wildman family. The phone suddenly felt too heavy. She couldn't bear to read it. It reminded her how they'd almost lost Luna.

"How have *you* been doing? I can tell you're close to Nick's daughter."

She shrugged noncommittally. "As fine as I can be. Trying not to think about it. It makes me feel awful."

"Yeah, I know what you mean." His voice drifted before he forced himself to cheer up. "To denial and suppressing. A healthy way to process things."

Mackenzie grinned. "Hear, hear."

They clinked their glasses again.

After that, conversation flowed easily between them. Austin talked about his time in Port Angeles. Mackenzie told him funny anecdotes of Sully. The bar was about to close, when they realized the staff were trying to kick them out.

Outside, mist rose from the ground, giving the dark town a spooky feel. Silver plumes swirled out of their nostrils; the air was crisp and nippy.

"You're okay to drive, right?" Austin checked.

"Totally. You?"

"Yeah." He fished out his keys from his pocket when something fell out of it onto the ground with a clink that hissed through the night air.

Mackenzie immediately swooped down to retrieve it. It was a wedding band: muted silver with a name engraved on the inside.

Sophie.

Suddenly, the band felt heavier and sharper between her fingers. She looked up at Austin who had gone pale. "I... I bought it a day before she went missing. I was going to surprise her. We always used to joke about eloping."

"Here you go." She handed it back to him, wondering if the wedding band meant more now than it would have if they were married. How when choice and control over a situation was stripped away, there was nothing out of focus anymore.

"I guess I have to let go now." He closed his fist around it and swallowed hard. "Accept that sometimes you never get any answers."

"Maybe not." Mackenzie blurted without thinking, "Someone close to me didn't know what happened to his brother for almost twenty years."

"In a way, he's lucky. Some people never find out."

"That's true. But I think you will." She didn't know where the words came from. It was some instinct roaring inside her. "I hope you find out soon."

A LETTER FROM RUHI

Dear reader,

I want to say a huge thank you for choosing to read *The Taken Ones*. If you did enjoy it, and want to keep up to date with all my latest releases, just sign up at the following link. Your email address will never be shared and you can unsubscribe at any time.

www.bookouture.com/ruhi-choudhary

I hope you loved *The Taken Ones* and if you did, I would be very grateful if you could write a review. I'd love to hear what you think, and it makes such a difference helping new readers to discover one of my books for the first time.

I love hearing from my readers—you can get in touch through Twitter or Goodreads.

Thanks,

Ruhi

 twitter.com/RuhiSChoudhary

ACKNOWLEDGMENTS

Writing is a lonely job, but publishing is all about teamwork. I'm extremely grateful to Therese Keating, my editor, for her hard work, sharp editing skills, and diligence. Laura Deacon for taking care of this story and seeing it through to the end. Lucy Dauman for always championing my work.

Big thanks to copy editor Jade Craddock, proofreader Shirley Khan, cover designer Chris Shamwana, and my publicist, Noelle Holten, for their commitment and brilliance. The entire team at Bookouture is talented and supportive.

My parents for always cheering me on. My sister, Dhriti, for always being in our hearts and looking after us. All my friends, especially Rachel Drisdelle, Dafni Giannari, Scott Proulx, Kaushik Raj, and Sheida Stephens for their excitement.

Most of all, I'm grateful to the readers. Thank you so much for taking the time! I appreciate each and every one of you and would love to hear what you thought of the book.

Lightning Source UK Ltd.
Milton Keynes UK
UKHW040636210222
398996UK00001B/110

9 781800 198883